"Have _____ debut toda_____

Maxine bit her bottom lip. "No, I didn't forget. I'm just not sure I want to go through with it."

"Not go through with it? You dare to stand there and tell me that?"

Tears stung the back of Maxine's eyes. "None of this was my idea! I never asked you to turn me into something I'm not. Before I met you, I didn't know anything was wrong with me."

She tried to pull away from his grip, but Dane held her fast. "I am simply trying to teach you some manners, to help you become lady enough to attract a large dowry."

"I don't care about dowries," she said. "I just want you to let me go!"

"I'm not done with you yet," he snapped.

Before she could react, Dane lowered his lips to capture her mouth with a soul-stirring kiss.

*   *   *

"Filled with delicious humor, witty dialogue, and good, strongly written characters, this one is a true delight."

—*Rendezvous*

Harper
Monogram

Wild Rose

Sharon Ihle

HarperPaperbacks
A Division of HarperCollinsPublishers

HarperPaperbacks *A Division of* HarperCollins*Publishers*
10 East 53rd Street, New York, N.Y. 10022

Copyright © 1993 by Sharon J. Ihle
All rights reserved. No part of this book may be used or reproduced in any manner whatsoever without written permission of the publisher, except in the case of brief quotations embodied in critical articles and reviews. For information address HarperCollins*Publishers,*
10 East 53rd Street, New York, N.Y. 10022.

Cover illustration by Jean Restivo Monti

First printing: April 1993

Printed in the United States of America

HarperPaperbacks, HarperMonogram, and colophon are trademarks of HarperCollins*Publishers*

❖ 10 9 8 7 6 5 4 3 2 1

In loving memory of my father,
Leith Cameron MacIver; for the way you were—
the way I'll always remember you.

and

Super Agent, Patricia Teal—you're a genius!

ACKNOWLEDGMENTS

Special thanks to Cathy Blanco de Jennings, Don and Betty Woo Martin, authors of *The Best of the Gold Country,* and The San Diego Historical Society.

1

San Francisco, California
March 1859

His smooth, tanned features impassive, Dane del Cordobes watched yet another poker player toss his cards on the table in defeat. Now only one gambler remained between himself and the enormous pot. With increasing confidence, Dane turned his attention to his ruddy-faced adversary and said, "What about you—in or out?"

Max "Dicey" McKain rubbed the scraggly stubbles on his chin in contemplation. Its sparse hairs, sprinkled with more gray than red, made the beard resemble a strawberry field gone to seed. Finding a painful lump as he fingered that ruined crop, he jerked an ingrown hair out by the root before he finally acknowledged the question.

Speaking in a voice dusted with a Scottish burr, he

smiled wanly as he said, "I'm afraid yur findin' me a wee bit short to call yur bet."

Dane arched his ebony eyebrows. "Then you're out?"

"Eh, eh—not so fast," Dicey said as the gambler leaned forward and reached for the pile of gold nuggets, dollars, and poker chips. "I'm sayin' I've been caught a bit short at the table. If you'll just be givin' me a moment's leave, I'll go fetch the rest of my purse."

Squinting his eyes as much in deliberation as from the thick blanket of smoke that hung over the group of men, Dane nodded to the dealer at his right. "Do you have any rules against that?"

The card room manager shook his head. "Nope. If you don't got a problem with it, neither do I."

Dane gazed thoughtfully at the Scotsman. The prospector looked in need of a bath and some new clothes, and most likely he had gambled his way down to his last pinch of gold dust. Should Dane relieve the unfortunate man of that too? His strong sense of fair play urged him to settle for what was already on the table.

Reading the indecision in the stranger's icy blue eyes, Dicey reached into his shirt pocket and pulled out his lucky golden dice. He rolled the cubes in front of him over and over again as he said, "My rig isn't far. Can't ya see yur way clear to give me a minute? It's somethin' less than a gentleman who won't give a fellah every chance to call his bluff."

For the first time since he'd strolled into the saloon some four hours ago, Dane smiled. He'd been many things to many people over the years, but never had anyone had cause to call Dane del Cordobes anything less than a gentleman. This unfortunate placer miner would not be the first. He reached into his vest pocket, withdrew his family heirloom watch, and laid it on the table.

"I can see you are in a hurry to lose everything you've got. If this leave brings you back to the table with five hundred dollars in no more than five minutes, the bet is still on. If you are tardy, I will have no choice but to claim the pot as my own." Again he turned to the dealer. "Sit right with you, Reid?"

The saloon manager nodded. "I'll keep one eye on the cards and the other on the stakes while you're gone, Dicey. And don't be dragging your feet, old man. The second them five minutes are up and you ain't back, I'm awarding the pot to Señor del Cordobes here."

"I'll be back," Dicey promised as he shoved his chair away from the table and leapt to his feet. "I'll be back quicker than you can say 'ante up!'"

With a short burst of laughter, Dicey wheeled around on his left foot and limped through the doors as fast as his twisted right leg could take him. He hobbled down the boardwalk to the alley and ducked around the corner to where his children awaited his return. Wheezing as he caught his breath, he said, "Quick, Maxie girl—how much we got in the sugar jar?"

Maxine looked up from the tattered magazine she was perusing and pushed the brim of her Palo Alto hat back from her forehead. Shading her eyes from the setting sun, she regarded her father's agitated expression. "Oh, hell's fire, Pa—what kind of woollybuggar you got us into this time?"

"Isn't a woollybuggar, girl. It's the best honest poker hand I've ever had. Come on, now." Dicey tugged his daughter to her feet. "Time's a wastin', and I can't spend any more of it explainin'. How much we got left?"

"You know there's more sugar than money in that jar—and just what do you need more for anyway?" Sparks of hope flared in her dark brown eyes.

Dicey sighed at the thought of losing the big pot. "I'm in a game the likes of which I've never been privy to, nor likely to be privy to again. I need five hundred to cover the bet."

Maxine brushed the dust from the dirty alley off her shirt and looked at her father. Loving and well-meaning as he might be, Dicey was not a man who always understood the percentages in a game like poker. She grumbled to herself, and not for the first time, about the injustices that kept her, a woman, from joining the gamblers and showing them a thing or two about poker.

Trying to keep censure out of her voice, she asked, "What are you holding that could be worth five hundred, even if we had it?"

Dicey slowly shook his head. "I've got me the most beautiful hand of clovers you'll ever lay yur big black eyes on. Looks like they'll be wasted if'n we can't think of somthin'—and fast."

"A flush?" she squealed, dropping her reservations as she picked up the scent of prosperity. "Hot damn! Why didn't you say so? You've really got an honest-to-God flush?"

"Aye, a loverly little bouquet of the prettiest little clubs you'd ever hope to hold. They'd be securin' a pot of at least ten thousand for yur dear old pa if I only had the means to cover 'em."

"Ten thousand?" Maxine cried out, her heartbeat accelerating. "Did you say, ten *thousand* dollars?"

"Aye, girl, but if we got no money—"

"We got something better than money—remember?" Maxine winked as she reached into her valise and pulled out her only skirt. She continued to interrogate her father as she pulled the garment up over her worn trousers. "How many players left in the game?"

Fairly sure what she was up to, Dicey knotted his bushy eyebrows and muttered, "Just one other fellah. What are you thinkin' of doin', Maxie? If it's what it looks like—"

"I'm just covering the wager, Pa. No need to get in a fret."

Dicey puffed out his chest and straightened his spine, but he still fell one inch shorter than his statuesque daughter. "I won't be hearin' of it," he said in his most fatherly voice. "Do I have to remind you about what happened in Columbia a couple years back? We *lost* you! I thought you'd never get shuck of that old miner and his demanding wife."

"Now, Pa," Maxine said with a wide grin, "that wasn't so bad, and have you forgotten the time before that? You won—and mighty handily, if memory serves!"

Maxine removed her hat and tucked the hem of the long shapeless man's shirt she was wearing inside the waistband of the skirt. Then, working to achieve the look that had always served them well in the past, she removed the pins securing her hair at the top of her head and let it spill down her back in an unruly tumble of waves and curls.

As she parted her mane of fiery red hair and began to braid it into two sections, she continued, "The other player—he pretty sure of himself? Did you have any trouble talking him into waiting for your money?"

Dicey ignored her questions. He stared at his daughter, uncomfortable and more than a little guilty about ever having used her in such a manner—even if it had been her idea the first time they'd tried it. Since then, she'd grown into a beautiful young woman, one who was becoming increasingly difficult to hide behind girlish manners and pigtails. It hadn't been so bad a few years back, but now, surely the stranger would realize that Dicey wagered not a shy young servant girl, but a lovely, full-grown woman. And if he did . . .

Unaware of her father's concerns, Maxine arranged the braids down the front of her shirt and then replaced her Palo Alto and pulled it down low on her forehead. She spread her arms wide, and said, "Well? How do I look?"

Dicey pressed his lips together and shook his head. "Like a twenty-year-old woman dressed up to resemble a lass of twelve."

Maxine frowned and tugged her shirt up from the band of the skirt until it bloused into a shapeless mass that hung around her hips. "Better?"

"Aye." Still hesitant, but wavering at the idea that her plan might succeed, Dicey worked a callused finger back and forth across the stubble on his chin. "We might get away with it at that, but you'll have to keep a pitiful pout about you and turn yur shoulders in to hide yur, ah . . . the fact yur a woman."

She grumbled inwardly about those miserable mounds of flesh she always struggled to conceal from the prying eyes of other argonauts, the completely worthless appendages she would never have use for even if she lived to be a hundred. A woman had to marry and have babies to find a use for breasts, and such a fate would never befall Maxine McKain. She already had all the children she could handle—her father and her twin brother, Max.

Dicey checked his watch and then glanced back at his daughter. "You look fine, I s'pose, but I'm still not sure we ought to be takin' such a chance with you."

Undaunted, Maxine shrugged. "I can take care of myself." She looked down to the far end of the alley. There, her gaze lingered for a second before she called out to her brother. "I'm going with Pa, Max. You stay put until—" She glanced over at Dicey and winked, "*we* come back to get you. You hear?"

Huddled with a group of boys around seven years of age—the approximate mental age Max had attained— he didn't look up or wonder where his father and sister might be going. He merely nodded vigorously and continued to coax his pet frog to jump the distance between himself and one of the boys.

Dicey paid no mind to the actual exchange between his children. He was listening to the sound of his daughter's voice, hearing its husky, womanlike quality. Her disguise would be for naught if the gambler heard it as well. Keeping her safety in mind, he advised her as they approached the saloon doors, "I think it'd be best

this time if you didn't speak, darlin'—nary a word.
Keep yur eyes cast down to the floor and smile sweetly
should the gentleman ask you to look at him. But other
than that, yur a mute. Got it?"

"Sounds fine to me." Then she added, "I know how
good it looks for us and all Pa, but just in case that fella
has an ace up his sleeve, I think we'd best have a plan."

Dicey furrowed his brow and checked the time just
before they reached the swinging doors. He had less
than a minute to produce his share of the pot. He whispered, "I got faith in that flush, I do, girl. I 'spect to be
a-winnin', but if somethin' should go wrong, don't
worry too much about a plan. Max will be close at
hand. Beg off to use the privy if you can, and we'll spirit
you away. If that don't work and this here stranger
proves a might stubborn, just cry out and yur brother
will be a savin' you. Ready?"

"As I'll ever be." She winked and hugged her valise
to her bosom. "Let's go rake in that pot!"

"That's my girl," Dicey said as he pinched her
cheeks.

The Scotsman pushed open the doors to the saloon
and propelled Maxine inside the dingy room. The piano
player abruptly stopped pounding on the ivory keys,
and the crowd, mostly miners down on their luck and
full up with whiskey, slowly began to quiet. Interest in
the enormous pot took precedence over the latest story
of lost treasure.

Keeping her head down as her father had instructed,
Maxine felt rather than saw the stares of the miners as
she passed by them. The air was fetid with the odor of
stale whiskey and heavily spiced tobacco, pungent with

the sweat and desperation of men too long in the company of other men. The scent turned Maxine's stomach, but she kept pace with her father and hoped her nausea would soon pass. As they neared the poker table where the crowd waited, she lowered the double rows of her thick auburn lashes until they practically rested on her cheeks. Playing the pitiful serving girl to the hilt, she jutted out her bottom lip.

Dicey patted her hand by way of comfort as he addressed the man sitting at the table. "Aye, and that didn't take too long now did it?"

Dane glanced from the girl to his watch, and then to the Scotsman. "Made it with less than ten seconds to spare. Where's your money? In the girl's bag?"

Dicey hooted his laughter and then turned to his daughter and made a grand sweeping gesture with his arm. "Any fool can match the pot with a few dollars, but I've brought you somethin' better than gold! It's a fine handmaiden I offer to cover my wager. She's perfeck. You couldn't ask for a more perfeck gal to tend to yur chores."

Surprise carved grooves in Dane's smooth, bronzed skin. He straightened his spine and propped his elbows on the poker table and then he studied the young girl, noting the patches in her cinnamon and russet gingham skirt, the slight trembling in her shoulders, and her subservient demeanor. Although he couldn't quite make out her features with her head hung low, he guessed her expression would be one of fear, if not downright terror.

His lip curled in a disgusted snarl, Dane turned his attention back to the Scotsman. "I don't wager on human flesh. Match the pot now, or fold."

"But you do na' understand!" Dicey argued. "This gal be worth every bit of what I'm owin' the pot. She can rustle up a gourmet meal outta rattlesnake hide, make a winter coat outta cactus needles and dandelions, or spot a gold nugget at the bottom of a bog. Best of all—she's a dummy. Perfeck."

"A dummy?" Again Dane's curious gaze raked over the girl. "Looks smart enough to me."

"Smart got nothin' to do with it," said Dicey. "She can't talk! She'll keep yur belly full, yur clothes mended, and best of all, she won't give you no lip in the process. When this little gal is full grown," Dicey added with a twinkle in his eye, "she will be the perfeck woman."

One of the card players who had dropped out when the stakes had gotten too high gave a bawdy chuckle. "How perfect is this little gal at keeping a man's bedroll warmed? Now that's the real question, ain't it fellahs?"

Maxine's fingers curled into fists as the other men joined in with their own ribald comments and lusty chuckles, but she kept her gaze on the pot, reflecting on what ten thousand dollars represented to her and her family. It would mean enough money for a new beginning, the real home she'd always dreamed of having. She yearned to bring an end to the nomadic McKain lifestyle and the years of uncertainty. She envisioned a cottage high in the mountains, where Max could flourish, far away from the taunts and cruelties of those who wouldn't accept him the way he was.

Although Maxie was ignoring the crude men, Dicey's gut rolled as their vulgarities burned his ears. He'd made a mistake, a dreadful error in judgment.

How could he have been so stupid as to let Maxie talk him into bringing her into this kind of atmosphere? What manner of abuse had his carelessness exposed her to? He glanced around the room, preparing to withdraw his bet, but then his gaze fell upon the huge pile of chips and gold, a bonanza just waiting for him to claim it.

He had a flush, he reminded himself. He thought of the games he'd be invited to with these stakes, of the pots ten times bigger than this drop in a miner's bucket. All the riches in the world were just waiting for a man with a pocketful of money.

His misgivings shrinking as his confidence grew, Dicey decided to forge ahead. After he won, he reasoned, he would make it up to Maxie and buy her some new boots or trousers. Maybe both. His sense of purpose and priority renewed, Dicey smiled across the table at the swarthy stranger. "Well now, sir—are we havin' a bet?"

Dane hesitated, weighing the inconvenience of accepting the girl against the miserable life she would lead if she remained a pawn of the Scotsman. "Tell her to look up," he demanded. "I want to know exactly what I'm betting on."

Dicey nudged Maxine in the ribs. "Have a smile for the nice gentleman and show him yur good strong teeth, girl."

Maxine lifted her chin and cast a lazy grin as impish as it was calculated across the table. When her gaze collided with those intense blue eyes, the sheer physical force of the man took her breath away. She reached for the chair in front of her to steady herself.

The stranger was quiet, deliberate in his appraisal. He stared back at her with an almost intimate expression—a look that seemed to go beyond her clothing to what lay beneath. Did he realize that he gazed on a fully grown woman instead of a young girl?

Uncharacteristically hesitant, unsure of her next move, Maxine gawked back at the handsome stranger. This was no grubby miner or down-on-his-luck gambler; this was a man the likes of which she had never seen. In her years of living on the fringes of decent society, Maxine had grown used to, and even expected, the rat-eyed stares and hollow expressions of hopeless desperation which were so abundant among her peers. But this man was different. He looked at her with all the reticence of a barn owl, and yet he was tense, coiled like the bullwhip he wore circling his shoulder, alert and prepared to strike at a moment's notice.

Chilled by his gaze, Maxine looked away from his arresting facial features to his clothing. In contrast to the men surrounding him, he wore a suit and vest of expensive black broadcloth and a matching flat-brimmed hat trimmed with a braided silver rope circling the crown. His attire suggested wealth, perhaps an aristocratic background, a class of person not usually found in the tenderloin area. Who was he, and what was he doing here?

Noting the girl's undisguised appraisal of him, especially her bold, adult stare, Dane twirled his index finger in the air. "Turn around, niña. I wish to see all of you."

The stranger's voice filled her senses. The sound was deliciously dark and rich, smooth as black velvet, and inflected by his Spanish heritage. Fighting a shudder, Maxine spun around in a slow, deliberate circle. When she came face to face with him once again, her pulse hammered in her throat, and her knees felt weak. She knew without a doubt that her features were flushed and far too womanlike for her own good. Working to achieve a more childlike expression, Maxine sucked in her bottom lip, forced her two front teeth to jut beyond her slight overbite and widened her eyes until they were round and properly innocent.

Caught by the sudden urge to laugh at the girl's facial contortions, Dane coughed into his fist as he made his decision. If he won, he reasoned, at least he could arrange a meal, a hot bath, and a way for the poor wretch to start her life anew. With a barely perceptible nod, he glanced across the table to the worried Scotsman. "She'll do."

With a triumphant grin, Dicey turned to the manager and proclaimed, "I call. Pot's matched, me good man!"

"Pot's right," the manager concurred.

Dicey plopped down in his chair and lifted the five precious cards off the scarred tabletop. After spreading the ace-high assortment of clubs into the shape of a fan, he looked up at the Spaniard. "Read 'em and weep, son."

"You're a little anxious, friend," Dane answered, his voice low and steady. "The obligation to show the first hand was mine." Then, with his dark face as unreadable as it had been during the game, he turned his cards over one at a time. After he'd revealed the last and displayed his winning full house, he fit the handle of the bullwhip to his palm and added, "But . . . better late than never, I expect."

Dicey gulped, and his already florid complexion turned bright and rosy. Beside him, he could feel Maxine's disappointment, hear her barely audible groan over the collective gasp of the crowd. He drew in a shaky breath, and said, "I can na' believe it. I was so sure. . . ."

"Happens to the best of us," Dane offered by way of grudging condolences. His chair screeched as he pushed away from the table and stood up. He turned to the saloon manager. "You mind collecting and holding the pot for me, Reid? I'd like to get this little girl out of here."

"No problem at all. Pick it up when it pleases you."

"Thanks. Keep a twenty-dollar gold piece for your trouble." Then he glanced at the girl and extended his hand. "Come on, niña," he said in a much gentler, softer voice. "You belong to me now."

Although her mind was busy calculating the best way to make her escape, Maxine kept her head low and meekly shuffled over to the stranger's side. When she ignored his outstretched hand, he slid his fingers along her waist and used them as prods against her back as he propelled her through the swinging doors and out into the fading glow of the sunset. Maxine could pick out the rhythm of her father's footsteps behind them.

Keeping a possessive hand at the girl's waist, the other filled with the thick stump of rawhide, Dane whistled for his buggy and then turned to Dicey. The Scotsman was backing down the boardwalk toward the alley, his gait more stealthy than casual.

Dane made a quick perusal of the area. Situated in the heart of the Barbary Coast, the Lucky Nugget Saloon graced the corners of Jackson and Gold Streets, a section of town long on brothels, saloons, and gambling houses, and short on morals or any sense of fair play. Fairly sure the Scotsman had an accomplice waiting for him in the alley, Dane tightened his grip on the girl's elbow as he addressed the older man. "Please be so kind as to remain here with us until the buggy arrives."

Though allowing Maxine to go with the man was the last thing Dicey wanted to do, he averted his gaze so the stranger wouldn't see the concern in his eyes. He shrugged. "If it pleases you, but you don't have a worry comin' from me. You won her fair and square."

Dane gave him a short nod and turned as a young Chinaman arrived with his fine piano box buggy. The covered black two-seater was pulled by an exquisitely beautiful gray mare.

Maxine's mouth dropped open as the Spaniard led her to the small enameled door. Never in all her life had she seen such a magnificent horse or so luxurious a buggy. She sighed, careful to keep the sound to herself, and glanced at her new "owner." Could he be as rich as he looked? Was it just possible that she and her father had stumbled across something better than the pot in that poker game?

After giving the boy a dollar, Dane turned to Maxine and reached out to relieve her of the valise. "This will ride better at the back of the buggy," he said.

She held it tightly for a moment, with instinct, not fear, driving her to keep her most precious—in fact, her only—possessions close to her bosom. She looked into his eyes, trusting her intuition to point out any signs of danger or evil in the man, but all she could see was the sharp contrast of blue against the warm nutmeg color of his skin and his midnight black hair. Maxine gulped as she allowed the stranger to stow her belongings.

When Dane returned to the side of the buggy, he fit his hands around her waist and said, "Relax and don't be afraid. No harm will come to you." Then he lifted her as easily as he would a child and deposited her on the tufted leather seat.

Stunned as much by the man as by thoughts of a new and possibly very rewarding woollybuggar, Maxine allowed him to position her. Then she sat back, jutted her teeth back out over her lip, and gave him the most pitiful expression she could manage.

Dicey ignored his daughter's antics. He was out of ideas and time and beginning to panic. With a slight tremor in his voice belying his words, he said, "She's all yours, me good man. I say, good riddance and good luck. You'll be needin' it with this worthless gal."

"Worthless?" Dane said with a careful grin. "I thought you said she was the perfect handmaiden."

"Well," Dicey muttered, his feet shuffling nervously, "might be I stretched the truth a bit, might be I handed you just the tiniest bit of a story. Truth is, girl's as useless as a milk pail under a bull. I'd only be playin' fair to you if I were to take her back and find another way to pay off the debt. What am I owin' you?"

Smiling inwardly, Dane climbed onto the rig and took the reins in his hand. "Bet's a bet, old man. I'm sure I can find some use for her." He winked, and then asked, "Does the girl have a name?"

"Ah." Dicey cleared his throat. "Ah . . . I just call her, ah . . ." He glanced at her braids, remembering the name few dared to call his volatile daughter, and then grinned as he drew in his breath and said, "Red."

Dicey reached up then, thinking for one insane moment of dragging Maxine down off the rig and facing the stranger's wrath, but one look from her brought his hand back to his side. She'd lost the sudden flash of anger the name "Red" had always brought to her dark eyes and was actually smiling, her creamy complexion fairly glowing with excitement. Then she quickly reversed her expression and frowned, waving him away with a tiny backward jerk of her head.

Dicey knew the look. Maxine wanted him to lay low, to let her go. Were he and Max simply supposed to follow her and wait until the opportunity presented itself to reclaim her? Or would she give them some kind of signal? Not quite sure what to do, the opportunity to effect a quick rescue was taken from him when Dane slapped the reins across the mare's back and the buggy lurched to life. As Maxine waved an exuberant goodbye, Dicey slowly shook his head and headed for the alley to collect his son.

After the rig had moved several feet down the rain-sodden street, Maxine glanced back to the corner. Her father, joined now by her twin, Max, stood waiting, preparing, she imagined, to track the buggy. Comforted by the sight of the two people she loved most, she twisted back around and let her gaze settle on the elegant horse bobbing along in front of the carriage. Tiny explosions of light caught her eye, and she noticed the reflections came from the silver rosette and diamond shapes embedded in the expensive leather bridle and harness. Hope glittered in Maxine's dark eyes to equal the luster of the polished metal. She drew in a sharp breath and began to calculate the rig's worth.

Cautiously turning her head to the left and looking out of the corner of her eye, Maxine snuck another peek at the man who thought he owned her. She could sniff the air and smell money, touch his jacket and feel it.

Money was elusive, at least to the McKain family, but very necessary. It was the ways and means to a new life.

Money was the only thing that could give Max freedom from ridicule and Maxine the peace of mind she'd never known.

Smiling as she imagined the riches the Spaniard might possess, Maxine relaxed and began to stroke the soft leather seat as if she already owned it.

2

An hour later, Maxine stood quietly as Dane's Chinese handmaiden helped her into a borrowed gown.

"You no little girl," the servant complained as she struggled with the buttons at the back of the dress. "You woman—plenty big woman, too. I have hard time squeezing you inside Señor Dane's lady friend's dress, but I can do. Miss Joy made like a sparrow. But you plenty big girl all right."

Struggling to keep her usually active tongue still, Maxine ignored the serving girl's remarks about her less-than-petite figure and gasped as she regarded her image in the fancy looking glass. The gown was fashioned out of white embroidered muslin and sprigged with tiny flowers and an all-over spot pattern in hues of green. Short-sleeved and cut low at the neckline, the dress was a couple of years behind the fashions of the day, according to the newest ladies' magazines Maxine pilfered from here and there during her travels, but she didn't care. It was simply the most beautiful gown she'd ever seen. And, for tonight at least, it belonged to her.

The girl, Ling Ling, clapped her hands together, almost jerking a cry of surprise from her "mute" charge, but Maxine managed to bite off the sound and tear her gaze away from the mirror. Raising her eyebrows as question marks, she cocked her head to one side and waited for her next instruction.

"Supper ready. You put on shoes, come to dining room. Chop, chop." Then she spun around on her satin-slippered toes and scurried from the room.

Alone for the first time in a home that seemed to Maxine a mansion, she turned back to the mirror. An almost, but not quite, pretty girl—*woman*—appeared, as if by magic. Could it really be her, Maxine McKain? She had never thought of herself as anything more than the freak her mother had said she was, what with her riotous mass of flaming red hair, height to equal most men, and feet too wide for dainty feminine slippers. Maxine was a lot of things, and most of those attributes she held dear, but pretty had never been a word she'd associated with herself. And while it certainly wasn't accurate even now, she did have to admit she wasn't quite as homely as she thought either.

What would the Spaniard see when he looked at her? A homely young girl or a pretty young woman? If he saw the latter, would he think he could keep her, and use her the way miners used saloon girls? Could she manage to—

"Psst. Psst."

At the sound, Maxine cocked her head in the direction of the stove which kept the bath water heated.

"Psst. Maxie, girl—you in there?"

Sucking in her breath as she recognized her father's voice, Maxine hissed a quick, "Shussh!"

She checked to make sure the door was tightly shut, tiptoed over to the satin-draped vanity, and removed the matching stool. After pushing the chair under the high privacy window and climbing up on the seat, she gripped the windowsill and peered out through the narrow opening.

"Pa?" Maxine whispered. "Where are you?"

The reply was a groan, the sound of something scraping against the wood exterior of the house. Then her father's bald pate bobbed into view for a split second before it disappeared. Again, there was a groan, and the top half of Dicey's face reappeared, wobbly, but apparently secure enough for a brief conversation.

Through a chuckle, she whispered, "What are you standing on, Pa?"

"Max's shoulders," he managed as he clawed at the narrow windowsill and struggled for balance. "You all right, girl?"

"I'm fine—in fact, I've just had a bath, Pa! A real bath—hot water and everything! And now the Señor is going to feed me a great big supper. I bet he's got—"

"Maxie, darlin'—I dona' know how much longer I can last on yur brother's shoulders. We come to get you. What's the best way? Right through the front door, or can we spirit you away through a side passage?"

"But Pa," she said, forgetting to whisper, "I don't

want to leave yet—I'm starved, and at supper, I'm sure I can make off with food enough for you and Max, too. After that, the serving girl said I could go to sleep for as long as I want. I figured then I could work out some kind of woollybuggar that'd keep us in clover for years. This fella's got more silver nailed to his harness than we've got tricks!"

Dicey shook his head. "You'll not be going to bed in that house. This Cordobes fellow seems gentleman enough, but I'm not bettin' on his intentions after the lights are blown out. I'll give you one hour to finish up yur bathing and get a bite. If'n yur not outside by then, yur brother will be fetchin' you."

"Oh, Pa, you know that I can take care of myself. Why don't you just wait until—"

A loud knock sounded at the dressing room door and it flew open. Maxine stiffened, and Dicey wobbled. Then he toppled out of sight. The thud of her father's well-padded body resounded against the earth below, nearly, but not quite hiding the sound of his moan.

Maxine was sure the game was up. Slowly, trying to give herself time to think of a story, she turned to face the intruder.

The serving girl stood in the doorway, her brows raised in puzzlement. Maxine hoped the girl had not heard her father's fall. By way of explanation for her position on top of the chair, she drew in a dramatic lungful of damp evening air, then smiled and hopped back down to the floor.

Apparently satisfied that her charge was only taking some air, Ling Ling shook her finger and scolded, "You

very, very slow. Supper ready. Señor Dane will be
angry if you do not come now." She clapped her hands
together loudly, and demanded, "You put on slippers,
follow me."

Maxine eyed the fancy shoes with their pointed toes.
She was half tempted to give them a try but far too
aware of her precarious position to chance wearing the
delicate footgear—even in the unlikely event they
should fit. When the time came to make her escape, she
would have to move fast. With a defiant shake of her
head, she marched over to her worn but comfortable
trail boots and tugged them on. Ling Ling sighed but
gave her no argument. Instead, she turned and opened
the door.

Keeping one eye on the girl's back, Maxine sidled
over to the vanity, grabbed an ivory-handled hairbrush,
comb, and matching mirror, and stuffed them into her
carpetbag before she followed Ling Ling out of the
room and down the hallway.

The serving girl, several paces ahead of Maxine,
entered the dining room and announced, "We have
plenty much trouble fitting dress, but Missy ready
now."

A grumpy feminine voice answered, "Thank God for
that—it's about time."

Dane shot his mistress a narrow glance before rising
from the far end of the table and addressing the servant. "You're dismissed, Ling Ling. Thanks for your
help."

The serving girl bowed and gave Maxine a little
push, sending her stumbling across the polished hardwood floor.

Dane intended to show the girl to her chair, but he stood locked in his tracks at the sight of her.

"*Niña?*" he whispered, unable to believe this lovely creature was the same girl he'd won in a poker game. "Is that really . . . you?"

The female voice, which Maxine discovered was attached to a lithe blond woman, resounded. "*This* is your idea of a little girl, Dane?"

But Dane wasn't listening to Joy, or even thinking about her. He was listening to his instincts, and to the warnings sounding at the back of his mind. Yet all he could think about was the beautiful young woman before him and what delights the night might hold.

Dane smiled and said, "Sit down, please, niña—although, since *niña* means young girl, I think the first thing I shall have to do is start using the Scotsman's name for you."

Clutching her precious valise, Maxine obeyed and slid onto the seat. After glancing nervously at the other woman, she propped the carpetbag against the legs of her chair. Then she sat up and cautiously eyed her host. He'd taken a seat across from her, his index finger, long and tanned, slowly stroking the cleft at the center of his chin, as if he were deep in thought. His fingers were dark and smooth, she noticed, yet thickly muscled. They looked like the hands of neither a miner nor a pampered aristocrat. What kind of man was this?

Dane broke into her thoughts as he made the introductions. "The lady to your left is Miss Joy Hunt. It was she who offered this dress to you. Joy, this young lady's name is Red."

Scowling at the name as she tore away from the Spaniard's gaze, she looked into the pale blue eyes of the woman who was offering her a limp, tentative hand. Maxine gripped it and shook it as if she were operating a rusty pump handle.

Joy snatched her delicate fingers out of Maxine's hand and turned to Dane to complain, "My Lord, this girl—this *woman*—is positively boorish!"

"Enough."

The word was a whisper, but Dane's tone cut off any further criticisms Joy may have had in mind. She dropped her hands into her lap and pursed her lips, her objections reduced to an occasional scathing glance in Maxine's direction.

Openly watching the exchange between her host and his mistress, Maxine was fascinated by the woman's unquestioning obedience. She lifted the heavy silver goblet next to her plate and sniffed its contents. Wine. Good wine at that, she guessed, and she was thirsty. Never taking her eyes off the Spaniard, she downed the wine in one noisy gulp and then reached for a nearby pitcher and refilled the goblet with water. As she swallowed the contents in the same manner, Maxine heard the dainty blond woman groan.

As amused by Joy's reactions as he was suspicious of the girl, Dane chuckled lightly as he said, "Tomorrow I will find a spot for you with the household staff, Red, but for tonight, think of yourself a guest in my home. Please, eat and drink your fill." He sat back to watch her reactions to that.

Maxine didn't have to be told twice. She reached across the table and gathered in a basket of rolls and a plate of crackers spread with something black and shiny. She took several of the crackers and dropped them onto her own china plate. Then, still staring into Dane's incredible eyes, and thinking how out of place the shocking blue color seemed against the backdrop of his rich caramel skin, she popped one of the little crackers into her mouth and began to chew. A second later, shuddering from the horrid taste, Maxine spit the foul offering back onto her plate.

"Oh, my Lord, Dane," Joy muttered. "How much of this am I expected to endure?"

Signaling for his mistress's silence, but never taking his gaze off his mysterious guest, Dane smiled and asked, "Am I to assume you do not care for Russian caviar, young lady?"

Maxine grimaced, wrinkling her nose and shivering at the thought.

Laughing at the gesture, Dane offered another plate of food. "Perhaps you would care to try the curried oysters?"

Oysters? Maxine sniffed but was unable to pick up any foul odor. She had once tried—and liked—the strange-looking mollusks in a concoction called Hangtown Fry, a crude bacon and oyster omelet that owed its origins to the newly christened city of Placerville. Too hungry to pass up anything now, Maxine accepted the offering and popped one of the appetizers in her mouth. It slithered across her tongue, feeling almost as if it were still alive. She quickly spit it out, leaving it to join the remnants of the caviar already on her plate.

Feeling forgotten, disgusted as well, Joy groaned.

"Puh-leeze, Dane. You simply must remove this street urchin from the table. She's absolutely making me ill."

He waved her off. "We just need to find something she likes." Dane rang a bell at the side of his plate. A moment later, a serving girl appeared with two large covered platters. He instructed her, "Please give our guest a new plate before you leave, Mary. I'm afraid seafood doesn't seem to agree with her."

Then he sat back in his chair and resumed watching her, studying her dark brown eyes, plumbing their depths for signs of deception or menace. She was, he decided, either a very well-trained actress bent on relieving him of his possessions, or an utterly guileless, feeble-minded wretch. If it was the latter, why wasn't she more afraid, more nervous about her new surroundings? Why did he feel as if he were looking down the business end of a double-barreled shotgun, instead of simply a pair of big brown eyes? She possessed, he decided, the absolutely fearless gaze of a woman more frightened of caviar than she was of her plight.

Still pondering the possibilities, Dane watched as Mary removed the covering on one of the large silver platters and offered it to his new charge.

Maxine's eyes grew round when she saw the huge mound of sliced beef surrounded by new potatoes, beets, and walnuts. She filled her plate and then threw herself into the meal, using only one of her three forks and her left thumb as a pusher. Between bites, when she was certain neither Dane nor Joy was watching her, she managed to drop much of the food into the napkin she'd stretched across her lap for that purpose. Once, she "accidentally" knocked the basket of rolls off the table, directing several of the baked goods to land inside her valise. At the meal's end, after a healthy portion of jelly puffs and ice cream, she folded the napkin over the pilfered fare and added the bundle to the growing contents of the carpetbag.

Throughout the dinner, the blond woman sat perched on the edge of her chair like an expensive canary, fluttering and groaning each time Maxine helped a slice of beef into her mouth with her fingers or took a noisy swallow of water. The Spaniard's expression flickered between amusement and curiosity, making Maxine feel as if he were gauging her reactions and making mental notes of her every movement.

As the girl finished her dessert, Dane finally directed his attention to Joy. She was sulking, with her small mouth drooped at the corners in the unappealing pout she'd been wearing far too often of late. Their relationship was nearing the end, he realized, and had been headed that way for some weeks. It was definitely time to do something about it.

Shaking off a vague sense of irritation, Dane said to Joy, "Go to the library and prepare our cognacs. I'll be with you in a moment."

"But we usually pour our brandy together," she said, her pout even more pronounced. "Why aren't you coming with me tonight?"

He answered in a voice no longer melodic, but taut as a bowstring. "I intend to see this young lady to her room myself. I think it would be best to set a few rules before she retires for the evening."

Joy shot Maxine a nasty look and continued to object. "But Dane, Ling Ling can do all that. Besides, I don't think you should keep her. She's much too old to be trained properly, and Lord help us, have you forgotten her abominable manners? Didn't you notice her—"

"I've informed you of my wishes," he said, the words deliberate, his expression rigid. "Go wait for me in the library. Pour us a brandy. I won't be long."

Grumbling under her breath, her mouth now extended to a scowl, Joy stood and swept from the room.

Dane moved to Maxine's side and pulled out her chair. "Please come with me." He reached down to collect her worn valise as she rose, but she beat him to it. "As you wish," he murmured. Then he took her firmly by the elbow and led her from the room.

Upstairs, Dane escorted her into a fluffy, feminine bedroom and closed the door behind them. "This," he said, prying the valise from her hand and dropping it on a rocking chair, "is your room for tonight only. We'll find a spot for you in the servants' quarters tomorrow, but for now, I hope you'll enjoy the use of whatever pleases you in here."

As he spoke, Maxine surveyed her surroundings. A huge four-poster bed swathed in floral curtains and crinkly bed coverings looked soft and inviting, and a vanity, skirted in the same billowing fabric as the bed and window, supported twice the toiletries as the one she'd used downstairs. Beside the dressing table stood a separate washstand holding a pitcher and bowl made of white ironstone. Such luxury and comfort, she thought, again marveling at the excesses in the home.

If only she could talk and ask the myriad of questions piling up inside her. Were all these rooms—the seven she'd counted downstairs added to Lord knew how many upstairs—here just for the comfort of two people? Where did he get the money for such finery? Gambling?

Dane moved behind her and took her shoulders in his hands. She flinched but did not try to escape his grasp. Puzzling over yet another enigma in her behavior, he said, "You may look and enjoy all you wish after I leave you. For now, I seek the answers to some very important questions." He carefully turned her, keeping her shoulders bracketed between his hands, and stared into her eyes.

Maxine looked up at him with an expression she hoped was innocent and properly subservient, but the Spaniard's countenance was unchanged, almost impassive. Her instinct deserted her, leaving her unsure of her next move, and, even more importantly, of his. He seemed to bore into her, seeking, it seemed, her very life story. He bent his head low, his gaze lingering on her hair and face, then drifted lower to the soft swell of her breasts pushing up and out from the tight bodice. He drew in a sharp breath and then casually looked back into her eyes.

Maxine's muscles tensed, and then weakened. Her bottom lip began to tremble, and she sensed that soon her entire body would follow suit. The Spaniard was too close. She felt his gentle hands on her naked shoulders, his warm breath, his male presence. She could breathe and inhale his very essence. She steeled herself against the Spaniard's gestures, against herself and her reactions to his touch, and worked at presenting a brave front as he continued to stare at her.

Beautiful, Dane thought, studying her bone structure, moist dark eyes, and attractive—if a little too flashy—red hair. Beautiful, but such a waste of unfinished womanhood. How many men before the Scotsman had owned this one, he wondered, used her body and then sold her or wagered her away? How welltrained had she become during her years of servitude in matters of the flesh?

At the thought, Dane had to give pause to sudden lustful sensations. Although he was not a man generally attracted to the help, he wasn't above spending a night in a particularly winsome serving girl's arms on occasion. His tastes usually ran more to refined and well-educated young women, but somehow, this ragamuffin, this woman of the streets, fascinated him. Was it a simple case of boredom with Joy? he wondered. Or was it that spark he saw in those dark brown eyes, that underlying sense of wildness he'd never experienced in himself or another before?

As thoughts of what might occur between them bloomed in his mind, Dane tenderly dragged the backs of his fingers along the young woman's jawline, and then slowly slid them down along her throat. She shivered at his touch. Almost certain now that she would go willingly to his bed, he brushed his fingertips even lower, across the soft rise of her breasts. Again, she shivered.

"Very good," Dane murmured from deep in his throat. "You feel it too."

Maxine didn't know exactly *what* she was feeling, or

what he was talking about, but she was sure that whatever it was, it most definitely led to nothing but trouble—the kind of trouble she might not be able to get out of. The Spaniard's eyes, she noticed, were no longer sharp and steely, but a soft, lazy, powder blue that seemed glazed and inexplicably more dangerous than before. Everything about him had become more dangerous somehow. She wanted to run away from him, but she couldn't seem to move. She felt cornered, trapped, a paralyzed fawn to his stalking cougar, and yet it was her own body holding her at bay. She didn't even seem to *want* to move.

Dane, sure now that moments like this were what she expected, crooned deeply and whispered, "Your skin is so creamy and unblemished, it is hard to believe that you have been indentured at all. If not for your hands, one might almost imagine dressing you up and taking you out on the town."

His voice, the black, velvet melody of his words; his gaze, so deep and penetrating, so full of mystery; his hands, gentle on her skin, teasing, arousing—all caressed and confused her, made Maxine feel hot and cold at once, a frightened child in the body of a fully grown woman. What was he doing to her? Was this the prelude to that lovemaking business Lola Montez had told her about a few years back, when the McKains were living in Grass Valley? Would he tear open his trousers and try to assault her next? And if he did, what manner of defense should she use? The eye-gouge her father had taught her or the knee-jerk Lola seemed to be so fond of? Or was she in more trouble than she thought and utterly defenseless?

Dane had no idea what the girl was thinking, but he sensed that her mind may not have been following his intentions after all. He dropped his head even lower, closer to her mouth, and said, "Is something wrong? You seem nervous. Surely you are not afraid of me—are you?"

Still captivated by his voice and the way he was making her feel, Maxine's lashes bobbed against her cheeks as she slowly nodded.

"Oh, no—do not be afraid. I will not harm or beat you, nor shall I force you to do anything you don't wish to do. Is that it? Are you afraid I will visit your bed uninvited?"

Visit her bed uninvited? Maxine squeezed her eyes shut and tried to make sense of his words and of her own feelings, but while her eyes were closed, the Spaniard's lips brushed hers, tasting and testing for one brief moment before they moved away, and she was more confused than ever. When her eyes popped open, he began to reassure her.

"Never fear for your physical safety from Dane del Cordobes, Señorita. When you and I succumb to one another, it will be with equal desire. *Comprende?*"

Maxine took a deep breath, thinking perhaps she ought to speak, to try and explain herself as well as she could without raising his ire. It wasn't as if he didn't know she was a full-grown woman now, so what could it hurt if he discovered one more little surprise about her? Hadn't he just said he would never beat her?

*   *   *

Downstairs, unheard by either Dane or Maxine, the bell rang. When the houseboy, Chang, opened the door, the first thing he saw was a young redheaded man whose bulk nearly filled the entrance. The second was that young man's very wide fist just before it connected with his jaw.

The servant leaned this way and that, as if wavering about which direction to fall. Before he could make the decision, Max caught him in his strong arms and gently deposited him on the marble floor. Then he stood up and called, "It's okay, Pa."

Dicey crept inside the foyer and made a fast survey of the area. "Go on upstairs, son," he whispered. "Open each door you come to until you find Maxie. You know what to do after that. I'll stay down here and make sure this fellow doesn't wake up and spoil things. Go on now—and be quiet."

Inside the fluffy guest room, Maxine had made her decision. She squared her shoulders, cleared her throat, and opened her mouth, but before she could form the first syllable, the door behind Dane opened. Her brother entered the room, his wide innocent face beaming with delight and relief that he'd found her.

When her twin's gaze shifted to the Spaniard, the smile twisted into a grimace as he realized the man held his sister captive. Maxine cried out, "No, wait, Max! Don't!"

Surprised by the sound of her voice, and by the odd and confusing announcement, Dane stood staring at her for a full moment before he realized she was talking to someone other than himself. He turned much too late, just in time to offer his chin to the biggest fist he'd ever seen.

Max's blow carried twice the punch of the one he delivered downstairs. Dane was catapulted backward across the room, where he crashed into the walnut armoire and then crumpled to the floor.

"Oh, my God!" Maxine cried, rushing to the Spaniard's supine body. "Why did you have to hit him so hard, Max? Didn't you hear me? I didn't want you to hit him at all."

Maxine bent over the injured man, pulled his embroidered handkerchief from his breast pocket, and carefully wiped the blood from the split in his chin.

With tears puddling in the corners of his eyes, Max shuffled up beside his sister and stood staring down at her while she tended to the stranger. "Pa said, Maxie," he explained, the words enunciated slowly, the sound hollow. "Pa said."

Maxine was sure now that Dane was out of danger and would only have a terrific headache and small scar to remember this night by. She glanced up at her twin and watched a tear roll off his cheek. Reaching out to him, she took one of his big hands in hers and softly said, "It's all right, Max. You done good. I didn't mean to yell—I thought for a minute you might have hurt this fellah. I just didn't want you to get in trouble."

Fortunately, Max was able to change his mood as quickly as most people could blink an eye. He grinned down at her. "I done good. Let's go."

"In a minute. Where's Pa?"

"Down the stairs with a Celestial. I done good on him too."

Maxine frowned and said, "There's at least one other Celestial working here—a girl named Ling Ling. Did you see her or anyone else?"

Max shook his head violently.

Maxine bit her lip, thinking ahead before she gave him his next instructions. "Go downstairs and wait with Pa. I'll be down in a minute."

"But—"

"Hurry, Max. Pa might need you. I'm in no danger. This fellah's going to be out all night long. Hurry."

All Max required to get him moving was to hear that his sister or father needed him. He turned slowly and shuffled out of the room.

Working quickly now, Maxine began to frisk the Spaniard. She started with his boots, carefully checking them for knives or guns, then worked her way up the pant legs to the apex. Blushing furiously as she admired his tight, custom trousers, she wondered what more he would have done if Max hadn't intervened.

Maxine closed her eyes at the thought of the Spaniard's touch, his brief kiss. She'd felt warm all over, mostly inside, as if coaxed to blossom by some internal sun. Had those feelings been a prelude, the beginning of the sensations Lola Montez had warned her she might one day have? If left undisturbed a few moments or hours longer, would Dane have done that special lovemaking on her? She laughed out loud at the idea. Why, with her circumstances and usually untamed looks, she'd be a fool to think that anyone so fancy as the Spaniard would ever do lovemaking on her. At least, not in the way Lola had described the act.

Shaking off her sudden sense of embarrassment, Maxine returned to her task and dug her hands into Dane's pockets, withdrawing the few coins he carried. Then she moved up to his waistcoat and found a beautiful gold watch tucked inside one of the pockets. She lifted it and impulsively draped the chain around her neck. Guessing this was but one of the Spaniard's many timepieces, she hooked the chain to the link on which the watch was attached, making a necklace out of it, and tucked it between her breasts.

Knowing they needed all the time they could get to make a clean getaway, Maxine moved to stand up, but she stopped as again her gaze swept across the aristocratic features of Dane del Cordobes. He was so handsome it hurt her eyes, and richer than any man she'd ever met or was likely to meet.

With a mischievous grin, she whispered, "Thanks for everything, Señor. You've been a real good sport about helping us out. Don't think for a minute the McKains don't appreciate it." Then, surprising herself, she leaned over and kissed him full on the mouth.

Downstairs, the McKain men were getting fidgety waiting for their third wheel to show up. Dicey had just about decided to drag his half-crippled body up the stairs to check on her welfare when Maxine came bounding down the steps.

"I was just comin' up for you, Maxie girl. What have you—" He choked on the words as his daughter came into view wearing a dress that showed more of her than he'd seen since she was five years old. "Stars, and what kind a costume is that fer a decent gal to be wearin'?"

"It's a lady's costume, Pa. The Spaniard's little gal gave it to me."

Dicey raised one bushy brow. "Well I think you'd best be givin' it back to her then."

Maxine snickered as she moved up beside her father. "No time, Pa—I think we'd better get out of here before that Spaniard wakes up. He's not going to take too kindly to us if he finds us here."

Dicey grumbled under his breath, but he signaled Max and the trio moved toward the door. Just before they went through it, a breathless female voice reached their ears. "Dane, darling—is that you?"

Maxine gasped and came to a halt. She had to think fast. Her main concern was to keep Joy away from Dane until they could make their getaway. She held a finger to her lips and motioned for her father and Max to keep moving out the door. Then she turned and tip-toed down the hallway to the library.

"Dane?" Joy said, taking a step toward the doorway.

"You looking for the Señor?" Maxine said as she strolled into the room. At the blond's surprised gasp, Maxine recalled a few bits of information from her scanty education regarding the private matters between men and women. Then she adjusted the bodice on her dress and pretended to fix her mussed hair. "I'm afraid Dane is—how shall I say it?—plum tuckered out."

Joy clutched her throat, her eyes wide with panic. "He said you couldn't talk, that you were a mute!"

Maxine tossed her head and laughed, the sound

hoarse and throaty. "Oh, that handsome fellah upstairs is better than a dose of laudanum for what ails a poor gal. I've flat out made a miraculous recovery, don't you think?"

In a swoon, Joy staggered backward and fell into a Queen Anne chair.

"Oh, now don't go getting your pantalettes all in a twist, Miss Hunt. You might hurt yourself." Her grin satisfied as she recalled some of the things the woman had said about her during the meal, Maxine strolled over to the sideboard and picked up two crystal glasses that were already filled with brandy.

Returning to the flustered blond, she carefully set them on a nearby occasional table and said, "Since it don't look like your sweetheart's going to be coming back downstairs tonight, you might as well have his brandy too. You look as if you could use a couple of belts." Then she turned and skipped out of the room.

Maxine caught up with Max and Dicey out front by the hitching post, and the three scrambled away in the cover of darkness. When they reached the warehouse where Dicey had hidden their small wagon, Max and Maxine dove into the back and pulled down the canvas flap, while Dicey climbed up on the buckboard and whipped the mules to life.

As the McKains drove out of San Francisco and into the fog-shrouded night, Dicey heard the vexation in his daughter's voice as she called to him from the back of the wagon.

"Hey, Pa? 'Member back in the saloon when you first brought me inside for the wager?"

Dicey nodded, still shaking off a residual guilt for pulling such a fool stunt. "Aye and I do, girl. Why?"

"Just what did you mean by calling me 'the perfect woman'?"

Dicey gulped and urged the mules to a faster trot.

"Huh, Pa?" Maxine persisted. "Were you trying to say that if I couldn't talk, that would make me perfect? Is that what you meant?"

Still no answer.

"Well is it, Pa?"

3

Amador, California
April 1859

Weary as much from the long ride into the gold country as from last night's endless faro game, Dane pulled his Andalusian stallion, Alazan, to a halt. He sat back, groaning in harmony with the squeak of his rich leather saddle, and glanced over his shoulder at the busy little creek hollow he'd just left. Down the road a few miles, at another, bigger, creek hollow, he would most likely find a repeat of last evening's activities. He would ride into the more productive boom town of Sutter Creek, check on his holdings in the impressive Central Eureka Mine, then wind up in a three-card Monte or faro marathon.

Simply thinking ahead to the festivities coaxed an echo of the headache he'd been trying to get rid of all day. With his pulse pummeling in his temples, Dane gazed toward the east. If he cut off the main road and slipped past the foothills for a few miles, he should be able to find the secluded lake he'd stumbled across last year on this same journey. The idea of a few hours of undisturbed rest in the waning daylight hours was too much to pass up. Dane wheeled the stallion around, clucking to the mare in tow at the same time, and headed up the side of the mountain.

On the south side of the same lake, nestled in a heavily forested valley, Maxine argued with her father while Max played a game of solitary marbles nearby.

"But Pa!" Maxine stomped her boot against the mat of pine needles carpeting the clearing. "How could you have sold one of those idiotic tapeworm traps to a fellah from Sutter Creek! I love that town—you *know* how much I love that town." She rolled her eyes and heaved a dramatic sigh. "Now I'll never be able to show my face in Sutter again, thanks to you."

"Now, Maxie girl, I dona' think it's quite as bad as you make out." At her scowl, he took a backward step and continued to justify the sale. "It weren't my fault, you know. If he'd just swallowed the baited trap, and not the string he needed to retrieve it, the surgery would not have been necessary."

"But he did—and it was. I heard," she hissed, leaning in close, "when the doctor opened that poor man up, his bowels were shot up with metal tubes and springs from one end to the other. It's a wonder he didn't die!"

"Aye," Dicey said, scratching his balding head. "I

dona' understand why the trap come apart like that, but look on the bright side, girl—the operation did give the doctor an uncommonly good look at that tapeworm, now, didn't it?"

Unable to keep her expression stern, Maxine had to turn and bite her lip to keep from laughing. Dicey found a bright side to everything, no matter how low the family got or how close to the last bean in their supply bag. He was the eternal light to Max's faint beam and the playful guard dog to her watchful shepherd. She wondered, and not for the first time, how long it had taken Dicey to find a bright side the day some fifteen years ago when Emaline Noland dropped her and Max on his doorstep.

They had just passed their fifth birthday when Emaline finally found Dicey in the small dusty town of Independence, Missouri. When Maxine first laid eyes on the man who had sired her, she had been a sullen, belligerent child, an oft-pummeled, verbally abused girl who trusted no one and nothing, not even that the sun would rise each and every day. Yet, strangely enough, she didn't harbor any ill will toward her mother. On the contrary, when Maxine thought of Emaline—an occurrence which happened less often as she grew older—her heart ached more with a sense of loss than with any hatred for the woman who couldn't seem to stand the sight of her own children.

After Emaline informed Dicey that he even *had* children, and that she intended to let him keep them, his reaction had been shock, quickly followed by the many excuses a nomad like himself had for begging off the pleasure of raising two young babes. Of course, Emaline wasn't interested in excuses, or in her children's welfare. She caught the first stage that happened along and went off to find a few adventures of her own. Her sudden departure was devastating to the twins, and a blow to the gut for Dicey, but it did force the new little family to find a way of surviving together.

If Dicey had reservations about raising the twins, Maxine was none too excited about the idea herself. She didn't take to her pa at first, grabbing Max and running off at every opportunity, confident, as only a five-year-old child can be that she could take care of herself and her twin with no one else's help whatsoever. But Dicey always rounded them up, promising to do better by them, vowing the next rainbow he chased would have the elusive pot of gold hanging from its tail.

It hadn't happened yet, but now there was word of a new strike near Pike's Peak in Colorado. Rumor had it that a find there could make the California Gold Rush of '49 look like a molasses spill in January, a mere drop in the bucket compared to the vast wealth hidden beneath the foothills of the Rockies. Maybe this time . . .

Taking her silence as censure, Dicey poked his daughter in the ribs. "Maxie, girl? You must know I did not wish the man a bad end."

Aware that she'd been daydreaming, Maxine allowed a grudging chuckle as the past faded from her memory. Suddenly aglow with love for her father, she turned to him and gave him a brief hug. "I know you didn't want him to get sick, Pa. Sorry if I seem a might waspish today. Must be the weather—it's too damn hot for springtime. I think I'll run on up to the lake and take a cool bath." As she walked to the back of the wagon to collect her valise, she added, "Keep a good eye on Max while I'm gone, hear?"

"Aye, girl, I hear you—just *you* be making sure the area's clear up there 'fore you strip down and get in the water."

Maxine laughed as she began the uphill climb. "Haven't you learned by now, Pa? I'm the last one in this mad little trio who needs looking after. I can take care of myself."

After Dane watered his horses, he led them down the north side of the slope to a sheltered meadow, where he tethered them and left them to graze. Then he returned to the crest of the hill and settled into a small grassy incline between a large scrub oak and a smaller pine tree. He could hear the nearby water teasing the shoreline, slapping at the rocks and pebbles that lined the banks of the lake. Jays and mockingbirds added their voices as they argued over the best berries, and the faint scent of a nearby dogwood plant drifted under his nose. Dane del Cordobes was asleep before his brain had a chance to identify the aroma.

As he slept, he dreamed of his home—the real one in San Diego, not the substitute he'd built in San Francisco. He thought of his deceased father as he was years ago, when the family rancho was one of California's largest and most successful cattle ranches. Life then had been good, good and easy. Perhaps, he reflected, too easy. Even the battle he and his elder brother had fought to reclaim title to the family's property after his father's death during the Mexican-American war, hadn't really kept his interest. Spanish family hierarchy prevented that.

At the death of Don Francisco Jose del Cordobes the father, Francisco Jose del Cordobes the son became head of the rancho. This left Francisco Dane, named after his English mother, Margaret Dane, untested and unchallenged. Shortly after he rode out of San Diego some nine years before to seek out his own personal fortune in the early days of the gold rush, Dane was dealt a blow from which he'd never fully recovered. In his absence, the girl he loved, his Caroline Buchanan, chose to marry the elder del Cordobes brother—a man whose rancho and wealth were secure—over the younger brother and his uncertain future. Caroline, with her laughing blue eyes and cornsilk hair, was the woman he sought in every woman he met but could never seem to find.

A telegram two weeks ago had changed all that. His brother Frank had died from a ranching accident. Their mother, ready to pull up her own roots and go back to England, asked Dane to return to the rancho and claim what was rightfully his. And Caroline, facing the future with two fatherless sons, was apparently prepared to offer herself to Dane in marriage—the way she should have done years ago.

Eager to return to the rancho, if less certain of his feelings about Caroline, Dane had accepted his responsibilities immediately. He sold his San Francisco home, bid Joy and the new life he'd built goodbye, and started the long journey back to San Diego. Now, as he made his way south and to the past, he lingered in the small mining towns along the gold country, dragging himself, it seemed, back to the woman he supposed he still loved. He did love her, he reassured himself, and yet he was having small doubts. He wondered if he would ever be able to rid himself of the bitter taste of Caroline's deceit, or forget the thousands of nights she'd spent in Frank's bed. Suddenly restless and angry, Dane rolled onto his side.

A loud splash brought him completely out of his slumber. He jerked up with a start and parted the branches of the scrub oak, looking for the source of the disturbance. All seemed as quiet and pastoral as when he had first laid down, but on closer inspection, he noticed a widening circle of rings spreading across the lake. Something or someone had fallen or dived into the water.

As a man who preferred the relatively bloodless nature of the bullwhip to pistols, not to mention the fact that a target usually lived after being "out-drawn" by Dane del Cordobes, he slid the coil of leather off his shoulder and fit the stump of the grip to his palm. Staying low, he parted the branches of the tree again and peered through the leaves.

A moment later, a mop of flaming red hair popped through the water's surface, bobbing for a moment before it dove back into the lake. That hair was the color of a blacksmith's fire, a pure scarlet he remembered seeing on only one head before. Could it be her? Was it possible he'd just stumbled over his little runaway handmaiden? Dane kept watch, following the ripples as the girl swam closer to the shoreline. Occasionally she would shoot to the surface, and then dive, exposing her round white bottom for a split second before disappearing, but her features remained a mystery to him until she finished her swim and moved toward the shallow water.

By then, there was no doubt that he'd come across his "stolen property," or that she was anything less than a full-grown woman, and an accomplished thief. Dane's anger at being used in such a manner ignited, and his thoughts turned to revenge.

Her dripping torso emerged from the water. Round and full, the girl's breasts were taut from the cold water. Dane's anger began to cool as his body heated, and he sucked in his breath and shifted until he had an unobscured view of her raw beauty.

She was unlike any woman he'd ever seen. Her flat stomach rippled like the water she left in her wake as she stepped onto the shore. Rivulets of water ran down from her hair, cascading off the rosy peaks of her breasts before making a dead run to the fiery triangle at the apex of her long, muscular legs. Her body was sculpted to athletic perfection, yet voluptuously rounded.

This was no soft, spoiled woman too weak to do any but the most menial of chores. This creature would be a match for the most primitive man, and capable, he suspected, of bringing even a savage to heel with a vigorous twist of her slim hips.

Overwhelmed with a sudden, intense desire, paralyzed by a sensation akin to basic animal lust, Dane drew in a painful breath and then let it out in an agonized moan as he whispered, *"Christo ... Dios mio."*

Somewhat disgusted with himself, with his reluctance to look away and his licentious reaction to her charms, he nonetheless continued to watch her. Despite his gentlemanly urge to allow her privacy, he vowed that she wouldn't escape him so easily this time. Exactly what he would do with her once she was back in his custody remained unclear, but regain her services, he would.

Unaware of those intense blue eyes upon her as she waded up to the shore, Maxine stuck her arms out at her sides and twirled around in a circle like a whirl-a-gig. When she stopped, she staggered for balance, the excess water from her long tresses sprinkling down on her damp body like raindrops. Laughing to herself, she quickly dried off with a small piece of worn toweling before pulling on the fancy new pantalettes she'd been given at the del Cordobes home. Then she struggled to stuff the yards of flouncy lawn inside the snug-fitting legs of her Levi's. That accomplished, she donned the feminine corset cover sans corset, also a "gift" from the Spaniard, and then slipped on her blue flannel shirt and buttoned it, leaving it open at the throat.

After tugging on her boots, Maxine looped the necklace she'd made of Dane's watch and chain over her head and dropped it down inside her shirt to rest between her breasts. She had just finished braiding her hair and pulling her hat down over her head when she heard it. A loud *pop* followed by an unusual, whistling noise. Before Maxine could look up to find the source or identify the sound, a leather snake lashed out at her, coiling around her waist and pinning her arms to her sides.

Taken off guard, Maxine was jerked off her feet just

before she flew across the small clearing and into the arms of Dane del Cordobes.

He quickly clamped his hand across her mouth and then issued both greeting and warning before she even had a chance to cry out. "So we meet again, my little handmaiden," he whispered, his voice dark and velvety. "This time I shall collect what's due me."

An hour later, as the sun finally disappeared behind the mountains for the night, Dicey shook his head one more time. "I dona' know what could be keepin' that girl."

"Let's get her, Pa. Let's get Maxie. I'm scared."

"Dona' be afraid, boy. Yur pa's here, yur not alone."

But having his pa near had never been any great source of comfort or security for Max. Tears sprang into the corners of his big brown eyes, and he began to pace. "Scared," he said, "scared, scared, scared. Let's get Maxie."

Dicey stroked his scraggly beard, knowing all the reassurances in the world wouldn't calm his son if he didn't lay eyes on his sister soon. "Aye, boy, and maybe you've got a good idea there after all. What's say we go see what's keepin' her."

Max nodded emphatically, a huge grin squeezing the teardrops from his eyes as he followed his limping father up the side of the hill.

At the crest, Dicey paused, wheezing and catching his breath. Then he called out, "Maxie? Maxie girl, are you still flappin' about in the lake?"

He waited several moments, but the only reply was the early evening breeze whistling through the pines and the incessant chatter of mockingbirds. "Maxie?" he called, louder and sharper as he stepped into the clearing and scanned the lake. The water, a glass-like reflection of the trees and twilit sky surrounding it, was as still as a cornered rabbit. Maxine was nowhere in sight.

"Maxie girl?" he whispered, alarm raising the hair on the back of his neck. "Come on out now—dona' be teasin' yur pa like this."

Catching the tone in his father's voice and the change in his posture, Max drew up close behind him and cried, "Pa? Did something happen to Maxie?"

"No, no, boy—now dona' get yourself all in a dither. She's probably gettin' dressed in the privacy of the trees."

But Dicey didn't believe his own words for a minute. He could almost feel the bad luck in the air. He took another step into the clearing, intending to call her name one more time, when he noticed Maxine's carpet-bag lying in the clearing. With his heart in his throat, he approached it and again made a visual sweep of the area. This was not a good sign at all. His daughter never *ever* left her precious few belongings unattended like this. Where could she have gone?

"Pa?" Max called out as he shuffled up behind his father. A full head taller than the elder McKain, he peered over his shoulder and asked, "Where's Maxie, Pa? Where is she?"

Dicey swallowed a sob and took a deep steadying breath before he trusted himself to speak. "I dona' know, Max. Looks like she be playin' a little game of hide and seek with us. Let's walk around the lake 'n see if we can't find her. Stay right behind me, son."

The pair slowly followed the shoreline, poking through the trees and bushes as they walked, hoping against all odds to surprise Maxine as they came upon her. When they reached the northern shore, Dicey pulled up abruptly as he spotted something in the dirt by a gnarled scrub oak. After cautioning his son to remain still, he hunkered down near the object and squinted his eyes. His heart sank when he recognized the ragged handle of Maxine's knife, which she always wore strapped around her waist. Pinned to the ground beneath the blade were five playing cards—three sevens and a pair of deuces. The same full house that had beat his flush in the San Francisco poker game the month before. The message was clear: Señor del Cordobes had reclaimed his property.

Groaning half in anger and half in fear, Dicey struggled to his feet and then spoke in a strained voice as he tried to explain to his son. "I dona' think we'll be findin' Maxie this night, boy. She, ah . . . she's most likely to be gone fer a spell."

"Gone? Maxie—*gone?*" Panic shot adrenalin through Max's body, but his feeble mind neglected to provide him with an outlet for the sudden burst of energy. He began to rock back and forth on his heels, holding his stomach with both hands as he cried out, "But Maxie can't be gone, she *can't!*"

Dicey was always terrified for his son when his fears gripped him like this. Maxine seemed to be the only person alive who knew how to calm him. Trying his best, Dicey tentatively reached out and patted Max's big shoulders. "Easy, son. You know yur sister—wherever she's gone off to, she'll be all right."

"But why did she go? Why did she go?"

Knowing the boy would repeat that same question over and over unless he got an answer, Dicey tried to explain without alarming him further. "She's gone with the man who won her back in San Francisco. It's his right to claim her." Dicey gritted his teeth at the thought of what might happen to his girl over the long dark night, but he managed to swallow his horror in order to reassure his son. "Dona' worry. We'll get her back—you'll see."

But Max was beyond seeing or understanding. He stared off into the twilight, muttering the same word over and over. "Gone? Maxie gone? Gone, gone, gone—"

"Easy, son. Try to remember what she said when she come up here to bathe."

Between his sobs, Max scratched his head, so upset he could hardly remember his own name, much less his sister's earlier remarks.

Used to Max's shortcomings, Dicey continued to stroke his son's shoulders, hoping he could make him understand and take some measure of comfort from her final words. "She said, 'I'm the last McKain who needs lookin' after. I can take care of myself.' Remember? She's right, you know. Nobody can get the best of Maxine McKain. Nobody."

Then, as Max tried to digest the message, Dicey stared off in the distance, and prayed to God that she was right.

4

Later that night, Maxine sat curled in a small grassy clearing amid overhanging cottonwood and oak trees and watched Dane snuff out the fire she'd used to prepare their supper of bacon and pan bread.

He'd barely said two words to her since he'd tossed her over the back of his pack horse and led her deeper into the Sierra Nevada foothills, but his expression had lost some of its edge, softened from anger to introspection. Was it safe to talk to him yet and try to bargain her way to freedom? If so, just how should she approach him, this man of great means and noble breeding?

Maxine continued to watch him as he moved about the campsite. Even though this Spaniard was more amorphous than most, she had a remarkable ability to see most people for what they were. She could spot glassy-eyed greed or the aura of evil, and recognize the self-serving motives behind any deed, good or bad.

These things were constants in her daily living, and because she understood her peers so well, Maxine had never really found a reason to fear the rat-eyed confidence men who lurked in the alleys of the tenderloin or along the riverbanks in the gold country. The McKains' lives were entwined with this kind, and they co-existed with them under an uneasy truce of professional courtesy, an unwritten law of "You stay away from my grabracket, and I'll stay away from yours."

But the privileged classes were something else again. Men of wealth, and women who not only knew where their next meal was coming from but had someone else to cook it, were as difficult for Maxine to see through as the fog rolling up from Yerba Buena Bay.

Dane turned then, catching Maxine off guard, and found her gawking at him.

"You have a question for me?" he said, trying to ease the awkward situation.

"I . . . I was wondering what name I should call you."

Keeping one eye on her, he began to spread his bedroll to accommodate two. He forced a stern tone into his voice when he answered, "My help generally addresses me as Señor Dane. You may also use that name if you wish."

Maxine's stubborn chin automatically lifted as she grumbled under her breath, "What I wish for is my freedom."

Dane dropped the blanket he'd been smoothing and turned to her, fists planted against his hips. "Do you now? And what of the Scotsman's debt—a debt, I might add, which your services were to repay?"

Cornered, Maxine exhaled loudly and shrugged.

"You got me there. Just what is it you expect of me, and how long do you figure I got to stay with you to work off that debt?"

Although his first impulse was to berate her for her insolent attitude and make certain she understood the way things would be between them, he couldn't help but warm to her sense of pride and apparently fearless nature. He already knew how cunning she could be, but did he also detect a certain amount of innocence in her expression? Or was it just another act, a deceptively clever way of presenting herself? With her long red braids hanging down from her shoulders and her shapeless figure in her worn men's clothing, Dane could see where anyone might almost believe she was the pitiful young girl the Scotsman had said she was, and not a grown-up, lying, thieving woman. Almost, he thought, suddenly recalling the sight he'd witnessed at the lake, but not quite.

Cursing to himself as the image of her nude, glistening body popped into his mind, Dane sank cross-legged onto the bedroll and then looked across the dying embers of the fire into her big brown eyes. She was anything but a girl—and not at all delicate with those strong, wide cheekbones, and that firm, stubborn jaw, even though these were softened by an exquisite widow's peak highlighting her forehead and fluffy red curls teasing the hollow at her temples. She was no innocent either, he deduced, remembering the way she'd melted against him in San Francisco. And honor, if she'd ever even heard the word, was definitely not on the list of rules she lived by. She bore careful watching, but from a safe distance.

On display long enough, and downright uncomfortable under Dane's visual assessment, Maxine tugged at a few shafts of grass and demanded, "Well? What are you looking at?"

Startled by her boldness, Dane almost laughed. "Forgive me if I seem to be staring. I was simply trying to decide how long to keep you in my employ. I suppose that depends on your talents. What can you do—and by that I mean, do well?"

Maxine shrugged. "I suppose about anything you want me to do."

"Really?" he said, his voice almost a whisper. "I think perhaps that remains to be seen. But now I am tired. Why don't we discuss what you can—and cannot do—tomorrow on our long ride. I would like to arrive in San Andreas before nightfall."

"San Andreas?" Maxine gasped. "Aren't we going back to San Francisco?"

Dane slowly shook his head as he stifled a yawn. "No, we are not. I have some business to check on in Sutter Creek, then we'll head south to San Diego."

"San *Diego?*" Alarmed, she popped up to her knees. "Why are we going all the way down there? I thought—"

"You ask far too many questions, Red. I liked you better when you were pretending to be mute. I think—"

"Don't call me Red," she cut in, her dark eyes glittering. "My name is Maxine. I'll thank you to use it."

"Maxine, is it?" he said, only slightly irritated at being interrupted.

"That's what I said," she snapped, terrified by the thought of leaving her home and her family. "Why are you going all the way to San Diego, and what makes you think you can drag me along with you?"

His patience waning, Dane drew a deep breath and said, "San Diego is my birthplace and the home of my family rancho. I am returning there to marry and live. You are indentured to me, so of course, you must accompany me wherever I go. *Comprende?*"

"B-but what about your big ole mansion in San Francisco? What about your lady friend, Joy?" She was frantic to find a way out of the long journey.

"Not that it's any concern of yours, but I sold the house, and Miss Hunt and I no longer . . . get along."

"Oh, hell's fire. Was it because of what I said to her? I didn't mean nothing by it, you know. I just wanted to make sure she stayed put a while longer. I hope I didn't get her too riled up at you."

Reminded of the incident, Dane laughed before he could clear up the misunderstanding. "Miss Hunt and I were preparing to go our separate ways before I brought you home. If anything, your little charade only hastened the inevitable. Now please come here to your bedroll."

Maxine tugged her shirt collar up around her throat and drew her brows together. "Why? Are you thinking of doing that uninvited bed business on me?"

"That uninvit—" Then he remembered what he'd said to her back in San Francisco. Dane began laughing, chortling in a way he hadn't done since he was a child.

Maxine was not disturbed or offended by his outburst. In fact, she was fascinated to see a tiny part of the otherwise unfathomable facade he usually presented. She could sense that the Spaniard was not a man who laughed often or easily, and for the first time since she'd met him she felt something other than curiosity, respect, or fear. She felt a little bit sorry for him.

Aware that she was watching him, Dane quickly gathered himself and set her mind at ease. "You have no worries coming from me—not this night, anyway. I am not a man given to accosting young women as they sleep. As for later? That also remains to be seen, Señorita Maxine. You see, I don't trust you, and I never share my bed with a woman I cannot trust. Now please come over here."

She believed him. The trouble was that she also felt disappointed, rejected somehow. Sighing, she crawled on her hands and knees over to the bedding and sat down beside him. A sudden gust of wind whistled through the grove of tall pine trees nearby and sent their fresh clean fragrance spiraling down over her. Maxine inhaled the scent, the one aroma she loved almost as much as her family, and suddenly felt homesick. There was no way she would go to San Diego, but what if she couldn't affect her own escape? What if the Spaniard dragged her south against her will? She would have to convince him to *let* her go.

Maxine glanced over at Dane and inched closer to him. That he was in a class so superior to hers that there was no way for them to find common ground was not in question. But back in the saloon, as he'd contemplated accepting her as part of the bet, she thought she'd seen a certain empathy in his eyes, a respect for her as a human being less fortunate than he. Could she count on that slender bit of compassion to help her gain freedom?

Dane moved to the far edge of the blanket and said, "Given our circumstances, I think it best if we stay in the foothills during our journey and not in the hotels along the way. I hope you will not be too uncomfortable."

Thinking of the hard wooden floor in her family wagon, Maxine padded the soft bedding and said, "No need to apologize—it's a damn sight better than what I'm used to."

Dane rumpled his brow. This was above the norm for her? He thought back to the way she'd eaten, from the gourmet delicacies in his home to the most basic fare they'd shared this evening. Maxine had stuffed food into her mouth without really tasting or relishing it. She had consumed her meals the way an animal might, with only one purpose in mind: survival.

The word turned over and over in his mind, and suddenly, Dane had to wonder, how far would she go to ensure that survival? He already knew her to be capable of lying and stealing . . . what else was she capable of?

Deepening the timbre of his voice, Dane warned her, "Know that I will not tolerate any attempts at escape. We are deep in the forest, and my horses have been trained to answer only to me. If you try to steal one of them, you will be thrown to the ground for your trouble. Have I your word that you will remain in camp, or shall I bind you for the evening?"

Maxine set her chin, and her eyes flared. "I am *not* a horse thief!"

Surprised by her outburst, Dane glanced away and

shook his head. She'd been offended! This woman who'd tricked, robbed, and caused physical injury to him, actually took umbrage at the suggestion she might try to "borrow" one of his horses. If the situation hadn't been so grave, he might have laughed, but Dane felt he was beginning to catch a glimpse of the real woman. She had a kind of aura about her, an identity she wore the way most women wore perfume. But Maxine's aura wasn't sweet like lavender or heady like rosewater. This young woman simply lived and breathed the modest goal of survival.

Thinking ahead to what might be a very long night, he said, "Forgive me for even suggesting such a thing, but what of your partners? The Scotsman and the man whose mark I carry?" He dragged a long tanned finger across the chalk-white scar just below the cleft in his chin. "I hope they will not be foolish enough to try and rescue you again. This time I will be ready for them."

His words punctured Maxine's confidence, and she leaked out her breath in a long sigh. Not only would Max and Pa be hampered in any rescue attempt by the mule-drawn wagon, neither of them had the ability to track a plow horse across the plains in the snow. Hell, they wouldn't have found her in San Francisco if they hadn't accidentally stumbled across the Spaniard's fancy horse and carriage.

Maxine said quietly, "They'll be looking for me all right, but you don't have to worry about them finding us. Neither one of them is much good at tracking. Seems I'm the only one in the family with any woods sense."

Dane whipped his head around. "The *family?*"

Maxine nodded as she slipped into a suitably pitiful expression. "Dicey, the gambler who had the flush? He's my pa. And Max, the fellow who laid open your chin, is my twin brother. He's real sorry he hurt you, too."

"Madre de Dios." Dane groaned and sank down on the bedroll. Lying on his back, he covered his face with his hands and thought only briefly of challenging her claims before he accepted them completely. How could he not? The one thing he remembered about his assault in San Francisco, other than that huge fist, was the glimpse he'd caught of a shock of bright red hair—hair far too much like Maxine's, now that he thought of it, to be unrelated. As for the prospector, Dicey, there was a certain resemblance there too, although Maxine's features were sharper, more defined, and her dark eyes contrasted with the pale color of her father's. He had no choice but to believe her.

Speaking slowly and wearily, Dane asked, "Why did you not tell me this before now?"

Maxine shrugged. "You never gave me a chance. Besides, I, ah, that is, I—"

"Thought you would have escaped by now?"

Her chin bobbed, but Maxine wisely kept her silence.

"Ah, well, there is nothing we can do about your family tonight. I assume your father will be at least a little concerned about your welfare?"

" 'Course! He's probably worried sick about me, and Max . . ." She paused, thinking of her brother's delicate mental processes, of the worry, panic, and rage he would probably be feeling, and decided not to elaborate. "Max is probably upset too."

Her words did not add to the guilt Dane was feeling, however. Instead, the more he thought about the entire episode, the angrier he became. "One night of wondering about your whereabouts is small punishment for any man who would use his daughter to cover a bet. The man does not even deserve to be called *father.*"

"Hey!" Her own anger flaring, Maxine scooted across the blanket. "You can't say things like that about my pa! Besides, it was my idea to cover the bet, not his. You leave him be."

Dane narrowed his gaze, pausing for a long moment before he lay back down. Then he slid his hands beneath his head and quietly said, "I do not believe you, but I am far too tired to continue with this conversation. Tomorrow, after I conduct my business in Sutter Creek, we will search for your family and work out some way to repay the debt. Now please lie down and go to sleep."

His words were clipped, final. Maxine sank down on the bedroll beside him and pulled the thin blanket across her shoulders.

"*Buenas noches,* Señorita Maxine."

"'Night," she answered back, even though her curiosity kept her wide awake. "Say," she blurted out, surprising even herself with her boldness, "you've been so busy asking all the questions, I almost forgot I had a couple of my own. Would you mind telling me why a fancy-faced gentleman like yourself was at a two-bit gambling hall like the Lucky Nugget Saloon the day you won me?"

"And if I do mind?" he said sleepily.

Maxine shrugged her eyebrows as she said, "I'd probably keep asking till you answer."

"Yes," he muttered, "I suppose that you would." After drawing in a long breath, he decided to answer truthfully. "I own more than just a little piece of that saloon. I like to play there occasionally to make certain the games are run honestly."

"You own a saloon? I've never known anyone rich enough to own their own saloon. You must be able to buy just about anything you want."

"I make do," he said, uncomfortable with the conversation. "Now go to sleep."

"In a minute—there's something else I wonder about." Ignoring Dane's low moan, she asked, "How come, if you got all that money and a big rancho in San Diego, you're riding through the eldorado? I can't see a dandy like you out panning for gold, and besides, there's lots quicker ways to get down south than this. What are you doing here?"

"You ask too many questions."

"My pa's mentioned that a time or two, but it's never kept me from asking 'em."

Feeling a sudden empathy for the woman, for the fact she had such a poor excuse for a father, he quietly said, "I will answer this last question, then we will sleep." He paused, waiting for her to agree, but she said nothing, so he went on. "I had some business to tend to up in Placerville, and I also have an interest in a gold mine at Sutter Creek. Since it may be a while before I'm back in these parts again, I decided to check on my holdings before I left for San Diego." He yawned and rolled over on his side. "Again, I bid you good-night."

Maxine led him to believe she was done with talk for the night, but a more personal question—one that had nagged her ever since he'd caught her at the lake—wouldn't let her rest until it was asked. In a deceptively light tone of voice, she said, "There's just one more tiny thing I've been wondering about, Señor Dane. When you caught me this afternoon? How long had you been watching before you actually tried to rope me in?"

The question prompted yet another image of her nude body as she'd stood dripping at the shoreline. Dane swallowed hard, feigning sleep, but he could almost feel her pointed gaze stabbing his back as she waited for some kind of reply.

Her curiosity stronger than ever, the pitch in her voice higher and more demanding than before, Maxine pressed on, "Well—what did you see?" When this produced no immediate answer—when, in fact, Dane's shoulders stiffened and he inched farther away from her—Maxine drew her own conclusions. "You saw me getting out of the water, didn't you?"

Dane tried to swallow the lump in his throat as quietly as possible, but in spite of his efforts, he gulped.

"Well?" she ventured, "how did I look?"

"*Christo,*" Dane muttered under his breath, "this is no conversation for us to be having. I am sorry if I disturbed your privacy, but I assure you, my only interest was in collecting what was owed me. I suggest we both try to forget that unfortunate incident and get some rest."

Determined to get the truth, Maxine rapped her

knuckles against his back. "But you didn't answer my question—"

"Nor shall I."

"But I'm just wanting to know what you think, you know, if I'm made like the fine ladies you see around the hills of San Francisco, or even shaped as good as that delicate little gal, Joy. Couldn't you tell me that?"

Embarrassed by her questions, ashamed that he had such knowledge of her body without her permission, Dane actually considered her request for a moment and then sighed heavily. "Gentlemen simply do not discuss such things with ladies. Please do us both a favor and go to sleep."

She knew it then. Not only was she not as fine a specimen as Joy Hunt, the Spaniard could not think of one thing nice to say about her. Sighing heavily, she rolled away from him and thought back to her short time in Grass Valley under the tutelage of Miss Lola Montez. Stories of this incredible business between men and women had completely fascinated her some four or five years ago. Now Maxine found herself wishing she'd paid more attention to the details, to all the little tricks Lola had mentioned about getting a man. Maxine had a feeling that this Spaniard might just be worth the trouble.

5

The following morning, in the town of Sutter Creek, Maxine tugged the brim of her hat lower on her forehead and strained for a glimpse of Dane through the window of Alvinza Hayward's home. She felt as if she'd been standing with the horses, waiting for him to conclude his business, for hours. How much longer did he need to discuss ways in which he and his partner could divide the piles of gold they were taking from the area mines? Her feet hurt, and she was hot and thirsty. And there was also the matter of her grumbling stomach.

With another hopeful glance, this time toward the front door of the house, Maxine sighed and plopped down at the edge of the pathway. She toyed with the idea of escape but quickly dismissed it. Although she couldn't see Dane, she just knew he was watching her from somewhere inside. Besides, even if she managed to slip away unnoticed, she would miss the meal he'd promised her at the American Exchange Hotel. And he'd vowed to begin the search for her family right after that. What good would escape do her now?

Wiping perspiration from her brow, Maxine closed her eyes and imagined herself splashing in the cool waters of the creek a few feet up the road. Why couldn't the Spaniard have trusted her enough to allow her to wait there, where she'd be more comfortable and so much more at home?

Home. Now there was a funny word. Most folks associated it with bricks and lumber, but for Maxine McKain, home was anywhere the family wagon happened to stop for the night. For now, it was wherever the Spaniard dropped the bedroll. That bedroll and the conversation she and Dane had had the night before popped back into her mind. Her plans to give life to those few hazy recollections from Lola's instructions had evaporated with the fog the second the sun had come up, Dane had seen to that. He'd been distant, uncommunicative, and surly all morning, utterly impenetrable. While she couldn't get the memory of his caresses in San Francisco out of her mind, she guessed that she wouldn't have a chance at igniting him again until he was in a better mood.

She tried to envision what came after the kissing and found herself picturing Joy and Dane in the midst of lovemaking. A sparrow and a cougar came to mind, a complete mismatch of frailty and strength. Then she conjured up a fancy lady, someone very much like Lola Montez, who would know exactly what to do and when. Would that kind of woman be a more suitable fit for such a hot-blooded man as the Spaniard, she wondered? A vision of Dane and herself coupling beneath a starlit sky drew an abrupt halt to her musings. But oh, what she wouldn't give to claim Dane as her own for a short period. To be Dane's woman for those few days, to be the one he dreamed of, the one he touched. Why, she'd even give the McKains' lucky nuggets!

As soon as this thought entered her mind, she felt ashamed of her selfishness, though excited by the idea. She jumped to her feet and stretched. Then, as she considered strolling over to the creek despite the Spaniard's orders to stay put, she spotted a familiar figure limping up the road from the south.

"Jumper?" she whispered as she walked to the rear of the horses. There, through the rainbow of dust kicked up by his wooden pegleg, she recognized the haggard features of a long-time, if not entirely trusted, family acquaintance.

"Hey, Jumper," she called again, louder, but not loud enough to reach the house. "Over here."

When the old man shaded his eyes and looked in Maxine's direction, she gestured for him to join her and then took a quick glance toward the window. Still no sign of the Spaniard.

Using the horses to shield herself from the windows, Maxine waited for the miner to approach. It had been something like six months since the McKains had crossed paths with this fellow and even though she'd never counted him as one of her favorite people, she was glad to see a familiar face. She gathered from his appearance as he came closer that he hadn't fared any better than they had in recent times. His clothing, dirty and grease-stained, appeared to be held together with bits of twine, and the sole of one of his boots flapped with every step.

"Good to see you, Jumper—how's tricks?" she said when he was finally standing in front of her.

"Danged few and far between," he answered, the words whistling out between his last two tobacco-stained teeth, "but a mite better than yourn of late, I guess."

That remark could only mean that Jumper had come in contact with her family sometime very recently. "You seen my pa and Max?" she asked.

"Shore have—your pa, anyways—earlier on this morning down Jackson way."

"Jackson? What are they doing down there?"

Jumper shrugged. "Dunno. Came down last night looking for you, I expect. When I mentioned I was heading to Sutter, Dicey axed me to keep an eye out for you. He seemed to think you might be having more trouble than you kin handle."

Maxine's heart lurched. She'd hardly given her family or their safety a thought this morning. Instead, she'd been daydreaming about Dane.

Her fingers involuntarily brushed her lips as she said, "I'm okay. How's Pa? And what about Max? Is he handling my absence all right?"

The grizzled old man shook his head and then took a surreptitious look around. "Your pa said you been claimed by some noble-type fella in a poker game. He around?"

Ignoring the stench of a man in desperate need of a bath, Maxine moved closer to him. "He won't give you no trouble for talking to me. Is something wrong with Max? He acting up some?"

Avoiding her gaze, Jumper wheezed as he dug into his shirt pocket and scraped up the last of his chewing tobacco. After stuffing the small wad into his cheek, he looked away as he said, "Hate to tell you this, you being, you know, tied up with this stranger and all, but your brother . . . well, he ain't doing so good."

"He ain't?" Alarmed, Maxine grabbed the sleeve of his shirt. "What's happened to him? He hurt?"

"No, no," the old prospector mumbled, tearing himself free of her grasp. "At least ways, not yet, he ain't."

"Dammit all, Jumper, cut out the cussed flapdoodle and tell me where they are and what's happened to Max!"

"Dad-blast it, get away from a fella and I will!" he sputtered, hopping backwards on his good leg. "Max ain't hurt a'tall. What he is is in jail."

"*Jail?*" Maxine clutched her throat, squeezing almost tightly enough to cut off her own breath. "Max? What could he have done to get himself tossed in jail? I can't believe—"

"Believe it, Maxie girl, cause it's true. Your brother went and beat the tar out of Sheriff Woods over to Jackson. Likely that boy won't be seeing the light of day till he's too old to load ore."

Kind-hearted Max? Why, he was afraid of his own shadow, not to mention the law. What could have made her gentle twin even think of striking the sheriff? "I can't understand it. Maybe someone else attacked the sheriff, then blamed it on Max."

"Don't think so," Jumper mumbled, spitting a stream of tobacco juice at the base of his stump.

"Then why? Why would he go after a sheriff, of all people? Max would never beat on a man of the law."

Jumper shrugged. "Nobody knows. Max won't talk, and Woods, well . . . he cain't."

Maxine groaned. "Hell's fire. Pa must be beside himself. Why hasn't he tried to get Max to explain?"

Jumper shook his head, and at the movement, particles of dirt rained down on his face like a fine mist. As if unaware of the dusting, he went on. "Told you—Max ain't talking. And your pa—well, he don't know which way to turn, if'n he ought to look for you or stay near Max. I tell you, he's plum wore out trying to decide which of you two needs him the most."

Maxine had heard enough. Without even bothering to glance toward the house, she launched herself up on the back of the packhorse she'd been riding since morning. She gathered the reins in one hand and pointed at Jumper with the other. "My brother—is he at the Jackson courthouse?"

"Sure 'nuff is. You gonna head on down there?"

"Of course, I am! Max needs me." No one but Maxine could understand how much her twin did need her, and nothing would stop her from going to his aid. "Thanks for letting me know, Jumper," she said, tugging on the reins. "Now back out of my way—I'm coming through." She kicked the mare in the flanks.

Inside the Hayward home, Dane stood just to the side of the lace curtain draped at the edge of the window. Alvinza droned on about ways in which he could keep Dane informed about his interests in the mine, but Dane's attention was captured by the fascinating young woman standing with his horses. She was stretching, reaching high above her head, pulling the thin material of her cotton shirt tight against the silhouette of her full breasts. Then she bent down, swinging her arms low, and displayed her very appealing heart-shaped backside. Dane's breath caught in his throat, and he knew he ought to turn away, but he couldn't seem to.

" . . . and, I suppose, that could be handled by wire as well." Alvinza cocked his head. "You listening to me, del Cordobes?"

The question forced Dane to tear his gaze from the window. "But of course I am, and I agree. I would think that monthly wires along with postings from the bank should be sufficient."

"Good. That's settled." Alvinza puffed on his cigar and then began to outline a fair distribution of the profits. "As for actually collecting your share, why don't I leave that up to you? You can either . . ."

The man's voice faded into the flowers on the wallpaper as Dane found himself captured once again by the sight of Maxine. Standing in back of the horses, she was almost but not quite out of his sight, and certainly in view enough for him to see the patches on her sleeves and the worn spots on her jeans. Even if she wasn't exactly a society lady, she should have decent clothing, *women's* clothing instead of the rags she wore. How would she look dressed in the finest silk from Paris, her glorious hair piled high on her head and topped by an exquisite velvet bonnet?

The sight his imagination supplied nearly sent

Dane reeling. She would be stunning, an absolutely superb figure of a woman, if cleaned up and dressed in the proper clothing. How difficult a task, he then found himself wondering, would it be to train her, to educate her and bring her out as a fine young lady?

"Well?" Alvinza asked. There was an edge to his voice now. "Does that sound fair, or not?"

Again, Dane snapped his attention back to his partner, but before he could comment, an abrupt movement from the yard caught his attention. Maxine had mounted Rocio. It didn't even take a second glance for him to see that she was trying to escape.

Dane's fist closed around the grip of his bullwhip. "I have no quarrel with any of your suggestions. Now, I must take my leave. I'll send a wire as soon as I reach San Diego."

Outside, Maxine kicked the mare again. Rocio tossed her mane but refused to budge.

"Blast your speckled hide, let's go!" Maxine punctuated the order with a harder kick of her heels.

The animal wheeled around in a burst of surprise but still would not move forward.

Maxine's frustration and panic grew as she visualized Max in his cell. She began to threaten the animal in no uncertain terms. "How'd you like to be strapped to the business end of an ore cart, you cantankerous, mule-headed—"

Then a whip cracked, sounding like high-mountain thunder. Maxine sat bolt upright and nearly fell off the horse as it sidestepped, then pranced around in a slow circle until it faced its master.

Dane sauntered down the pathway, slowly looping the length of leather back into a manageable coil. Without looking up at Maxine, he mounted his stallion. Then, with a brief, wicked glance in Maxine's direction, he wheeled Alazan around and, with just the slightest nudge from his knee, instructed the horse to rear up. The movement brought the animal's hooves high above Maxine's head before they slashed back down to earth, narrowly missing her. When the dust had cleared, Dane's face was inches from hers, and the mare's reins were bunched in his fist.

With eyes devoid of all humor, he locked her gaze with his and said, "And to think I believed you when you said you were not a horse thief. That is a mistake I will not make again."

"But you don't understand! I wasn't—"

"You will be quiet unless otherwise instructed! As I told you last night, Rocio, and my mount, Alazan, answer only to me. They are well-trained—as I expect you to be before the day is out. *Comprende?*"

Maxine scowled, the corners of her eyes twitching with rage. "*Comprende!* Can I talk now . . . *master?*"

Her tone and the set of her jaw filled him with vexation. She made him see red. *Rojo,* a translation of the very color, was a good name for her. Allowing a half grin as he settled on it, Dane dropped his voice to a whisper and said, "If you can *comprende* anything, *Rojita,* you'd better know that we go only where I say we go and ride only when I say we ride. If those things are understood, then yes, you may speak now."

Jumper had stood by, witnessing their confrontation, without a word. A man who'd gained a nickname and lost a leg during his claim-jumping days, he had learned his lessons well during his years in the eldorado, and avoiding trouble at all costs was number one. With a slight tip of his ragged old hat, he offered Maxine a half-hearted smile and said, "Nice seeing you again, gal. Ah . . . good luck to you on down the road." Then he spun around on his pegleg and hopped away toward the center of town.

Maxine glared at the miner as he passed her. Then she turned back to Dane. "As I was trying to say, I wasn't running away from you. I got business to tend to. Shouldn't take too long. Just tell me what to say to ole Rosy here, and I'll be on my way. You can catch up with me after breakfast."

Dane muttered under his breath and then said, "This mare is from fine Andalusian stock, and her name is not Rosy, but *Rocio*. This is a Spanish word meaning— how shall I say it—silvery, like the morning dew. As for you riding off alone, apparently you weren't listening to me a moment ago."

Maxine rolled her eyes but kept her tongue. She didn't care about horses or their names. All she cared about was getting to Jackson, and fast. She eyed the bullwhip still coiled around Dane's shoulder and willed herself to calm down before trusting herself to speak. Then she quietly said, "Look—I have to go on down the road for a spell, and I've got to go now. You'll just have to trust me with the horse. I promise, I'll be back." She clucked her tongue and renewed her efforts to get the mare moving.

"Still you do not seem to understand," he said in a low and dangerous voice. "I said you will go only where I say you—"

"Excusing me, and meaning no disrespect, Señor, but it's you who doesn't understand. I really got to get on down the road to Jackson. It's—it's my brother. He's in trouble."

"Ah, yes, I think I remember him." Dane stroked the scar at his chin. "Max, correct?"

Maxine pressed her lips together and nodded, wondering how much more she ought to tell him.

"And you say this brother of yours is in trouble?" Dane issued a hollow laugh. "That cannot be too much of a surprise or worry to you. I suggest we rejoin your family after we've eaten. Max can wait."

"No!" she cried, no longer caring what he thought. "We can't. Max has gotten himself tossed in the Jackson jail. I don't know if you've ever seen that hanging tree at the west end of town, but if you had, you'd want to ride lickety-split to make sure your brother wasn't the next in line. I can't do any less for mine."

At the word brother, Dane thought of Frank and sagged back against the high seat of his Spanish roping saddle. Shaking off a twinge of loss, he furrowed his brow. Surely this Max had a very good reason for being in jail. What possible difference in his fate could a couple of hours make? "What has this brother of yours done? Murdered someone?"

"No, it's not that bad. I guess he got himself in a fight of some kind."

Dane released Rocio's reins. "Then he can most definitely wait. I am hungry."

"No, please!" she begged. "Thing is, Max—well, Max gets a mite fidgety without me around to calm him. He's . . . he's not exactly like you and me. Max is a little *different* than most folks and he'll be needing me real bad. Please—can't we go to him now?"

There was something behind her words, some little piece of truth, even though he suspected she was hiding as much as she was telling. The glimmer of panic in her eye made the decision for him.

With a strong sense of family honor prompting him, Dane said, "I doubt there is anything you can do to help, but I suppose it wouldn't hold us up too much if we stop by the jail and see to him."

"Now?" she asked, her voice a squeak.

Dane chuckled to himself, thinking of the mayhem her male counterpart might have caused, and then nodded and gave his horses their command. "Alazan, Rocio! *Vamanos.*"

As they began moving south, Maxine glanced over toward the Spaniard and smiled. She wanted to thank him, to show her appreciation in some way, but she felt tongue-tied when she caught sight of his profile against the midday sun. Light seemed to sparkle around his dark features and clothing, making him appear as if he were wearing a cloak of firelight, a glowing backdrop to set off his handsome face.

With a sudden shiver, Maxine forced herself to look away. She finally spoke in a brisk, clipped voice. "Thanks for understanding about my brother, Señor Dane. Now would you mind talking your horses out of this fancy trot and into something a little faster? I have a feeling the sooner we get to that jail, the better."

* * *

In less than an hour, they stood in Jackson at the entrance to the courthouse basement, which led to the jail. Still concerned about Dane's reaction to her brother, Maxine turned to him and said, "You might as well wait out here. What the sheriff's got to say can't be of much interest to you anyhow."

But Dane pushed the door aside and gestured for her to descend. "I am as anxious to learn of your brother's fate as you are. Besides—I wouldn't dream of allowing a young lady to visit a jailhouse unescorted."

"I never said I was a lady," she grumbled under her breath.

"I stand corrected." He bowed at the waist. "I wouldn't dream of allowing a young *woman* to visit the jail unescorted. Shall we?"

Left with no option, she followed the dark stairwell down into a surprisingly well-lit room. An officer of the court sat at a desk near the far wall, and as she and Dane approached, he looked up in their direction.

"Can I help you?" the man said, his voice as dull as his disinterested gaze.

Leaping past Dane, Maxine rushed up to the desk and said, "I heard you got my brother, Max McKain, locked up in the jail. Can I see him, please?"

From only two steps behind her, Dane added, "I am Dane del Cordobes from Rancho Cordoba in San Diego. I am with the young lady."

The guard looked from Dane to Maxine and wrinkled his bulbous nose into a disgusted frown. "Ain't up to me. Have to ask the under-sheriff." Turning his head toward the inner office, he yelled, "Hey, Darby! Got some customers!" Then he turned back to the visitors and said, "Got to remove your weapons—hats, too."

Maxine tore off her Palo Alto, smoothed her mussed hair, and draped her long, single braid down the front of her shirt. She was toying with the idea of tucking her shirttails inside her Levi's in an attempt to look more feminine when a man emerged from the smaller office.

"Afternoon," he said, stepping into the room. "I'm filling in for Sheriff Woods while he's down. What can I do for you folks?"

Before Maxine could open her mouth, Dane stepped between her and the undersheriff and offered his hand. "I'm Dane del Cordobes, Sheriff Darby."

"Pleased to make your acquaintance," he said, accepting the handshake. "Who are you looking for?"

"The young lady," Dane gestured behind him, "is in my employ. She was told you might be holding her brother, and she'd like to see him."

Maxine elbowed her way between the two men and said, "It's Max McKain I'm looking for. You got him?"

Darby looked past her to Dane. "I got him all right. He thrashed Sheriff Woods to within an inch of his life. Pretty serious charges. Don't know if I ought to let you and the—" Darby eyed Maxine from head to toe and lifted one incredulous brow as he finished the sentence "—the lady in to see him or not."

Dane offered him a solicitous smile. "As you can see, Miss McKain is quite concerned about her brother. I would consider it a kindness if you would allow us to speak with him."

Darby shrugged. "Oh, all right. Don't see what it'd

hurt. Maybe she can find out what got him so riled up at the sheriff. Have to remove your weapons first." He gestured toward the bullwhip and the small pistol sheathed at Dane's hip.

When the Spaniard reached for the coil of leather, Maxine covered his hand with hers in a last attempt to keep Max's dignity from suffering any further blows. "Listen, you don't have to go in there with me. I ain't afraid."

But Dane shook his head as he slid his hat and weapons across the desk. "As I've already said, the bowels of a jailhouse are no place for a lady, much less an unescorted lady. I will accompany you on this . . . this mission of mercy, or you will not go."

With a sigh of resignation, she looked into his incredible blue eyes and bit down on her lip. "If you insist, I guess I got no choice. Just remember what I told you about him, all right?"

Before Dane could answer, Sheriff Darby squeezed past them. "Excuse me, folks," he said as he fit a key into the huge padlock securing the door to the cells. When it clicked open, he called to the jailor through the high, heavily barred, peephole, "Coming through, Wiley. Man and a woman to see prisoner McKain."

"Let 'em come on through, Darby!"

This was followed by the unmistakable sound of a shell slamming into the chamber of a shotgun. Then the under-sheriff eased the five-inch plank of oak aside and gestured for Maxine and Dane to enter.

Maxine no longer cared what conclusions Dane may have drawn about Max. She walked without a backward glance into the jailhouse. The area was poorly lit, its only illumination—and ventilation—coming from several narrow slits high up in the thick walls of solid masonry. Maxine heard Dane's approach, followed by the ominous slam of the heavy door. At the hollow sound of the key turning in the metal lock, she gulped.

"It's all right, Rojita," Dane's voice comforted her from over her shoulder. "You are safe. Remember I am with you."

Maxine opened her mouth to speak, but before she could, the jailor called out, "Follow me," and began to walk away.

Startled by his voice, Maxine jumped, and Dane took her hand. They slowly followed the guard. At first glance, the inside of the jail seemed to be a maze of bars, some vertical, some horizontal, and still others at odd, intersecting angles, looking like the weapons of a ghostly fencing match. As Maxine's eyes became used to the semi-darkness and she could separate the bars from their shadows, she realized she was walking along a sort of solid moat, an expanse of mortar separating the outer rectangle of walls from the inner cubicle of cells.

"Hey, girlie," called a disjointed voice. "Over here— come visit me!"

Maxine jumped again but managed to contain a squeal of surprise at the prisoner's request.

"Say nothing to them," Dane whispered into her ear, his grip still firm. "Do not appear as if you can even hear them."

"That ain't no girlie," another shouted out, "it's a Celestial!"

"Ain't neither," hollered another, "lookie at the

color of that braid! No Chinaman I ever seen got anything but black hair. It's a girl, what it is!"

Then they all seemed to be shouting at once, some grunting and hooting, others offering vulgar requests to her burning ears. Finally, when the jailor reached the end of the first row, he turned, propped his back against the wall, and pointed the shotgun at Maxine and Dane.

"There's the fellow you're looking for. Last cell there. Have at him. You got ten minutes."

Ignoring the other inmates now, Maxine fixed her gaze on the cell, searching for her twin. She finally detected some movement, then the heartbreaking figure of her brother as he sat hunched in a ball, rocking in time with the ever-present drummer in his mind.

"*Max.*" The name was a whispered cry as a sudden swelling tightened her throat. "Oh, Max—how could they do this to you?"

Forgetting about the Spaniard, even though his fingers remained looped through hers, she called out, "Max? Look up here—it's me, your sister Maxine. Max?"

The frightened giant continued to rock, occasionally striking his head on the stone wall to which his wrists were manacled.

"Come on, Max," she pleaded. "Look over here, Froggy boy—it's your sister, Maxie. Come on, Froggy, look at me!"

Her voice finally reached into the depths of his injured brain. Raising his hands to his face, Max peered through the jumble of chains and fingers and struggled to identify his visitor. He gasped and then sobbed when he recognized his sister. With equal parts of shame and joy filling him, he slowly climbed to his feet and reached out as far as his restraints would let him.

"Maxie," he cried, teardrops rolling down his apple cheeks. "I done bad. The man said I done real bad."

Maxine thrust her hand through the bars, but the distance between them was too great. She couldn't reach far enough to touch or comfort him. "It's all right, Froggy," she assured him, struggling to keep her own tears out of her voice. "Don't you fret. I'm gonna get you out of here. Don't cry. Maxie's gonna make it all right."

Max sniffed a couple of times and then wiped the tears from his face with the back of his hand. "Then let's go. Let's go, Maxie." He began to march in place. "I don't like it in here. Let's go now."

"We can't go just yet, Max," she said. "I have to know if you hurt the sheriff before we can go. You gotta tell me—what happened?"

Max's pacing increased, and he became more agitated as he tried to remember. Then he looked up, preparing to answer, and spotted Dane standing in the shadows behind his sister. Max gasped and flattened himself against the wall. Unable to verbalize his new terror, he pointed at the stranger and began to cry again.

Maxine glanced at Dane and then turned back to her brother. "It's all right, Max. This here is Señor Dane. He's a good man. He . . . he helped me find you. And now he wants to help you get out of jail. It's all right, Froggy, you can talk in front of him." She turned then, imploring Dane with her gaze as she whispered, "Please say it's all right. If you don't, there's no telling what he might do."

Dane understood now what she'd been hiding, the burden she now faced. Struck by Maxine's strength, the inner beauty he hadn't seen before, he had to clear his throat of emotion before he could say loudly, "Of course it's all right. Go on, Max. Tell your sister what happened and try to forget I'm here."

Maxine lingered a moment, as surprised as she was warmed by his words, more, in the way he said them. Then she turned back to the cell and made a quick survey of Max's quarters. She spotted two untouched plates of food and a full cup of water, confirming what she'd already guessed. Her brother, a man who possessed meager survival instincts in the best of times, would not eat while imprisoned. He would not last long if left in this miserable cell. She had to get him out, and get him out now.

"Froggy," Maxine began again, her voice soft, nurturing, "you gotta tell me. Did you hit Sheriff Woods?"

Max brought his hands to his face, as if, somehow, the gesture would hide his entire body.

"Come on, Max. I'll give you my cat's eye marble if you tell."

This produced the desired results. Max dropped his big hands to his sides, chains rattling like broken glass, and said, "Promise, Maxie? Promise?"

She held up her right hand and waved it so he could see. "I swear. Now tell me, what happened with the sheriff?"

Max stabbed at the brick floor with the toe of his

boot and slowly began to swing his arms as he explained. "I might a hit him a little bit."

"That's good, Max," she said, struggling to keep the concern from her voice. "Now tell me why you done it."

Max dragged the toe of his boot from brick to brick, polishing this one, sweeping that one, convincing himself it was a job he must perform before he could answer any more questions.

Maxine had seen this ploy before, but the jailor hadn't. He waved the shotgun in the air and said, "You folks got less than five minutes to go anyway. Why not give it up? This idiot don't know shit from his bootlaces."

Blind rage consumed Maxine. She jerked out of Dane's grip, whirled around in a fury, and advanced on the jailor.

"Max ain't no idiot!" she screamed into his face. "Don't you *ever* call him by that name again! Now take it back—take it back now, or I'll bust you in the mouth!"

"Shhh, Rojita." Dane held her firmly by the shoulders now, restraining her. To Wiley, he said, "I must apologize for the lady's behavior. You can imagine how difficult it is for her to see her brother imprisoned."

Maxine persisted. "Nobody, but *nobody,* calls Max an idiot—leastways, not around me. This fella here's lucky I didn't get my hands around his scrawny neck."

Dane slid his hands across her back. She was trembling, struggling to fight the panic he assumed would frighten Max even more. A wave of admiration swept through Dane as he lowered his mouth to her ear and whispered, "Why don't you let me try to talk to him."

That black velvet voice, and Dane's hot breath bathing her ear, gave her goosebumps. Her voice came out strangled as she answered, "Thank you kindly, but you don't know Max or understand his ways. Most often, I'm the only one he'll talk to, even when he ain't upset. You'll only scare him more. Ah—*comprende?*"

Dane laughed quietly, softly, at her imitation of him. "*Yo comprendo*, Rojita. Please continue, but try to hurry him along if you can. We don't have much time."

"I'm doing the best I can," she said, frustration seeping into her words.

He gently squeezed her shoulders. "I know you are. Go on, speak to him."

At his gestures, his touch, Maxine felt spellbound, but she managed to turn back to her brother. Using her most authoritative tone, she threatened softly, "The cat's eye, Max. I'm gonna have to give that marble to the sheriff instead of you if you don't tell me what happened, and I mean now."

Max jerked his head up and his eyes seemed to brighten. "Not him! He's bad. He hurts people!"

"You mean the sheriff lit after you first?"

Max shook his head. "Not me. It was you he hurt."

Maxine glanced over her shoulder, catching Dane's eye, and raised one auburn eyebrow. He shrugged, as puzzled as she. She spun back around and pressed her face against the bars. "I don't understand what you're talking about, Max. The sheriff never hurt me."

Through a heavy sigh, he muttered, "Pa said I could

look for you while he set the wagon up to sell medicine over by the hotel."

"Medicine?" Dane blurted out. "I thought your father was a placer miner."

Maxine raised her chin and dismissed him along with the inquiry. "He is most times, but there's lots of things Pa can do besides pan for gold and play cards. He's a sort of . . . doctor sometimes."

"A *doctor?*" Although it was a struggle, Dane restrained his laughter, the urge brought on by a sudden vision of Dicey wearing a white smock, a stethoscope around his neck—and a pair of aces up his sleeve.

From behind her, Maxine could almost swear she heard a snicker. Fiddling with her braid, she ignored the sound and went back to questioning her brother. "Okay, Max. So you went to look for me in Jackson town, and then what happened?"

"Then I seen him." As he remembered what happened just before the men took him away, Max's expression sobered and turned grim. "I seen the sheriff, out back in the bushes near the spring, and he was hurting a lady real bad. Her hair, it was all big and red like yours. I thought it was you." Max looked away and began dragging his toe across the bricks again. "I *did* think it was you. He was hurting you, so I done him real good."

The answer to one puzzle prompted another. Again Maxine glanced at Dane. "I don't get it—sounds to me like he did what any good brother would, smart or not. Why'd they arrest him for saving a gal he thought was his sister?"

"Isn't the spring over near a few of those, ah, 'female boarding houses' at the end of town?" Dane asked.

"Boarding houses? You mean the whorehouses?"

Dane sighed. "I suppose that I do."

"That's where they are all right, and the spring is out back of the Louisiana Hotel. Why?"

Trying to find a delicate way to question the young man, to get to the truth in the most discreet of manners, Dane said, "Ask him what the sheriff did to hurt the woman. Find out what made him think she was injured."

"All right." Maxine turned back to her brother, coaxing him with a smooth, even tone this time. "Max—what'd the sheriff do to the red-haired lady? Was he beating on her or whipping her?"

Max scratched his head, then shook it. "Sort of. Mostly she was moaning, and screaming for God to come help her. The sheriff," he continued, his voice high and excited, "he'd gone and tore off all her clothes, and some of his own, too—"

"The sheriff took off his *own* clothes, Max?"

"I swear it's true, cause I seen it!" Max started for her, forgetting he was manacled to the wall, and the movement jerked him back hard against the slab of mortar. Absently rubbing his head, he went on, singular in his purpose. "I *seen* it—I seen his big white butt jumping up and down on that poor lady, and her clothes was—"

"That's enough, Max," Dane cut in. "I think we understand."

"Damn right we do!" Maxine whirled around, facing Dane, hands on hips. "Max caught the sheriff whoring—

and he thought the man was whoring on me. It ain't fair they went and locked him up for that."

"Maxine, please." Dane took her shoulders in his hands and drew her to him. "Let me explain Max's behavior to the under-sheriff. It isn't a proper subject for you to be discussing—not with him or me."

"I appreciate your kindness, señor." Maxine lifted his hands from her shoulders. "But proper really ain't got much place in this business. He's my brother. I'll see that he gets out of this hell-hole."

Behind them, disturbed by the argument between his sister and the stranger, Max began to whimper. "I swear I'm not lying. I'm *not!* I *seen* it!" Then he clamped his mouth shut, retreated to the corner of his cell, and slid down the wall until he was curled in a fetal position.

Although she'd observed this behavior from Max many times in the past, it hurt even more when Maxine realized she was in part to blame this time. "Max?" she whispered, even though her efforts were useless. "My poor, poor baby. It's gonna be all right. Maxie guarantees it."

Wiley cleared his throat. "Time's about up, folks. Come on, let's move it out." He gestured with his pistol.

This time, as Maxine walked down the narrow corridor, the taunts and filthy suggestions of the inmates didn't register. She was too busy plotting Max's release—or escape—if it should come to that.

When they were out of the cellblock and into the outer office, Dane nudged Maxine and whispered, "You go outside and wait with the horses. Leave this to me."

"I can't."

"You can and you must," he warned in a husky voice. "The fact that Max stumbled across the sheriff during a … a private moment with a red-haired woman who must have resembled you demands your absence. That situation is something that only I or your father should discuss with the sheriff. Since Dicey is not here, the chore falls to me, *comprende?*"

Not entirely, but she did understand that she was fighting a losing battle. Getting in her last shot, more of a complaint than an objection, Maxine snapped, "I don't know why I can't explain it as good as you. The sheriff was whoring, pure and simple."

"*Callate—silencio!*" Dane lashed the words at her, stunning her as surely as his whip might have. "If you wish to secure your brother's freedom, you will do as I say and you will do it now. I give my promise that I will find a way to secure your brother's release. Now please—go outside and wait by the horses." With that, he gave her a none-too-gentle shove toward the stairs and then turned and strode confidently back to the sheriff's office.

Maxine knew deep inside that she did not belong at the discussion which would follow, but still she worried. Would the Spaniard fight long and hard enough to secure Max's release? How could he possibly make as passionate or convincing plea as she could? The Spaniard didn't even *know* Max.

Maxine stood on the bottom step, wavering. Dane wheeled around when he reached the sheriff's doorway and pointed a long finger at her. "Forget it. Do not even consider following me in here."

"I—I was just gonna get my hat." Chin high, she marched across the room and snatched the Palo Alto off the scarred oak table. Then she turned and bolted up the stairs, two at a time, and walked out onto the boardwalk.

6

"*Maxie?*" *Unable to believe* his eyes, Dicey called again from down the street. "That you, Maxie girl?"

At the sound of her father's voice, Maxine twisted around and found him tying the family mules to a rail not far from where she stood. "Pa!"

After knotting the rope, Dicey crab-walked along the rotted boardwalk to where his daughter stood and crushed her in his burly arms. "Aye, and it's good to see yur sweet face, Maxie girl. I weren't sure I'd e'er lay these poor tired eyes on you again."

"P-Pa," she stammered, touched by the emotion in her father's voice, and shaken by the depth of her own feelings. "I don't know why you're carrying on so. I wasn't gone but a day or so, and besides—I told you that I can take care of myself, didn't I?"

Holding her at arm's length now, Dicey looked her over. "I know, girl, but this was a little different. I've been worrin' after yur health. How's the Spaniard been treatin' you? He ain't . . . hurt you none, has he?"

" 'Course not, Pa." Pretty sure she understood what he was talking about, Maxine blushed and kicked a few pebbles off the walkway. "He ain't done me wrong except for an occasional high-handed streak where he thinks he's king or something and can tell me what to do. Most times though, he's a right nice fellah." Her thoughts lingered on Dane's handsome face for a moment. She pushed the image to the back of her mind and softly added, "In fact, I kinda like him, Pa. I like him a lot."

Dicey lifted his brow, alarms ringing in his head, and glanced toward the doorway leading to the basement. "You been downstairs at the jail checking on yur brother's troubles?"

She nodded. "Jumper run across me in Sutter's and told me what was going on down here. Dane—the Señor," she corrected herself, "brought me right on over to help out. He's down talking to the under-sheriff now, says he thinks he can get Max sprung. I guess if anyone can, it'd be him. He's real smart."

"Right nice of him, considerin' the circumstances." Dicey tugged off his worn hat and dragged his handkerchief across his nearly bald pate. Refreshed, he sighed and faced the jailhouse door. "Guess I'd best get on down there and see what's goin' on."

"I found out about a couple a things already," she said. "Max told me what got him in this mess."

"Did he now?"

Maxine saw the expectant look in her father's eyes, and even though she knew he was waiting for the explanation, she understood even more why the Spaniard had forced her out of the discussion downstairs. There really was no easy way to explain it, not even to her own father.

"Well, girl, and what happened? Got to be a mistake of some kind. I know Max didna' have it in him to hit Sheriff Woods."

"Sorry, Pa, but yes he does, and yes . . . he did." At her father's surprised gasp, Maxine averted her gaze and explained as best she could. "Max come across the sheriff and a red-haired lady from one of those whorehouses over by the spring—you know about them?"

Dicey nodded. "Aye and I do."

"You do?"

"Ne'er mind about that, girl," he grumbled, adjusting the collar of his shirt. "Get on with yur tale."

"Well . . ." Maxine hedged, trying to find just the right words. "It's this way, Pa. It seems this whore woman was hollering and carrying on, and Max thought she was me and that she was crying 'cause she was hurt, but I guess it was just that the sheriff was doing some lovemaking on her, and she was carrying on 'cause of that, but she wasn't hurt."

Dicey sputtered as if he'd choked on a piece of jerky. When he regained his ability to speak, he quickly said, "Thanks for gettin' Max to talkin', girl. You dona' have to tell me anymore." Folding his arms across his chest, he struck a thoughtful pose. "It's lookin' like our Max has gone and made a wee bit of a mistake, but I dona' see why it canna' be explained away. I'd best get on down there and try to spark a bargain."

"Not a good idea, Pa. I told you, the Spaniard's a little lordly about some things. Thinks he can do every-thing himself. He told me he was gonna get Max out alone, and not to bother him."

Dicey jabbed a gnarled finger against his own chest. "Dicey McKain is that boy's father, and Dicey McKain's the one's gonna see to him." Then he spun around on his good leg, limped over to the doorway, and disappeared down the staircase.

Maxine hated the idea of missing anything. She took a few halting steps after him, even though there was no question that she did not belong in the discussion downstairs. Then her father suddenly reappeared in the doorway. Directly behind him came Dane and the under-sheriff.

As the trio approached Maxine, Darby tipped his hat. "Back in a minute, folks," he said. He started across the rutted street.

"Hey!" Dicey called after him. "Where're you going? What about my boy?"

Dane supplied the answer. "Darby's on his way to ask Sheriff Woods if he'll consider releasing Max."

The Spaniard's voice, powerful and unyielding, startled Dicey. He wheeled around and stared up at the much taller man.

"So we meet again," Dane said, offering his hand in greeting.

Cautious, as a man with Dicey's background had to be, he inched tentative fingers toward the Spaniard but never took his gaze away from those intelligent blue eyes. After the briefest of handshakes, he asked, "I can't say I thank you for snatchin' my girl away, but she says you've been down tryin' to get Max sprung.

For that, I'm beholdin' to you. Now what might they be plannin' for my boy?"

Keeping his voice low, out of Maxine's earshot, he asked, "Do you know why your son was arrested?"

Dicey offered a curt nod. "Aye, and my girl told me. Max made a wee mistake all right, but that'd be all he did. Can'no punish a man for that . . . can they?"

Dane shrugged. "I rather doubt they really want to. I think they'll let him go."

Tired of being excluded from these discussions, Maxine stepped between the two men. "Really? Honest to God true, really?"

Maxine stood before Dane, her features as bold as her manner. He found himself smiling as he said, "Darby understands that Max made a mistake. I think the sheriff will too. Between that, and the offer I made to pay the sheriff's medical expenses, I believe they'll release your brother."

"Did you hear that, Pa?" She impulsively threw her arms around Dane and hugged him, and then she wheeled around and did the same to her father. "Everything's gonna be just fine. Just fine and dandy."

"Not everything, girl," Dicey said, his voice muffled with worry. "If'n that bill comes to more than six bits and a pair of mules, yur brother's most likely gonna be calling the jailhouse home for quite a spell."

Maxine's bright expression faded at his words, but then Dane spoke, lifting them again.

"I have already sent one thousand dollars with the under-sheriff. I'm quite sure that amount will secure your son's release."

"Hot damn!" Maxine slapped her forehead with the

palm of her hand. "A thousand bucks ought to secure the release of every jailbird in Amador County! What kind of fancy doctor did the sheriff hire?"

Dane narrowed his eyes, thinking for one brief moment of censuring her language, but in deference to her father, he ignored the outburst. "I decided," he explained patiently, "that in a part of the country where a dollar is the going rate for a single egg, or a slice of bread, one thousand dollars ought to be about right for the purpose of freeing your brother. The doctor's actual bill is probably no more than a hundred dollars; the rest is meant for the sheriff's peace of mind. *Comprende?*"

Feeling left out, Dicey leapt into the conversation. "It's boodle, what it is. Boodle, pure and simple."

Dane shrugged. "I can't argue that if you're talking bribe, but I was under the impression Max wasn't doing too well down in that cell. I thought his freedom might be worth whatever it took."

"Aye, and you did no wrong, young man. In fact, I'm owin' you more than coin." Dicey wheezed out a tired sigh. "It's grateful to you, I am, to be sure. I just dona' know where I'll be gettin' the money to repay you."

Over the miner's shoulder, Dane could see Darby approaching rapidly. "Why don't we worry about a way to settle our bill after it becomes a fact? Let's hear what the sheriff had to say."

Darby leapt up on the boardwalk, with his hand extended toward Dane. "Got yourself a deal, Mr. Cordobes. Sheriff thought about making the kid stand trial, but then he thought about McKain being an idio—" Darby cut himself off, but not before a scathing glance from Maxine set the hair on his scalp on end. Scratching his head, he amended his words. "When he thought about him being kinda slow and all, he decided it wouldn't be worth the trouble. One of you folks come on down to the jailhouse with me now in case we have a problem getting the kid out of his cell. He's free to go."

Maxine let out a war whoop. "Hot damn and hallelujah! I told you, Pa! I told you Dane could do it!"

Dicey's excitement about Max's release was dampened by his daughter's obvious admiration for the Spaniard. He reached out to Dane and shook his hand. "Thank you kindly again, sir. We'll figure out a way to settle up after we collect my boy."

"You are welcome. Now go on ahead with Darby. I'll stay out here and . . ." he glanced at Maxine, grinning. "And try to keep your daughter out of trouble."

"Uh, well, thank you again anyways." Then, still troubled by Maxine's reactions to the Spaniard, he limped over to the stairway where the deputy stood waiting for him.

After her father and the under-sheriff were out of sight, Maxine leaned toward Dane and whispered, "I'd like to thank you, too. Can I kiss you?"

Her voice, softer and more feminine than before, surprised him, as did the request. Dane turned to her, caught in a surge of tangled emotions, and found himself corralled by the sight of her. Several lengths of her hair had escaped her sloppy braid, and the rays of the noonday sun merged with those colorful strands. She was an image of flames, a fiery goddess. Captured by her stark beauty, by the strength of her long wing-shaped brows above her intensely curious eyes, Dane indulged his imagination. Once again, he envisioned her draped in a fine Paris gown.

"Well?" Maxine demanded, embarrassed by his perusal. "Can I or not?"

Dragging in a surprisingly difficult breath, Dane forced himself to say, "You don't need to thank me. I was glad to help out."

"But I want to." She took a step closer, determined to have her way. "I was a mite cantankerous down there in the jail, and I want you to know how sorry I am. A kiss is about the best I can offer."

With that, she grinned up at him, dropped her hat to the ground, and looped her arms around his neck.

"Maxine," he objected mildly, "this is not expected or proper."

"I'm none too interested in what's proper, and maybe you're not expecting any thanks, but I got to do it anyway. That's the way I am."

Slowly, partly because she was so new at it but mostly because she wanted to keep this memory with her always, she inched up on her tiptoes until her gaze was level with his. Twisting her head from side to side, she grinned again and positioned her head at what she thought would be just the right angle.

Her lazy, deliberate movements were driving Dane wild. Honor and decency demanded he remove her from his person, that he reach up and disengage her arms from around his neck, but before he could move—if he'd really intended on doing so in the first place—her sweet lips were upon him. The words he'd planned to say slid down his throat as Maxine's mouth began to move against his, and Dane knew for sure that he had lost his skimpy battle with honor. But oh, how sweet were the spoils of defeat.

Maxine offered no slight gesture of thanks, no brief encounter of lips. She plunged in, all gusto and curiosity, and engaged his tongue in a teasing dance that sparked a kind of earthy passion he'd assumed he was too civilized to have. He began to groan like a wild beast as he matched her thrusts, plumbing her fiery depths.

With a final moan, he pushed her away.

"*Christo,* Maxine. Take pity on a man who is trying to salvage himself as a gentleman. Far too much has passed between us already. Please—I beg of you—don't say, or do, another thing."

Her mouth fell into something resembling a pout, but she kept her gaze locked in his. Dane had a strange look in his eyes, a kind of glassy shine to his skin that made him appear feverish. His expression was as confusing as the strange sensations colliding inside of her. He looked almost angry . . . or was it something else?

Maxine cocked her head and picked out another curiosity in his expression, something that had nothing to do with anger. There was a certain warmth in his eyes she'd never seen before, the blue of a summer pond instead of an icy winter lake. There was something else as well, some other message she couldn't quite decipher. Whatever it was, whatever it meant, she only knew that the look, like the kiss, made her feel weak all over, as if she'd just climbed out of her sick bed. Except that being sick had never been such fun.

Dicey, who'd just reached the top step, stood on the boardwalk and watched the silent exchange between his daughter and the Spaniard for several seconds. He recognized the look instantly, and he understood it all too well.

Dicey yelled over his shoulder, "Get on up here with me, Max. I think your sister's gonna be needin' yur help to get shuck a that Spaniard after all."

7

When she heard Max's shuffling gate resounding against the boardwalk, Maxine forced herself to step away from Dane and ran to greet her brother.

"Maxie! Maxie!" he cried, flinging himself toward her.

Even though Max was easily twice her size, Maxine gathered him in her arms. "You done good, Froggy. It's gonna be all right now. How do you feel?"

Max stepped back and rubbed the heels of his hands against his watering eyes. "Hungry," he said, with a grin that split his face in two.

The twins' father stepped up close and said, "We'll just be takin' care o' that in a minute, son. First we got business to attend to."

Dicey looked over his shoulder and found Dane standing next to him. A sudden burst of possessiveness shot through him, and he reached out, grabbed Maxine's hand, and jerked her to his side before he addressed the Spaniard. "So what am I owin' you, me good man? And you'd best be addin' my foolish gamblin' bet in the tally while yur at it. I canno' allow you to take my daughter away again."

"Pa," she protested. "He isn't—"

"Please, Maxie girl, I'll thank you to button your lip. Let me take care o' this."

Tired of being told what to do by both Dicey and Dane, her eyes flashed, but she kept her silence. For the time being, anyway.

Pleased to find Maxine obeying him for a change, Dicey puffed out his chest and continued. "As I was sayin', sir, please go on with your cipherin'."

But Dane was in shock, still flabbergasted by his reaction to Maxine's charms, stunned to think he'd allowed their embrace to happen at all. Hard as he tried, Dane could only half-listen to the miner's request. He stood silent, incapable of mathematics, and used the moment of confusion to study the odd trio surrounding him. Glancing first at Dicey, he noted the worn spots in his checkerboard shirt, the white fringed tears in his jeans, and knew for sure that the miner would never be able to repay him—not, at least, for a very long time. Then he turned to the giant man the Scotsman called son.

The young man was made like the thickest of trees from his long arms to his proportionately shorter legs, and although he was approximately the same height as Dane, his bulk and enormous chest made him seem twice as big. A formidable obstacle, Dane observed, and one to remember should he make another mistake with this curious family. Max suddenly grinned at some random thought, or perhaps simply because he was the object of Dane's attention, and Dane was struck by his conflicting features. Heavily splattered with dark freckles, Max's face was wide and square, boldly featured like Maxine's, but his teeth were the oddity; they were small, perfectly shaped pearls, almost babyish compared to his sister's larger, somehow more interesting arrangement of overlapping eyeteeth.

With his attention fixed on Maxine, he glanced at her enticing mouth, those full satin lips. A quiet warmth spread throughout him at the memory of her dripping wet body, glistening in the sun. Here he was now, a man of honor, a man who would soon carry the respected title, *Don* Francisco Dane del Cordobes. If anyone had told him before this day that he would be standing in the middle of town, in broad daylight, *kissing*—and quite passionately at that—a woman dressed in men's clothing, he'd have given them a taste of his bullwhip, at the very least.

Dicey cleared his throat, anxious to be on his way, and prodded the Spaniard for a decision. "Sure and I canno' be owin' so much you canno' add it up! What's my bill?"

As he thought of never seeing Maxine again, Dane shook off a stab of disappointment and pulled a figure from the air. "It comes to about fifteen hundred dollars, but I believe you owe me a little more than that. What happened to the things you stole from me in San Francisco? I'd either like their return, or the cash equivalent if you have sold them."

Dicey puffed his chest and took a halting step closer to Dane. "Now see here, my good man. We McKains may catch a fella with a little woollybuggar now and again, but we are not common thieves. I'll be a thankin' you to take that back."

Dane frowned, preparing to raise his objections, but before he could bring the man to task, Maxine confessed.

"I might a borrowed a thing or two, Pa." She turned her attention to Dane. "Wasn't exactly stealing, you know. You said to help yourself, and more than once. Besides, you have more hairbrushes in that house than women, and as for the few coins I got out of your pocket—well, I guess I didn't figure a rich fella like you'd even know they were gone. Wasn't much."

"You think not?" Dane shot her an incredulous glance. "And what of my watch—my *solid* gold watch? Is that too petty an item for me to reclaim also?"

Disheartened, Maxine drew her hand to her breast. She held it there, her fingers pressing against the time-piece, hoping against all hope that Dane would tell her to keep it, that he didn't want it returned after all. The watch had been special to her since the night she took it, but now it was even more so, as a kind of memorial, a remembrance of her first honest-to-God kiss, a link she would have to Dane and his touch forever. How could she give it up?

"I don't know what you're talking about," she said in a small voice.

Dane's eyes narrowed as he said, "I do not believe you, Rojita—the watch, *por favor.*"

Dicey hobbled closer, his expression indignant. "What's that yur a callin' my girl—Row-sometin'? She might accidentally pick up a thing or two don't belong to her now and again, but my Maxie's a good girl. I will not be standin' here havin' you call her bad names!" Then he raised his fists.

Dane answered the Scotsman, but his dogged gaze remained frozen to Maxine's. "I did not defame your daughter. I simply called her Red—Rojita."

Relieved, mostly because he wouldn't have to back up his threat and take the Spaniard on, Dicey laughed. "Best step away from her then—Maxie dona' take to folks commentin' about her hair."

"The name," Dane explained, his gaze still riveted on hers, "has nothing to do with her hair. It means color, red like the cape of a matador. Your daughter seems to enjoy waving that cape at me—as she is doing now— and like *el toro,* I grow impatient. One last time: where is my watch . . . *Rojita?*"

That was that. She wished she could find a way to challenge him, to force Dane into allowing her to keep that which she'd come to think of as hers, but she was fresh out of woollybuggars.

Sighing irritably, Maxine grumbled, "Oh, all right!" Then she looped the chain over her head and pulled the watch from between her breasts. When Maxine dropped the heirloom into Dane's open palm, she impulsively offered a final rationale, an excuse for her less-than-honest behavior. "It's not like I meant to take anything of value, you know. I figured you must have a thousand of these. Didn't think it'd matter if you had one less. Excuse me if I cut into your supply."

Smiling now, wondering why he continued to be so attracted to such a woman, Dane's fingers closed over the warm metal. Feeling envious as he thought of the lush valley where his family heirloom had been hiding, he slid the watch into the breast pocket of his shirt and tried to ignore the fact that his heartbeat was picking up the tempo of the timepiece where hers had left off.

Aware that Dicey's eyes were upon him, Dane stiffened his spine and spoke in formal, clipped tones as he set Maxine straight. "You are mistaken about this timepiece. There is only one watch like this, Miss McKain. It has been in my family since the early years in Cordoba, the town we are from in the Andalusian region of Spain. It means a lot to me. I thank you for its safe return."

Less than humbled, but stung by a twinge of guilt, Maxine's gaze fell to the boardwalk. She really ought to apologize, but she was unused to apologizing to anyone for anything. She searched for the correct words and proper manner before she finally settled on a small oration which seemed like it might do the trick.

Keeping her eyes downcast, she spoke in little girl tones as she said, "I had no idea that watch was so special, Señor Dane. I—I really and truly am sorry I took it, and I promise nothing like that will ever happen again." She took a quick peek at him then to see if she'd gotten the reaction she sought. She hadn't.

Dane rolled his eyes and slowly shook his head.

Maxine snickered, unable to stop herself.

She chanced another peek at Dane, and they both burst out laughing.

That was it for Dicey. He'd seen all he intended to

between his daughter and the Spanish nobleman. Trying to sound as in control of the situation as he could, he toughened his voice, and said sharply, "Am I to understand, sir, that once Maxine returns yur ivory goods, our debt's settled except for the cash?"

With surprising difficulty, Dane turned his attention away from Maxine and faced her scruffy father. "She can keep the toiletries. I really don't have any use for them now."

"I can?" Maxine blurted out. "You mean like a gift? A real gift?"

Dane shrugged. "I suppose you could call them a gift if you like. In any case, they're yours to keep."

"Really? Really mine to keep?" Maxine marveled at the thought, the very idea of someone other than her father offering her a gift, a *real* gift, not some little toy or discarded object.

Dicey pointed a gnarled finger at her. "Get hold of yurrself, girl—a person'd think you never saw a brush before." He brought that same finger to the tip of his chin and added, "Come to think of it, yur lookin' a bit like you've never used one. Where's yur hat?"

Scowling as her father pushed her out of yet another conversation, Maxine marched to where she'd let the Palo Alto fall, picked it up, and jerked it down over her head. Then she hurried back in to the men in time to hear Dicey working at a settlement.

"Then we be owin' fifteen hundred, complete?"

Dane nodded, glancing at Maxine, looking at the ridiculous hat and suddenly feeling robbed of the unfettered view of her beauty. Then out of the corner of his eye, he noticed Max slowly moving toward his horses.

"Max," he called, his tone a clear warning, "please don't get too close to my horses or try to touch them. They can be very dangerous."

But Max continued walking in his usual labored, shuffling manner as if he hadn't heard a word.

Dane turned to Dicey, concerned. "Why doesn't he stop? Those horses are highly strung, and trained to resist strangers. He could be seriously hurt."

Dicey glanced toward his son, then shrugged. "You do'na have a worry about your stock or my boy. He's got a real way with animals. Now then, we have a deal?"

In spite of Dicey's assurances, Dane felt uneasy and kept one eye on Max as he repeated, "Good enough. Do you have any of it," he asked, distracted, "or something I can take as collateral until you have the rest?"

Even though he knew exactly how much money and possessions the McKains had, or more correctly, *didn't* have, Dicey gave his stubbles a thoughtful rub. "Ummm," he finally admitted, "I'm afraid yur a findin' me a wee bit short."

"How short?"

"Ummm." He stalled another moment and then came out with the truth. "Right close to fifteen hundred short."

Dane heard the confession but couldn't seem to tear his gaze away from what was happening at the hitching post. Amazed at how easily Max had approached Alazan, he wondered how long it would be before the stallion would explode and lash out at the young man. Dane absently said, "You must have something, some way to settle this. Perhaps you can secure a loan?"

Dicey and Maxine laughed in unison at the very idea of finding anyone fool enough to loan them money, and then another, even more perfect, solution popped into her mind. There was one more option in the McKain bag of tricks, one which they reserved as a kind of last resort—and more importantly, one that had always served them well in the past. It could certainly work again, she decided. The plan would not only ease them out of their debt, but it would keep Dane around a little longer as well. It was, she thought using her father's word, the *perfeck* solution.

Even though she was brimming with excitement, Maxine managed to find a sorrowful tone as she suggested, "Then I guess there just ain't no getting around it—we got to repay you. We have a way you know, one that we swore to keep as our little family secret, but under the circumstances—"

Dicey cut her off with one drawn out, perfectly enunciated word. "*Max . . . ine.*"

The use of her given name, coupled with the stern pronunciation, should have been more than enough warning that her father wouldn't consider the plan, but she went ahead anyway. "We got to, Pa," Maxine insisted, hoping he would understand. "There ain't no other way to settle this. You wait right here. I'll be back with what's due you before you can blink three times."

Then she made a dash for the back of the family wagon and launched herself inside. By the time she'd dug through the family's meager belongings and found what she was looking for, her father had joined her.

He waited patiently for her to climb down the two steps at the back of the wood-sided wagon. Once she stood before him, Dicey challenged her decision. "Maxie girl," he said, pointing at the black objects in her hand. "I can'no believe yur capable of such a terrible thing."

She canted her head in her father's direction, glancing first at the nuggets she carried, then at him. "I admit it ain't the kindest thing we ever done to a fella, but that never stopped us before. Why should it now—especially since we owe this Spaniard so much money?"

Dicey sighed. "It ain't the woollybuggar so much, girl. What it is . . . it just ain't the right thing to do." Dicey slammed his fist into his open palm and tried to make her see how much the idea disturbed him. "We ain't *never* woollybuggared the same man twice. 'Tain't fair, and 'tain't right. We got to find another way to get even."

"But, Pa, this is the only way! Besides, he's the nicest, smartest man I ever met. I . . . I was hoping he could stay with us a while longer. I promise when the time comes I won't let him get too lost in the desert— hell, I'll draw arrows pointing the way in the sand if I have to. I'll make sure we leave him where he can find his way home to San Diego. *Please*, Pa," she begged, her hands clasped in front of her, rocks and all. "I don't ask for much, you know I don't. So can't we just keep him around a little longer?"

"Maxine," Dicey blustered, embarrassed to think of

the conversation ahead, of the things he should have told her long ago. "Y-you—you can'no be keepin' a full-grown man. I-it just ain't done."

"Oh, Pa. I don't want to hurt him or nothing, and besides if we keep him around long enough, maybe . . ." She hesitated, trying to think of a good enough reason, something that would sweeten the idea for Dicey, yet get her what she wanted at the same time. It struck her like the tail of Dane's bullwhip. "Well, who can tell? Maybe I can talk him into teaching me to read words! He can't do that if we're up one road and he's down another, can he?"

Maxine's final prod took the punch out of Dicey's objections. Of all the guilt he felt over the manner in which he'd raised his children, their lack of education bothered him the most. He'd figured that by now, at least one member of the McKain family would know how to read and write, but they'd never been able to settle long enough for schooling, what with chasing one strike after another.

It wasn't that he hadn't planned to see to the family's long-term needs, or try to find some kind of permanent home, it had just never happened. Neither had that little talk he'd figured on having with his headstrong daughter—the one about men and their notions, and especially about a few of the things they might try to talk her into doing. Coward that he was, he'd assumed—stupidly now that he'd seen what it garnered—that keeping such information from Maxine would also keep her from harm. It sure wasn't that he didn't *think* of the things he ought to do to be a good father. He just wasn't too good about acting on those thoughts. Was it too late now?

He finally said, "It's this way, Maxie girl; and danged if I dona' know that I might a dawdled too long in teachin' you a few lessons about men—dandies like the Spaniard, in particular. I dona' have the time fur details now, so you just got to trust yur pa when I say that it ain't a wise idea to keep that man around."

Maxine laughed, guessing at the next warning or bit of information he would try to relay. Beating him to it, she said, "Don't worry, Pa. I know plenty about the ways of men—Lola told me—so you don't have a worry there. I can take care of myself, remember?"

Dicey hesitated, remembering Lola Montez and her wild, wicked ways, wondering just what she'd revealed, and how she'd explained the facts of life to his impressionable daughter. He glanced into Maxine's dark eyes, hating to dash the bright glimmer of excitement he saw there, knowing what might happen to her if he didn't. Gently, he said, "I dona' want to see you hurt by this fellah. He might think a puttin' notions in yur head, notions about livin' a high fancy life with him, but they'd just be lies to get you to do his biddin'. Did Lola tell you about men like that?"

Maxine laughed. "Is that what's bothering you? Don't worry," she said, "because Dane is on his way to San Diego to get married! He don't have any interest in me—none he can lie about, anyway."

"The man's betrothed, you say?" Dicey began fingering his stubbles, seeing a tiny light of hope in the family's woollybuggar of "last resort."

"Yes, he's about to be married! Don't you see how

perfeck all this is? Why, even if were he to take a notion to get his revenge after we dump him in the desert, he wouldn't go chasing after us up in eldorado country—not with his sweetheart pining away for him down in San Diego!"

Dicey was pensive now, his mind weighing his daughter's relative innocence against what seemed to be an increasingly good way out of the enormous debt.

Maxine leapt on his moment of indecision like a rattler on a ground hog. "Let's get back to Dane with these nuggets before he decides to have us *all* tossed in that jailhouse for thieving. This is gonna work, Pa—it's an absolutely perfeck plan!"

Then, before her father could change his mind, Maxine spun on her heel and ran off.

"I'm back," she said breathlessly as she sprinted up beside Dane.

He was standing near the horses, watching as Max examined each of Alazan's hooves. Without a glance in her direction, he whistled his appreciation and said, "I can hardly believe this. Your brother has Alazan under his spell. This horse seems perfectly happy to do anything he asks!"

Maxine shrugged it off, far too excited about her plan to gush over Max's affinity with animals. "Pa told you not to worry about him, didn't he? Now, if you'll excuse me for butting in on you two, I got something to show you. Before I do," she warned Dane, nudging him away from Max until she had his full attention, "you got to promise never to tell another soul you saw these or who had them. Promise me."

Only mildly curious about what she might have balled into her fist, Dane shrugged. "I promise. What is this valuable commodity you possess?"

With practiced excitement, she began her fabricated tale. Grinning broadly, Maxine dropped the black nuggets into his palm, and whispered conspiratorially, "Have a look at these and see if they don't make a good start at ending our debt."

Dane was staring at the large pebbles, unable to believe his eyes, when Dicey limped up beside him. Dane glanced away from the treasure, noting the sour, defeated expression on the elder McKain's craggy face, and wondered if perhaps he wasn't mistaken about their origin.

Giving Maxine the benefit of the doubt, Dane said, "I fail to see how these can reduce your debt."

Max, who was usually contented just to observe conversations he barely understood, jumped at the chance when he realized he might actually be able to contribute to the discussion. "Them's our lucky nuggets!" he exclaimed, clapping his hands. "They're the lucky ones that I can never play with or show off to folks. Lucky, they are."

Max broke into his broadest grin ever. Unable to do less, Dane gave him a warm smile and said, "Thanks for clearing that up, Max. I didn't realize they were lucky."

"Yessir," he beamed. "Luckier than anything we got—luckier than Pa's magic dice, even."

"Magic . . . dice?" Dane asked, more than curious.

"Ah," Dicey cut in, his tone as shifty as his suddenly nervous gaze, "you dona' want to be wastin' your precious time about anything but how to get back that money we owe you. Now let us discuss these nuggets—"

Maxine stepped on his words as well as his left foot as she crowded back into the scripted conversation. "You got to give a fellah a chance, Pa. We haven't even told him what they are or how much they're worth." When Dane's attention was back where she wanted it—on her—Maxine cried out, "They're gold! Pure, honest-to-God gold!"

Drawing back, Dane studied the nuggets, lifting each one and turning it over. On one, he found a tiny scratch, a blemish that revealed a small yellow creek running through the black ash coating. He held it up into the sunlight, noting the luster of that scratch, the pure golden color beneath, and then palmed them again. They were, he thought, somehow disappointed, exactly what he'd first suspected they were.

"Go on," Maxine encouraged, "dig some of that black off the other one. You'll find the same thing. Gold, thick as a man's finger, and more where those come from too."

"Is that right?" Playing along with her absurd story, Dane lifted the nuggets in the air. "They're gold all right, but still a long ways from fifteen hundred dollars' worth."

"There's more where those came from!"

Her practiced enthusiasm beginning to wear thin, Dane gave her one more chance to come clean. "Then why haven't you good folks mined it out? Lose your map?"

Maxine was taken aback for a moment. Hearing something in his tone but disregarding it, she went on, "No, silly. It's just not so easy to work the claim. Hard-rock mining takes more than a strong back—takes lots of money for supplies, too. Besides that, we've had a speck of trouble finding the exact same location again, but I'm sure—"

"Then what you're saying is, you've staked a claim, but now you can't find it?"

"Yes," she hedged, "and no. Our mine is down your way near San Diego, in the Borrego desert. And, well, I guess you might say we did have a little trouble finding it the last time we looked."

His brows cinched tighter than Alazan's saddle, Dane glanced to the Scotsman, hoping Dicey would at least offer some small bit of truth. What he got was another dose of McKain flapdoodle.

"The site's a wee bit hard to get to," Dicey said, easing into his usual role, "and I admit, tough to find, but I'm certain we can locate it together." He pointed to Dane's Andalusian horses. "You got some fine horse-flesh there, and cash enough to keep us all in supplies. That'd be the number one reason we ain't found it again ourselves—no cash!"

Still juggling the nuggets, certain he was being tricked, sure even where the confidence game had originated, Dane's smile was tight as he asked one final question. "If that's true, why haven't you taken on a business partner, someone with enough money to outfit you, before now?"

Preening in his role like a man with a new coat, Dicey struck a proud pose and said, "Because, me good man, we McKains tend to be a mite close with what's ours. We ain't much for sharin'."

"That's right," Maxine added. "We never wanted a partner, but now that we owe you so much money, looks like we got one whether we want it or not." She lifted her chin, giving her profile a properly scrupulous tilt as she tossed in, "Instead of doubting us, I think you ought to be right honored that we've taken you into our confidence."

"An excellent choice of words," Dane snapped back, weary of the game, angry as well. "Let me see if I can't guess the name of your previous partner. Could it be Peg Leg Smith?"

Both McKains gasped and took a backward step.

"I thought it might be." Dane jiggled the nuggets and recited what he could remember of the stories he'd heard around San Francisco. "Let's see—the black coating, as I recall, is caused by copper oxide from the small amount of that mineral mixed in with the gold, but there is definitely gold beneath. The trouble, I believe, is that there is no such claim. These rocks and a few others like them are the sum total of this 'missing mine.' I can only assume that once we arrived in the desert, you fine folks—in the tradition of your good friend, Peg Leg—planned to abandon me and take off with my goods and horses, debt unpaid. How am I doing so far?"

Maxine and her father glanced at each other, one as guilty and chagrined as the other, but neither stepped forward to offer an explanation.

Lifting the hand holding the nuggets, Dane tested their weight again, figuring they would assay out at around three hundred dollars. His tone serious, annoyed, he said, "Enough of your games. What do you have besides these to cover what is due me?"

Maxine wasn't concerned about their debt just then. She was watching Dane, horrified as his fingers curled, then began to close over the nuggets. Before he could even see her coming, she reached up and snatched them out of his hand.

"Sorry," she said, backing away, "but these don't leave this family for any reason, not even if we don't have a bean to cook nor a spoon to stir it—they're our lucky nuggets. We'll never, *ever*, give them up. They ain't gonna be part of any bargain we strike."

"*Bargain?*" Exasperated, Dane heaved a sigh and tried to talk sense to the family's patriarch. "You people have not tried to bargain or reach an agreement with me. Instead, you continue to trick me, to try and cheat me out of what I am owed. Do none of you McKains have a sense of honor or fair play?"

Wearing his guilt and shame like a hat dipped in mud, Dicey pressed his lips together and slowly shook his head. "Yur right to be takin' offense at us about now. Dona' know what got into our heads, but Maxie's on the up and up about one thing. Each and every one of us'd have to be dead and burried fore we'd turn loose of them lucky nuggets. We can'no be bargainin' with them."

"Our lucky ones," Max echoed, pleased to find another part of the conversation he could understand. "Lucky is what they are."

Nuggets tucked firmly into her back pocket, Maxine

inched up closer to her father and peeked over his shoulder as she said, "Looks like we're just plain indebted to you. She chuckled at the thought. "Indebted and indentured, I guess."

Dicey raised his bushy brow and beamed at the first ray of hope. "Now there'd be an idea. Why not let us work off our debt?"

"No." Dane shook his head firmly, with conviction. "No, no, absolutely *not*. I won't be having the lot of you under my roof. One of you," he added, spearing Maxine with his gaze, "was more than I could handle. Three— no."

"But," Dicey challenged, "as I see it, kind sir, it's the only way out."

"He's right," Maxine said, delighted with the new plan. "Why, the three of us can have that debt paid off in no time."

Although Max had lost a good bit of the conversation, he added his two cents. "Right," he echoed. "We're the lucky ones."

Dane groaned and rubbed the back of his neck. He was actually considering the idea, in spite of all he knew about this family of thieves, he was thinking of taking them on, of hiring them, a ram enlisting the aid of a wolf pack to help guard his ewes. Had he lost his mind?

Dicey watched the Spaniard carefully, hoping to catch some idea of what the man was thinking, regretting the decision to try the Peg Leg mine woollybuggar on him. This Dane del Cordobes was a lot harder to fool than most, and not as easily touched by his family's plight as others were either. In fact, the last time they'd tried the game, Dicey had done most of the talking with the twins standing by his side. Silently, they usually lent validity to his claims, looked every inch a properly pitiful pair of angels who didn't know the meaning of the word *fraud*. By the time the McKains finished this act, more often than not, they had a new "partner" eager to invest in an imaginary gold mine somewhere off to the south. And the twins could count on eating a few decent meals for a spell. This time, though, he'd known deep in his heart it was no good, that it wouldn't work. Why had he been fool enough to let Maxine talk him into it? And now that he had, how would he ever regain the Spaniard's trust?

Taking his hat in his hand, Dicey humbled himself and pleaded. "And what do you say, my good man? Will you be a willin' to allow this family its self-respect? Might we work our debt away?"

Although he feared he would regret the words the instant they were out, Dane heard himself say, "Perhaps. What are your talents? What can any of you do that might possibly earn the kind of money you need?"

"Well . . ." Dicey hedged, then noticed what Max was up to. "Take my son for instance. He's a right handy stable boy. Isn't a horse or a mule he canno' talk into jumpin' off a cliff if he set his mind to it. And they love him, they do, cozy right up to him like that big stud of yurs is doin' as we speak."

Dane glanced over at the horses, and sure enough, Alazan not only had his black muzzle buried in Max's big hand, Dane could swear he heard the stallion nickering. Looking back at Dicey, he nodded. "All right.

Max certainly seems to be able to handle the job, but it will take a very long time for him to work off the whole debt himself. What about you? What can you do besides pan for gold?"

Dicey studied his blunt fingernails and dug them into the whiskers along his jaw. "Well, I'm mostly good at plannin', you know? Cipherin', figurin' out the best trails to take and where to ford a river, things like that."

Useful perhaps, Dane thought, but only for the two weeks or so it would take them to arrive in San Diego. Dane shook his head and sighed. "I don't know. I don't see how you can pay your debt in this manner. There simply—"

"What about me?" Maxine plowed between the two men. "You didn't ask me what job I could do. I can cook, you know, and do lots of handy things. You name it—I can do it."

Dane shook his head. "No, Maxine, I do not need another cook or servant. I'm afraid there is nothing—"

"How about I write your letters and such? I could be one of them secretary people for you. What about that?"

Dane's eyebrows inched together. "You read and write?"

Shrugging, Maxine admitted, "Not yet, but Pa and I thought you might like to teach me on the way to the desert—excuse me, on the way to your rancho in San Diego. I'm a real fast learner. What do you say?"

"Teach you?" Dane began to laugh, the sound rumbling up from deep inside, but then he abruptly stopped as quickly as he'd begun. *Teach her*—as in educate? As before, Dane imagined Maxine cleaned up and coifed like a lady. His mind's eye dressed her in an exquisite emerald gown of shimmering silk, and then added a lush velvet cape in forest green to complement her fiery hair. Perhaps it might just work.

Smiling broadly, Dane said, "If each of you can abide by my terms, there may be a way to accept your offer after all."

Maxine let out a war whoop.

That set Max off. He clapped his hands, hollering along with her as if the curtain had fallen on a really good puppet show.

Their father turned skeptical. "Just what might those terms be, my good man?"

"I'll take Max on as a stable hand and find suitable work for you, but Maxine will be the one to pay off most of your debt, and she might do it much sooner than any of us expect." Dane now had the family's complete attention. "I'll take the time to school her socially as well as academically on our journey south. My mother and Caroline can complete the job when we reach Rancho Cordoba."

"We're going all the way to your *ranch?*" Maxine thought of the many days and nights she'd be spending with the Spaniard and added a resounding, "Hot damn and hallelujah!"

But Dicey was still skeptical. "How's all this teachin' gonna pay off the debt? I'm not understandin'."

"It is very simple." Knowing somehow in the back of his mind that the task would be anything but simple, Dane explained it to them.

"San Diego is a growing town. Women of breeding

are in short supply." He smiled at Maxine, then at her father. "My family has many friends, many high-placed, wealthy friends. I believe that once your daughter is properly finished, she will bring in a dowry that will more than pay off your debt."

8

Jackson City sat in a kind of hole, with its wooden buildings spread throughout the pleasant little valley at random. The day was not exceptionally warm by springtime standards, but not even a light breeze had been able to sneak through the little pocket town, and the temperature soared toward one hundred degrees.

Overheated, Max had lost interest in both the horses and the conversation. He sat on the edge of the boardwalk, panting and fanning himself with his hat. Dicey, a consummate desert rat, felt no discomfort from the heat. His was a fever of the mind as he pondered the Spaniard's proposal, weighing the pros against the cons, finding far more reasons to accept the new plan than drawbacks to defeat it. Dane, while not generally affected by temperature changes, hot or cold, was unaccustomed to conducting business in the noonday sun, and he continually blotted dots of perspiration from his brow with the sleeve of his shirt.

Maxine felt cold inside, however, even though she wasn't quite sure what the Spaniard was asking of them or of her. She stared at Dane, accusing him with a long hard gaze before she turned to her father and whispered, "A dowry? Just exactly what is that anyways?"

With a thoughtful, calculating expression, Dicey answered his daughter, "If I'm rememberin' correctly, a dowry is a pile a goods or nice fat purse a fellah is willin' to part with in order to gain a bride."

"A bride?" Maxine wrinkled her nose. Then, as the possibilities loomed in her mind, she blurted out, "A *bride?* You mean *me?*"

"Yes, *Rojita*. As I explained earlier, my family has many wealthy friends in San Diego, some of whom—"

Panicked, Maxine grabbed her father's arm and ducked behind him. "He's trying to sell me off, Pa!"

Dicey patted her hand but kept his attention on Dane. "Now, now, Maxie girl," he soothed, eager to hear what the Spaniard had in mind, seeing not just a way out of the debt, but the possible means with which to give his daughter—both of his children—the things he'd never been able to provide himself. "I say we hear the man out. Ain't nuthin' carved on the side of a mountain yet. Go on, kind sir."

Over Maxine's exasperated groan, Dane explained. "Your father was right, *Rojita*. I believe that once you're presentable, many fine young men will be lining up for the chance to claim your hand in marriage. The offering of a dowry is simply a gift, the proof of the gentleman's honorable intentions and compensation to her family for her loss. *Comprende?*"

Maxine understood completely. She took another step behind her father. "See, Pa? It's just like I said—he means to sell me to the highest bidder!"

"No, Maxine," Dane said, "it is not like that at all."

"If you'll just be excusing us," Dicey said, "I'd like to be talkin' to my girl private like."

"Take all the time you need."

"We will not be long." Dicey spun around on his good leg and took Maxine by the hand. "Come take a walk with me back to the wagon, Maxie." Dicey winked as he faced his daughter, and, as he'd hoped, she winked back and followed along without balking or questioning him.

The McKain rig, a homemade cross between a prairie schooner and a medicine wagon, featured high wooden walls with long canvas flaps covering a pair of window cutouts at each side. Dicey lifted one of these "curtains" and propped it open with a long walking stick, creating enough shade for both himself and his daughter.

Easing into what he knew would be a difficult conversation, he said, "Please dona' be so quick to say no about this dowry business, girl. I know how it must sound to you, but think a what we might get out of it should we play along. The Spaniard said he'd teach you writin'—isn't that what you've been a wantin'?"

Maxine sighed. "Sure it is, but I don't want to have to get *married* to learn!"

Dicey stroked his chin, considering the best approach to use on her. Straight out with it usually got the best results, so he only fibbed a little as he said, "I'm not sayin' you *got* to get hitched, girl, I'm just wantin' you to think about it, that's all. I shoulda seen to it you had a man of yur own by now, maybe even a family—"

"I got a family!"

Dicey blushed. "Babies and such is what I'm talkin' about, and dona' go interruptin' me again. I just want you to consider the fine things a wealthy man can provide for you. Think a what he might provide fur yur brother, too."

Babies and such? Maxine almost laughed out loud, but at the gleam in her father's eye, that rare spark of hope, she reached into the wagon for the water scoop instead. Dicey was talking about more than a family for her; he was looking for a home for Max, a safe place, where he wouldn't be apt to find himself at the end of a noose, as he almost had in Jackson. Maxine wanted those same things too, but did she have to sacrifice herself to get them?

Encouraged to see that Maxine was at least considering the idea, Dicey pushed on. "As I see it, Maxie, if'n we go along with the Spaniard's plan, you'll be a gettin' all that educatin' you been wantin'. After that, what's the harm if'n you let him show you off to his rich friends? Who knows? You might even find one you take a likin' to, then we'd all be set."

Maxine, who'd lifted the lid on the water barrel and filled her mouth with the cool liquid, swallowed hard as she said, "But Pa—I don't want no man telling me what to do and when to do it. I don't want no man, period. Isn't there some other way?"

Slowly shaking his head, Dicey came up with an out. "I'm thinkin' not, but dona' worry yur head—I won't be askin' you to go takin' on a husband if you dona' want one. After you get benefit of the Spaniard's teachin', if you can'no find a man you've a hankerin' for, we'll just be spiritin' you off in the middle of the night like we done in San Francisco."

Maxine's eyes lit up. "Really and true, Pa?"

"Really and true. If you find yur ready to move on, just say the word. We'll head on out to Pike's Peak 'fore you can blink. Now what do you say to that?"

"Oh, Pa!" Maxine dropped the wooden scoop back inside the wagon and threw her arms around her father's neck. "Thanks for understanding how I feel—and for figuring out a way to keep Dane around a little longer, too."

Although Maxine's final words gave him pause, Dicey slipped his arm around her shoulder and urged her to walk along with him as he said, "Shall we go tell the Spaniard he's got hisself a deal, then?"

Once the deal had been struck, Dane agreed to add to the debt the cost of supplies needed to make the McKain rig sturdy enough to stand the long journey south. When they finally pulled out of Jackson, the wagon sported new wheels all around and more goods than it had carried since the family had headed west some ten years ago. Maxine rode ahead of the rig on one of the Spaniard's fine horses, while Dicey and Max stayed behind on the wagon. The idea had been to give Maxine as much time alone with Dane as possible in order for her lessons to begin, and from Dicey's vantage point, it looked as if class was in session.

Up ahead, he could see Maxine laughing, tossing her head as she rode alongside the Spaniard, behaving like a schoolgirl having the time of her life. A thought he hadn't considered earlier blossomed in Dicey's mind as he observed the pair; what if Maxine should fall in love with *him*? Men like Dane del Cordobes didn't entertain themselves with coarse tatterdemalions like Maxine, unless there were no other options. If he bothered with her at all, it would only be for a few moments of pleasure. What if the Spaniard won her heart, used her for his own, and then discarded her? Would the man break her spirit, snuff her McKain fire forever? What, Dicey wondered much too late, had he asked of his innocent young daughter?

Aware that her father was directly behind her, Maxine kept her conversation with Dane alive. "I've never ridden on a horse so fancy as Rocio. Do you think my brother is too big to ride her too? You know, would he squish her down or sag her back some?"

Laughing, as he found himself doing more and more, Dane said, "Not at all. Don't let Rocio's smooth gait fool you. She is quite strong and agile, a match for the strongest, most clever of bulls. I believe she can withstand your brother's bulk. Why—did he ask to ride her?"

"Not exactly." But she knew he would love the feel of such a well-bred animal beneath him as much as she did. "He didn't come right out and ask me, but I know what he's thinking. It's kinda my job to know what's going on in Max's mind."

Relaxed, enjoying the lazy pace the wagon set, Dane slipped his boot out of its stirrup and hooked his free leg across the saddle horn. "Max is welcome to ride her anytime he wishes." Using a lower, softer tone, Dane asked the question which had plagued him since he first saw the young man in jail. "If I'm not being too personal, would you mind my asking what happened to your brother? Why is he so slow to speak and learn?"

Maxine turned to Dane, surprised and delighted at the erotic way he was lounging across his mount's long back. Although she had no saddle, she copied his posture by leaning back against Rocio's rump. "Max was born that way. He pretty near died when he come into the world. I took up all the air or something, from what my ma told me—held him up and damn near killed him, I guess. Anyway, that made his brain slow."

Wondering how a mother could tell her child such a dreadful story, even if it were true, Dane said, "I'm sorry."

"No reason for you to be sorry—Max ain't." Pleased that he was interested in her family, Maxine went on, her husky voice hardening as she moved farther back in the past. "Our ma used to say he'd be better off if he'd died, said he was an idiot, too. Now, I guess there's nothing to stop a ma from calling her child an idiot if she takes a notion to, but when other folks try to call my brother that . . . well, I just get madder than a rain-soaked banty rooster."

Through a quiet chuckle, Dane said, "I know. I have borne witness to this side of your nature."

Maxine laughed with him. "I might get a touch jumpy sometimes, but it just ain't right for folks to act like that around Max. They ought to think before they open their mouths and fling hurtful talk about a nice fella like him. He never hurt no one—well, excepting Sheriff Woods, I guess."

She looked across the dusty, well-worn trail, expecting Dane to comment, but he remained silent. He just sat there, smiling, studying her it seemed, still sprawled across his saddle in a kind of half-sitting, half-lying pose.

Growing self-conscious, feeling womanly thoughts bloom in her cheeks, Maxine looked away from the sight of Dane's hard, lean body, and said, "I guess I haven't given you much chance to start teaching me, what with all this rambling I'm doing."

"On the contrary, Rojita. The more I know about you and your family, the easier my job will be. Besides," he said with a chuckle, "I think it will be in my best interests to know what sets you off and why."

Maxine shrugged. "I just do what I have to."

"Perhaps, but I think Max is pretty lucky to have a sister like you—very much so. You must be the best little lucky charm your family has ever had."

Maxine's grin was sheepish and wobbly as she struggled to reply to the rare compliment. "Thanks for saying so, but I'm nothing special. I'm just a good sister. Wherever I go, Max goes. You've seen what happens to him when I'm not around. Taking care of Max is my lot in life. I've known it since I was old enough to walk, since the day I found out that if Max was gonna learn to walk, too, I'd have to be the one to teach him."

Dane was humbled in the face of such utter devotion and selflessness. He slid his leg back off the saddle and drove his boot back into the stirrup, slipping into a more serious demeanor as he continued his questions.

"Where is your home, Rojita, the place where you set-tle down between travels?"

"Home?" she echoed, looking over her shoulder at the wagon behind them. "It's following us."

The words had been spoken nonchalantly, without hesitation, as if this traveling house was a piece of land. Sure she must have misunderstood the question, Dane persisted. "I realize your family travels a great deal, and that the wagon serves as your home when you're on the road, but what I am asking about is your permanent base, the place you revere as I do Rancho Cordoba."

Maxine had never really felt it before, this sudden sense of inadequacy, of inferiority. The sensations swept through her like the hot dry winds of the desert which lay before them, singeing her, stinging her. How could a small thing like a home make such a big difference between high-falutin' folks and those like the McKains? And how was she to behave in the face of such superiority? Should she acknowledge shame for her lowly circumstances and humble herself before the man who held the treasured key to a more respectable future? Maxine's stomach did a flip at the very idea.

Jutting her chin out, she turned away from the Spaniard and took in her surroundings. They'd trav-eled south since noon, past the mining towns of Mokelumne Hill and San Andreas. The countryside from here to Murphys, their general destination for the night, was peaceful and serene, a series of green hills dabbed with clumps of shrubs and scrub oak. Beyond that lay a forest thick with huge aromatic pines and split by the raging, icy waters of the Stanislaus River. If there was a more beautiful place to call home, she couldn't imagine what it might be. How dare he suggest she was lacking!

Maxine swept her arm across the skyline. "This is my home, and all the home I've ever wanted. I happen to think it's grander than your mansion in San Francisco, and probably more valuable than anything you've ever owned or could *hope* to own, you . . . you fancy-faced jackass."

Dane wisely kept the sudden urge to laugh inside. Maxine's dark eyes were lit with righteous indignation, and her proud jaw was rigid, set like a cornerstone. Her haughty, rebellious attitude should have brought his own temper to boil, but it didn't. She was bold, this one, as bold as her incredibly beautiful features, and saucy too, impudent. If she were a man, there was no question that Dane would admire her grit, her belief in herself and her family. Confronted with such spirit in a woman, he found himself wondering if he might find more than just a pretty little agate after she was polished. Had he stumbled across a rare gem instead?

Dane went ahead with the lessons. To ease her temper, he began with an apology. "Forgive me if I did not understand your situation, *Rojita*—I meant you no disrespect. Know, however, that I will not tolerate such language from you in the future. Ladies do not speak to gentlemen in loud, obnoxious tones, and they never, ever swear. *Comprende?*"

He was so polite, and so very condescending. Maxine bristled. First he slighted her home, her very lifestyle, and now he was arrogantly attempting to bring her to heel. It was too much. Maxine McKain never answered to anyone and certainly never entertained the notion that she needed to be censured. She shot the Spaniard a steely gaze, preparing to tell him exactly what she thought of his attempts to civilize her, but then she remembered the promise she'd made to her father. She couldn't ruin everything before she'd even given it a chance, though it wasn't in her nature to simply roll over on command. In a quandary as to what her next move should be, her mouth drooped into a frown, and her gaze plummeted to the mare's withers.

Seeing that his pupil was less than receptive to his instructions, Dane added a little incentive. "I would appreciate an answer when I ask a question, Señorita Stubborn. Of course, I cannot force you to accept my instruction if you wish to ignore me, but what shall I tell your father? I saw the look in his eye when I told him of my wealthy friends. I know how much he wishes to see you married to a man who will take care of both you and your brother. The money your family owes me will not affect my future one way or the other, but what of yours? Do you mean to rob your father of this dream?"

Maxine gasped, and actual tears burned the back of her eyes. How did he know such things? And what would he think or do if he knew how repulsed she was by the idea of marrying *anyone*, nobleman or not?

It occurred to Maxine that in order to ease her father's mind and acquire the kind of security Max required, she might actually wind up wed to one of Dane's friends, no matter how she felt about it. As she thought of her future, tears no longer burned Maxine's eyes but rushed in, soothing them, exposing her. Next they would roll down her cheeks. Then she would be sitting on Rocio, a blubbering, helpless female for all the world—for Dane—to see. Determined not to let that happen, Maxine gave the mare's belly two quick, hard jabs with the heels of her boots, and she took off galloping down the road.

Dane hadn't foreseen her reaction, and the movement caught him off guard. As Rocio's stride stretched into a dead run, Dane slid the bullwhip down off his shoulder and fit the grip to his palm. Before launching the coil of leather, he hesitated. Maxine seemed to be an excellent rider, even if she wasn't atop a proper sidesaddle, but if he cracked the whip and the mare slid to a stop as trained, what would happen to her rider? Could Maxine hang on, or would she be thrown?

Deciding it wasn't worth the risk to find out, he wheeled Alazan around and raced back to the wagon. Before Maxine's father could even inquire about her, Dane said, "Your daughter has ridden on ahead to locate a good place in which to camp this evening. I think it best that I accompany her. Just look for us on down the road a little ways."

Dicey was not sure how to broach the subject. He only knew that if he were to rid the burden from his mind, now was the time to bring it up. He raised a hand and said, "A moment of yur time before you go chasing after me girl?"

Dane glanced down the road, more worried about Maxine than he wanted to let on, and said to her father, "Only a moment, if you please. Maxine is a strong rider, but Rocio is very spirited. I do not wish to see either of them harmed."

"Maxine will be all right, least ways where that mare is concerned."

"What do you wish to discuss?"

"Me girl . . . she's not been around men like you before. She . . . ah, she only knows our own kind, and even with them, well, she ain't never been around 'em without Max at her side to protect her, if you get what I'm a sayin'."

Dane smiled warmly, understanding that which he'd already deduced for himself. "Maxine is innocent."

"Me," Max said, pounding his chest. "I take care of Maxie."

"That'd be about right." Dicey nodded toward his son, then addressed Dane again. "What I'm askin' of you, what I'd like is yur word. I'd enjoy the trip to San Diego a whole lot better if'n I had yur word as a gentleman that you intend to honor yur good name by promisin' me you'll not be layin' so much as a finger on me sweet, innocent girl."

Distracted by the sound of fading hoofbeats, Dane made the vow without even considering what he might be asking of himself. "You have my word as a gentleman."

His bottom lip quivering, Dicey extended his palm. "Then I'll just be thankin' you for the sleep I'll be gettin' at night."

When Dane clasped the miner's hand, he found himself nearly pulled off Alazan as Max latched onto the sleeve of his shirt and began tugging on it.

"Me too!" Max said, still pulling at Dane's shirt. "Me too."

Dicey shrugged his eyebrows. "Max likes to shake hands. It makes him feel like he's conductin' business just like the rest of us."

Because he could do no less, Dane offered his hand to Max, holding tight as the young man squeezed and pumped it, and said, "My word—your sister is safe with me."

Some three miles down the road, Dane found Rocio tied to a gnarled oak tree. After doing the same to Alazan, he worked his way to the crest of a small knoll, where he spotted Maxine sitting, her legs tucked beneath her, near a small mound sprouting a weather-worn cross.

As he approached, she inclined her head slightly, letting him know she realized he was there, but made no further effort to acknowledge him. Sensing her need for privacy, Dane made a careful survey of the area. There were, as far as he could tell, six graves, each of them sporting some kind of plant or rosebush, but the plots were untended, overgrown with weeds and tall grass. He turned in a full circle, shading his eyes from the glowing ball of the sun, and then settled his gaze on Maxine and her own incendiary halo. She looked pensive, almost downtrodden, and the thought that he might be the cause of her mood spread more than a little guilt through him.

Moving quietly, Dane walked to the edge of the grave and sat down beside her. "A friend of yours?" he asked, his voice soft and low.

Maxine glanced at him, her tears already shed, her eyes dry now, and slowly nodded.

Disconcerted by her silence, Dane strained to read the crudely scrawled grave marker. "'Billy Hall—1838 to 1852—a fine son and friend to all.' I guess that makes him around fourteen when he died, right?"

Maxine sighed, ready now for the conversation she knew was coming. "Right. He was the same age as me. Got killed during a cave-in while he was working in his father's mine. Old man Hall gave it all up after that. Squatters took over what was left of his mine, and Billy . . ." She looked back at the gravesite. "I stop by now and again to make sure he's being looked after."

Dane saw the sadness in her dark brown eyes, the pain, and could think of nothing to do but offer his condolences. "It is a shame for one to die so young."

"Um," she agreed. "Terrible for him of course, but not too good for me either. Billy was my best friend in the world, a fellah I could talk to about anything." She laughed. "We even talked about getting married one day. Can you believe it? He give me my first kiss standing under the bridge at Sutter's." At the memory, Maxine closed her eyes and drifted back to the past.

Billy's kiss. She almost giggled. They'd planned it, discussed it for weeks before actually touching lips. She could almost smell him now, that pungent combination of damp earth and brackish water, the essence of a compost heap. At the time, she'd wondered why she'd never noticed his aroma before.

Maxine turned then, reminded of a more interesting embrace, of a far more enjoyable scent, and looked Dane right in the eye. " 'Course kissing Billy wasn't anything like kissing you. He didn't go putting his tongue in my mouth or nothing, he just squashed his lips flat against mine, and boom—we were fianceed."

"Maxine . . . about the kiss we shared—"

"It was wonderful," she said, cutting him off, her eyes aglow with the memory. "Pure and simple wonderful, and I thank you for showing me how it's done. I liked it, Dane. I liked it a lot."

An apology hardly seemed appropriate now, and even a repeat of the vow he'd made to her father seemed out of place, more cruel than assuring. That he had to discourage her was not in question, but how could he do it without hurting her feelings? She was looking down at her friend's grave, her fresh profile steeped in confusion and sadness. Dane's gaze wandered down to her mouth, to the lush full lips he knew were so eager to learn, to experience. Lips made for kissing, for caressing. A chill rattled his spine, and then heated him just as quickly. The promise he'd made to Dicey loomed large in his mind, and Dane guessed this would be the first in a series of regrets he'd have over so rash a vow.

Her gaze lingered on the wildflowers dotting the grave as she went on, "I'm a mite stubborn sometimes, even Billy used to complain about that. Stubborn as an old mule with a case of the colic, but I'm willing to learn, Dane, really I am." She faced him then, apologetic and remorseful for the way she'd behaved. "Pa and I do appreciate that you're set on teaching me manners. I guess I just don't see how anything you've got to show me is gonna help."

Glad for the change of subjects, Dane said, "Not help? I am afraid I do not understand."

She plucked at a long shaft of grass. "We McKains got a saying: You can put a hat and coat on a mule, but under the finery, you still got a mule. I guess that's what I mean. How you gonna fool one of your fancy friends into thinking I'm a fine lady? One peek under my hat's gonna tell 'em what they got is a stubborn ole mule. I appreciate all you're trying to do, but I just don't see how this is gonna work."

Maxine's lack of confidence in herself seemed to be a crack in her otherwise indomitable spirit, a spirit he was determined to keep intact even as he smoothed the ragged edges of her character. Dane glanced around the graveyard. A splash of bright yellow near Billy's marker caught his eye. He reached into the wild rose-bush and snapped off a single bud from the profusion of blooms.

Pinching each spike between his forefinger and thumbnail as he spoke, Dane stripped the stem of thorns. "I have seen this rosebush before. It is called a Harrison's Yellow. In fact, I cultivated this variety in my garden at Rancho Cordoba, and again later at the house in San Francisco."

Maxine leaned forward and sniffed the heady scent. "I've seen them before, too—they're everywhere," she said. "The bush gets real big sometimes, and so thick, I swear you could lose a good-size goat inside one of them."

Dane shrugged. "Perhaps, but the size isn't what interests me about this particular bush. There is something special about this rose, a feature that reminds me of you—of you and of your beauty."

Maxine's lungs filled, and her breasts rode high as she gasped and said, "*Beauty?* I ain't beautiful."

"You *are not* beautiful," he said, correcting her.

Maxine nodded sharply. "That's what I just said. There ain't one beautiful thing about me."

"No, no." He shook his head, deciding to give up on the English lessons for the time being. Capturing her gaze with his smile, Dane swept the yellow bud across her lower lip. "Just be quiet for a moment and listen to what I have to say. This rose is special, beautiful like you because it thrives even here, in this atmosphere of the worst kind of neglect. It will continue to thrive even when others, more fragile in beauty and constitution, die. *Comprende?*"

Maxine's mind spun with the words, and her heartbeat became erratic. "I—I think so."

"And do you not also think this rose is beautiful?"

"Well . . . yes, of course I do."

"Does the fact that it grows wild, survives in surroundings that are, shall we say, less than hospitable, make it any less beautiful?"

Spellbound, as much by his rhetoric as the lush sound of his velvet voice, Maxine could only shake her head and offer the barest of whispers. "No."

"This, Rojita, is why the rose reminds me of you. It is

a survivor—and it is beautiful. Like you." He took her hand in his, opened it, and lightly basted her palm with the bloom before positioning the stem between her fingers. "Never forget that, and never think you are anything less than the beauty you see here in this rose."

Speechless, Maxine's spine went rigid, and her eyes grew moist. She drew in a fractured breath, and the whole world seemed to whirl around her. An ache—sorrow and happiness all jumbled together—spiraled up from inside her, coiling around her heart, filling her throat with an exquisite pain. Somehow, through it all, she managed to squeak out, "I'd appreciate it if you'd just leave me alone for a spell."

Faced with the sudden urge to hold her, to crush her against his chest and bury his face in her fragrant hair, Dane forced himself to his feet. In a voice harsher than he'd intended, he said, "Take all the time you need. I'll go wait down by the road for your father and Max. They should be along any minute now."

Maxine nodded and listened for his footfalls to fade down the other side of the ridge. When she was certain Dane was out of earshot, of sight, she threw herself in the sweet grass alongside Billy's grave.

"I miss you," she whispered, wishing there were someone, anyone who could understood the kind of person she was, a friendly ear to listen and help her sort out her feelings, her confusion. But she had no one, not even her family. Max, God love him, would never be able to understand what she was feeling, and neither would her father. Oh, Dicey might understand, but she suspected he would get all twisted up in knots, turn red, and babble the way he did whenever she thought to inquire about the goings on of men and women. She studied the rose and thought of Dane, of his touch and the wonderful things he'd said.

Then, in yet another rare display of what she considered weakness, Maxine McKain began to cry, for what she'd been given, and for what she understood she could never possess.

9

Over the next two weeks, the group fell into a proper, if slightly uneasy, routine. Following along the Butterfield Stage Route, Dicey and Maxine spent most days riding on the wagon, and Max rode ahead with Dane on the pair of Andalusians. Evenings usually found Dane tutoring Maxine, while the Scotsman and his son looked after the supplies and prepared the meals.

On this night, a particularly warm evening along the fringes of the Mohave Desert, Max, overheated and swollen, had burrowed a small den for himself in the cool earth beneath the wagon and refused to budge. Dicey, his twisted knee throbbing from too many days propped against the wagon's sideboard as it bounced down the trail, was stretched out beneath the shade of a smoke tree.

This left the chore of collecting water up to Maxine and Dane. On foot, with Maxine in the lead, they'd followed a rocky, zig-zag course up a narrow canyon for several hundred yards when Dane stopped and wiped his brow with his shirtsleeve. "Wait up a moment, *Rojita.*"

Maxine slid to a halt and glanced back. "What's the matter, fancy man? Heat getting to you?"

Dane laughed and blotted his brow once again. "It seems I am not as well suited to the desert as you. Is this hike really necessary? We still have over half a barrel of water left in the wagon. We cannot be in any real danger of running out before we come to the next stage stop, can we?"

Maxine barked a laugh and then forged ahead, berating him from over her shoulder. "You're *never* out of danger in the desert. That's a pure and simple fact of life. You can't have too many supplies or too much water. If I don't miss my guess, we're right close to some. Come on—you won't melt."

Grumbling to himself, Dane caught up with her. "I don't know—all I see is rocks and sand. I think you have me chasing after a mirage."

Her smile satisfied, happy finally to know something he didn't, Maxine pointed out the shrubs lining the wash. "Take a look at them plants. You just look for the greenest shrubs and bushes, things like mesquite, and you either find water close by or get it by digging a little. It's there somewhere if you got greenery."

Around the next bend, almost as if by her decree, a small, but healthy fan palm rose up like a protective banty hen. Huddled beneath its fronds was a tiny pond.

"*Dios,*" Dane whispered. "You were right."

"Damn straight." She dropped down to her knees to

check the water's potability, swishing the flies and mosquitoes from the water's surface with her hat. She sniffed for foul odors and then scooped up a mouthful with her palm. Maxine made a great show of tasting and testing, and then finally swallowed.

"Pure and fresh from an underground spring," she proclaimed, filling her hat before she regained her footing. "And plenty more bubbling up from below, near as I can figure. Help yourself."

Before he could move, Maxine dumped the contents of her hat on top of her head and stood there, eyes closed, moaning softly as the water trickled down her overheated body, cooling her. Maxine's clothing sucked up the moisture, sketching the woman beneath, and Dane had to stifle an involuntary groan. With a flash, the image of her emerging from the lake, nude, suddenly returned to his mind. He drew in a sharp breath. What was it with this woman and water?

He'd tried so hard during these past days to think of her as nothing but a student. He'd worked with her, tutored her, all the time trying to convince himself she was but a girl, a sister of sorts who looked to him for her training. It had very nearly worked, this farce of patiently teaching her the alphabet and ways of the genteel, but Dane could no longer fool himself or pretend. He wanted her—and badly.

What of his promise to her father? How much of this indulgence could he allow himself and still remain a gentleman? Maxine's eyes were still closed, her face rapturous, as she unwound her braid and then shook her head, freeing the damp strands, flinging a few of them across her cheeks, where they stuck to her satiny skin. She stretched luxuriantly.

"Lord almighty," she breathed, unaware that Dane's eyes were on her, or that their bright blue color had darkened as if by storm clouds. "If that ain't the best thing that can happen to a body at the end of a long hot day, I don't know what is."

Dane resisted the impulse to tell her exactly what *was* better and struggled to cling to his control, his honor. The only feeling he could manage was anger. "What do you think you are doing?"

Maxine blinked up at him. "Huh?"

"Huh is not a word," he snapped back, no longer sure he could control even his anger.

"Excuse me, *sir,* I meant, What? What are you talking about?"

"This." He flipped his fingers toward her wet shirt, unable, perhaps even unwilling, to tear his gaze away from the perfect outline of her breasts. "*Ladies,* women of breeding do not parade around in front of others with their . . . their attributes showing for all to see."

Maxine glanced down at the front of her shirt and gulped when she realized her nipples were practically poking through the thin material of her damp blouse. Pulling the cotton away from her skin, she turned her gaze back to Dane and grinned. "Sorry if I was being indelicate and all, but I didn't mean for that to happen. Why are you so mad?"

"Mad?" Dane's voice sounded higher, especially to himself. "I am not mad. I simply want to make sure you understand the spectacle you're making of yourself.

This is not proper behavior for a young lady in *any* circle of society."

Maxine's grin widened as she sensed the underlying reasons behind his discomfort and anger. Her brown eyes sparkling, she took a step toward him. "I don't see why it's so wrong for a gal to slop a little water over her when she's hot. I told you—I didn't mean to do anything but cool off a little."

Dane read it in her eyes and in the way she moved her body. She was mocking him, teasing him, as if she knew she was safe, that he was honor bound to keep her at arm's length. Drawing on a renewed burst of anger, he gripped her shoulders and jerked her close. "Do not play these childish games with me, *Rojita*. You will be making a very big mistake if you think to tease me and then run. A very big mistake."

Maxine's expression sobered, and she drew in a difficult breath. No one had ever treated her like this, touched her in such a manner, or made her feel so downright weak and helpless. She was jittery all over, especially around the knees. Would she topple and fall? No, she thought, not as long as Dane had hold of her. His hands were strong, so very strong. She splayed her fingers out against his chest, enjoying the feel of him, testing the muscled planes and ridges, and then leaned her head back and gazed into his eyes. He was staring at her, trying to look mean but not quite succeeding.

Grinning up at him, she confessed her sins in a breathless whisper. "I guess maybe I was teasing you a little, but I never planned on running away. I was hoping to learn a few more things about this man and woman business. You know, about lovemaking and such."

"*Sangre de Dios.*" Dane groaned, adding a few more curses in Spanish under his breath as he tried once again to bring her to task. "Is it possible you do not realize what you are doing to me, how difficult you are making my job, my very life?"

"I'm not trying to make things harder for you. I just want you to teach me everything there is to know, more than just alphabets and ciphering." She pressed herself against the length of his body. "How will I know what to do with one of these rich fellahs when I get my hands on him if you don't teach me that part, too?"

This walk had been a mistake, as was taking her into his arms, as was trying to talk some sense into her—it was all a very big mistake. Was he still capable of turning back? Dane tightened his grip on her shoulders, as if to push her away and rid himself of temptation, but he hadn't the strength. Maxine remained crushed against him, her wet shirt bleeding into his, the heat from her breasts warming his chest. He met her gaze and then felt his eyes plummet, directing their own path to that eager mouth. Her lips were slick, wet like the rest of her, and her pink tongue lolled at the corner as if waiting to catch the tiny rivulets of water as they skittered on by. It would be so simple to cover that mouth with his, to educate it to give him pleasure, but how could he just forget his vow to her father?

Dane inhaled, hoping the act would purify his thoughts, but this was yet another mistake. Her essence was all around him, surrounding him, drawing him in like a magnetic field. He'd been in tune with the subtle delicate perfume of feminine arousal many times before, but this was different. Like the woman herself, there was nothing delicate or subtle about her. He didn't simply catch a whiff of Maxine's scent, it was all around him, permeating him, heating his blood so, he wasn't sure his heart could tolerate the temperatures. How could he break away from her now?

Maxine was tired of waiting for her lessons. She stood up on tiptoes and slid her mouth across his before he could accept or discourage her advances. Then she parted her lips, her teeth as well in bold invitation, and Dane was hers. He kissed her tenderly, exploring gently, and then exploded with a burst of passion that rocked her down to her toes.

When Maxine matched his passion and encouraged his explorations, Dane slid his hands down her back to her bottom where he gripped her and ground her hips against his groin. He was like a wild man, an animal, a thing he'd never been before, and he was lost in the sensations. This was no mere urge, no hunger so simple as desire, but a raging need, a need so intense and primal that it terrified him. What was he doing? He, a gentleman, a man of his word. What more *would* he do if he didn't find some way to regain control of himself? This had to stop—and stop now before even the shredded remains of his honor were gone. Dane finally found the strength to tear away from Maxine and turn his back to her.

"Go back to camp," he ordered hoarsely. "Go now and don't say another word."

"But Dane—"

"You have pushed me too far, woman! Now go—leave me!"

Her breath coming through as a sudden sob, Maxine mashed her knuckles against her swollen mouth, turned, and ran down the wash.

Angry with himself, Dane dropped to the ground and plunged a canteen into the pond. If he could have, he would have taken his bullwhip to himself. It was the least he deserved after so blatantly ignoring the promise he'd given the Scotsman. Was he becoming a madman out here on this hot dusty trail? He was certainly behaving as if he were one.

Dane buried another canteen into the pond and held it there. As it filled, he worked at a way to end this ever-increasing attraction to Maxine. Although he suspected his feelings for her were infinitely more complicated than sheer lust, he decided he simply would not think of the intimacies they'd already shared. Instead, he would think of something else when she was around; he would concentrate on . . . concentrate on *Caroline!* Yes, he would think only of the woman he planned to marry once he returned to San Diego. The image of Caroline would rid him of this need, this obsession for the red-haired wildcat.

Dane screwed the cap on the final canteen and flung the containers over his shoulder as he climbed to his feet. "Caroline," he whispered to himself, wondering how she could have slipped his mind so completely. It would work, he thought, starting down the wash. He could do it.

Dane had gotten only halfway back to camp when he came across Maxine. She was kneeling by a mesquite bush, her face buried in her hands, and as he approached, he thought he could hear her crying. He smiled, the expression more grim than pleased. Ridding himself of these lusty thoughts was going to be easier than he imagined. If there was one thing Dane del Cordobes couldn't abide in a woman, it was the tendency to weep when things didn't go her way.

"Maxine? If you're done crying, we should return to camp before the others begin to worry."

At the sound of his stiff voice and his sterile words, Maxine leapt to her feet and wiped the tears from her eyes. Facing him, she spread her feet and slammed her hands to her hips. "I ain't crying."

Dane inclined his head, giving her the lie. "I am not crying is the correct way to phrase that sentence."

"I don't give a damn about English lessons, and I don't give a damn about you." She sniffed, hoping to keep yet another round of tears from spilling over her lids.

"Caroline," Dane muttered under his breath, "Caroline." Then louder, with more compassion in his tone, he said, "I can't blame you for being angry, Maxine, and I don't. What I did back there . . . taking advantage of you like that, well, it was an unforgivable breach of trust. I hope you can find it in your heart to excuse my behavior and try to understand it a little."

"I understand it plenty," she said, "and it's just like I thought—there ain't a decent man in the entire state of Californy who wants a mess like me as his woman, and all your fancy teaching isn't gonna make one whit of difference. I might just as well forget about the writing and ciphering lessons, 'cause it's a pure and simple waste of time!" She stomped her boot for emphasis. "You don't have to bust a board over my head 'fore I get the idea—Maxine McKain just ain't pretty enough for a man to want to do lovemaking on her. No need for you to go apologizing for that."

"Oh, you're so wrong, *Rojita*." Dane spread his arms, but as he approached her he drew an imaginary line he vowed he would not cross. "What you don't understand is that I am just a man—a man without a woman, his woman, for too long. The fact that you *are* so attractive is largely responsible for my loss of control. *Comprende?*"

She sniffed, and looked away. "Flapdoodle. Pure and simple."

"You think so?" He took another step, and then one more until the toe of his boot touched the line, just short of touching her. "I think you are not so innocent that you do not know when a man desires you, and you know I wanted you back at the pond."

Although she kept her head turned, Maxine's gaze slid sideways until she caught his. She knew it all right. She shrugged in surrender. "Maybe so, but if you wanted me so much just now, why'd you holler at me and tell me to go away? Why didn't you just show me what I want to know?"

Dane groaned and shut his eyes. *Caroline, Caroline, Caroline.*

Since he hadn't answered one way or another, Maxine closed the small gap between them and stood not a horsehair away from him. "Dane—if you want me, why don't you just—"

Breaking yet another vow, Dane took her face

between his hands. "Please, Maxine—listen to what I have to say. Try to understand the way things must be. Lovemaking is a more complicated thing than what you may imagine, and certainly more than just the simple coupling of a man and a woman." Dane paused, thinking back to his past relationships, and added, "At least, it should be."

His powerful hands slid down her face until they rested at either side of her neck, and Maxine's legs weakened in response. "I must be dumber than I thought. I still don't see what can be so all-fired complicated about lovemaking that you can't just show me."

Dane sighed heavily. Trying to ignore the silky feel of her skin, wondering why he couldn't seem to let her go, he tried an avenue that any member of the McKain family would understand. "If you can't imagine the complications of the act, perhaps the results to your purse will make better sense. A pure bride will bring your family a far bigger dowry than one who has known another man."

She hadn't considered that, but now that he brought it up, Maxine remembered Lola's tales of virgins and how much stock men seemed to put in them. Grumbling to herself, her mouth fell into a pout.

Adding a little more incentive, perhaps in an effort to convince himself it was just as well, Dane said, "I'm sure when you think this over, you'll be glad you saved yourself for your husband, for the man you love." The minute the words were out, Dane had the urge to take them back, to toss them as far from his mind as possible. He shrugged, the movement sharp and jerky, hoping to rid himself of this sudden sensation, this dark, ugly emotion that felt a lot like jealousy.

Those strong hands had slipped further, and now they cupped the hollows at Maxine's shoulders, sending shivers of excitement through her body. Suddenly, money and her future didn't matter. She looked into Dane's eyes, eyes that sparkled with conflicting messages, and said, "I don't care about dowries or other men. I just want you."

"What of my word to your father?" he blurted out, frustration and desire waging a battle within. "Do you think a man's honor is so easily dismissed?"

"My father? Pa? What's he got to do with us?"

"Then . . . you didn't know?"

Maxine wrinkled her nose. "Know what?"

Dane sighed and looked away. Was nothing ever easy with this woman—or with her crazy family? Would he too become a crazy man before this journey was over?

"Know *what?*" she repeated.

Slowly returning his gaze to her, Dane said, "That I made a promise to him shortly after we left Jackson, a vow that I would not touch you or take your innocence."

"*What?* Why'd you go do a fool thing like that?"

Suddenly, he didn't know. Stumbling around for words, Dane said, "Because he asked it of me, that's why. I could do no less as a gentleman."

"Oh, hell's fire!" Defeated, Maxine dropped her hands to her side and whirled around. She began to kick at stones and pebbles, splattering mud rocks against the canyon walls as she worked out her frustrations. Then she kicked something soft and squishy. Something which moved and made a soft noise.

Maxine jumped and fell back against Dane.

"What is it?" he whispered, feeling the tension in her body.

"I don't know—I stepped on something, a snake maybe from the feel of it, but I just don't know." Cautioning him to remain still, she circled around the creosote bush which obscured her view and spotted the object. It was a human hand. "Lord almighty," she breathed, waving Dane over by her. "It's a person. Someone's dug himself under that ledge and got blown over with sand."

Preferring to remain cautious, Dane took his pistol from the holster and motioned for Maxine to step aside. For once, she did as he asked. Then he called out, "Identify yourself, please. We have no wish to harm you."

There was a feeble cry. The hand strained visibly but could not seem to move.

"*Christo*," Dane muttered under his breath as he sheathed the gun. "I think this man is injured, perhaps badly. Help me dig him out."

Maxine dropped to her knees beside him, and together, they brushed the sand away and extracted the person. When they got him out in the clearing and rolled him over on his back, he winced, too weak to cry out in pain.

Leaning over the body, Maxine noticed the soft mounds rising up from the stranger's chest. "This ain't no man—it's a woman, and I think she's an Indian." Using the tail of her shirt, she began to wipe the smudges of dirt and mud from the woman's face. The skin beneath the grime was young, although cracked and dry, and mottled with welts and bruises in various stages of healing. Maxine glanced at Dane. "Give me the canteen. She needs water real bad."

Dane felt sickened by the sight of the woman's battered face and the pungent odor drifting up from her. "Will she live?" he asked.

After ripping a strip of cloth from the woman's shirt, Maxine took the canteen from Dane and dipped the material inside. "I don't know for sure," she said, worry creasing the skin near her eyes, "she's about half-dead."

As Maxine gently slipped the wet cloth between the Indian's lips, she studied her for clues to her identity. Her face, sunburned to the point of blistering, was boxy, the nose long, but not flat or spread out toward her cheeks, and her lips, cracked and bleeding, were full, yet small in proportion to the rest of her features. The skin which hadn't been burned was a light doeskin color, not the coffee color of the Apache or even the dark sienna of the Mexicans scattered throughout the gold country. The woman's long ebony hair gave no clue to her tribe either. It hung down to her waist in two tightly pleated braids, but no ornamentation could be found there or on her person. Who was she? How had she come to this?

Keeping his voice low and unthreatening, Dane said, "Can you tell what tribe she belongs to?"

Maxine shook her head as she carefully added more water to the material between the woman's lips. "Could be Diegueño, I suppose, but I'm not real sure."

As the squaw began to suck the moisture from the

cloth, Maxine gently ran her hands along her legs, arms, and torso. Gaining clues from the occasional flinches and soft moans, Maxine sat back and said, "She's beat up pretty bad. Got a couple a broken ribs, maybe smashed up her knee too, hard to tell when she can't talk. Between that and her being all dried out the way she is, I'd say she needs a lot of help."

Dane raised his brows and pushed his hat up off his forehead. "We cannot just leave her here, that is true. Perhaps if we can get her to the next stage stop in time, her life can be saved."

One of those war whoop laughs Maxine had little control over slipped out as she said, "What do you think they'll do with her, fancy man?"

"Why—get her some medical attention, I suppose."

Again she laughed, this time, the sound a little more ladylike. "You've been living high up on the hill with them rich folks for too long, Señor. Ain't nobody at no stage stop gonna care one way or the other if this Indian gal lives or dies. We're her only chance. We got to put her in the wagon and take her to your ranch with us."

"I . . ." Dane hesitated only a moment before he said, "But of course. Go get Max to help me move her. I'll stay here and see that no further harm befalls her."

Maxine winked. "Be right back." Then she sprinted away.

After he dipped the cloth back into the canteen then positioned it between the Indian's lips, Dane shaded her face with his hat and sank down into the sand. For the first time, and much too late, he thought of his return home—of the actual moment. In just a few days, he would be greeting his family, Caroline, and the *vaqueros* who would look to him for guidance at Rancho Cordoba.

How in God's name was he ever going to explain this bizarre entourage he'd collected along the way—to any of them?

10

Dane and his new friends reached the outer pastures of Rancho Cordoba in just over five days. They traveled slowly to keep from jarring the squaw who, while no longer in danger of losing her life, remained uncommunicative and withdrawn. Max, using the special touch he usually reserved for injured wildlife, along with several doses of the McKains' homemade animal compound, tended the woman in the back of the wagon. Dicey, who'd insisted Maxine ride with him most of the way, had allowed her to spend the final day of travel ahead on the Andalusian mare alongside Dane.

When the party reached the last plateau before descending to his property, Dane pulled the horses to a halt and said, "We are finally here. Welcome to Rancho Cordoba, Rojita."

Following his gaze, she looked out over the ridge and saw a large, shimmering lake shaped like a three-pointed star, dominating a narrow, grassy valley below. The mountains to the south, carpeted with chaparral, sage, and mesquite were basically treeless, a monotone landscape compared to the spring green slopes of the mountains and foothills along the eldorado. But it was lovely in its own way, and new to Maxine's eyes, which gave it an extra attraction.

Turning to Dane, she said, "That lake looks mighty inviting. I could use a swim about now. How far is it to your house from here? We got time?"

Dane laughed. "That won't be necessary, Rojita. Just to the southeast of the lake, up on that plateau." He pointed into the noonday sun. "See the rancho? We will be there in less than a half hour, where you can have a real bath."

She strained her eyes to see the groves of trees and smattering of outbuildings which surrounded a large, U-shaped ranch house.

"That's not too far off." Maxine's eyes grew wide at the thought of meeting Dane's mother, and the woman he planned to marry, so soon. Feeling more disheveled than usual, she slid down off Rocio, walked to Alazan's side, and handed the mare's reins to Dane. "I'll ride the rest of the way in the wagon, if you don't mind. I suppose you'll be wanting to say hello to your family alone, anyway."

Then she spun on her heel before he could object and raced back to the wagon.

Far from objecting, Dane was actually grateful for the privacy, for a brief time alone in which to consider his homecoming. He'd been so completely involved with the McKains—Maxine in particular—that he'd hardly given any thought to a reunion with the mother he hadn't seen in nine years, meeting the nephews he'd never laid eyes on, or his obligation to Caroline. Now, as he rode the final two miles to the main house, his thoughts were interrupted again, this time by the decided calm of the meadows. Where were the great herds of cattle he remembered, the hundreds of *vaqueros* to tend and oversee them?

That there had been a decline in the cattle market was not news to Dane, nor was the fact that drives to the north, to the gold country and San Francisco, were becoming smaller and less profitable, as the number of mining towns and prospectors decreased. But what of the new ties his brother Frank had made to the east, to Fort Yuma and its hungry soldiers? Why were there not more spring calves, or even greater numbers of purebred horses grazing on his land? What of the men, the decided drop in employees?

Even those thoughts evaporated as Dane, riding ahead of the others, approached the rancho and saw a small blond woman dressed in black awaiting his arrival on the long wood-beamed porch of his adobe home. She waved as he rode up and stepped out from the shade and onto the brick walkway.

In a voice still dusted with the inflections of her English upbringing, she called to him. "I saw you coming from a distance, and I just knew it had to be you, son."

Swamped by a surge of emotion, of pleasure at seeing her again, Dane climbed down off Alazan and quickly gathered her in his arms. "Mother," he whispered, kissing the top of her head as he swung her in a circle. "Are you well?"

When her feet hit the ground again, Margaret Dane del Cordobes stepped out of the circle of her son's arms but kept hold of his hands as she said, "I am now. I expected you at least a week sooner, you know. I suppose I shouldn't have, but I've worried about you. I was afraid—"

"There's no need to be afraid for me. As I wired, I had business to tend to along the way."

"I know, but it's just that since your brother's accident, I've been a little too, too—" She cut herself off, unable to go on.

"I am here now, Mother. Don't think of the past. Think to the future."

"I will—I do," she corrected, barely aware that an odd little wagon had pulled up under the carriage entrance of the rancho. "At least I do most of the time. It's just seeing you again, I suppose, knowing that you're finally here and safe and looking so healthy." She beamed then, all traces of sadness gone from her bright blue eyes. "For heaven's sakes! Here I am going on and on and I haven't even had a good look at you. Step back, give your mum a better view."

Although he felt self-conscious and ridiculously young, Dane backed away and spread his arms.

Margaret gushed her pleasure. "Oh, Dane—you do look wonderful! I knew you would be a fully grown man by now, but I had no idea how handsome you'd become—even if you are a little shaggy around the ears."

Laughing, Dane slid his fingers through the long black curls which had grown down past the collar of his shirt and measured the growth. "I have not had occasion to have a haircut since I left San Francisco," he explained. "I'll see to that—and a hot bath—immediately."

Maxine, who'd been walking up behind him, overheard Dane's reply. "Oh, please don't go cutting your hair," she said. "I like it hanging down like that—it makes you look . . . I don't know, less like a fancy-face and more like a pirate."

Surprised to hear a feminine voice and shocked at what that voice had to say, Margaret peeked around her son's shoulder. She looked back into her son's eyes and raised a perplexed brow.

"Maxine," Dane explained with a crooked grin. "Maxine McKain and her family." He turned, gesturing for her to come up alongside him. "This is my mother, Margaret."

When the woman extended her hand, Maxine gripped it between both of hers and shook it with her usual gusto. Reciting the speech she'd practiced these past few days, she said, "It is a pleasure to meet you, ma'am. My pa—my father, that is—and my twin brother, Max, they'll be out in a minute, and I know they'll be wanting to meet you too." When Maxine remembered their newest member, she added an unscheduled postscript. "We're all just pleased as can be that you're putting us up like this, but you might have to wait a spell to meet that squaw. She's giving us a speck of trouble."

Dane released the breath he'd been holding slowly, loudly, and Maxine turned to him, no longer certain she should be discussing such business in front of his mother. Whispering so only he could hear, she explained. "That squaw's doing a whole lot better, but we can't seem to get her out of the wagon. Want me to have Max pick her up and carry her out?"

Dane rolled his eyes, but before he could reply, his mother's voice rang out.

"Son? What is going on? Who are these, ah, Indians, brothers . . . fathers she's talking about? When I saw that wagon coming up the road with you, I assumed you had brought your staff from San Francisco. I can see I was mistaken about that, but who are these people?"

Once again, before Dane could form an answer, another voice took his place.

"We've having one *hell* of a time back there," Dicey complained as he limped up to the group. Tipping his tattered hat toward the blond woman, he gave her a short nod and then addressed the Spaniard. "Might be we're gonna have to leave that little Injun in the wagon. She ain't comin' out fur love or money—'course, we canno' offer either to the poor wretch. Fact is, she just ain't—"

"Excuse me," Dane said, cutting him off, still hoping to make the McKain integration into his family home as painless as possible. "Why don't we just leave her be for the moment. I'd like you to meet my mother, Margaret. Mother, this is Dicey McKain, Maxine's father."

The elder McKain wiped hands sweaty and grimy from handling the mules on his trousers, which were even dirtier, and then poked his hat between his knees and offered his hand.

With a nervous look in her son's direction, Margaret

brushed the Scotsman's fingers with her own and gave him a little curtsy. "So nice to meet you—both." Then she turned back to her son, the previous question still mirrored in her eyes, and folded her arms across her breasts.

Before Dane could even think of a way to explain his accomplices, Max shuffled up and joined the crowd. "Hi, Dane. My friend won't come out. I don't know what to do. What do I do?"

"Son?" Margaret moved to Dane's side and slipped her arm through his. "Perhaps you didn't hear me. I would like to know who these people are and why they're traveling with you. And what's all this about putting them up?"

"We thank you kindly for yur hospitality, ma'am." Dicey bowed, tipping his hat again.

"That makes two of us," Maxine added, not wanting to miss any courtesies that might be expected of her.

"Me too. Me too," Max cried.

Stifling an urge that was becoming second nature, Dane swallowed his laughter and said, "Mother, it probably won't surprise you to learn that this is Max, the brother Maxine told you about. Max, this is my mother."

Max didn't offer his hand in greeting. Instead, he linked his fingers together and began swinging his hands in front of his body, grinning as he blushed and said, "Your ma's pretty. She's real pretty." He began dragging his toe across the bricks as he added, "I don't got no ma. Wish I did, but I don't. Yours is pretty."

"Ah," Margaret stammered, "th-thank you, young

man." Then she looked back to her son, completely confused and utterly speechless.

"The McKains," Dane began, wondering how to encapsulate the family and the bizarre circumstances which had brought them to the rancho, "and I met in San Francisco. There was a poker game, and then . . ."

The rest of the sentence died in his throat as the wide front door opened and a younger, blonder woman stepped through the entrance. At each side, hiding behind her skirts, a small boy peeked out at the strangers in the yard.

"Caroline," Dane whispered, more to himself than to her.

The name, the way he said it, froze the blood in Maxine's veins. Following his gaze, she pinned her own on the blond vision perched at the edge of the stairway. Then, gracefully, as if she were some kind of angel from heaven, this Caroline descended the steps. She walked with such grace, such feather lightness, that Maxine could almost swear her feet didn't touch the adobe stairs. She gulped, feeling shamefully dirty and unkempt, and took a step back toward the wagon. Even though she'd gone to the trouble of combing and re-braiding her hair, putting on a clean shirt and tucking it inside her only skirt, Maxine knew she couldn't begin to compare with such a radiant, well-groomed beauty.

Caroline was a pure, finely made woman, her features small and perfect, a near match to the ones Maxine had seen painted on a porcelain doll in a store window some years back. But more distinctive than her beauty, or the coil of silky blond hair shining

through her black lace mantilla, was the fluid, elegant
way she moved. A feeling akin to envy washed over
Maxine, a sensation as foreign to her as it was ugly.
She brought her hand to her mouth and bit down on
her knuckles.

Watching silently, her heart leaden as Dane and the
woman exchanged a brief hug, Maxine listened as he
made the introductions to her family. When she finally
heard her own name and understood that Dane was
waiting for her to acknowledge his lady friend, Maxine
blinked her eyes and stared into the other woman's
face.

"Nice to meet you, ma'am," she began reciting
woodenly. "Dane's told me some about you, and I want
you to know that I'm pleased as can be to make your
acquaintance. I might also like to—" Maxine paused,
wondering why Caroline seemed so familiar. When it
struck her, she abandoned the script and blurted out,
"Say—did you know you look just like Miss Joy Hunt!
Don't she, Dane?" Maxine turned to him. "Don't she
look just like Miss Hunt to you?"

"Doesn't," he corrected her, irritably.

"*Doesn't* then," she said with a sigh. "But ain't it just
the most amazing coincidence?"

"Isn't," Dane said, this time with a smile tugging at
the corner of his mouth.

Caroline glanced from her to Dane and said, "Miss
Hunt?"

"A friend from San Francisco," he said, brushing
them both off. "Why don't we all go inside out of the
hot sun. I think most of us are in desperate need of
refreshing. Shall we?" He had started to herd the entire

group into the house when Max's voice filled the air behind him.

"Look, Dane—it's my new friend and she come outside all by herself!"

The entire group turned just in time to see the frail, battered Indian woman. Still dressed in baggy cotton trousers and a long flannel shirt, and limping painfully, she dragged herself up beside Max. Once there, she buried her head in the valley between his arm and chest and leaned against his body.

"Whew," Caroline whispered to Dane, her fragile features puckered into a grimace. "What on earth is that horrid odor?"

Maxine, who heard her as well, supplied the answer. "Creosote, ma'am. She was hiding, or maybe even buried, behind a creosote bush. There's some sticky, stinky stuff all over the leaves that kinda jumps right on you if you get too close to the plant. Might take a while to get the stink out of her hair, but the rest of her ought to come clean enough."

Caroline shuddered and looked up at Dane. Keeping her voice lower than it had been before, she said, "Who are these people? Why are they here?"

Dane's gaze swept the group. His mother, standing on the porch, still wore that very same question in her expression. The two boys, nephews he had yet to meet, had scrambled back up the steps and now hid behind their grandmother's skirts. Dicey was fingering a lump in his scraggly beard, apparently more concerned about finding that ingrown hair than a place in which to bathe and clean up. Max was petting the woman's head and humming to her as if she were an injured puppy, and

Maxine—Maxine was pacing in place, her mind turning over faster than a pair of loaded dice.

Unequal to the task of explaining his unusual charges, Dane started up the steps, motioning everyone to follow. "The McKain family," he said to his mother and Caroline as he strode into the house, "will be staying with us for a few days or weeks, however long it takes for the woman we found on the trail to heal, and for Dicey and myself to settle an outstanding debt. For now, each of us is in need of a hot bath and a meal. We can talk more later—tomorrow perhaps."

Slipping easily into his new role as head of the house, he addressed his mother, "Who is our *mayordo-mo* now? He's going to be very busy the next few days."

Margaret joined her son in the foyer. "Ernesto is still with us. I'm sure he can take care of your friends and their needs."

Dane spotted Maxine fingering the solid silver candelabra hanging near the entryway and laughed. "I hope Ernesto has been resting well of late. I believe he's going to lose a little sleep in the nights ahead."

An hour later, after he'd bathed, shaved, and dressed in fresh clothing, Dane made his way down-stairs to the sitting room, where his mother awaited him. He regarded her from the doorway as she worked the stitches into her quilt.

Margaret Dane had embraced her Spanish hus-band's lifestyle yet managed to keep her own English

heritage as well. She dressed like a fashionable *doña*
but usually wore a little English chatelaine attached to
her belt. The chatelaine, which had once belonged to
her grandmother, sported an ornate silver triangle from
which an ivory memory aid, thimble holder, scissors,
needle case, pin cushion, and silk tape dangled from a
series of silver chains. It was an heirloom, like Dane's
watch, but in Margaret's case, because of a complete
estrangement from her parents, it had become much
more. It was her only link to the family which disowned
her the day she chose to mix her blood with that of a
Spaniard.

As he thought of the sacrifices she'd made to be with
his father, to become his mother, Dane smiled warmly
and said, "I've missed watching you work."

Margaret's head jerked upward. "Oh, Dane—I'm
sorry. I didn't hear you come in." She set the quilt on a
small hardwood table and patted the sofa beside her.
"Come sit down. Tell me what's been happening in
your life. Your letters home have been little more than
financial reports."

"That's because my financial status is the only thing
I am sure of these days."

"These days?"

He sighed. "I thought I knew exactly what I wanted
and where I was going when I left San Francisco, but
now, I'm not so sure. Now . . . maybe I don't know
what I want anymore."

Her expression troubled, she said, "You're not talking about leaving the rancho again, are you?"

Dane hesitated only a moment before he slowly
shook his head. "No, that's one of the things I am sure

of, and I know it's something that's been missing in my life. I belong here. I intend to stay."

"That's a relief," Margaret said, lightly fanning herself. "Then your reservations must be of a personal nature. Caroline?"

Avoiding her gaze, Dane slumped back against the couch.

Margaret accepted his silence. "There's no hurry there, son. Until you know what you want in your heart, you simply cannot make any decisions regarding your future beyond running this rancho. Take your time with the rest, allow no room for error. I learned that much when I ran off with your father. Just make sure your decision feels as right in your heart as it does in your head." Her pulse quickened as she thought of her dead husband. "If you find that you cannot forget about Frank and Caroline, about the bitterness, the hurt you must have felt when they—"

"This is not something I wish to discuss with you— or anyone just now."

Margaret relaxed against the cushion and studied her son. They'd all lost so much during the past few years of his self-imposed exile, Dane in particular. He'd lived as a man without a family, an orphaned adult, and she as a woman with only one child. She didn't know this son, her youngest, her baby. He was a stranger to her. Was it too late to rekindle the bond they had once shared?

"You may be feeling uncommunicative, Dane, but there are a few things that need to be said." At his heavy sigh, she went on. "I want you to know that I was none-too-pleased about the goings on after you left, and I understand why you had to go. But I have to make this clear to you—your brother and Caroline made a good marriage. They loved each other, of that I have no doubt, and they produced my only grandchildren. I don't—can't—harbor ill feelings any longer about what happened in the past. I hope for your sake, that you won't either."

Dane now realized that somewhere along the road between San Francisco and San Diego, he'd managed to misplace those bitter feelings, the utter sense of betrayal. Even more surprising, now that he was home again, it didn't seem to matter so much. With an honesty that startled him, he said, "I am at peace with the past."

Margaret squeezed his hand. "Have you told Caroline you feel this way?"

Dane shook his head. "We have not yet had the opportunity for a private moment."

"I suspect that's because you've avoided each other so studiously," she laughed. "She's been feeling a little awkward about this situation, too. I hope you'll talk soon—before I leave next week."

"You're going that soon? But I've just returned home. I expected you would stay here with me a while longer."

"No, son, I can't. I planned my departure for Europe around your return—around that and the *fiesta* I've arranged in your honor this Saturday, which, due to your late arrival, I feared might not include the guest of honor!"

Dane drew his brows together. "A party?"

"Please don't be angry. It was something I had to do.

You know your father would have insisted on my seeing to your official introduction as Don Francisco del Cordobes before I sail for England."

He waved her off, wondering if five days was enough time to get Maxine ready for her debut. "The party is fine with me. I want to know more about your trip. Are you really that set on going back?"

"Yes, I am." She straightened her spine, increasingly convinced she'd made the correct decision. "Nine years without you taught me a lot about heartbreak. I've decided that thirty-three years is long enough for my stubborn parents to forget they have a daughter. If they won't come to me or answer my letters, I shall go to them." When she guessed the objections forming in his clear blue eyes, eyes so much like her own, Margaret smiled and reassured him. "And don't think for a minute you have to worry about me. Aunt Penelope is meeting me at shipside, and she will put me up should my parents remain bullheaded. I will be quite well taken care of, in any case. You just worry about running this ranch—and taking care of Caroline."

Caroline. Lord, why hadn't he been more enthusiastic when he'd first seen her? She was everything he remembered and more. Their years apart had added to rather than subtracted from her classic beauty, and her fragile skin was still a pristine blend of satin and porcelain. Dane thought of her hair, that beautiful blond hair which still shined like the morning sun and smelled of lemons. Why hadn't he been more moved when he'd held her in his arms again at last?

Margaret looked at her son, so deep in thought, and

noticed that although he was fresh and clean in every other way, long black curls still hung over the collar of his shirt. "Why didn't Ernesto trim your hair?"

Avoiding her gaze, he shrugged and said, "I asked him not to just yet."

Margaret broached the other subject which had been on her mind. "Let's talk about your guests—the girl, Maxine, in particular."

Dane glanced up with a start. Some things never change, he thought, somehow warmed by the realization. Even as a young boy, he could never put one over on his mother. She always knew when he'd been up to no good or if he was hiding something. The trouble was that he wasn't even sure if he knew what it was, himself.

With as little explanation as possible, he said, "I need your help with her."

"Oh?"

He nodded. "Maxine's family owes me a great deal of money—why is not important. We have decided to see what kind of dowry she will bring. To that end, I was hoping that you and—" He bit his lip just before Caroline's name slipped out, and in that moment, Dane realized that whatever he was hiding was no small thing. It was a dark, nebulous secret inside him, and the sensation sent a chill up the back of his neck.

Margaret was watching him closely. "Dane? Is something wrong?"

"No." He shook off the troubling thoughts. "I started to include Caroline in this little challenge, but I think perhaps it would be better if you handle Maxine's introduction into society yourself." He winked and added, "I've been working on her language for the last few weeks. Do you think you can teach her some manners before Saturday's party?"

Margaret let her breath out. "Oh, Dane—that sounds like a challenge, all right, but I think I'm equal to the task."

"Oh! There you all are!" Maxine popped into the room. "Howdy, Dane, ma'am. I've been wandering around this big ole house for ten minutes looking for someone who wasn't a maid!" Bubbling with nervous laughter, she crossed the cavernous room to where they sat. "There must be at least five servants for every man, woman, and child in this house. You always have this many people waiting on you, ma'am?"

At Margaret's amused nod, Maxine added, "Then I'd say it's a good thing we showed up—I don't know what all those folks would do to occupy themselves if we hadn't."

Although his mother chuckled, Dane wasn't quite so amused. Disturbing private conversations was one area he thought he'd schooled her in. With a tight smile, he said, "Please, do come in, Señorita Maxine. And by the way, we accept your apology for interrupting us so rudely."

"Oh," she said in a soft voice. "Excuse me. I didn't mean to—I mean, I forgot about that interrupting thing."

With his features less rigid, Dane said, "I believe we've already accepted your apology."

Maxine stood quietly for a long, awkward moment, and then curtsied and canted her head toward Dane.

"Want me to go back out and start over again?"

Chuckling to herself as she thought of the days ahead, Margaret said, "That won't be necessary. Please, Maxine. Come have a seat. We'd love for you to join us."

"Thank you, ma'am—don't mind if I do." Maxine tipped her nose toward Dane triumphantly, stomped over to them, and sank onto one of the leather chairs across from Margaret del Cordobes.

Dane's displeasure showed in his expression, but his attitude had nothing to do with her boorish entrance. It was her manner of dress. He'd expected Maxine to be outfitted as a lady when the maids finished with her, but she was dressed no better—actually worse, to his eyes—than she'd been when they'd first arrived at the rancho. In place of her man's shirt, she wore a loose fitting blouse with a low cut neckline and flouncy sleeves. Her skirt, while not much different in style from the patched russet gingham he'd first seen her in, was blood red with bright yellow flowers splattered across the background in a free-flowing pattern. Yards of black lace petticoats lay beneath it, some peeking out from under the hem of her skirt, others hugging her slim, muscular thighs.

Except for her hair, that glorious mop of curly red tresses which was arranged into a large waterfall spilling down her back, Maxine could have passed as one of the servants. She was dressed like a peasant—a voluptuous, desirable, fresh-faced serving girl, a woman who begged to be touched, whether she voiced that desire or not. Trying to keep his gaze off her loose red tendrils, spirals of fire which corkscrewed down the sides of her long, inviting neck, Dane finally snapped, "Why are you dressed like that?"

Taken aback for a moment, more by his tone than by the question, Maxine smoothed the colorful material draped across her legs and said defensively, "Your maids did it. They wouldn't let me wear my own things because they were too beat up and dirty." She glanced down at herself, just in case she'd been mistaken about the pretty dress she'd been given, and leveled a pair of incredulous brown eyes on her host. "Hell's fire, Dane—I thought I looked right fancy just the way I am."

With a muscle at the corner of his mouth twitching, Dane said, "I'd appreciate it if you'd mind your language in front of my mother."

Realizing her error, and sensing her inadequacy, Maxine whispered, "Ah . . . begging your pardon, ma'am. Sometimes I forget where I'm at."

At her expression, which resembled the look of a cornered calf, Dane almost apologized right back. Swallowing the urge, he said, "And what of the gown I gave to you in San Francisco? You could have sent one of the servants out to the wagon to retrieve it for you and worn that."

"Oh, no—not anymore I couldn't." Maxine's expression lit up as she explained the demise of the fancy ball gown. "I thank you again for the dress—it was one of the best presents I ever got, but Pa—"

She turned to Margaret, as if she would understand, even if Dane didn't. "It was kinda small, especially around here—" She dragged her hands across her breasts and then continued, despite Dane's muffled groan. "Well, my pa took one look at it and said he'd sooner drop over dead than see that much of me exposed again. I sure didn't want to burn it like he suggested, so I went and made a mattress out of it."

Margaret's fingers fluttered to her breast. "A . . . *mattress*, my dear?"

Maxine nodded. "I cut the top off—wasn't much material there anyway—stuffed the skirt with the petticoats, then stitched up the sides. Softest bed I ever had." She smiled at Dane. "I thank you again for your generosity."

Margaret pressed her quivering lips together.

Dane shook his head and muttered, "One can only imagine what she must have done with the corset."

"No need to," Maxine said, proud of the family's ingenuity. "I'll tell you right out. Max tied a couple of ropes to it and made a tree swing for me. Nice and bouncy, you know?"

"Made a—" Margaret, who'd lived in a grim world of mourning for the past few weeks—years, if one included the loss of her husband—burst out laughing.

Maxine didn't know if she'd made another blunder or found a small niche in the heart of Rancho Cordoba's mistress. She picked her fingernails and shifted her restless gaze between mother and son.

And Dane, who wasn't sure what to make of any of Maxine's revelations, coughed into his fist to battle his own laughter, but he lost the fight.

This caught Margaret's attention. Her son was a man who'd never laughed much, even as a boy, and yet he seemed positively in tune with his free-spirited houseguest. Was this the source of his confusion, and not

Caroline, as she'd supposed? If that was the case, how should she proceed with Maxine's lessons? Train her as she would a daughter to suit any young man, or tailor her lessons to suit Dane, and Dane alone?

11

The next few days saw a flurry of activity at the rancho. Manuela, the head cook, gathered up all the available help and worked around the clock to prepare food for the throngs of visitors Doña Marguerite had invited. Servants who were spared from this duty worked on a suitable wardrobe for Maxine and her family, none of whom could fit into anything already hanging in the del Cordobes' closets. And Dane's mother struggled along with her very challenging assignment.

On the morning of the fiesta, an unusually subdued Maxine found herself covered up to her throat in an appropriate day dress of crisp gray calico. She restlessly wandered through the sprawling house, looking for something, anything, to occupy herself. Sniffing out an absolute melange of aromas, she headed for the dining table and found it burgeoning with hams, turtles stewed in the shell, haunches of deer, wild turkey, and geese. She stopped for a moment to admire the center-piece, a large peacock pâté surrounded by tail feathers from the bird's gaudy plumage, Maxine poked her finger into the mass for a little taste.

"No, no, no, Señorita Maxine!" Catalina, the servant most often assigned to meet Maxine's needs, scurried up beside her. "Doña Marguerite will be angry if the food is touched before her guests arrive. Come to the kitchen. I will prepare some warm tortillas for you."

"No thanks. I'm not hungry. Just curious. Where is everybody?"

Catalina smoothed the pâté, rearranged the flowers and decorative fruits surrounding the centerpiece, and shrugged. "The men, I do not know. The ladies, they are beginning to dress for the fiesta—as you should."

"Dress? But I thought the party didn't start for another three hours."

"*Si*—three hours. You should go to your room. I will come help you soon."

"It won't take no three hours for you to stuff me into that getup. I'm going outside for a breath of air." Still grumbling, Maxine walked through the dining room to the immense doors leading to the inner courtyard.

"Don't be too long," Catalina called after her. "We must fix your hair, too!"

"My hair is just fine," Maxine muttered to herself as she stepped out into the bright morning sun. She stood at the fringes of the courtyard, watching the servants scurry back and forth between the house and the great stone fireplace where most of the cooking was done. Some were grinding corn for the hundreds of tortillas that would be consumed before the day was over, and others, higher in rank, were busy setting out champagne, French liqueurs, and an assortment of fancy coffees and teas. Everyone, down to the lowest of servants, had something to do. Everyone except Maxine.

She checked the sun's position through the latticed patio cover. Pausing long enough to admire the huge bunches of green grapes hanging beneath the leafy vines, she decided she had time, plenty of time, to go see what her brother was up to. She was heading across the courtyard toward the outbuildings when her father emerged from the barn, leading a pair of Dane's fine horses. Attached to their rigging was the McKain wagon.

"Hey, Pa!" she shouted as she lifted her skirts and ran to meet him. "Does Dane know you're stealing his horses?"

"Mornin', Maxie girl," he said, avoiding eye contact as he climbed up on the wagon. "Don Francisco was good 'nuff to make the loan of his horses so our mules could rest up. Now if'n you'd be so kind as to step outta the way, I'll be goin' into town for a spell.

"Town?" Maxine circled the horses. Shading her eyes from the morning sun, she looked up at him. "You're going into San Diego? What about the party?"

"Oh now, Maxie, you know I canno' abide such things. I'll just be playin' a little poker, probably be gone fur a day or two. Nothin' fur you to get roiled about."

Curling up her fists, she brought them to her hips and narrowed her gaze. "Where did you find a stake to get you in a poker game, Pa? We ain't got the means for you to make any kind of showing at a saloon, and besides—" she patted her dress pocket. "I got our money right here. Where'd you get yours?"

Dicey blew out a noisy sigh. "Our very generous host give his vaqueros their freedom whilst the fiesta's goin' on. They started up a right friendly game last evenin', they did, one that's gonna last on through tonight and maybe even into another day. I used my lucky dice to get in the game, and after that?" He shrugged and winked. "Stakes weren't much, but neither were the talent! My winnin's ought to get me a wee bit of attention in town."

Dicey was still laughing when one of the ranch hands, a man named Carlos, walked around behind the wagon and climbed up beside him. "Señorita Maxine," he greeted, touching the brim of his sombrero.

Maxine returned the favor with a hollow "How'd you do," and then resumed the conversation with her father. "It's not fair—you running off and leaving me at this fancy party all by myself. If you're going, I'm going too."

Dicey wagged a stern finger in her face. "I'll just be puttin' my foot down on that, girl. You made a promise, remember? Yur supposed to be findin' yurself a nice young man." He straightened his collar and took the reins in his hand. "'Sides, time and again a man's got to go off alone. Ain't no place fur you on this trip. You got yur brother to keep you company if you don't take to nobody at the party. I'll just be sayin' goodbye now. Take care of yurself and try to have a little fun."

"But Pa," she cried, sensing she had lost the battle. "I don't think I'm gonna like this party or Dane's friends, and they sure as hell ain't gonna like me."

"Oh, now, Maxie—that just ain't true. You'll be the prettiest gal in the room."

"I don't care about that, but what if I make a fool of myself? I never know what to say or when to say it, and even after all the Doña's teaching, I'm still afraid to eat in that house. I never know what spoon or fork to use on what, or what's food and what's decoration. Everything I do or say is wrong. You gotta take me with you."

"Sorry, Maxie, but not today. See the party through, and if yur still feeling that way, we'll head for the hills like I promised. Take care, girl."

Done with explanations, Dicey slapped the reins against the horses' backs, and the wagon lurched to life. As the rig rolled past her, Maxine impulsively kicked the back wheel. Then she whirled around, cursing her new shoes and the fact she'd hurt her toe, and stomped into the barn.

When she reached the paddock area, Maxine called out, "Max? You in here?"

"Over here," came his reply from an empty stall.

Maxine rounded the corner and saw the squaw sliding a brightly colored *serape* over her brother's new white shirt. After she'd adjusted it so the shoulders hung evenly, Max spun around, his broad grin in place, and said, "Hi, Maxie. Look what I get to wear. Dane said I could. He said I could take care of his friends' horses, too. Me. Just me."

"That's good, Max," she said, appraising his new look, shiny black trousers and new boots. Even though he wore a perpetually vacant look in his eyes, Max was an appealing young man when properly cleaned and dressed—a fact reflected in the squaw's expression as she smiled up at him. Then she ducked behind his powerful shoulders and hid.

Something in the squaw's manner showed more than gratitude. Not sure how she felt about the changing relationship, Maxine strolled over to her brother's side. "You look real good, Max. Handsome, too. Good as any of them fancy people you'll be helping."

"Really?" Max's naturally rosy complexion positively shone. "Really and true?"

"Really and true. I'll bet your new friend agrees with me too—don't you?"

At the direct question, the woman retreated even further behind the immense barrier, but Max sidestepped, exposing her as he whispered in her ear. "My sister is okay. Maxie's good. I told you before, Maxie's good."

Taking one tiny step at a time, the squaw crept out from hiding. She stood silently for a long moment, measuring Maxine through her sloped, ebony eyes. Then she finally said, "I am called Rosa."

Startled, Maxine took a backward step before she collected herself enough to reply. "You can talk! I thought, well, we kinda figured someone cut out your tongue, or something like that."

"I talk."

"She talks to me," Max said, proud of his role in her recovery. "She talked to me yesterday."

"Why didn't you tell us, Max?"

"I asked him not to." Rosa moved a step closer to Maxine, her tired eyes rimmed with red, the purple bruises beneath them now evolved to a pale mustard color. Her tone was feeble and not too confident. "There is no one else I wish to speak to."

Maxine shrugged. "Don't then, but it's time you came on up to the house. Dane has maids who'll give you a nice bath and a real soft bed. There's a room just waiting for you. You won't have to say a word—I'll do all the talking for you if you like."

Rosa shook her head. "No," she whispered. "I cannot."

Maxine glanced at Max, who'd placed his big hand on Rosa's shoulder. Shaking her head slowly, she said, "But you two can't stay out here all alone—it just ain't fitting, you know? Dane's mother says that it not only has to be right, it's got to look right, too. Now come on up to the house."

"Max is free to go to the house. I will stay here."

Maxine shook her head again. "I think you know that ain't gonna happen. You also know we can't just leave you out here by yourself, and having someone else—another man—stay with you, well, that ain't right either."

"She don't need nobody else," Max piped up. "I like the barn. I like to sleep with the horses. I like it. I like Rosa, too. I like her a lot." At this, Rosa squeezed Max's arm, and his grin got so huge, he could hardly go on. "Rosa is good like you, Maxie. She's from coyotes."

Maxine rolled her eyes. "*Coyotes,* Max?"

"I am from the coyote people, the Cahilla tribe."

"From the Borrego desert? Then why were you wandering around by yourself?"

Rosa dropped her chin and lowered her gaze.

Max, noticing his new friend's discomfort, turned on

his sister. "You leave Rosa alone. She don't like to talk. Leave her alone."

Maxine swallowed, trying to loosen the sudden tightness in her throat. Max had *never* spoken to her like that, and he'd certainly never taken another's side against her. First her father's abandonment, and now this. Had her entire family deserted her, just when she needed them most?

Knowing there was no reasoning with Max when he took a stand, Maxine began to back away. "You be sure to take good care of those horses when the guests get here, Max. You have any trouble at all, come on up to the house and get me, hear?"

His earlier irritation forgotten, he repeated, "Come get you."

Maxine nodded, even though she suspected that her brother would turn to Rosa first before he thought of her now. Swallowing the ache in her throat, Maxine said softly, "See you both later, then."

At Rosa's firm, almost sympathetic nod, Maxine turned and rushed out of the barn. Once she was back in the yard, exposed to the bright sunshine and the sprawling rancho, she made her way to one of the oak trees gracing the property and gripped a low-slung branch. She glanced to the west, to the trail and the dot which her father's wagon had become in the distance, and then looked back at the barn. It wasn't until she swung her gaze around to the house, to the second floor, with its bedroom windows in particular, that she realized the full measure of her loneliness.

Her family had other plans or other people to keep them occupied, happy. Dane and his Caroline were upstairs in that house somewhere, probably getting ready for the party. Or maybe, she thought, her imagination running wild, they were together, his arms around her, his lips—

No, what was was bad enough. Maxine had never been the kind of woman to add to her troubles by making things up, and she had more than enough reality to deal with. Instead of wallowing in her troubles, she needed a way to rid herself of this overwhelming sense of loss, this feeling of complete and utter isolation. Sniffing back a tiny sob, Maxine pushed away from the tree and began roaming the grounds, searching for something, anything to take her mind off this terrible and foreign loneliness. As she neared one of the bunkhouses, the sounds of boisterous laughter reached her ears.

Remembering her father's description of the protracted poker game and the decided lack of talent, she straightened her shoulders, climbed the two steps to the door, and pushed it open. Five vaqueros huddled around the dining table, each buried up to his eyebrows in a fan of playing cards. If that sight wasn't a cure for the blues, Maxine couldn't think of what was.

Patting the dress pocket in which she'd hidden the McKain savings, she smiled sweetly and said, "Hi, fellahs—I ain't too good at it, but if you're playing poker, I'd sure like to give it a try. Got room for one more?"

Inside the house—its furnishings as eclectic as its English, Spanish, Mexican, and Indian occupants—Dane and Caroline sat on an English settee built into a small alcove below the wide, arched windows that overlooked Otay Lake. He was staring down at his hands, searching the nail beds as if they might contain the answer to her question.

He finally raised his head and looked into her soft gray eyes. "I honestly cannot think of what to say. That I agreed to marry you is not in doubt. I am a man of my word."

"I know that." Caroline pushed her skirts to the side and moved closer to him. "I wasn't asking if you still plan to marry me, Dane. I'm more interested in knowing if you actually *want* to. You've hardly said two words to me since your return. I don't like this tension, the feeling that you're avoiding parts of your own home just to make certain that you won't bump into me." She covered one of his hands with hers. "What is it? Frank and me?"

Dane snatched his hand away and shook his head. "No." Much to his surprise, that really didn't disturb him. "But you are right—I don't know for sure what is bothering me, but something does."

Again, Caroline slid her hand across the back of his. Dane flinched but made no attempt to move it. "You once told me you loved me. Was that a lie?" she said in her melodious voice.

Suddenly, Dane didn't know. When he tried to think back to the past, everything seemed wooden, emotionless. Had he even known what love was back then? Did he know now?

Trying to be as honest as possible, he said, "I only know that I thought I loved you, but that it was a very long time ago. I was little more than a boy." He turned, finally looking Caroline in the eye. "How can I know how deep my true feelings ran then—and what do they matter now?"

Caroline nodded, smiling. "I wasn't much more than a baby myself. I know I was sweet on you, but when you left, I . . ." Her words trailed off.

With a rashness he usually kept in reserve, Dane finished the sentence for her. "Figured one del Cordobes brother was as good as another?"

This time, it was Caroline who jerked her hand away and Dane who reclaimed it. "Forgive me," he said, wishing this conversation were not taking place. "That was a cruel, unnecessary remark. Perhaps there is some bitterness after all, some bad feelings I wasn't aware I still had."

She squeezed his hands, forcing his gaze back to hers. "I can't say I blame you for those bitter feelings, if that's what they are, and I do want you to understand that I wasn't looking for someone to replace you. I—I fell in love with Frank. It just happened."

She was looking at him the way she used to, those soft blue eyes filled with wonder, and yes, with even a certain amount of innocence. Dane used to love that look as much as he loved the woman. Now that she, the Caroline he'd coveted for so many years, was here, so close by, he had to wonder: Where was his triumph? His joy? Why couldn't he bring himself to embrace her, to allow himself even a small measure of pleasure with her company?

Perplexed, Dane stood and turned, facing the window. Hooking his thumbs in the waistband of his trousers, he stared out at the lake as if he might find the answers he sought. His gaze picked up a pair of ducks as they skimmed across the glassy pond, and a light breeze carried the fresh scent of chaparral to his nostrils, but his mind seemed as muddled as ever.

Still sitting below him on the settee, Caroline watched the confusion building in Dane's expression, the darkening storm in his mind. He'd changed in many ways since she'd last seen him, grown from a strapping young boy to a sculpted man worthy of any woman's awe. She observed the strength in his hands, the way his lean body had expanded with fine ridges of muscle since she'd last seen him, and startled herself with a burst of desire. It was then that she realized what was missing between them, what he was withholding. It was more than love—much more.

The Dane del Cordobes Caroline remembered was hot-blooded and sensuous, a man who left a woman with no doubts as to how much he wanted her. Where was his passion, the look that promised his fire? Was there another woman, one who still had a hold on his heart? Surprised by her wandering mind, by thoughts she knew were inappropriate for a widow of three months, Caroline pushed propriety aside and decided to seek out his passion. She slowly rose up off the couch and glided to his side.

"You haven't even kissed me hello, Dane. I think that's permitted, isn't it?"

He blinked as if he'd just awakened and then shifted his gaze to Caroline's. "Forgive me, my mind was elsewhere. What did you say?"

Caroline's sigh was soft, nearly inaudible, as she rephrased her question. "Who is she, Dane?"

" 'She'?"

Caroline gave him an indulgent smile. "I believe that not something, but *someone,* is keeping us apart. If it's not Frank, I wonder if it couldn't be the young lady you left in San Francisco—Miss Hunt is her name, I believe."

Dane almost denied the accusation but wisely turned back to the window and kept his silence. Caroline was right, he finally acknowledged, if only to himself. There was another woman distracting him, keeping him from her, but she was no one so shallow as Joy, or so genteel as Caroline. A veritable wildfire of a woman had tossed her *riata* around him, and flipped him upside down before he even knew what had hit him. Even now, as he spoke of a life with Caroline, Dane could feel Maxine tugging on the lasso, prodding him to keep her fiery red hair and chocolate brown eyes first in his thoughts. No wonder he couldn't concentrate on his future, on the woman he assumed, until now, he would wed one day.

Sure now that another woman occupied his thoughts, Caroline squared her shoulders and said, "We can talk about this later, if you wish. I can see that your mind and your passion are elsewhere."

Startled, Dane spun around. "My passion?"

Caroline looked away, blushing. "It's a delicate subject, I know, and nothing I think that should be of concern for now. Perhaps what we once felt for each other will come to us later. We'll have plenty of time to discover that, if you decide you want me to stay."

Dane didn't even want to think about passion—not his, or hers, and especially not theirs. He had all he could worry about with Maxine. Wanting nothing more than a quick end to the conversation, he thought to reassure Caroline. "I have not, nor will I ask you to leave your own home. You and the boys belong here as much as I do."

She shook her head, objecting. "I can't stay here with you if we're not married. Once your mother leaves, you'll have to make a decision about me, about us."

Feeling much older than his twenty-nine years, Dane sighed and said, "Let me think about it some more. I will not leave either of us in doubt for long." He glanced back out the window, noticed two carriages in the distance, and added, "Now if you will excuse me, I see the first of our guests are about to arrive."

As he turned to leave, Caroline stood on tiptoe, quickly kissed his cheek, and whispered, "Welcome home, Dane. We all missed you very much."

As troubled as he was warmed by the gesture, Dane returned the sentiment. "It is good to see you again, too." Then he gave her delicate shoulders a gentle squeeze and left the room.

On the way to the courtyard, he passed Catalina and asked, "Where is Señorita Maxine? Some of our guests are almost here and I want to be sure she's properly introduced."

Catalina shook her head. "No Señorita Maxine, Don Francisco. I cannot find her anywhere. She has disappeared."

"Disappeared? What do you mean by that?"

Her black eyes darting nervously, she shrugged and said, "Gone, I do not know where. She did not come back to the house. Her dress is still in her room."

"What?"

"I am sorry—I looked, but I cannot find her."

The servant's apology was lost on Dane. Assuming Maxine was out helping her brother prepare for his assignment, he bolted from the house and headed straight for the barn. When he didn't find her there, he began to search the outer perimeters of the ranch, his panic growing.

As he passed the row of bunkhouses on the way to the carriage house, a round of raucous laughter from one of the buildings gave him pause. It took Dane a full minute to realize that something about that laughter disturbed him. When he realized what it was, his search came to an abrupt halt. Incredible as it may have sounded, even to his own ears, he could almost swear he'd heard feminine giggles sprinkling the male guffaws.

"It cannot be," he said to himself. "She would not. She *could* not." Could she?

In long, purposeful strides, Dane marched back to the bunkhouse and up the steps and glanced through the open door.

There, like a Baccarat champagne glass amidst five chipped beer mugs, sat Maxine in the middle of his drinking, swearing *vaqueros*.

His hot Andalusian blood surging to the forefront, Rancho Cordoba's newest Don stormed into the room.

12

"Your two bits, and . . ." Maxine chewed on her lower lip as she calculated her hand's worth and then said, "raise you a dollar."

As she plunked the coins into the growing pile, one of the *vaqueros,* a Diegueño Indian named Jesus said, "A dollar? Oh, Señorita Maxine, you are too reckless for me to keep you honest. You win." Then he folded his cards and added them to the pile of coins.

Laughing, she reached toward the center of the table and then froze. A shadow, dark and foreboding, seemed to glide overhead. Feeling as if she were moving in slow motion, a single moment seeming to take an hour, she turned her head and found the danger.

It was Dane. An angry Dane, nostrils flaring, hands on hips, legs spread apart, testing the strength of his tight black trousers. He was all fancied-up, wearing a short black jacket and a white ruffled shirt with gold trim and filigree buttons of silver. Would his gentlemanly exterior help to keep the rage she saw glittering in his blue eyes in check?

Smiling wanly, she said, "There's room for one more—how lucky do you feel?"

His jaw tightened as he swiftly closed the distance between them. "A lot luckier than you will be feeling for a very long time, Señorita Maxine."

When he reached the table, Dane turned to his men and snarled, "*Estupidos ignorantes!* You should know better, even if *she* doesn't!"

To a man, they each muttered, *"Perdona me,"* before lowering their gazes to the floor.

Far from appeased, Dane turned to Maxine and demanded, "Come with me—now!"

"B-but I'm winning," she protested, knowing it was not only futile, but probably a mistake to argue with him in front of his men.

It was. Dane grabbed her arm and jerked her to her feet. "There will be no further discussion. You are coming with me."

He started to drag her away, but she planted her feet and gripped the table's edge. "You got to let me get my money!"

Although it took all the patience he possessed at that point, Dane relaxed his grip long enough for her to scoop her winnings up off the table and drop them into the wide pocket of her dress. Then his fingers closed around her arm, and he led her from the bunkhouse out into the deserted grounds between the carriage house and the corral.

Tapping her forehead with his knuckles, he demanded, "What do you keep in that head of yours where the brains should be, Miss McKain—*frijoles?*"

"Hey—*hey!*" Incensed, Maxine slapped his hand. "What the hell do you think you're doing? And what's wrong with a little game of poker, anyhow? I was winning!" She turned then, as if to stomp back to the bunkhouse, but Dane stopped her cold by reclaiming her arm, angrier this time.

"The bunkhouse," he growled, his face inches from hers, "is no place for a lady—even if the lady in question is trying very hard not to be one."

She bristled but had no retort.

"You are supposed to be dressed—dressed, *comprende?* My guests are arriving. Have you forgotten that you are to make your debut today?"

Of all the things she had forgotten, this fact was not one of them. She lowered her lashes and bit her bottom lip. "No, I didn't forget. I'm just not sure I want to go through with it."

"Not go through with it?" Dane's temper exploded. "You dare to stand there and tell me that after I have troubled myself to bring your family here, after my mother has spent hours preparing you for this day? Does nothing we do hold any value for you?"

Tears stung the back of her eyes, but Maxine wouldn't give in. "None of this was my idea! I never asked you or your mother to turn me into something I'm not. Hell—before I met you, I didn't know anything was wrong with me!"

She tried to pull away from his grip, but Dane held her fast. With her accusations burning in his ears, he narrowed his gaze. "My mother and I are simply trying to teach you some manners, to help you become lady enough to attract a large dowry. Have you forgotten that along with all you learned here?"

Maxine jerked out of his grip, but Dane managed to hook her arm again and spin her around. "I don't care about dowries or debts," she said. "I just want you to let me go!"

"I'm not done with you yet!" he snapped.

"Well I'm done with you." She tilted her chin upward. "In fact, there's nothing I want or need from you."

"Nothing?" Dane echoed, out of control. "Not even this?"

Then, before she could react, he crashed down on her mouth with his, smothering her with a kiss so brutal she could hardly believe the lips assaulting hers belonged to Dane. When he finally released her and stared down at her with glassy eyes, his moment of confusion gave Maxine an opportunity to retaliate.

"You bastard." Her voice was low and guttural as she swung her arm back and drove her palm against his cheek as hard as she could.

When she realized what she'd done, hot tears finally erupted, and her cheeks burned. Unwilling to let Dane see her in such a state, Maxine broke away from him and ran toward the barn.

Dane, more dazed and confused than ever, stood rigid for a full minute and then marched back to the ranch house.

From an upper bedroom window of that home, a blond woman dressed in black stepped back out of view. As she turned to head downstairs and greet her guests, an amused grin lit Doña Marguerite Dane del

Cordobes' features, from her mouth to her eyes. "Price-less," she whispered to herself as she descended the stairs. "Utterly priceless."

Out in the barn, racing from stall to stall, praying that Dane had not followed her, Maxine was feeling anything but priceless. She felt utterly worthless, in fact. She swallowed sob after sob, wiping her tears as she searched for her brother, and finally came across him and Rosa in an empty stall. Max's back was to her, but even with his bulk, she could see that he held the woman in his arms, and that they were sharing a kiss that went beyond the bounds of friendship.

Maxine gasped, as much from shock as from the hic-cups her sobs had become.

Max released Rosa and awkwardly wheeled around. Blushing furiously, he swung his hands in front of his body and lowered his head. "Hi, Maxie. Rosa. She— she . . . and I—"

"You kissed her," Maxine said wearily. "It's all right, Max. Don't worry. Sometimes people . . ." She swallowed the anger which swelled in her throat, then forced herself to say the suddenly loathsome word, "*kiss* when they like each other. It's not a bad thing."

He brightened and raised his head. "I do like Rosa— I like her a lot! I like Dane, too. He done good things for us." Max scratched his head, then frowned. "Do I have to kiss him, too?"

Even though her heart was heavy, and her thoughts about the Spaniard were as black as his hair, Maxine wasn't so angry that she didn't laugh at the image of her brother kissing him. With a quiet chuckle, she said, "No, you don't have to kiss him, too."

With his huge grin in place, Max beamed. "That's good. I like Dane a lot, but I don't want to kiss him. I like kissing Rosa."

As her brother spoke, Maxine began to see him in a new light. There was a fire in Max that had never been there before, a sense of self-worth. He'd grown here at Rancho Cordoba, blossomed in a way he never could have in the eldorado, and Maxine realized what Dane had been trying to provide for them all: security. For the first time, her family had something they'd never had before, and what had she done? Slapped opportunity in the face.

Vowing to do better by Dane and her entire family, Maxine took her brother's hand and squeezed. "Walk me up to the house, would you, Max? Then you got to go to work. Dane said his friends are almost here."

Max didn't question his sister. He began to shuffle from the barn, following alongside of her.

A voice called after the twins. "Be happy, Maxine."

Still surprised to hear sound coming from Rosa, Maxine jumped and looked back toward the Indian. Although she wasn't quite sure what the woman meant, she smiled and said, "Thanks, Rosa. And listen, if there's anything you want—food, clothes, anything— just have Max come get me. I'll bring it out personal."

Rosa offered a barely noticeable nod and then lowered her head. "Thank you."

"You're welcome." With her spirits lifted a notch, Maxine marched back to the house with her brother— and bodyguard—in tow.

She didn't need him, though, as Dane was no longer in the yard. When she stepped through the front door at the house, she ran squarely into Catalina, who'd been sent to the barn to retrieve her. Without giving her so much as time to blink her eyes, the servant pushed her up the stairs and into her room.

An hour later, Maxine was bathed, perfumed, powdered, and clinging to the solid oak post of her four-poster bed as Catalina lashed her into a satin corset.

"Hell's fire!" she said, struggling to draw a full breath. "You're squashing the very life right out of me! Are you absolutely sure I got to wear this thing?"

"*Si,* Señorita Maxine. You must. All fine ladies wear corsets under their clothing."

Catalina gave the lashes another yank and her charge cried out, "Holy hell!"

A light tapping sounded at the door just before it opened. Caroline peeked inside. "Are you decent?"

Maxine glanced down at herself, at the layers of petticoats, the heavy linen chemise, and the fancy lace pantalettes beneath all that. "I got enough unmentionables on me to be decent for the rest of my life. Come on in."

Chuckling as she crossed the room, Caroline addressed the servant. "Go downstairs, Catalina. You're needed in the kitchen. I'll finish dressing Maxine."

Without a word, the servant made a little curtsy and scurried out of the room.

"I'm sorry."

Caroline cocked her head. "What on earth for, dear?"

"For being so late and taking you away from Dane and the party. You ought to be downstairs greeting the guests with him instead of up here trying to turn me into a lady."

Again, Caroline laughed. "You are laboring under several misconceptions. First of all, greeting Dane's guests is not my place—not yet, anyway. Also, I'm still in mourning for my husband. Our visitors will not be expecting to see much of me." Offering Maxine a bright smile, she spun her around, studying the corset, and added, "Besides, dear, I want to help you. Are you laced tight enough?"

"So tight I can hardly breathe—will you loosen the danged thing for me?"

Caroline shook her head. "If I do that, you won't fit into this lovely dress." She took the white muslin gown off the bed, and slipped the yards of material over Maxine's head.

After Caroline had finished fastening the back, Maxine walked to the mirror and studied her new look. The gown, sprigged with embroidered pink flowers and lots of long green leaves, had a low, rounded bodice which fit snugly to her rib cage, then tapered off to a V at the waist. The sleeves were short and puffed, and the skirt was full. The gown, and the way it clung to her body, were decided improvements over the costume she'd been forced into during her brief stay in San Francisco, but a self-conscious Maxine could only bear to look at herself for a couple of minutes.

When she turned away from the mirror, Caroline remarked, "That dress is absolutely perfect for you."

Maxine shrugged. "It's all right, I guess, but I'm sure not used to seeing myself like this."

"Well, get used to it." Caroline directed Maxine to

sit on a bench in front of the vanity. "After you attract a beau this evening, you'll be able to dress this way all the time."

Maxine bit her tongue and stifled a groan at the thought.

Caroline, busy twisting and tying long strands of vermillion hair, was unaware of Maxine's displeasure. She worked and worked until she was finally pleased with her efforts. "There. You'll have the most fashionable coif in the room. What do you think of it?"

Maxine twisted her head and regarded her reflection. Caroline had parted her hair down the center, made two neat coils along the sides of her head, and tied them in a knot at the back of her neck. Jabbed into the knot was an elaborate silver comb, and below that, the coils hung down in two long spirals. She looked fancy and fashionable, she supposed; even a little like Lola Montez. But nothing like herself.

"Don't you like it?" Caroline asked, bringing one of the coils across her shoulder and arranging it down the front of the dress. "It's the newest style. I think it's stunning on you and really sets off that gorgeous red hair."

Gorgeous? Maxine took another look in the mirror. She'd always thought her hair was too bright, too red, and made her look as if her head might burst into flames at any minute. Gorgeous? No, she didn't think so, but all fancied up as it was, she had to admit that her hair was more attractive than it ever had been.

Her lessons on becoming a lady prompting her next move, Maxine stood up and extended her hand. "Thank you for helping me out so much. I may have a long ride ahead of me in learning how to be a lady, but thanks to you, I almost look like one."

"No thanks are necessary." Caroline brushed Maxine's fingers away in an effort to discourage the fierce handshake she knew she'd receive. "I had a beautiful subject to work with. Anyone could have made you look like a lady."

Very uncomfortable with this flattery, Maxine started to head for the door, but a commotion in the yard caught her eye. Moving up to the window for a better look, she leaned over the sill and asked Caroline, "What's going on out there? Why is everybody gathered around the corral?"

Joining her at the window, Caroline glanced into the yard. "The men are showing off for each other."

Maxine craned her neck, looking for Dane, wondering what it was the men were up to, when all her questions were answered at once. Dane emerged from the barn riding Alazan. The stallion, dressed as gaily as his rider, was sporting a silver mounted saddle embroidered in gold and silver with matching bridle and reins. Sunlight glinted off the silver *conchos* decorating the leather goods, and an *anqueta,* a leather drape in the shape of a half-moon, covered the top of Alazan's hindquarters. More silver and inlaid gold were evident on the thick wooden stirrups in which Dane rested his boots, which she noticed were accented by large silver spurs.

The stallion and his trappings were impressive, but not nearly as impressive as his rider. To the costume Maxine had seen him wearing earlier, Dane had added a low-brimmed hat made of quality *vicuña,* a *poncho* over his jacket which was heavily trimmed with gold fringe, and a pair of soft deerskin leggings tied at the knee with a silk cord which had been wound around each leg several times first. Heavy gold and silver tassels hung from the cord at the knee, swaying in time with Alazan as he pranced up to the corral.

When the crowd drew back and opened the gate, Maxine spotted a large bull snorting and pawing the ground. Horrified, she turned back to Caroline. "Dane's not planning to mess with that big ole bull, is he?"

Her delicate mouth twisted into a grimace, Caroline nodded. "Oh, yes, he is."

"B-but, won't the bull try to kill him? Can't he get hurt?"

Caroline laughed. "Of course. That's why they do it. Putting themselves in danger, my dear, is what men do to prove to one another that they're *men.*"

Her eyes wide, Maxine swung her gaze back to the yard. Dane had entered the corral, and the crowd was cheering him on. Using only his knees to guide his well-trained mount, Dane held up a cape made of brilliant red cloth and waved it, working to attract the bull's attention. The animal charged, and Alazan, his movements slick and graceful, dashed to one side as Dane, with a dexterous swing of the *capa* across the bull's face, temporarily blinded him. The snorting, incited animal realized he'd been fooled. He slid to a stop, spun around in a cloud of dust, and charged again.

Maxine turned her back to the sight, and covered her eyes with her hands. "How can you stand there and watch him so calmly? Don't that just scare hell out of you?"

Caroline laughed, in spite of the salty language. "The *corrida de toros* can be a thing of beauty to watch. When it's done right, it can look like the most beautiful of dances." She gazed at Dane as he made another pass at the bull. "Dane is an excellent horseman who has a mount to be envied as well. Others will try today, but I think none will come close to his performance."

Almost afraid to look, but too fascinated not to, Maxine turned toward the window again. Finished with his exhibition, Dane was riding out of the corral, leaving the bull to catch his breath and await the next *ranchero* and his horse. As the gate closed behind him, Dane glanced up at the window. Although he wasn't smiling, he took off his hat and waved it toward her. Maxine was sure that the gesture was meant for Caroline, who was standing beside her.

"You must be the luckiest gal I know," Maxine said wistfully.

"Lucky?" Caroline continued to wave at Dane. "In what way?"

"You got him—Dane. Except for that ornery streak, I think he's the most wonderful man I ever met. Can't be too many like him hiding in the bushes waiting for a gal to pounce on him."

Caroline laughed. "No, I doubt there are."

"Was Dane's brother as wonderful?"

As she considered whether she ought to answer such a personal question, Caroline slowly turned away from the window. "I suppose you could say that he was, but in a different way. Frank was a lot calmer, slower to boil than Dane, and not nearly the perfectionist. If Dane has a fault, it might be that he expects everyone and everything to conform to his way of thinking."

Maxine didn't need her imagination to know what Caroline was talking about. She knew that much to be true. Chuckling to herself, she said, "Well, I hope you understand his way of thinking then, 'cause if you don't, you're gonna be in for a long, rough ride."

Caroline's instincts picked up on something she hadn't noticed before. "Oh? You sound as if you've gotten to know Dane quite well during your travels."

A mere apprentice at woman-talk, Maxine was unaware that this conversation might be way over her head. "I think I understand him pretty good now, good enough, anyway, to know how lucky you are to be on the receiving end of his great kisses."

Caroline gasped.

Understanding too late that this was no conversation for her to be having with the man's intended, Maxine blurted out, "Don't get me wrong—I didn't mean nothing by it, and neither did Dane. I made him do it."

Caroline began fanning herself and stopped in midswing. "What does that mean, you made him do it?"

"I asked him if I could kiss him." Maxine watched as those soft gray eyes turned stormy, and her words practically ran together as she tried to explain. "I hope you don't mind, but I never had a man kiss me before—not like he can anyways . . . oh, you know what I mean, with his mouth open, and . . . oh, that's not what I should say. What I mean to tell—"

"That's quite enough," Caroline said, cutting her off with a brisk reply. "I think I understand what happened. You wanted a kiss, and Dane, being the fine gentleman he is, was only too happy to oblige you."

Maxine missed the hint of sarcasm in Caroline's voice. "Yeah!" she said, excited. "That's exactly right. He was happy to oblige me. I never saw him so happy as he was when he kissed me." Realizing she'd blundered again, as Caroline's expression darkened, she added, " 'Course, I'm sure he's a damn sight happier when he kisses you. You're the lucky one all right."

Caroline resumed fanning herself, considering Maxine's words. Then she thought of Dane's reaction to her and the kiss they'd shared earlier. Could this unkempt, untrained ragamuffin be the object of Dane's affection, the reason he wasn't ready to give himself to her? It seemed impossible. Dane del Cordobes had been, and still was, from what she'd seen of him, an exacting, honorable, high-bred nobleman. What could he possibly have wanted from this unfortunate girl, other than a little "relief" after his long weeks in the saddle? He simply couldn't have lost his heart to a woman of such low character and position. The very idea went against everything in his nature.

Certain that she'd been mistaken to consider Maxine as the one who stood between her and Dane, Caroline said, "May I ask you a personal question, Maxine?"

A personal question? Confident that she knew what

was coming, and eager to push those thoughts from Caroline's mind, Maxine's denial fairly tumbled out. "He didn't do no lovemaking on me, Caroline, I swear on the McKain lucky nuggets it's true! Only a kiss or two, that's it!"

"A kiss . . . or two?"

Wishing now that the conversation had never begun, and frantic to find a way out of it, Maxine said, "Honest, nothing happened—not even that night I slept on his bedroll with him!"

Her flawless white skin puckered at the bridge of her nose, Caroline stared at Maxine for a long moment before she was able to comment. "*Slept,* dear? You were sleeping with Dane?"

Lowering her gaze, Maxine began to pick at her fingernails. She'd never meant to do or say anything wrong, but apparently she had. Caroline was getting very angry. How should she proceed now? Shut her mouth, or try to explain one more time?

"Maxine—I'm talking to you. Has Dane taken advantage of you in any way?"

Her gaze jerked up and met Caroline's. "Advantage? I don't know what you mean. I just don't want to get him in trouble. Please don't be mad about anything I said, and don't be mad at Dane either. He didn't do nothing wrong, and I'm real sorry if I made it sound like he did."

Her suspicions far from assuaged, Caroline pursued the truth from a different angle. Her voice softer, less accusing, she asked, "Perhaps you'd tell me how you feel about Dane? You sound like a woman in love. Are you?"

Maxine blushed, her scalp, her face, every part of her glowing the same red as her hair. She *never* blushed, but she was so completely unprepared for the question, she didn't know what to do or what to say. Even worse, as she worked at avoiding Caroline's gaze by looking down at the floor, she noticed that she was imitating Max, and dragging the toe of her new shoe across the polished tiles. Knotting her fingers together, Maxine forced herself to look up and offered Caroline a watery smile. "I—I d-don't—"

"It's all right, Maxine," Caroline said, keeping her voice soft, non-judgmental. "I think I can see that you are. I only hope that Dane hasn't made any promises, or made you think that he loves you, too."

"Oh, gosh, no!" Maxine laughed, the sound loud, almost hysterical. "Why, that's just ridiculous—half the time he can't even stand the sight of me. Love me?" Again she laughed. "The idea is just too funny to even think about!"

Although she still didn't like the implications of what she'd heard, Caroline was convinced Maxine was telling the truth. This time, her soft, gentle tone was genuine as she said, "I sincerely hope you understand just how ridiculous the idea of a man like Dane falling in love with a woman like you is. He has certain obligations and a family name to uphold, not to mention the obvious differences between you."

"Yes, ma'am, I understand." Anxious to end the conversation, she added, "Can we please not talk about this anymore? I'm getting real fidgety and starting to feel a little sick."

Caroline smiled and patted Maxine's shoulder. "I

didn't mean for you to become upset—I just thought it prudent to make certain you weren't being led astray."

Maxine shrugged. "I'd just be happy if you led me downstairs."

Touched by a sudden empathy for the poor girl, Caroline linked her arm through Maxine's. "That sounds like a fine plan. Let's go make our grand entrance."

Feeling awkward and ungainly, like a mule hitched up alongside one of Dane's fine Andalusian horses, Maxine allowed herself to be taken down to the festivities.

After Caroline had introduced her to the neighboring Doñas and ladies from San Diego, and she'd picked her way through the huge assortment of fruits and pastries spread out in the courtyard, Maxine backed into a far corner, much more comfortable observing the proceedings rather than taking part in them. Content just to listen to the musicians tune their instruments, to inhale the atmosphere redolent with spiced citrus, floral arrangements, and the comforting aroma of warm tortillas cooking on the grill, she noticed the men were beginning to trickle into the courtyard.

It wasn't long before Dane strode under the grape vines and scanned the huge patio area. When his gaze met Maxine's from across the room, he offered a short nod—no smile—and then slowly, greeting guests as he moved, he made his way through the crowd.

Watching him approach her safe little observation

point, equal parts of fear and joy split her emotions like a scythe. Would he still be mad at her?

"Rojita," he whispered as he neared, his voice a dark, luscious croon. "You look very beautiful. Are you pleased with the dress?"

Determined to be the lady he'd trained her to be, she said, "Yes, sir, and I thank you very much."

Dane's gaze swept her features and came to rest on her mouth, on the little swollen area at the corner. He thought he'd tasted blood after the brutal way he'd kissed her earlier. Had he cut her lip?

Watching the direction of his gaze, and guessing what he was looking for, Maxine took a quick glance at his cheek and noticed a fading welt along his jawline.

Their apologies began almost in unison. "Forgive—"

"Sorry—"

"Me."

After a long moment of silence, Dane said, "My behavior toward you was inexcusable. I hope I did not hurt you too much." Then he brushed his finger across her swollen lip.

Maxine shivered. Awash with pleasure, she looked up at him and said, "I'm fine. I just hope you ain't gonna hold—"

"Aren't going to hold," he said softly.

"I'm sorry. I hope you aren't too mad about me popping you across the jaw. I really am trying to do better with my temper."

"As am I." Dane rubbed his cheek and grinned. "But perhaps I had that one coming."

"Oh, no—never. You're just trying to help me, to help my family. I know that now, and I promise to behave from now on. Where's all them—*those*—dandies I'm suppose to set aflutter?"

If his heart hadn't constricted at the same moment, Dane would have laughed at the words. Instead, he took a deep breath and glanced around the room. He didn't want to introduce her to the neighbors. He didn't want them to even lay eyes on her. What Dane wanted, crazy as the idea might be, was to put her in a glass case where only he could see and visit her.

Sensing his reluctance, Maxine sighed heavily. "It's not going to work, is it? All the baths and English lessons in the world won't change the fact that I'm just not good enough for your friends."

"Oh, but you're so wrong—they will be honored to make your acquaintance." Dane caught her hands with his, bringing her fingertips to his mouth for a kiss, then lingered a long moment before he finally got hold of himself and let them go.

Dreamy-eyed and stunned, Maxine gazed up at him. Spanish guitars began strumming softly in the background, and the room seemed to spin around her. For a split second, she thought she'd never been happier in her life. Then a shadow seemed to pass over her. She tensed and whipped her head around to see the source of that danger. She found it over by the punch bowl: Caroline was staring at her, her expression narrow, sharp, her brow bunched, shading her eyes. Maxine shuddered and then ducked under Dane's arm and began to back away from him.

"Where are you going?" he asked, turning toward her.

"I, ah, thought I was supposed to meet some of your

rich friends. How am I going to do that if I stay in this corner?"

Although he was less than enthusiastic, Dane offered his elbow. "How, indeed? Allow me to begin your introduction into society, Miss McKain."

But Maxine hesitated. She could still feel Caroline's eyes on her. She glanced around, looking for help, a friendly face, anything or anyone who might get her out of this tangle. Her gaze fell on a gentleman at the opposite end of the room who was engaged in animated conversation with two other men. She blinked, trying to focus her eyes, but the picture still remained the same.

All color drained from Maxine's face, and her breath caught in her throat as she fixed her gaze on the man's hands, on the objects he was showing the others. Sheer panic blotted out everything but that sight. Dane, Caroline, and even the enormous room and all its guests, were blurred images, watery mirages through which she could easily pass.

Maxine advanced across the room, calling to the stranger as she moved, *"Hey!* Hey, you! Where'd you get them nuggets?"

Maxine was shaking an angry fist in the air when the man finally understood that she was talking to him. Startled, he lurched, tripped on an Indian rug, and crashed backward to the floor.

With only her father's whereabouts in mind, the very preservation of her family in her heart, Maxine bore down on him. When she reached the fallen man, she dispensed with reason and allowed impulse, fear, and instinct to guide her.

With no thoughts of Dane or his guests, Maxine leapt on the man while he lay stunned on the tiles and straddled his chest. Then she grabbed the collar of his shirt with both hands.

Jerking his head up off the floor, she demanded, "What have you done to my pa?"

13

"*Maxine!*"

Oblivious to everything, including the sound of her own name, Maxine's finger's slipped, and the man's head dropped to the floor with a thud. Renewing her grip on his collar, tearing the material in the process, she jerked him back off the tiles.

Her dark eyes sparkling with cinnamon flares, she threatened, "You'd best tell me and tell me *now!* What have you done with my pa?"

"Maxine," Dane implored, "for the love of God, let him go!"

Hands tore at her, dragging her up and away from the man, but she hung onto the collar of his shirt with the tenacity of a mink. Then, to a background accompaniment of Spanish guitars and shrieking fabric, Dane finally pulled her free of the man and stood her on her feet.

Panting, her gaze and attention riveted on the

stranger, Maxine was barely aware of what was happening. All she could think of was her father—and the fact that he was probably dead.

"Answer me!" she demanded, watching as the man struggled to his feet. "Why won't you answer me?"

"Maxine!" Dane gripped her shoulders and shook her hard until she finally looked up at him. "What is wrong with you?"

"The nuggets," she cried, her eyes clouding with tears. "He's got our lucky nuggets! Pa would never have given them to him, or even wagered them. He musta stole them! And to get them, he must have killed my pa!"

"*Christo.*" Keeping a firm grip on Maxine, Dane turned to the startled man. He was standing nearby, brushing himself off. "Forgive Maxine her poor manners, but she is . . . a little impulsive. Please be so kind as to tell her where you got the nuggets she is talking about."

Governor John Weller cleared his throat, shaking his head at the same time, setting off a chain reaction of jiggling jowls. Rubbing the back of his head, he said, "That's some welcoming committee you've got yourself, Don Francisco. Some little committee, indeed."

"Just answer the question!" Maxine blurted out, lunging toward the man.

Dane jerked her back into the circle of arms, squeezing her shoulders to the bone as he narrowed his gaze and said, "Do not open your mouth again unless I ask you to, *comprende?*"

Her frantic gaze darted to the governor and then

back to Dane. Maxine ground her teeth and gave him a terse nod.

The governor, more curious than shaken, asked, "Is this one of your neighbors, Don Francisco, or just a small hurricane passing through?"

Dane cleared his throat, but before he could form an answer, he noticed that Caroline had moved up close, several friends in tow, and stood just a few feet away. Studiously avoiding her gaze, he quietly explained Maxine the fastest, and most succinct way he could. "Miss McKain and her family are guests of mine, as you are. Because of that, I would appreciate it if you would tell her where you found those nuggets, or who you got them from as quickly as possible. We are drawing a crowd."

Weller shrugged. "A friend up in Los Angeles gave them to me. They came with what is usually a very entertaining story—until today, that is."

"And that story would be?" Dane encouraged, only half listening as he watched the size of the curious audience grow.

Weller went on. "My friend was duped by a confidence man a few years back. Took him for a couple thousand dollars, then left him in the desert to die, all because of these black gold nuggets. Who knows— maybe the fellow is your . . . *guest's* father, I wouldn't know. I never met the man."

Dane groaned, sure that he knew who the confidence man was. "Did your friend mention this man's name?"

Weller nodded, his gaze flickering between Dane and Maxine. "Said his name was Pegleg Smith."

Maxine gasped. Her voice squeaked like a rusty ore cart as she said, "Pegleg? Your friend got tricked by Pegleg?"

Frowning at Maxine, still rubbing the back of his head, Weller directed his words to Dane. "I believe that's what I just said, isn't it? Is Pegleg her father?"

"No," Maxine answered quickly, "ah, he ain't—isn't." Mortified, feeling dumber than ten lumps of coal and just about as wanted on this sultry afternoon, she quietly added, "Sorry if I hurt you any."

Weller adjusted his jacket around the neck of his collarless shirt. "And I guess you should be. I've never seen a lady come flying at a person like that. For a minute," he added, chuckling at the memory, "I thought I was being attacked by Indians."

Several guests joined in with the governor's robust laughter, and through the din, Maxine strained to make herself heard. "I said I'm sorry. I didn't mean for it to happen—I just made a little mistake."

Then she made another. She looked up into Dane's ice blue eyes. Never in all her life had she seen such blazing fury, such cold rage, in another's expression. Her mouth dropped open, and her mind went blank. Should she run away? Try again to apologize, or gag herself with the man's collar? Realizing then that she still clutched the shredded cloth in her hand, Maxine let it slip through her fingers onto the floor.

Dane noticed the gesture, glanced into Maxine's eyes, and saw her shame. What had ever made him think that he could take a woman as wild and free as Maxine and tame her so easily—in five days, no less? He'd been crazy to think it might work, a fool to even try it. Now look what he'd done. His guests were shocked, laughing at him behind his back, and there was the damage he'd caused to Maxine as well. Her sense of humiliation must know no bounds.

So angry with himself he could hardly talk, Dane turned to the governor and said, in a clipped, dry monotone, "Please excuse us for a moment. I will return and see to your comfort after I attend to Miss McKain."

Then he spun her around, unintentionally pointing her in a path which left her facing Caroline, and gripped her firmly by the elbow. As he guided her along the way, he whispered into her ear, "For once in your life, Maxine, please do as you're told. Do not fight me—just go where I point you and don't say another word."

Criticism or censure usually provoked her, but Maxine struggled against the urge to vindicate herself and clamped her lips together as he suggested. When she passed by Caroline, with her cheeks flaming and heart pounding, she looked to the lady for reassurance. But what she got was a look of pity. She could have taken anything from Caroline—a scowl, a frown, even laughter, or Dane's obvious displeasure—anything but pity.

Angry and humiliated, Maxine jerked out of Dane's grasp and tried to flee. He caught her and whispered harshly, "What did I just ask of you? Can you *never* listen to those who try to help you?"

The matriarch of the respected Estudillo family walked by them at that moment, paused and studied them under a furrowed brow, and then clucked and continued on her way.

His jaw rigid, his voice harsher, louder, he said, "We are making a spectacle of ourselves. Is it too much to ask that you please come quietly with me? Haven't you been embarrassed enough?" Without waiting for a reply, he tightened his grip on her arm and resumed guiding her toward the stairway leading to the bedroom wing.

Maxine allowed herself to be dragged up the stairs and away from the guests. A moment later, he kicked open her bedroom door and pushed her into the room.

Still too angry with himself for gentle conversation, he said, "I want you to stay in here until I come for you, *comprende?*"

Maxine found her voice, "B-but what about the party?"

"I think you have suffered enough for one day. I suspect the governor feels the same way."

"The governor?" she asked, horror wriggling up her spine. "W-what's he got to do with your party?"

"Since you sat on him? Probably not much."

Maxine staggered backwards until the backs of her legs hit the edge of her bed. Falling onto it, she cried, "I—I sat on a ... a *governor?*"

"The governor of California to be precise." Dane turned on his heel. "Now, if you'll excuse me, I think I'll go see if he's decided to allow Rancho Cordoba to remain in the state."

When he got to the door, he turned back to Maxine, searching for some way to console her. She looked shocked, dazed. It would be better to have this conversation later, when they both had a firm grip on themselves.

Trying to soften the hard edge in his voice, he said, "I have never been more serious than I am at this moment. Do not come back downstairs, *Rojita*. We will talk later, but for now, I forbid you to leave this room. *Comprende?*

On the verge of tears, Maxine chewed her bottom lip and nodded slowly. After Dane had stepped into the hall and closed the door behind him, she fell back against the pillows, pushing her face into the ticking to mute the sobs she could no longer repress. As she cried, the family motto rang in her ears: *You can put a hat and coat on a mule, but beneath all the finery, you've still got nothing but a stubborn old jackass.*

Dane hurried back downstairs, stopped briefly at a refreshment table, and went to look for the governor, carrying a glass of champagne in one hand and a fine Cuban cigar in the other.

Reaching the courtyard, his spirits and hopes for resuming the *fiesta* with little or nothing said about the incident dimmed considerably as he noticed Caroline standing beside John Weller. She was holding a cloth to his head and patting one of his beefy shoulders.

Offering the champagne as he walked up beside his most esteemed guest, Dane said, "Please accept my humble apologies for your unfortunate experience, Governor Weller. Maxine is not used to our kind of society. She's had a rather . . . hard life. I hope you can understand that and find it in your heart to forgive her."

"Oh, it really wasn't too bad a fall." Weller slapped

Dane's back with a big meaty hand, chuckling from low in his throat as he added, "In fact, I can't say it was an entirely unpleasant experience." Careful to keep his expression from Caroline, he shrugged his eyebrows for emphasis.

Dane's hands clenched, and every muscle in his body seemed to tense, but he managed to keep the sneer off his lips as he said, "Maxine is as much my guest as you are. She's been quite shaken by this entire episode. I only hope you've come through it less distressed."

Caroline shifted her attention from the governor to Dane and saw the look she'd been dreading. It was obvious to her now that he had fallen in love with Maxine McKain. While she wasn't particularly surprised, or even defeated by a battle which had never really begun, Caroline couldn't help but feel a stab of disappointment.

Trying to keep those emotions out of her voice, she said, "Shall I go see to her, Dane? Maxine and I have become somewhat friendly. Maybe another woman's council will help."

He didn't think long about the suggestion. If Maxine was as upset as she had a right to be, heaven only knew what she might *say* or do to anyone who burst in on her now. Shaking his head, Dane said, "I appreciate the offer, but I think Maxine is best left to her own devices for the time being. Perhaps Governor Weller would appreciate some more of your excellent nursing skills."

Caroline gave Dane a long, pointed look, smiled her brightest smile, and turned to the governor. "I'd be more than happy to get another cool cloth for your head." As she spoke, she ran her gloved fingers across his balding pate. "I think we'd better—you've got quite a nasty lump."

Dane watched only long enough for Caroline to link her arm through the governor's. Then he turned and headed for the refreshment table, where he poured himself a large brandy. He was listening to the strumming guitars, picking up bits and pieces of conversations all around him centering on the topic of the day—cattle rustlers and border bandits—when he noticed his mother strolling up the hallway which led to the back of the house.

Raising his glass as she approached, he said, "*Salud!*" Then he downed the drink in one long swallow.

"Son." Margaret lightly touched his arm and then leaned in and spoke in hushed tones. "I'm glad you're alone. I'd like to speak to you about some disturbing things I just learned. Can you spare me a minute?"

"Of course." He could spare her the entire rest of the party if she wanted. Anything to keep him from facing his guests. After refilling his brandy glass, Dane led her to a quiet corner. "What troubles you?"

"One of my friends from town, Marianne, whose husband is a member of the San Diego Board of Trustees, says she heard that bandits were somehow involved in Frank's death, that it was no accident. Could that be true?"

Dane thoughtfully sipped his liqueur. He'd never lied to his mother, and he wasn't going to do so now. Softening what at this point was only hearsay, he said, "Some of the *vaqueros* seem to think so, but they cannot be sure. It may make you feel better to know that the Estudillos and myself have arranged a meeting with the board, so that we might discuss this bandit problem. Perhaps once we unite, we can get at the truth."

Margaret wrung her hands. "They frighten me, these bandits. They stop at nothing—perhaps even murder— to destroy us and take what is ours."

Dane nodded, troubled by the steady depletion of cattle and horses from the border ranges, by the fact that between his rancho and the neighboring Otay Rancho, they had lost at least three thousand head of cattle to rustlers since Frank's death. He finished his drink and draped a comforting arm across his mother's shoulders. "Do not worry so. That is my job now."

Margaret leaned her forehead against her son's broad chest. "My only worries now are for your safety. After what happened to Frank, just the thought of you out on the range—"

"Do not worry, *Madre*. I am here now, and here I shall stay."

Catalina, hurrying toward them on the way to the kitchen, stopped and inquired, "Excuse me, Don Francisco, but do you wish for me to take a tray of food to Señorita Maxine?"

Watching his mother out of the corner of his eye, Dane brushed the servant off. "That's very thoughtful of you, Catalina. I'm sure she'd like that."

After the girl had scurried away, Margaret stepped out of her son's embrace. Her slender eyebrows raised suspiciously, she asked, "Has Maxine taken to her room?"

Glancing at his empty glass, wishing he'd brought the entire bottle with him, Dane sighed. "Yes, she has."

"Oh, goodness—did she take ill? Perhaps all the rich food and excitement didn't agree with her. I'll just go see to her."

Dane reached out, blocking his mother's path. "No. I think it's best if we leave her to herself."

"But Dane, that's not very—"

"She's had a little trouble." His mother's attention captured, Dane leaned against the wall. She would hear about it sooner or later, he reasoned. She might as well hear it from him while the facts were still fresh and untainted by gossip. He began the story quickly, and when he finished, his proper mother's mouth was agape.

"She actually *sat* on the governor?" Margaret said, baffled. "Straddled him, you say?"

"Like she was riding a runaway pony. Ripped the collar right off his shirt, too."

Margaret's laughter bubbled out of her, catching Dane with its effervescence. Struggling to keep his expression grim, he said, "It was not particularly amusing at the time, I can assure you of that."

"Oh, but Dane—the sight, it must have been . . ." She began laughing again, picturing not the incident, but the look that must have been on her son's face, the complete horror he must have felt.

Misunderstanding, he took umbrage at her response. "It is not so difficult to understand. Maxine thought her father had been injured, perhaps even murdered. Dicey and that brother of hers are all she has to call her own—all she's ever had, from what I've learned about the McKains. The thought of losing a member of her family must have terrified her."

Hearing the edge in his tone and noticing the suddenly defensive stance he took, Margaret had to hide a knowing grin as she remembered the scene she'd witnessed in the courtyard earlier. "I still don't understand. How could she be so upset over a couple of nuggets? Miners sell their gold every day, and from what I've seen of Dicey, it's just as likely he gambled them away."

Dane shook his head, adamant. "He wouldn't have wagered these. The—" Dane cut himself off, wondering where his mind had gone. He'd almost said, "Them's the lucky ones." Regrouping, he explained, "Those are the McKains' lucky nuggets. They symbolize some kind of lifeline, a bond that keeps them together. I honestly believe each of them would rather part with their life than give up those nuggets."

Smiling warmly, Margaret said, "It sounds as if you're finally learning to see people—Maxine, in particular—for what they are, not what you want them to be."

Dane drove his hands into his pockets. Is that what he'd been doing? Driving Maxine for more selfish than charitable reasons? Perhaps his mother had a point: His efforts to change Maxine had not necessarily been for her own good, but more to meet his own standards of what a woman should be. Was that really so wrong?

Margaret brushed her fingers across his arm, whispering, "Want to know what I think? I think Maxine touches you more than you know, more than you care to admit."

She was reading him again, glimpsing into his personal diary before he'd even had a chance to study it himself. Dane abruptly changed the subject.

"We should be tending our guests. At least one—"

"Don Francisco?" Catalina cried, cutting him off as she scrambled down the stairs, "Don Francisco?"

Annoyed by such an overt breech in protocol, Dane wheeled around and prepared to chastise the servant for interrupting his conversation. By then, Catalina was upon him, still chattering.

"It is Señorita Maxine," she said breathlessly. "She is not in her room."

Alarmed, Dane glanced toward the top of the stairs. "Perhaps she has gone to her father's room."

Catalina shook her dark head. "No. I have checked all the bedrooms. Señorita Maxine is nowhere."

"Impossible!" Dane had been in view of the stairs since he'd left her. She had not come down. "She must be there." Deciding to have a look for himself, he turned back to his mother. "See that our guests are comfortable. I'm going to check on Maxine."

He started for the bedroom wing, taking the stairs two and even three at a time in his haste to find her. When he got to her room, Maxine was nowhere in sight, and yet there were few hiding places. Furnished much like the rest of the house, this guest room was sparse, with only a heavy wooden bed, utility table, and bed stand to decorate it. Maxine's precious valise sat open on a spindle-back chair. There was no closet, and no piece of furniture large enough to contain a fully grown woman.

Dane crossed over to the only possible hiding place

in the room—the four-poster bed—dropped to his knees, and looked beneath it. Only a thin layer of dust met his gaze.

"Maxine?" he whispered, even though he knew only he could hear the name. "Where the devil have you gone?"

Climbing back to his feet, Dane spotted a bit of color on an area rug near the window. He approached it, his heartbeat accelerating as the object took shape. When he recognized it, he came to a halt and drew in a sharp breath. Lying between his boots, as pitiful as a broken doll, lay a single yellow rose, its dried petals and leaves shattered, fractured as if someone had ground the heel of a shoe against them.

"Oh, Maxine," he groaned, feeling a twinge of guilt as he gripped the windowsill and looked out on his property. "Where have you gone?"

Dane was considering the possibility that she might have climbed down the trellis and rejoined his *vaqueros* in their poker game when he picked up some movement in the distance. Narrowing his gaze to focus on the object, he could see that a small dust storm was traveling at the approximate clip of a galloping horse, and that it was heading steadily south like a great puffy tumbleweed.

If that dust storm contained Maxine, and Dane suddenly had every reason to believe that it did, she was headed straight for Mexico. For the border, and the bandits.

14

Maxine scooped a handful of water from the small stream and began to wash the blood and dirt from her scraped elbow. Glancing down the road at Rocio's rapidly disappearing rump, she hollered, "Coward!" Then she resumed her doctoring, checking first to make sure that the rattler which had spooked the mare had slithered off to its den.

Maxine was alone, more alone than she could ever remember being. Angry at herself for her indiscretion with the governor, and at Rocio for running off without her, she grabbed a handful of pebbles and hurled them into the slow-moving stream. When they hit, pellets of muddy water exploded as if blasted from a shotgun, spraying her face and the bodice of her dress. Would nothing go right for her this day? What would she do now?

She knew her impulsive leap to freedom had been a foolish move. She'd run away from Dane, from his proper and very offended guests, and, most of all, from herself. Now it was too late to rectify it, and she was lost.

She'd planned to ride south, until she intercepted the army mail route, and then head west to San Diego and the shelter of her father's arms. Could she have passed the road in her haste, somehow missing the deep east-to-west ruts? Or was it just a mile or two down the road from where she was now?

Dane had told her his rancho was four miles from the Mexican border. She knew the Army route couldn't be much more than another four or five miles once she crossed the border, but she couldn't tell exactly how far she had traveled. Was she closer to San Diego or Rancho Cordoba? Of course it didn't make any difference now where the mail route might be, or how far she'd traveled from Dane's home. She couldn't go anywhere without a horse or a decent pair of boots.

A rare hint of fear tickled Maxine's spine as she looked down at her new shoes, her first honest-to-God pair of ladies' boots. They were made of soft white kid, lined in cotton, and heelless, which made them very comfortable—as long as she was inside on the polished tile floors of Rancho Cordoba. Out here in this rocky arroyo, she might as well have been barefoot, for all the protection they provided.

Maxine glanced at her dress, which she hadn't been able to get out of without assistance, that fancy, frothy gown with yards and yards of material. Then she realized she didn't have so much as a hat to cover her head or hide her hair and the fact that she was a woman.

She'd never been in such a predicament, a woman alone and decidedly vulnerable.

Fighting off panic, she looked around at the country-side, toward the canyons and the grayish green vegetation saved from blandness only by several scattered patches of wild mustard. God, how she missed the lush, rolling slopes and contrasting greens of the eldorado country, the huge aromatic redwoods and thick fragrant pines deep in the Sierra Nevada Mountains. She'd know where to hide and how to survive if she were back there. Of course, if that were the case, she wouldn't be in this mess, and she wouldn't have to worry about finding a hiding place to begin with.

A tear ran down her cheek, veering into the corner of her mouth. Never before—not when Emaline Noland had dumped her and Max on their surprised father, not when the family had nearly died in the desert, and not even when she saw other young women her own age with husbands and children—had Maxine McKain ever felt so much as a sliver of self-pity. She almost laughed through her tears as she remembered the day a self-righteous minister's wife had wagged a stern finger in Dicey's face, lecturing him about dragging his two darling twins through mining town after mining town.

"Just pitiful!" the old biddy had exclaimed. "These babes belong in an orphanage where some decent family can claim them."

The woman had reached out, as if to grab Max by the hand, but Maxine had rushed up between her father and the woman, pushed her brother aside, and shaken her fist at the do-gooder as she shouted, "We ain't pitiful and we ain't going to no orphanage! Mostly, we're lucky is what we are!" Then she'd banged her foot on the ground, displaying her shiny new leather footgear. "Just take a look at them boots—brand new, they are, and Max got a pair just like 'em! Ain't nothing for you to pity about us McKains—we ain't pitiful!"

Maybe not then, she thought with a heavy sigh, but she sure as hell was today. What was wrong with her? Back at the rancho, when she'd seen the lucky nuggets, common sense had deserted her faster than her mother had the day she'd caught that stage. Why hadn't she simply questioned the governor, spoken to him in a calm ladylike manner—the way Dane's mother had instructed her—instead of squashing him flat and jumping him as if he were a horse she was breaking in. Even she was appalled at the memory, and if Maxine was appalled, Dane's opinion had to be something she couldn't bear to contemplate.

Her heart seemed to twist in her breast when she thought of how disappointed Dane must be. She'd fallen in love with him, she suddenly knew above all else. She'd fallen for that Spaniard as sure as a full house beat a flush. And all she could possibly hope to get out of that love was this sick-to-her-stomach, heart-aching numbness brought on by just the thought of him.

She had the love-sick, pure and simple. The no-cure-for-it-love-sickness. The trouble was that neither that nor self-pity would help get her out of this mess.

Maxine snapped to her feet and assessed her situation. She took a deep breath—shallow, actually, due to the damnable corset—and pushed her long, loose hair back over her shoulders. The beautiful coif that Caroline had worked so hard on had been jarred loose during the ride, and somewhere back on the trail, the silver comb had escaped as well. Shaking off a pang of guilt over losing the expensive hair ornament, Maxine braced herself for a very long and painful walk.

Even though she knew her only real option was to head back to the rancho and hope to run across someone looking for her on the way, Maxine glanced both north and south as if she were just now making the decision. On the pass south, her gaze picked up a group of men, around a dozen riders, heading due east, following, she supposed, the Army mail route she hadn't quite gotten to.

Had they seen her? Her survival instincts taking over, Maxine dropped to the ground as if she'd been shot. Watching the cloud of dust accompanying the men, she waited until it was out of sight before she scrambled back to her feet and made a dash down the road to the north, toward Rancho Cordoba. As she ran, she searched the small valleys between the foothills for a place in which to hide in case she'd been spotted, but in this terrain, she couldn't find a bush to duck behind, much less a cave or fissure in the mountainside. She was dressed in white, puffed out with more petticoats than she'd ever seen, quite simply a walking target for even the most incompetent gunman.

Her only chance was that she hadn't been spotted, but even that hope was dashed as she heard a group of riders approaching from behind. Guessing that her best defense would be composure, Maxine lifted her chin and stepped out into the road. The horsemen stopped a few feet from her, except for one, who continued riding toward her on a big, lathered buckskin stallion.

Making a fast appraisal of the men, she sensed hunger and desperation about them. It was a look she recognized instantly, but never before had it been directed at her. Struggling to remain calm on her trembling legs, Maxine swallowed her fear as the man drew near. With a terse smile she said, "Good afternoon."

"*Buenos dias, Señorita.* Are you lost?"

Maxine gave him a sideways look, ignoring the arrogance in his expression. "No, I know exactly where I'm going." Then she began to walk down the road, her stride forced but unhurried.

The man kicked the horse's sides, urging it to lope on by until he was several paces in front of Maxine, then he brought the animal to a skidding halt sideways across the road. After climbing down off the oversized saddle, he circled his mount and propped himself lazily against the stallion's haunches as he waited for her to reach him.

Maxine slowed her steps, knowing she was trapped between the riders behind and the man directly in her path. Fighting panic, she came to a stop and decided to continue with her brave, unruffled facade.

"Please move your horse, sir—you're blocking my way."

The man, close enough now for her to get a good look at his features, threw back his head and laughed. His hat, wide of brim and low of crown, was weather beaten and held in place by a chin strap that fit beneath the ends of his thick, drooping mustache. As he laughed, Maxine could see the sunlight glinting off several gold crowns in his mouth, and when he brought his head forward again, she saw the hatred belying that laughter in his small black eyes.

Discarding all pretenses of his previous good humor, he approached her, stalking her as if she were prey. "*Hola, Señorita,*" he said, tipping that hat, revealing a large red kerchief bound about his head. "What a nice surprise you are to these tired eyes."

"Please move out of my way," she said, still working to appear undaunted, fearless. "My horse and my friend are waiting just up the road for me. I should get back to them before they start to worry and come looking for me."

"A horse—*and* a friend?" He raised his bushy black brows and then laughed and spun around on his heel.

Drawn by the jingle of his rusty spurs, Maxine glanced down to the ground and kept her gaze there as she tried to think of what to do next. She didn't have long to wait. Those spurs, and the leather buckskin shoes they were attached to, began to retreat. Looking up, Maxine watched as he mounted his horse. Then, laughing to himself, he began riding up the trail toward Rancho Cordoba.

"I think you are lying, Señorita," he called over his shoulder, "but if you are not, I will make sure your friend does not worry about you."

Maxine shot an uneasy glance behind her and discovered that the men were still there, slouching in their saddles, watching her with hooded eyes, waiting like buzzards to swoop down on her. Her panic growing, Maxine labored to think of a plan, but a surge of adrenalin crippled reasoning powers. Several minutes later, when the man came galloping back down the road, she still had no idea if she would live to see another day.

"I bring bad news, Señorita," he said with a smug grin. "Your horse—she has disappeared. Your *amigo?* He has disappeared, also." He clucked his tongue and turned his attention to his men. He barked an order, "*Largense el campamento! Esperenme alli.*"

Maxine heard the horses moving behind her. She didn't need to turn around to know that the stranger had sent his men away, leaving her alone with him. When the riders were out of sight, he dismounted. Then, with an evil grin, he advanced on her.

In spite of her determination to appear undaunted, Maxine took a backward step. The outlaw was dressed in a torn, dirty white shirt and leather leggings, the dusty buckskin trousers beneath held up by a wide leather belt sporting a huge gun and holster. In addition to his clothing, the man wore a sneer, a perpetual snarl fueled by a hatred which, she suspected, had been forming over a period of time. What were her odds against such malevolence?

Gathering all her courage, she began to walk by him, brushing him aside as she said, "I really must be on my way. People are expecting me."

"*Perdona me,*" he growled, his sour breath assaulting her as he gripped her arm and dragged her close to him. "I said your *amigo* has left without you." Still holding her prisoner with one hand, he dragged the callused fingers of the other across her tear-stained cheek. "Perhaps you and your sweetheart had a fight, no? *Pobracita peliroja*— where do you come from? Where do you live, *gringa?*"

Taking as much time as she dared, Maxine quickly decided that because Dane's home was relatively close, the truth would best serve her purposes. "I am a guest at Rancho Cordoba."

"Ah?" This news seemed to impress him.

"Yes, and I'm afraid I have been gone for too long. They will be worried about me, so please let me pass."

He ignored her request and asked, "Are you a friend of the recent widow, Doña Caroline?"

"I, ah—no," she answered automatically. "I am a guest of Dane's—of Don Francisco's."

"*Dane?*" he exclaimed, losing his aloof tone. "Dane del Cordobes has returned?"

Maxine's gaze darted nervously from side to side as she fretted about whether she'd helped or hindered her cause with this information. Fighting to keep the desperation out of her voice, she said, "Yes. Dane has returned and I am his guest. Now, if you'll please—"

"Shut up, *gringa!*"

Startled by his horrid, vicious sneer, Maxine kept her silence and allowed him the next move.

"So you are Dane's *puta,*" he said with a thoughtful leer. "The other del Cordobes men always preferred *gringas.* I see the little brother is no different."

Maxine lifted her chin, very aware he'd called her a whore, but managed to keep her calm manner as she said, "I am Dane's guest, not his . . . woman."

"Of course you are," he said. "I have often thought of the del Cordobes men and their taste for *gringa* women and wondered about the fascination. Perhaps I should find out what I have been missing . . . no?"

Imagining the kind of trouble she would face next,

Maxine gave up the soft ladylike approach. Hoping to catch him by surprise, she tried to jerk her arm out of his grip, but he held fast.

"No, *gringa*—you will go nowhere until I am finished with you."

In the next moment, everything happened so fast that Maxine barely knew what happened. The bandit's free hand struck out, grabbing the front of her dress. Then, in one quick movement, he tore open the bodice.

"Hey!" she cried, glancing down to her exposed breasts. She jerked her head up and met his vicious laughing gaze with a fury of her own.

"You stinking son of a *bitch!* How *dare* you touch me like that, you *bastard!*"

The man was so stunned by her sudden change in manner that he stood frozen for a moment—long enough for Maxine to push him away and break into a run. She made a dash for his horse, launched herself onto the saddle, and kicked the animal's sides as hard as she could. It took off in a dead gallop but had only traveled a few yards up the arroyo when Maxine heard a shrill whistle cut through the air. The horse came to an abrupt halt, catapulting her over his head and onto the hard earth below.

Struggling back to her feet, wiping dirt from her face, Maxine worked to steady herself, but by the time she got her bearings it was too late. The man was upon her, twice as enraged as he'd been before, more determined than ever to have his way.

"*Puta!*" he screamed. "I will show you how Chubasco tames a no-good whore!"

Then he smashed his fist into her jaw, and she

thought her head had exploded. Coldness washed over her, as if she'd fallen into an abandoned mine shaft. Then she felt nothing.

In the barn at Rancho Cordoba, Dane was using every drop of his patience to try to elicit information from Max without alarming the young man.

"Did Maxine tell you anything at all about where she was going or why?"

Max, who was cinching Alazan's saddle, paused and scratched his head. "Maxie said to get Rocio."

"Yes." Dane's jaw was so tense he thought it might break. "You told me that. Where was she going?"

Finished with the saddle, Max circled the horse and stood watching as Dane slammed a rifle into the scabbard and looped his bullwhip around his shoulder. "Maxie had to go. She had to go *now*."

"That's it? She didn't say anything else?"

Max began to rock back and forth on his heels. "She had to go." Then he looked down at his feet and wrung his hands.

A feminine voice came from nowhere. "Maxine went to San Diego. She wanted to see her father."

Dane swung up onto the saddle, using one precious second of time to search out and discover Rosa peeking around the corner of a stall. "Are you sure?"

Mute again, Rosa nodded and ducked back inside the stall.

Directing the words at Max, Dane said, "If anybody asks, tell them I've gone after Maxine. And don't worry about her, Max—I'm sure she's all right."

Then he gave the order, and Alazan took off at a dead run. He rode hard until he reached the border crossing and then slowed just enough for Alazan to regain his wind before setting off for the Army mail route, the only clearly marked trail to San Diego that Maxine would have taken.

Less than a mile into Mexico, he saw Rocio racing toward him. Obeying his shouted order, the mare trotted up beside Alazan. "Easy, girl," he said, noting that the reins were still looped over Rocio's neck. Had Maxine been thrown? Or had she dismounted and inadvertently let Rocio get away from her?

Thinking back to Maxine's stubborn nature, her strong will and skillful handling of the horse, he chose to believe the latter. But if she had fallen off the mare, Dane imagined he would find her just around the bend, spitting and cursing.

His hopes were dashed another few miles down the road. Just before he reached the bend leading to the intersection, Dane heard a woman's cries—no, not cries, screams. Terrified, agonized screams.

"*Maxine?*" he yelled, bringing the horses to a skidding halt.

When the only answer was more screams, Dane kicked Alazan into a gallop and fit the grip of the bullwhip to his palm. As he rounded the mountainside, what he saw twisted his gut into a hard knot. A bandit was sprawled atop a mop of flaming red hair and white muslin, and his exposed backside told Dane exactly what was happening.

Consumed by a rage he'd never known, Dane leapt down off the stallion and unleashed the whip. It whistled through the air and struck its target with blinding speed, slicing a diagonal gash across the bandit's buttocks.

Chubasco screamed and stumbled to his feet, but as he groped for his trousers, the whip found its mark again, this time by carving a valley down the middle of his back. He cried out in pain as he wheeled around, one hand clutching his trousers, the other drawing his pistol.

Again the whip cracked, snatching the gun from Chubasco's hand, tearing flesh from his thumb as well. Falling to his knees in pain, the bandit drew his hands together like a tent, begging in a plaintive wail, "*Por favor*—enough!"

But as far as Dane was concerned, he hadn't even begun to mete out this animal's punishment. He bore down on the man, recoiling the whip, glimpsing at Maxine out of the corner of his eye as she stumbled to her feet, still screaming, hysterical. When he looked back at the bandit, Dane's face was contorted with rage. "Prepare to die!"

"*Amigo?*" Chubasco said, feigning surprise. "Dane del Cordobes, is that . . . you?"

Dane's arm froze in midair as he tried to sort his rage from this new confusion. Narrowing his still seething gaze, he stared at the man, recognizing that they had met, but unable to remember when or where.

Offering just the hint of a friendly smile, Chubasco said, "Remember me, *amigo?* Antonio Sanchez— Rancho del Sol?"

Distracted by Maxine's cries of distress, which were growing fainter, Dane's memory managed to supply him with a fast picture of his boyhood, of the days before the war between the United States and Mexico, before sides were taken and many family-owned ranchos were lost, or in some cases, stolen. The face he gazed on now, even though one cheek was marred by bloody scratches, was the same as he remembered from long ago. He lowered the whip to his side and quietly said, *"Chubasco?"*

"Si," he answered, moving slowly as he rose and adjusted his clothing. "It's your old *amigo,* Chubasco. The lady—she is a friend of yours? *Perdona me*—how could I know?"

His rage renewed, obliterating everything else, Dane grit his teeth and spat. "You knew all you needed to— that you were taking something which was not offered. For that, you will die." Again he cocked his arm, and again, it froze as Chubasco pointed out Maxine's retreat.

"You waste your time on me—I think it is your lady who needs your attention more than I do."

Dane quickly glanced around and saw that she was stumbling down the road, limping toward Alazan as if each step was agony. He spun back around and found Chubasco mounting his horse.

"Go after your woman," the bandit said. "You and I can settle our differences some other time, no?"

Caught between the urge to take a measure of revenge now and be done with it and the need to go to Maxine, to comfort her and somehow make things all right again, Dane hurled a wad of spittle toward the man. "Settle we will, Chubasco—make no mistake about that."

The bandit wheeled his horse around and narrowed his eyes. "You can be sure we will settle, *amigo*. No matter if it is my land or your woman, it hurts, doesn't it? It hurts deep in your gut to have something you love taken from you, to have it used for another's pleasure regardless of your wishes. *Comprende?*" Then he gave his horse a vicious jab with his spurs and galloped off.

His thoughts murderous but his heart breaking for Maxine, Dane turned on his heel and went after her. He caught up with her just after she passed Alazan. By this time, she was weaving, crying, babbling incoherently, but apparently dead set on getting away.

Dane reached for her, murmuring, "Maxine—Rojita, come here to me." He gathered her in his arms.

The minute he put his hands on her, she began screaming again. "No—*no!* I can't take any more— leave me alone—get away from me!" Between sobs, she kicked his shins, beating her unprotected toes against the leather of his boots.

Dane held fast as she struggled, whispering in her ear, "It's all right now, Rojita—he's gone. It's Dane. You are safe. Come to me, *querida*—let me hold you and keep you safe."

"He hurt me!" she screamed, hot tears flowing. "I didn't do nothing—*nothing!* Why'd he want to hurt me?"

Before he could offer his compassion, she collapsed against his chest, her sobs wrenching, the anguish in her voice almost more than he could bear. When Maxine's hysteria had eased to intermittent bouts of weeping, Dane gently nudged her away from his chest and examined her. Her jaw was swollen and blue from the tip of her chin to her earlobe, and below, her dress was torn, exposing her breasts.

Forcing himself to swallow his renewed rage, he whispered, "Raise your arms, Rojita. I'm going to cover you with my *poncho*."

Ashamed, and unable to look at him and read the disappointment she was sure to find in his expression, Maxine closed her eyes and obeyed. After she felt the garment drop over her head, she clamped her lips together and clasped her hands at her waist.

Unsure of how to proceed, Dane decided to get her out of the area before trying to get her story. Vermin like Chubasco didn't always travel alone. If he came back, he might return with help. He gently lifted Maxine and scooped her into his arms. She kept her eyes closed and her face buried against his chest, dampening his shirt with a continuous flow of tears as he walked back to Alazan. After catching the stallion's reins between his fingers, he walked a little further down the road to collect Rocio.

When he reached the mare, Dane set Maxine on her feet and cupped her face in his hands, forcing her to look up at him. "Rojita? Listen to me. I'm going to prepare the horses for the ride back. Can you stand by yourself for a minute?"

She looked up at him, blinking and wiping the seemingly endless flow of tears from her eyes.

"Can you stand alone?" he repeated.

Feeling listless and worthless, she gave him a miserable, anguished nod, then lowered her head again so he wouldn't have to see her shame.

Kissing her forehead, Dane whispered against her

damp skin, "I will try to make you as comfortable as possible." Thinking of how bruised and torn she might be, and hard-pressed to keep his rage in check at the very idea, Dane transferred the saddle from Alazan's wider back to Rocio's. Keeping the bullwhip coiled around his shoulder, he went back to Maxine. "I'm going to put you on Alazan just like you were sitting in a chair—*comprende?*"

She didn't understand the need for such an arrangement—it wasn't as if Chubasco had succeeded in raping her—but Maxine was as afraid to ask stupid questions as she was of the censure which was sure to come. Her voice barely audible through her soft sobs, she said, "Yes."

Gingerly, as if she were made of eggshells, Dane deposited her just past the stallion's neck, on the softest part of his back, then he swung up behind her. Gathering her body close to his, he said, "Lean on me, Rojita, balance yourself." When she complied, he tucked her head in the hollow beneath his chin, kissed the top of her head, and asked, "Are you comfortable?"

In the midst of a deep sob that surprised even her, she nodded. Why was he being so kind? She'd insulted and assaulted the governor of California, taken one of Dane's best horses without his permission, and then ridden off into a dangerous situation which had forced him to follow her, leaving his guests and the party behind. Why hadn't he lit into her yet?

"We'll go now," Dane said, cutting into her thoughts, "but we'll ride slow. If you need to stop or something is hurting you, don't hesitate to tell me."

He grabbed Rocio's reins and urged Alazan into a

smooth, easy walk. They hadn't moved more than a couple of yards before Maxine jerked her head up, smashing into Dane's chin. "Where are we going?"

"Home. Back to the rancho."

"*No!*" she cried out, struggling as if she meant to leap off Alazan's back.

Dane pulled the stallion to a halt. "Maxine! Hold still. What is wrong?"

"I can't go back there!" She looked up at him, her dark eyes pleading, her bottom lip trembling. "Please, *please,*" she begged, "don't make me go back there yet—I can't face them, not your guests, and Max—Max would go crazy if he saw me like this, and—oh, God— what if Pa's come back from town?"

Maxine thought of the others—mainly Caroline and Dane's mother—and of the questions they would ask about her reckless decision to run away. They would say it was her own fault she'd been assaulted, because of her stupid, impulsive behavior. She shuddered, ashamed and embarrassed by the idea of facing any of them. Her sobs renewed, Maxine buried her face in her hands.

Dane thought of objecting, but the basic truth of her words stopped him cold, and he understood. It was enough that she had to endure herself in such a state— she couldn't bear the idea of subjecting her family to her humiliation as well.

Stroking her loose, unruly hair, he whispered against it as he said, "All right. We'll take the long way home, around the back of the San Ysidro Mountains, and approach Rancho Cordoba from the east. Will that make you happy?"

Maxine lifted her head and nodded slowly. "That," she said between hiccups, "and a lake. I need a swim."

"You mean you want a bath? Before we go back to the rancho?"

Maxine sniffed and wiped the tears from her cheeks with her palms. Thinking of her torn, soiled dress, the grit on her legs, she said, "I—I just want to wash up."

"Of course." He was annoyed at himself for not thinking of her needs on his own. "I shall find you a pond or something."

Then, nudging Alazan back into action, he made a silent vow. He would find his Rojita a bath and help her repair her shredded dignity, and after that, he would hunt down the *hijo de puta* who had done this and find vengeance for her as well.

15

If Dane kissed her once, he kissed Maxine a thousand times during the ride. He kissed her hair, her forehead, her cheeks, and yes, even her lips, not with passion, but rather out of something so deep, so personal, he couldn't put a name to it. Whatever it was, until today, he'd been unaware he possessed the capacity for such feelings.

It took Dane just over an hour to guide the horses to the northeast corner of Rancho Cordoba. There, tucked away in the heavily shrubbed foothills of the San Ysidro Mountains, he relocated the secluded spring-fed pond he remembered from his youth. Even in the most abundant of years, when thousands of cattle roamed the rancho's boundaries, the generous creeks and overflowing banks of Otay Lake made this pond a rarely visited oasis by man or beast. Its pristine appearance today suggested that nothing had changed.

They dismounted, and at Maxine's request, Dane

helped her out of her dress and underpinnings, save for her knee-length chemise. Then, in order to give her some privacy, he left her at the edge of the water and turned his attention to the horses.

She'd been silent and completely withdrawn during the ride, and Dane had allowed her that much, convincing himself he'd followed the most gallant route. Now, as he led Alazan and Rocio to a spot in which to graze, he realized he might well have another Rosa on his hands if he didn't speak to her—and speak to her soon. But what to say, and how to say it?

That she'd been ravaged horribly and brutally would be difficult enough for him to address, but what about her mind? Had Chubasco penetrated her very soul when he used her body, and robbed her of that innocence as well? Dane thought back to her tears, the seemingly endless flow, and knew without a doubt she'd never before had cause to cry so long or so hard—in fact, as he considered her strength of character and her confidence, he was sure that not even the most insignificant of tears ever fell from her dark brown eyes.

When he returned to the pond, Maxine was bobbing near the center, her right hand clutching the knot she'd made of her hair and holding it fast against the top of her head. As she tried to maneuver in the water, her balance tenuous at best, she nearly slipped and fell several times.

Dane watched her awkward attempts at bathing for as long as he could. Then, painfully aware of the temptation but unable to do any less for her, he stripped down to his trousers and waded into the water.

"Let me help you, Rojita."

Maxine stiffened when she realized he was coming up behind her but said nothing when he slid his hand up her arm, gathered the mass of her hair, and pushed his own hat down over the top of her head to secure it.

Regaining her footing in the waist-deep water, Maxine kept a firm grip on the torn bodice of her chemise as she slowly turned to face him. She was amazed and deeply touched by his continued attentions. "Would you tell me why you're being so nice to me after the mess I've made of everything?"

Stunned as much by the incongruous question as by the irresistible sight of those big brown eyes peering out from beneath his hat, he said, "Do not think poorly of yourself for what's happened. If anyone is to blame, it is me."

Averting her eyes, Maxine backed deeper into the chilly water. "I figured you'd have turned loose on me by now, at least called me a few of your Spanish names for being so stupid as to run off like that."

"How can you honestly believe anything you did back at the rancho matters now? Do you imagine I care about anything at this moment except for you and your terrible ordeal?"

Up to her neck now, Maxine released the ragged edges of her chemise and allowed the waters to soothe her scraped skin. She was still too ashamed to look him in the eye, unable to understand what he was trying to say. "What I imagined was that sooner or later you'd light into me. Everything I've done since we got to your house is wrong or stupid, or, like today, both."

Dane reached her and slid what was meant to be a

reassuring arm across her shoulders. "I have pushed you too hard, tried to turn you into something you can never be. It was my mistake, not yours, that brought you to this. Try to forgive me."

Very aware of the intimate way he held her and the suggestion of affection, she rambled on. "But if I hadn't run off after making such a fool of myself, I wouldn't be in this mess, and you wouldn't be missing your welcome party. I—I know it probably doesn't mean much now, but I am sorry. I'm real sorry for all the trouble I caused you and your family."

His reservations and his needs no longer of any concern, Dane gathered her in his arms, pushed his hat up from her forehead until it cupped the back of her head, and pulled her close. A few loose strands of damp auburn hair clung to her shoulders, and her eyes, no longer tear-stained, held their usual cinnamon fire once again.

"Madre de dios," he said, his velvet voice rich with emotion. "It is I who apologizes to you; don't you understand that and know how deeply it pains me to see you in such misery?"

"Really?" she said, her breath caught in her throat. "Really and truly?"

"Really and truly," he confirmed, caressing her back, her tense shoulders.

She moaned at his ministrations, allowing herself these feelings, the luxury of experiencing his sensual touch, the gentle yet firm manipulation of his fingertips. Arching her neck and raising her shoulders in an exaggerated shrug, she sighed. "Oh, that feels so good. I swear since my troubles down the road, my body feels like it's been rolled end over end down a dried-up sluice, then dumped at the bottom with the tailings. I must be black and blue from one end to the other."

His pulse racing, his thoughts dark as they returned to what she must have endured, Dane tried to keep the anger out of his voice as he asked, "Is there any other way I can help you? What are your injuries?"

Maxine flexed the muscles in her arms and legs, then gave herself back to Dane's strong fingers as he continued to knead her knotted muscles. "My back is sore. I think that might have happened when I tried to steal the bandit's horse. It threw me—but then so did Rocio, now that I think of it."

Dane tried to ignore the way her silky skin felt beneath his fingertips. "I wouldn't have thought even Alazan could manage that—what happened?"

Fully relaxed now, Maxine let her head fall back and her gaze rest on Dane, on his mouth, as she grinned and said, "Thanks for the compliment. It wasn't Rocio's fault she tossed me, though, it was mine. I ran her right over a coiled-up rattlesnake. Never even saw it, but she did."

"Where does it hurt?" he asked, running his fingers down her spine.

"There," she said, stopping him, wishing he would go on. "Anyway, I think that's when I hurt my back, but I can't remember. After I met up with the bandit, he punched me in the jaw. See?" She angled her chin, giving him a clear view.

"Yes, Rojita," he whispered, afraid to raise his voice any louder, no longer sure he could control the anger in it. "I saw the bruise there as well as the scratches on your breast."

"Oh, yeah—those." She raised up out of the water, checking the marks, forgetting herself and exposing her rigid nipples for a moment. When she realized what she'd done, Maxine glanced shyly at Dane, who'd averted his gaze, then sank back down in the pond and finished her story.

"The dirty bast—the bandit scratched me with his fingernails when he ripped my dress. After he knocked me out, I don't know what happened for sure but I guess he must have dragged me out of the road because my legs are all scraped up. Next thing I knew, I woke up and he . . . well, he was poking at me, trying to hurt me."

"I know, Rojita," Dane cut in, unable to hear anymore. "He will pay for what he's done to you, for what he cost you. You have my word on it."

"He's already paid some—as much as I could manage anyway. Right after I woke up, I guess about the time you came along, I got a pretty good hold on his gizzard and hurt his throat some." For the first time since her ordeal, she laughed. "I think you have some idea about what strong legs I have. I kicked him pretty hard, so who knows? I might have gotten away by myself."

Smiling in spite of the subject, Dane warmed, admiring her resiliency. Borrowing a McKain expression, he said, "From what little I saw of him, I'd say you done him pretty good."

Relaxing, her body forgot its aches and pains, and Maxine no longer concerned herself with Dane's reprisals or disappointments. Instead, she began to concentrate only on him and his sensual touch. "I remember you told me that the goings-on between men and women could be complicated. Is what happened to me what you were talking about? Did you mean that sometimes this lovemaking business is hurtful?"

The corner of Dane's mouth twitched, and his jaw was as unyielding as one of his wooden stirrups, but he managed to keep his tone soft as he said, "What Chubasco did to you has nothing to do with lovemaking, Rojita. He is filled with hatred, and hatred cannot see your innocence or beauty. Hatred is blind."

Dane traced a gentle fingertip across her sweeping brows, down along her broad cheek, and allowed his gaze to linger a long moment on her exquisitely bold features before he added, "Some men, animals like Chubasco, confuse desire with hatred. What this man took from you had nothing to do with desire. The honest passion between a man and a woman should never cause pain, only pleasure."

Even though daylight was fading and the sky was turning an almost unnatural shade of pink, Maxine could swear the morning sun was rising inside of her. His words healed her the way no balm ever could. She cast off the final pallor of regret, shunned her remorse, and beamed up at Dane, really looking at him for the first time since he'd come to her aid.

That's when she realized that he was at least half-naked. His powerful chest, slick and wet, sporting just an angel wing of coarse black hair above each nipple, was the most beautifully erotic sight she'd ever seen. Maxine slid her hands up along his sculpted back and then slithered her fingers along his ribs until they came to rest at his collarbone.

The gesture took Dane by surprise. He staggered backward, clutching Maxine to his chest, and slipped on the bottom of the pond. He somehow regained his balance before he could fall. As he steadied himself, he realized Maxine was no longer up to her neck in the pond, but up to her waist—and that now he could not only feel her sweet, upturned breasts pressed against his chest, but see them as well.

Drawing in a ragged breath, he suggested, "If you are done bathing, I think we should go. It is getting late and it will be dangerous for us to travel in the dark."

"No, please, not yet." Nestling her head in the hollow between his shoulder and neck, she pressed her lips against his throat and said, "I want to know more about the difference between hatred and passion."

"Maxine . . . please—we must go."

"Soon," she whispered as she molded herself to him, lightly rubbing her breasts against his bronzed skin, amazed at the impulses, the shocking signals the motion sent to every part of her body. Then Maxine became aware of Dane below the water-line, of the heat generating between them. Gripped with an intensity, a need she'd never known before, she hooked one of her legs behind his knee and instinctively nudged against his thigh.

Dane's mind reeled with her words and suggestive gestures. He reached down and filled his hands with her nude bottom. She moaned, and squirmed against him, and Dane lifted her, whispering beseechingly,

"Please, Rojita—we must go. I cannot take this any longer. I—I am only human."

"But how can we go now?" she gasped, barely able to hear her own voice over the frantic beat of her heart, the sound of her pulse roaring like waterfalls in her ears. "You told me once I was smart enough to know when a man wants me—you want me now, Dane. I know you do."

"*Christo*, Maxine." His melodic voice was reduced to a strangled, garbled rasp as he tried to reason with her. "Do you hear what you are saying? Do you know what you are doing to me—what you are asking of me?"

"I—I think so," she stammered, not quite as sure as she'd been a moment ago. "I was thinking you wanted to do lovemaking. I thought you desired me; I know I desire you. Is it so very wrong to want you the way I do?"

"Oh, Maxine." Dane groaned, his sanity dangling by one silken strand of her scarlet hair. "I would have thought after your terrible experience this afternoon, the last thing you would want is me. How can I possibly—"

"How can you not?" she cut in, daring to hope that he only meant to spare her feelings, not deny his. "If what happened to me today was my last, my only memory of part of what goes on between a man and a woman, I don't think I can stand it. Only you, Dane, only you can give something I'll live on forever." She brought her hands to his face and stroked his tense jaw as she made her final plea. "If you care about me at all, how can you not?"

He thought of objecting, of trying to convince her that someday another man, one who would offer to share her life as well as her body, would replace those dreadful memories, but the thought sickened him almost as much as the sight of coming upon her and Chubasco had. Lifting her from the water, pulling her close, he stared into her eyes, searching their sable depths, and whispered, "Are you sure you can live with this? What of regrets?"

Maxine didn't even have to think about it. She arched her neck, melting against him in spite of the chilled water, and breathed from deep in her throat, "Yes, oh yes, Dane. My only regrets will come from the sadness I'll have if you don't give me this moment."

Dane's breathing was a low rumble deep in his throat. Unable to deny her—or himself—any longer, he slid his mouth across hers with a tenderness that surprised even him. Careful not to hurt her, slowly, so she wouldn't sense so much as a hint of violence, Dane caressed her, soothing her with his lips, gently parting hers with his tongue.

Maxine loved the sensations, the marvelous texture of his chest brushing against her breasts, his mouth more tender, more giving than it had ever been before, but it wasn't nearly enough. Her lips still clamped to his, again she hooked her leg around him, this time higher on his thigh, then shimmied up his body until they were hip to hip.

Startled, Dane tore his lips from hers. "What are you doing, Rojita?"

"I—I don't really know."

"Then why don't you relax and let me show you?" At her unexpectedly shy nod, he scooped her into his arms. The movement sent his fine vicuña hat into the pond, and her hair tumbled down over both their shoulders. Aware of the mishap but unconcerned, Dane kept his attention, and his heated gaze, on Maxine. When he reached the small incline where their clothing was scattered, he set Maxine on her feet, grabbed his *poncho,* and spread it to accommodate them. Then he deposited her in the center and lay down beside her.

"You are cold," he said, noting the tiny bumps on her forearms, the delicate hairs at half-mast.

Full of anticipation, Maxine's voice was tiny, her eyes big, as she said, "I wasn't a minute ago."

"Nor shall you be for long. Let's get this wet camisole off of you." Answering her soft giggle, Dane slid the garment over her head and tossed it over a shrub to dry. Then he reached for his shirt and began to wipe her damp, chilled skin.

He expected at least a few shy reactions as he lavished his gaze on every inch of Maxine's beautiful body, but never once did she coyly try to hide herself from him. She was completely refreshing, not inhibited or concerned about her nudity, and so confident in herself as a person, if not yet as a woman, that he had to wonder which of them was actually the more civilized.

When he tossed the shirt aside, Maxine touched his chin, fingering the cleft, and leaned up to the small white line below it and gently kissed the scar. It was an innocent gesture from a basically innocent woman, and yet the act inflamed him. Eager to possess her, to wipe the memory of her assault from her body and soul, Dane rolled over, half-covering her, and drove his hands into her riot of hair. "Do not be afraid," he murmured, "I will try not to hurt you in any way, *comprende?*"

"Yes," she gasped, growing impatient. "And I'll try not to hurt you, too."

Dane laughed, and slid his fingers into the hair at each side of her head. "Kiss me, Rojita. Kiss me like only you can."

Here was something she could do, and do well, if his recent reactions to her kisses meant anything. Maxine linked her hands behind his neck and brought his mouth to hers, tentatively exploring at first, and then probing deeper, intimately. Dane's gentle hands left her hair and began to move across her, flitting from one part of her body to another, lightly touching the surfaces like a dragonfly on a pond, skimming her slick skin, leaving tiny ripples of pleasure behind.

When she thought she could stand it no more, when she thought to cry out and beg him for something, anything, Maxine's voice deserted her, and all she could manage was a hoarse cry.

Understanding she was ready to move on, Dane stripped off his trousers and then gently eased her thighs apart. "Maxine," he whispered, using every ounce of his control, "I am coming to you now—tell me if there is pain."

Her mouth opened, but still she couldn't form words. Her answer was in her hips as she lifted them, then opened her legs even further to receive him. Dane accepted the invitation immediately. Carefully, slowly, he began to slide into her, to make her his. Then something unexpected, a barrier, drew him to an abrupt halt. He tried again, adjusting the angle, this time thrusting harder, but again he was unable to penetrate her.

"Maxine?" he whispered, his tongue thick. "I thought—didn't Chubasco . . . tear you?"

Dazed and panting, almost overwhelmed with need, she tried to focus her gaze as she looked into his eyes and said, "Why are you stopping—what's wrong?"

"Chubasco—didn't he force himself inside of you?"

"Inside of me?" she echoed, still in a daze. "No, I told you—I hurt him with my legs. Why? Is something wrong with me?"

"No," he breathed, the air rattling in his throat, "of course not." There is something wrong with me, he thought. There had to be, or he would move away from her now, draw on his last drop of chivalry and decency, and back off. He had no more right to take her virginity than Chubasco had. But how could he deny this urge to possess her, to make her his in a way no one else ever could? How could he ask it of himself?

Maxine shifted her impatient hips and then abruptly raised them in one swift movement, and the point was moot.

"There," she whispered, her pleasure reflected in the timbre of her voice, "did that take care of the problem?"

"Yes, *querida*," he murmured through a groan. "Now you and I are a part of one another." Then he began to move inside her, slowly, gently, with respect for her tender flesh.

After only a few moments of this, Maxine took those strong legs of hers, wrapped them around his hips, and set a new, more frantic and deeper pace. Dane tumbled into her, aware that he was no longer leading but following. His earlier suspicions about her had been right on the mark, he realized, but he'd lacked the foresight to guess at how completely uninhibited and fluid she could be, how strong, yet fragile and feminine in his arms.

She was an absolute wildcat, testing each sensation at every turn, unabashedly relishing every move. She took the controls, and Dane allowed her this, and more, as he followed her lead, surprised when she would occasionally take an unexpected turn and catch him with a burst of pleasure he'd never before experienced. When she crested, surged to the very highest peaks, Dane heard her cries, the sound of his own name, and he thought he'd go mad. On the verge of insanity, driven by love, lust, and every emotion he'd ever had all rolled into one, Dane burst into the wildfire, the flames consuming him and his last lucid thought.

Moments later, swamped with pleasure as awareness of her surroundings slowly crept back into her senses, Maxine felt as if she were floating above herself, looking down on her own body, which was glowing from head to toe. Her nerve endings were so close to the surface, it seemed that even the slightest movement caused another tiny burst of pleasure somewhere. She tried to recall what had happened, to experience once again, each and every sensation, but all she could think of was the sound of Dane's velvet voice, Dane invading her, surrounding her, becoming a part of her.

She glanced down at the top of his head, at the damp ebony curls bobbing in time with her breathing, and a wave of love swept over her, filling her throat with an unexpected tide of tears. She was on the verge of crying!

Coming to his senses, Dane rolled to his side, caught his breath, and propped his head with his hand and looked into Maxine's eyes. "You are beautiful, Rojita, absolutely the most beautiful woman I've ever known. How are you feeling?"

The urge to cry grew even stronger at his words, and still, Maxine couldn't understand the reason why. She couldn't seem to think or speak, and even breathing was nearly impossible. Dane had said this lovemaking business was merely complicated. Such a small, small word for such enormous emotions!

"Rojita?" he coaxed, tracing her lower lip with his free hand. "What is on your mind?"

Feeling ridiculously shy, she shrugged and quietly said, "Lovemaking, I guess."

"Really?" He raised an amused eyebrow. "And what do you think?"

Her embarrassment grew, and this suddenly shy Maxine had trouble forming the words. "I liked it. I really, really liked it a lot."

Dane rolled onto his back. A sense of freedom he hadn't known before liberated his unrestrained laughter. The sensation, the honest-to-God, heartfelt emotions shooting through him were almost as pure, as intense a release as he'd experienced inside Maxine a few moments ago. Who had been the actual virgin here? he had to wonder. Which of them had had the most to learn, to gain?

"Dane?" she said in a small voice as she leaned up

on one elbow and looked down at him. "What's so funny?"

"Nothing," he said, still laughing. "Everything."

She chuckled along with him, daring to believe he cared more than just a little, and then leaned over and whispered against his lips, "Thank you. Thank you for staying here with me, and thank you for . . . you know."

Thank you? Breathing heavily, Dane sat up and nudged Maxine back down on the *poncho.* "Why do you thank me? Don't you know that you are more precious than all the gold in the eldorado, more beautiful and exciting than any woman a man could ever hope to see or know?"

Any man? Him? Maxine didn't believe it. Oh, how she wanted to, but what she was and who she was were facts she couldn't ignore. Happy just to hear the words, even if they couldn't be true, Maxine gave him a wan smile, and again, her lashes bobbed shyly to her cheeks.

Dane's blue eyes grew dark, indigo like the sky behind them, and he tickled her chin, forcing her gaze to meet his. Hoping to erase the doubt mirrored in her eyes, he softly said, "I've wanted you since that first night on the trail—did you know that?" She bit her lip and shook her head. "It was you I dreamed of, you I wanted." At the memory of the sight of her bathing that time, Dane's hot blood thundered in his veins, and he was jolted by desire far stronger than any he'd ever known. "I wanted you then and I want you now. Can you see that?"

His voice, the black velvet magic in it, its honest passion, was almost too much for Maxine. She swallowed, once, twice, but still felt as if she had a mouse in her throat when she squeaked out, "You do?"

"*Es verdad, dulcinea mia*—I want you more now than I've ever wanted anything in my life. Do you still want me?"

His voice was lower now, darker, strumming her senses like a Spanish guitar, and Maxine endured a violent shudder before she could say, "Yes, Dane, oh, yes. I—I'd . . . love to." *I love you,* she thought.

Lowering his head, he nuzzled the hollow at her throat and whispered against her skin, "Help me remember—what part did you like best, Rojita? This?"

Dane's hands skimmed over her breasts, his fingertips tracing the outlines of her nipples. Desire lit a fire inside of her, and Maxine had to catch her breath before she could say, "Yes—no, I mean . . . I liked that, don't get me wrong, but . . ."

"Ah," he crooned, "then perhaps this was the part you liked best?"

Those fingertips, feather-light but heavy with passion, slid off her breast and blazed a crooked trail down her belly to her thighs where they began a slow, intimate exploration between her legs, stroking her, feeding her fire until she feared she might ignite.

Gasping, Maxine bit down on her bottom lip, then moaned, "I—ah, t-that's almost it. Almost."

"If that wasn't your favorite part, then it must have been this," he suggested, nearly strangling with passion as he parted her legs and slowly, ever so carefully, slid back inside of her.

"Oh my God," she groaned, the sensations ten times more pleasurable than they'd been before. "Oh, God, that's close to the best thing, that's very, very close."

"What then?" he said, teasing her, watching her face, the rapture reflected in her expression as he moved his hips, rocking inside of her ever so slowly, so deliberately. "What else could there be?"

Her cheeks matched the roots of her hair, and her breath was coming so fast that she barely had time to feed her hungry lungs. "I, well . . ." She trailed off, pausing to drag in a breath, then said, "I guess what I liked best, what made me the happiest, was . . . the end."

"The end, Rojita?"

"Yes, the end." Shuddering as she felt her body surging toward that very goal, she murmured, "I thought I was gonna burst into a million pieces."

His thrusts coming harder, faster, Dane whispered, "And are you willing to risk such a tragic end again?"

"As often as you're willing to risk taking me there."

Then he fell on her mouth, bestowing a kiss so powerful, so emotional, that Dane could feel his entire body tremble with the shock, the absolute fulfillment. He increased the pace, the depth of his strokes, and took them both to utter and complete chaos, to where neither was able to speak or even think, as a new more intensely satisfying ending overtook them both.

16

Later, as Dane and Maxine lay in each other's arms, they slowly became aware of the sound of something other than their own heartbeats or labored breathing.

The pounding, earth-shaking reverberations, it finally occurred to Dane, were not caused by their ebbing passion after all. He sat bolt upright when he recognized the sound.

The thunder belonged to at least a dozen horses. Riders, traveling at a steady gallop, were heading up the narrow valley below them. Maxine bolted upright beside Dane. "Oh, my God! Did I mention that the bandit wasn't alone when he found me? What if he and his men followed us?"

Amazed to think he could have forgotten the danger so easily, Dane tugged on his damp trousers and began gathering the rest of his clothing as he questioned her. "How many were with him, and why weren't they with him when I rode up?"

She picked through the memories of her ordeal. "I don't know for sure, but I think there was at least ten and maybe as many as twenty men with him, every one of them looking mean and ornery as him. He hollered at them in Spanish when he saw that I was alone. I don't know exactly what he told them, but they took off to the south in a hurry, like they didn't want to get him mad."

Bandidos? What other explanation could there be? Yet how was it possible that his old boyhood friend had become the leader of a group of cattle rustlers? And what of Chubasco's anonymity? Now that he'd been recognized, how far would he go to protect his identity from Dane's neighbors?

Renewed suspicions about his brother's death crept into his mind, but Dane brushed them aside. Dressed now, he picked up his bullwhip and looped it over his shoulder. "Wait here for me, Rojita," he said. "I'm going to ride down and have a look around."

Maxine leapt to her feet, oblivious of her nudity. Clutching the edges of his jacket, she pulled herself to him. "You can't go down there alone! I couldn't stand it if something happened to you, not now."

"Nothing," he assured her with much more conviction than he felt, "will happen to either of us. The horses we hear are probably just a small band of Rancho Cordoba mares who have broken away from the main herd. You wait here"—Dane's gaze flickered over her nude body—"and do the best you can to dress yourself while I'm gone."

"But what if it is the bandits and they trailed us to this spot?" Panic latched onto the base of her spine like a bloodsucker, and Maxine went pale as she speculated further. "What if they've come to kill us?"

This was precisely what he'd been thinking, but in an attempt to calm her, Dane offered the only small ray of hope he could see. "I used to know Chubasco quite well, and I can't believe he'd want to kill either of us. Please promise you'll do as I say. Remain here, quietly, and I will go find out exactly who, or what, is there, *comprende?*"

As difficult as it was for her to accept direction, Maxine bit down on her lip and nodded. Once Dane had made his way back to the horses, she collected herself and began to do as he asked. She donned her damp camisole, torn petticoats, and shredded pantalettes. Even if she could find a way to strap herself into the corset, her torn dress made its main purpose—squeezing her until she fit inside the tight bodice—unnecessary. After only a moment's hesitation, Maxine heaved the satin prison into the lake, where it joined Dane's hat in a muddy grave.

She had just slid the ruined dress over her head and covered its torn neckline with Dane's *poncho* when he returned. Although he'd been gone less than fifteen minutes, he not only had both horses with him, but he'd taken the time to transfer the heavy saddle from Rocio's back to Alazan where it belonged.

Riding up to where she stood, he dismounted quickly and said, "You are safe, Rojita. The riders are a group of my *vaqueros* out looking for us. They are waiting below to escort us back to the rancho."

Although Maxine heaved a relieved sigh, the thought of returning to Dane's home and facing his guests gave her pause. "Do I really have to go back already? I'd just as soon stay here and . . . rest up for another day or so."

Dane took her hands in his. "My men told me that the party is over, Maxine. Apparently my mother wisely called an end to it when I did not return immediately. There won't be cause for many explanations once we get back. Now, if you are ready, we really must be going."

Maxine glanced up at him quickly, shyly, then looked away. "I know we have to leave," she said so softly, so wistfully, she could barely hear her own voice. "But I wish we could just stay here all night—forever, even. I'll never forget this, Dane. I'll never forget you."

Prudence told him to lift her onto Rocio's back and be off, but Dane gave in to the moment and took her into his arms instead. His lips against her hair, he murmured, "I feel the same, Rojita, but I have compromised your reputation enough for one day. We must return home before too many eyebrows are raised by our long absence."

Even though she couldn't make sense of all the words, Maxine did understand what he was talking about. "I guess I've already raised enough eyebrows to cover the ceiling of your house. I don't want to cause any more trouble for you, but do you think we can take the time for just one more kiss before we leave?"

Just one more kiss? And then what? Dane considered their arrival at the ranch, the future. How would they carry on when they returned? Certainly neither of them could pretend that things hadn't changed between them—at least Dane knew he couldn't. His mother would see to that. He'd never be able to hide his feelings from her, emotions that were becoming increasingly clear to him, even though he had no idea what to do about them at this point. There was also the matter of Maxine's father. How would they be able to avoid him? What if—

Thunderstruck by the realization, Dane wheeled around, turning his back to Maxine. Where had his sense of honor flown? He'd promised the man that he wouldn't so much as lay a finger on Maxine, given his word as a gentleman, and what had he done? He had betrayed them all—Dicey, Maxine, and even himself.

Behind him, Maxine chewed on her lip and blinked back the tears. She'd pushed too far, asked too much of him. She'd told him that all she wanted was a few stolen moments, the chance to experience this thing called lovemaking. No promises, no complications, just the chance to satisfy her curiosity. He'd done that, and more—so much more. Why did it hurt so bad to think it could never happen again? To know that he couldn't even bring himself to give her another kiss?

Swallowing her tears and her pride, Maxine moved to walk past him, muttering as she went by, "Sorry I asked. I guess that wasn't a very ladylike thing to do. It won't happen again."

Dane could barely contain his rage as he slid one hand behind Maxine's neck and pulled her tight against his body. In a voice husky and filled with emotion, he said, "Whatever happens from here on out, do not think for one moment that what happened here today meant any less to me than it did to you—*comprende*?"

Maxine's knees buckled, and she began to tremble.

The fury in his eyes was as bright as their color, and yet she sensed it was not directed at her. Humbled and confused, she said in a low, tiny voice, *"Comprende."*

Dane finally granted her request. He kissed her, briefly, his lips rigid and unyielding. Then, with no further communication between them, he fit his hands to her waist and swung her up on Rocio's bare back.

Although the group managed the ride back in less than an hour, all the guests had left by the time they reached the outbuildings of Rancho Cordoba, and the night had grown dark. The grounds had to be illuminated by several lanterns.

They came to a halt, and Dane, still silent and brooding, climbed down off Alazan and assisted Maxine. She turned to him, waiting, hoping for some kind of acknowledgement, but Rancho Cordoba's *mayordomo* approached, cutting her off as he directed a long list of questions toward his employer in Spanish.

"Un momento, Enrico," Dane said, his voice taut. "I want you to tend to Señorita Maxine first. She has had a very exhausting and upsetting experience. We will talk after she has been taken care of."

"No," Maxine said, planting her foot. "I'm not ready to go inside yet. I want to see Max and let him know I'm all right before I do anything else."

Dane glanced at her, noting the stubborn set of her chin, her usual confident, feisty manner, and breathed a sigh of relief. Determined to keep his men from speculating about what may have happened out on the trail, he offered a terse, "As you wish." Then he turned away from her and resumed his conversation with Enrico.

Her thoughts with her twin, Maxine didn't dwell on the slight or Dane's formal attitude. She picked up her soiled skirts and hurried into the barn. Pausing to light a lantern, she called out his name, "Max? Where are you? I'm back."

From the last stall, the one in which he slept, she heard the thrashing of straw and the rustling of fabric just before Max stumbled out into the aisle. He was disheveled and shirtless, covered from the waist up only by the *serape* Dane had given him, and even that was askew. Below, he wore his Levi's, but his feet were bare.

"Were you sleeping already, Max?" she asked, moving closer to him. When she saw his expression, the glee mingled with an odd embarrassment in his eyes, the flushed condition of his deeply rosy cheeks, she studied him closer. "Max?" she said, bewildered. "What is it? Were you worried about me, or is something . . . wrong?"

Although he kept his silence, Max's lips burst apart in a grin and he began to swing his hands back and forth across his body. When he glanced not once, but three times back inside the stall, Maxine stepped forward and followed his eyes. She caught a flash of Rosa's nude body just before the woman's buckskin dress dropped down over her like a window curtain at twilight.

What was going on here? When Maxine's shock eased enough for her to look back at her brother, she noticed he was dragging his bare toe through the straw, his face even brighter, the color almost too red to be true.

Even though she was beginning to boil inside, Maxine kept her tone cool as she suggested, "You know, Max—Dane and I rode Alazan and Rocio pretty hard today. What they need is a good rubbing down. Why don't you go on outside and help Dane with the horses? He needs you."

"He does?" Even though his riotous color was beginning to fade, Max beamed as he turned to Rosa and said, "Dane needs me. I got to go."

She gave him a short nod, dismissing him, and then quickly returned her wary gaze to his sister.

As soon as Max was out of earshot, Maxine charged into the stall. "What's been going on in here?" she demanded, hands on hips.

Submissive and humble, Rosa lowered her head, but she wisely kept a watchful eye on the red-headed ball of fire standing before her. The word accented by her native Uto-Aztecan language, she murmured, "Nothing."

Maxine rolled her eyes. Uncomfortable with the subservient posture of the woman at her feet, she said, "Get up off the floor."

Rosa's glance moved to Maxine's hands. "I do not wish to fight you."

Until then, Maxine hadn't realized she was standing with her fists not only clenched but raised as well. Releasing the tension in her fingers, she sighed and slid down the stall's partition until she was sitting beside the other woman. "I don't want to fight you either, Rosa. I'm not really mad at you, but I am worried about my brother. I can't just let you do Max like this—I can't."

Rosa blinked, her deep-set eyes slits as she asked, "What have I done that is so wrong?"

Too weary to mince her words, Maxine came right out with it. "You've been doing some lovemaking on him, and don't try to tell me different."

If she was surprised by Maxine's bluntness, it didn't show. Rosa lowered her gaze and shrugged. "I would not lie about this. I wish only to make him happy."

"But Rosa—can't you see that Max is a little ... *different* from most folks? With him, nothing, not even a little kiss is little. Understand what I mean?"

"I think so."

"I don't think you do." Maxine shook her head, not missing the irony in the fact that she and Max—born together—had experienced another sort of milestone on the same day as well. She closed her eyes and sighed, but the sound came out as more of a soft wail.

Rosa brought her blunt-nailed fingers to Maxine's shoulder and patted it gently. "My heart is for Max the way your heart is for the Spaniard. I think this is good."

"I appreciate that, really I do, but it's not the same thing."

"It seems the same to me."

"No, no. You don't understand. You see, when Dane and I, when he kisses me or says fancy words, I know in my head that I can't have him forever, that I can never, ever—" Maxine's throat clamped shut, making it difficult to continue. Swallowing again, she took a deep breath and slowly finished the sentence. "I can never . . . have him . . . for my own. I know that, Rosa.

I may not like it much, but I can accept it and find a way to live with it."

Rosa's amber eyes, usually hard like the resin of their color, softened as Maxine spoke, and grew slightly moist. "I do understand." Again, she touched Maxine's shoulder. "But I still do not see what I have done wrong to Max."

The frustration showing in her voice, Maxine practically shouted, "Max will never get over it when you leave. He must think you're his own special toy or something by now, and he'll expect you to be there for him as long as he lives. That's the way he thinks, and I can't just stand by and watch how tore up he'll be the day you get well enough to take off."

"I will not leave Max."

"You say that now, but there will be a later—for both of us." Maxine's eyes hardened then, as much for her own plight as her brother's. Suddenly feeling half-dead herself, she numbly whispered, "It'll probably kill him when you leave."

To that, Rosa did something Maxine had never seen her do before. She smiled. The gesture was slow, secretive, almost smug, but it was most definitely a smile. "How do you think I came to be in the desert?"

Maxine shrugged.

"White men—miners. They took me from my home, stole me even though I was still a little girl."

"How little?"

Rosa couldn't remember in years, so she explained through her tribal rituals. "I was not yet old enough for my initiation as a woman, for the time of bleeding, but they took me anyway and used me as if I were."

Aware now of what that entailed, and able to imagine how dreadful it would have been had Chubasco succeeded, Maxine took the hand from her shoulder and held it. "I'm sorry, Rosa, really I am. But Max—"

"Max is good. I have never met anyone—man or woman—as gentle as your brother. He may not have all his head parts, but inside of him, in here"—she paused and touched her breast—"he has *?iva?a.*"

Maxine tried to pronounce the word, to make the gulping noise that preceded and seemed to end it, but it came out sounding like a belch.

Laughing, Rosa said, "*?iva?a* is a strong special power, and only special people have this. Max is strong this way."

Maxine smiled into the woman's dark features. Not many took the time to know this about Max or recognize the good in what he did. Still, she remained skeptical. "You've been good for Max, too, Rosa, but—"

"You are not convinced." Rosa looked away and paused before revealing the rest of her story. "The last miner who bought me was a very cruel man. I stayed with him until our child was born."

Maxine gasped. "You have a child?"

"I had a child." Rosa's voice was flat, and she looked away from Maxine, to the ground as she finished. "The miner relieved us of that burden after the child's birth. He took a rock to my daughter's head."

"Oh, Rosa! You mean he ..." But Maxine didn't finish the sentence. She saw the answer in Rosa's eyes, that and a well of unshed tears, buried just beneath the surface like a desert hot spring. Maxine slid her arm across the Indian's shoulders and whispered, "I'm sorry."

Rosa didn't acknowledge the gesture. She went on with her story, her voice that same emotionless monotone. "I escaped the next day, but I was too weak to get far. The miner caught me and beat me fiercely."

"The bruises and busted ribs?"

Rosa nodded. "I waited one more day and left again. I ran until I could not run, then walked until I could not walk. You found me as I searched for water and shelter from the sun, but I was not dead. I would not die. Understand that I could have died and that I thought of death often, but I would not. Understand?"

Above all else, Maxine understood survival. She nodded.

"Know then," Rosa continued, "that if I should ever cause Max pain, I will gladly end the life I have tried so hard to preserve. I would drive a dagger into my heart before I see his first tear fall. I swear this on *Mukat*, the father of all my people."

Maxine was speechless. She and Rosa were two of a kind, she realized, tough and hard like a desert tortoise on the outside, soft and vulnerable beneath that impenetrable shell.

She was ridiculously close to tears, again. She swallowed them and said, "Then I hope this *Mukat* is the kind of God who'll watch over you if you ever do leave my brother. You're going to need all the help you can get hiding from me if you do."

Rosa threw her arms around Maxine's shoulders and squeezed. Then she said one simple word. "Deal."

Maxine chewed on her lower lip and nodded as she whispered, "Deal."

The following morning—actually, closer to noon—Maxine stretched like a cat, twisting and turning in the soft bed, and worked to convince herself that this time she simply had to get up. She'd awakened to at least a semi-conscious state several times during the morning hours, but each time she would start thinking about the lovemaking she'd shared with Dane, daydreaming about every mouth-watering memory until she dropped back off to sleep.

Now hunger and thirst compelled her to sit up in bed and rub the sleep from her eyes. As if the gesture had rung some kind of invisible bell, the door opened, and in came Catalina carrying a tray.

"*Buenos dias,* Señorita Maxine. Are you hungry? I bring your breakfast—your very late breakfast."

Maxine yawned. "Can't it wait a little longer so I can have it downstairs with Dane—with the family?" she quickly added.

Catalina shook her head as she set the tray on the bedside table. "Don Francisco has taken his *madre* to San Diego where she will meet her ship tomorrow morning. He said to tell you that he also plans to call a meeting of the Board of Trustees to discuss the *bandido* problem, and that he might be gone until late this evening."

Maxine tried not to let her disappointment show. "That's too bad. He had such a long day yesterday."

"*Si,* but he is a very strong man with a very strong

mind." Catalina shook a linen napkin open and draped it across Maxine's lap. "Since Doña Caroline and the niños have already eaten, and there is no one else to share your meal, I thought you might enjoy eating in here. You are the only late riser in this house."

Doña Caroline? Maxine squeezed her eyes shut, groaning, and threw herself back on the bed. *Caroline.* She hadn't even given the woman a thought yesterday— or this morning. She hadn't thought of anyone or anything but herself and her excruciating need to be with Dane. How in God's name could she face that woman today? Maxine remembered how the lithe blond had questioned her before, the way Caroline's instincts had ferreted out her deepest feelings for Dane, and she cringed at the thought. Caroline would know! She would take one look into Maxine's eyes and know that she had betrayed her, that she had taken something which did not, and could not ever, belong to her.

Not that Maxine had a problem with taking things that didn't belong to her—she had done so before, on several occasions. Hats, shoes, chickens, any kind of survival items; all were fair game, admissable "thefts" to the McKain way of thinking in the family's ongoing quest for survival. But how in the craziest of suppositions could she equate those stolen moments with Dane to a struggle for survival? Was there any way at all to rationalize her behavior and come away with her self-respect intact?

"Señorita Maxine?" Catalina said, breaking into Maxine's thoughts. "Are you in pain?"

Opening one eye to a bare slit, she feigned sudden illness and nodded. "I—yes. I have a headache."

"Perhaps this will help." Catalina reached for something on the tray. "This is from Don Francisco. He chose it from the courtyard gardens just this morning and said to make sure you received it with your breakfast."

Maxine looked up to see what the servant held, and her breath caught in her throat. She couldn't move. As if reading her mind again, Catalina leaned forward and deposited a perfect yellow rose in Maxine's palm. "*Es muy bonito*—beautiful. Don Francisco is a very thoughtful man, too—no?"

"Uh-huh," was the best Maxine could manage. Hypnotized, so deeply touched by the gesture that she couldn't tear her gaze away from the flower, she bit her bottom lip and prayed that the servant couldn't see the tears welling up in her eyes.

Going on about her business as if Maxine's reactions or feelings were perfectly normal, Catalina said, "Enjoy your food, Señorita Maxine. I will return when you are finished and help you prepare for the day. I have made another dress for you."

Finally able to look away from the rose, Maxine blinked and looked over to the chair, where Catalina pointed to a robin's egg blue day dress with a brand new corset draped across it. Thinking fast, determined that she would never be strapped into one of those contraptions again, she moaned dramatically and said, "Oh, thanks, Catalina, but I'm afraid my ribs are much too bruised to squeeze into a corset or that fancy dress. Can I wear the skirt and blouse you gave me the day I arrived?"

Catalina frowned. "Don Francisco did not like that.

Perhaps I can find something as comfortable, but more suitable." Nodding to herself, she added, "Yes. I think I have just the thing." Then she scurried out of the room.

Maxine collapsed against her pillow. Even if Catalina found something she would wear, what good would it do? How could she possibly leave this room and face Caroline? What could she do, and what in God's name could she say?

Above all else, why hadn't she listened to Dane when he tried to explain what a complicated thing this lovemaking could be? The answer to that was quite clear, of course. Maxine had never been much good at listening to anyone. Not since her mother had abandoned her, she realized, had she put stock in anything anyone had to say, not even her father. As long as she was looked upon as one of Dicey's wild twins, she could do and say just about anything she wanted to.

But she wasn't a child, and no matter how hard she tried, Maxine knew she could never pretend to be one again. In fact, it occurred to her that all along, she'd been living in a make-believe world.

As that world closed in on her, crushing her with its weight, the tears that fell on the rose were anything but pretend.

17

In just over an hour, headache and all, a nervous Maxine stood at the top of the stairway leading down from the bedroom wing. She listened intently for Caroline's voice or the tattoo of the boys' shoes against the tile floor. All was quiet. Should she take the chance and flee to the barn? What if she ran into Caroline? What would she do—what would she *say* if she were unable to slip past her and the boys?

The decision as to whether she should stay in her room or venture downstairs had been made for her when Catalina returned to help her dress. Maxine had tried to explain that she intended to stay in bed and nurse her headache, but the servant had said that if that were the case, she would get Caroline to come take a look at her. After all, Maxine was an honored guest of Don Francisco, and if she had taken ill, a member of the family had to be notified at once.

Feigning a miraculous recovery, Maxine had allowed

Catalina to dress her in a costume similar to the blouse and skirt she'd requested, and with the exception of long sleeves and the matching shawl she was required to wear, she was reasonably comfortable.

Satisfied there was no one below in the living room, she quickly descended the stairs and then glanced around. From the courtyard, she heard the high-pitched giggles of the young boys set off by their mother's delighted laughter. Sprinting across the floor on tip-toes, she ducked out the front door and headed straight for cover in the orange grove.

Maxine dawdled there for over an hour, picking fruit, tearing the rinds from oranges and eating the wet, sticky, flesh, and generally trying to keep herself occupied. It hadn't worked. All she could think about was the mess she'd made of things. She'd been so wrong, so very wrong about lovemaking—and hadn't Dane tried to tell her? Hadn't her father, for that matter? And what of Caroline?

Caroline above all had tried to tell her how ridiculous the idea of a man like Dane falling in love with her was, because of the "obvious differences" between them. Yes, it was obvious: He was a gentleman, and Maxine was a . . . a what? A child—no, a woman. A woman with no home, and with no family honor. A bastard of the streets, as her mother used to say. A woman to be pitied.

Growing tired of hiding, Maxine decided to risk a stroll around Otay Lake. She stepped out onto the roadway, scanned the grounds, and spotted her father's wagon coming up over the rise. She caught up with the wagon and followed alongside until it came to a halt at the barn.

Although she had planned to offer a simple "hello, how's trick's?", the minute Dicey's feet hit the ground, she flew into his arms instead. "Hi, Pa," she choked out, her voice muffled. "I missed you."

Surprised by his daughter's overt enthusiasm and the touch of desperation in her voice, Dicey kissed her cheek and then held her at arm's length. "Maxie girl? Everything okay here?"

"Everything's fine, Pa," she said, averting her gaze. "I'm just glad to see you're back and healthy and all."

Frowning, Dicey began to pick at his scruffy beard. "I've barely been gone fur two days. What's wrong? Where's yur brother?"

"He's fine, Pa, really. He's in one of the stalls, I expect."

"Well, then, I guess I'll just go see to him."

"Ah, no . . . don't do that." She snagged his arm before he could turn away. "I wouldn't go barreling in there without announcing yourself. Max is, well . . . Max has got the love-sick."

Dicey screwed up his features and looked at his daughter. "The love-sick? My boy, *Max?*"

Glad to be discussing anyone but herself, Maxine followed along behind him, supplying as much information as she could without being too explicit. "It's true, Pa. He's got it bad for that squaw woman. Her name's Rosa, and she can talk, too. Max has the love-sick something awful for her." She blushed and lowered her head. "You'd best knock and call his name a time or two before you take another step. No telling what they're up to in there."

Dicey stopped in his tracks. "What's this yur sayin'? You don't mean to tell me . . ."

She nodded. "Max—Max and Rosa . . . they, uh . . ." She looked away. "Best knock, Pa."

Dicey's breath whooshed out in a warm sigh. "You don't say!" Glancing back toward the barn, equal parts of surprise and pride coloring his already ruddy complexion, he added, "I can't hardly believe that Max—my poor boy, *Max*—is all growed up that way. I can't hardly believe it a'tall." Then another thought occurred to him, and his wondrous expression turned grim. "That Rosa—what's our Max gonna do when she lights out? How's he gonna—"

"Rosa ain't—*isn't* going anywhere, Pa."

"But Maxie, what if she—"

"She *isn't* gonna leave or hurt Max. I made sure of that right off." Maxine gave him a confident grin. "You don't have to worry about Max's happiness. He's gonna be just fine."

Dicey regarded her a long moment, then softly said, "And what about you, girl? Can you say the same about yurself?"

Maxine's answer was to lower her head. Dicey turned back and hollered into the barn, "Max? You in there, boy? It's yur pa come back. I'm a needin' you. Get on out here."

In less than the time it took for Dicey to glance back at his daughter and see her still somber demeanor, Max shuffled out through the barn doors.

"Hi, Pa. Look what me and Rosa can do." He held up a leather bridle dotted with silver conchos for his father's inspection. "Rosa showed me how to rub the leather, and she's good at shining up the silver. Look and feel it, too."

Dicey gave the halter a cursory examination. "Feels just like a baby's ass, son. You done good."

"Rosa does good, too," he said, his grin huge. "She showed me. We're gonna fix up all of Dane's saddles and halters. I can do it. I can do it all good, Pa."

"I know you can, son. Now take care of Dane's horses. They're a sight more important than what goes on them. I got to go sit with yur sister a spell."

"Okay, Pa. I can take care of them. I do that good, too. I do everything good. Rosa says so. *Everything.*" Then he went to work unhitching the team.

Dicey was satisfied by his son's state of mind but decidedly suspicious about his daughter's. He limped over to Maxine, took her by the elbow, and guided her away from the barn. Whispering under his breath as they walked, he said, "I swear if'n I didn't know better, I'd say that boy growed himself an extra set of teeth since I left for town."

"I told you he's real happy, Pa. I don't think I've ever seen him happier than he is now."

"What about you? Just how happy are you these days? I swear you look like a squirrel got into yur valise and made off with all yur pine cones. What's happened to you, girl?"

Maxine glanced toward the house, worried that Caroline would sail out the door any minute. If she did, she would greet Maxine, look into her eyes, and know immediately what happened between her and Dane at the pond.

"I have to talk to you, Pa," she whispered under her

breath, her voice strained. "There's a couple of things to explain, too, but I can't talk here. Will you walk on down to the lake with me?"

Dicey slid his gnarled index finger under her chin and lifted it. "Somethin' mighty bad come down on my Maxie, I can just—"

Dicey strangled on the next word as the side of her face came into clear view. The bruise, no longer fresh, had darkened into the color of a brewing storm on the horizon of her jawline. "You've been hit!" he cried, sickened by the sight. "Who'd a put his fist to my girl? Tell yur pa, Maxie—who hit you?"

"Hush," she whispered, racked with guilt, still glancing around the yard. "I can't stand it if I cause one more commotion around here." Her desperation was mirrored in her eyes. "Will you please come on down to the lake with me? I'll tell you all about it there, I promise."

His blood was heated with anger and indignation, moving through his sluggish body faster than it had in years. Dicey gave her a short nod, reversed his direction, and followed her down the long path which led to Otay Lake.

When they were out of sight of the house, he turned to Maxine and demanded, "Out with it, Maxie. If that Spaniard—"

"Oh, gosh, no! It wasn't him, Pa. It was a stranger."

"A . . . a *stranger?* You mean one a them fancy friends of his went and—"

"No, Pa. I got myself into a little trouble since you went to town. Truth is, I got myself into a lot of trouble after you left." Drawing in a long breath, she glanced out at the lake, the sparkling water looking like tears, and started her story at the beginning of the party.

"And so?" Dicey limped closer to the shoreline as she finished. "You sat on the man—weren't like you didna' have cause."

Maxine sighed heavily. "Dane was none too happy about it. He put me in my room, saving the rest of his guests, I suppose, and well . . . I guess I went a little crazy. I climbed out the window, borrowed Rocio, and took off for San Diego."

Dicey's bushy brows shot up. "Did you now? Alone?"

"For a while, anyways. Not long after I passed the border, Rocio tossed me, then I ran into a bandit. He's the one tried to beat the tar out of me."

Dicey swallowed hard, working to keep the jitters out of his voice as he asked, "What'd that fellah do besides sock yur jaw, Maxie? You can tell yur pa, you know. I want you to know that you can tell me anythin' what's on yur mind."

What was on her mind was guilt and shame, but mostly guilt. Those ridiculous tears crept up her throat then, robbing her of her voice, and Maxine had to look away from her father and take several deep breaths before she was finally able to say, "He just roughed me up some, Pa, I swear it. I know what you're asking, but it's okay. Dane come along and scared him off before the bandit did much more than tear up my dress and throw me around some." She paused. "After that, Dane and his men brought me on back to the rancho."

Dicey's breath whistled out of him as he reached for her and gathered her in his arms. "Each time I think I'm about to get square with that Spaniard, I wind up owin' him even more. I'm owin' him a lot for this one, Maxie—lots more than all the gold we've e'er laid claim to."

Maxine began to cry then, hard, as if her very soul had been pummeled along with her body. Dicey was at a loss over what to say or do in the face of such misery, the utterly extraordinary fact that his strong-willed daughter was crying at all. He patted her shoulders and held her until her sobs became manageable. When he released her, she quickly turned her head and stepped away from him.

"S-sorry, Pa," she said through a hiccup. "Don't know what got into me."

But he was determined to find out *everything* that had happened to his daughter since his departure. He made a guess. "This got to do with more than a run-in with a bandit, don't it?" When she didn't answer, but kept her head down and wiped her nose instead, he made some more assumptions. "It's the Spaniard, isn't it?"

Uncomfortable with the turn in the conversation, Maxine began to fiddle with the loose strands of her hair. "None of this is Dane's fault, Pa."

Dicey wasn't assuaged. "Answer me, girl—has he been fillin' yur head with fancy notions? What's he been tellin' you?"

That I'm beautiful, as tough and beautiful as a Harrison's yellow rose. "Not much, maybe said that I'm kinda pretty once."

And couldn't Dicey just hear it, Dane whispering sweet temptations into her innocent ears. Angry, more at himself for ever having brought his family to this, he grumbled, "Pretty—humph!"

"What's that mean, Pa? Don't you think I'm the least bit pretty?"

"'Course I do!" Realizing his blunder, Dicey limped a few steps closer to her. "Haven't I made mention a that 'fore?"

Answering softly, with a fresh shower of tears, Maxine whispered, "No, Pa, you haven't. Until Dane, nobody ever did."

Taking a long look at his daughter, Dicey began to feel a sting, a dampness burning behind his eyelids that he hadn't felt in years. "I'm right sorry about that, Maxie. I guess I should a told you sooner. Yur more than pretty. Yur a beauty, girl, a real beauty."

Maxine smiled, squeezing the tears from her eyes as she whispered, "Thanks, Pa. Even if it isn't true, thanks."

Still hearing more from her tone than the words themselves, Dicey raised a suspicious brow. "There's more, Maxie, I can feel that there's more. What else has that Spaniard been filling yur head with? Is he making promises, saying things best kept for his intended?"

Unable to look him in the eye, she glanced down at the ground. Forcing a casual manner, she bent over, pulled up a shaft of wild wheat, and began chewing on it.

"What's he said or done, girl?" Dicey asked, persisting. "You kin tell yur pa."

But she couldn't, of course. She gave his arm a little pat. "He gave me a rose, that's all. A pretty yellow rose from his garden 'cause it reminded him of me. Nothing much to that now, is there?"

Dicey grumbled under his breath. "I suppose not, but I hope you ain't takin' it too serious. You got to remember folks like him feel kinda sorry for folks like us—you know, us not having a chicken or a pan to cook it in. Just feels sorry for us, that's all."

She'd known it was true. She'd known it all along, but why did it still hurt so much? The blood rushed to Maxine's head, and a sob escaped from her throat. Embarrassed again, at her own folly as well as the display she was making of herself, she dropped to her knees and hid her face in her hands.

"Oh, Maxie," Dicey said softly, afraid to approach her. "I was right about there bein' more—Max ain't the only one round here that's got the love-sick. Got it pretty bad yurself, don'cha, girl?"

Then she fell apart. Unable to hide her feelings from her father or herself any longer, she cried, "Oh, Pa, I don't know what's happening anymore. I'm all twisted up inside, and feeling real funny, like a sucked-out orange, you know? Hollow, empty in here," she beat on her breastbone, "but kinda squishy, too."

Dicey nodded, his mouth set in a grim line. "It's the love-sick, all right. Pure and simple."

She wondered briefly if her father had ever had these feelings for her mother. Her own pain ebbed for just a moment, and then rushed in, the tide higher than ever. "I didn't know—I never knew this love business could hurt so much."

Although he could barely stand to see the pain in her eyes, in a way, Dicey was relieved by her words. He had thought it would be much more difficult to approach the topic. "I tried to tell you, Maxie, tried to warn you off the Spaniard, remember?"

At her miserable nod, he went on. "I ain't blamin' you for that, girl—you shoulda had yur own man and a passel of kids by now. If I'd been a good pa and give you the chance for that, you wouldn't be tailin' along behind that Spaniard with yur tongue hangin' out and yur eyes rollin' back in yur head 'cause yur all twisted-up with the love-sick."

Maxine shook her head violently. "But I never want-ed a man and a passel of kids, and I don't want that now. I just want—hell's fire, Pa—I just don't know what it *is* that I want anymore."

"Well I hope what yur wantin' *ain't* that Spaniard! You canno' have him—you must realize that you canno' have a fine gentleman like that."

"I know I can't have him—I do! But knowing that doesn't make me love him any less. I kind of hoped it would, but it doesn't."

As difficult a maneuver as it was for Dicey and his twisted knee, he eased down beside her. "Why don'cha let me decide what you might be a wantin' fur a spell. I'm gonna make everythin' up to you, Maxie. Yur gonna forget you e'er laid eyes on that Spaniard 'fore I'm done!"

Maxine dried her tears with the hem of her skirt. Trying not to sound too skeptical or ungrateful, she asked, "How you gonna do that, Pa? It seems Dane's all I can think about anymore."

"I know, I know," he said, patting her hand. "'Twas a foolish idea trying to get you hitched to any of his friends, too. So here's what we'll be doin'. How about we head for Cherry Creek, Colorado, and that big strike at Pike's Peak? Once we file our first claim, the very next thing I'm gonna do is build you yur very own home—outta pine logs and everythin' just the way you always wanted high up in the forest."

Maxine caught her breath and said, "Our own house—really and true, Pa?"

Egged on, Dicey piled up the promises. "I swear it on our lucky nuggets! After the house is built, I'm gonna set out to find you a man of your own, a miner like us. Someone who can understand what we McKains are about. What do you think of that?"

The thought of any man besides Dane so much as looking at her made Maxine's stomach turn, but she smiled at her father, warmed by his unconditional love. "Gonna have to be a mighty tough man—tough and dumber than mule fodder to willingly become part of this family."

"If'n I have to," Dicey answered, chuckling, "I'll just be making you a man outta all the gold we find. Bet you'd like that just fine, now, wouldn't you?"

"Sure, Pa." More herself now, she leaned over, wrapped her arms around Dicey's neck and gave him a big, sloppy kiss on the cheek. "Just one problem I can think of with all your plans, though—since none of Dane's fancy friends are going to be tossing a fortune at my feet, how are we gonna get out from under that huge pile of money we still owe him?"

"Glad you asked," he said, slapping his thigh. "Got a little surprise fur you, Maxie—a *big* surprise, that is." He reached into his shirt and pulled out a leather sack tied shut with a strip of rawhide. Waving it like a pendulum beneath her nose, he said, "I had me a lucky streak wider than yur brother's shoulders while I was in San Diego—got enough here to pay the Spaniard, plus five hundred or so to get us to Colorado! Whadda you think of yur old pa now?"

"Two thousand dollars?" she cried, her misery brushed aside for the time being. "You telling me you got two thousand bucks in that bag?"

"Thereabouts," Dicey said, shades of a grin like Max's peeking through the stubble on his chin.

"Hot damn!"

"And hallelujah!" Struggling to get his footing, Dicey's voice reflected pure enthusiasm. "Now let's get on up to the house. We'll give that Spaniard his due, then be on our way. Things is lookin' up for us McKains— I don't want to take no more chances. The sooner we get on out of San Diego and off this rancho, the better off we'll be."

Trying not to think of what it would be like to leave, to never see Dane again, Maxine climbed to her feet and brushed off her dress. "Have to wait till morning, Pa. Dane's in town trying to get some help rounding up those bandits. Catalina says he won't be back until tonight."

Dicey was undaunted, sure that he would be soon leading his children to a new, more rewarding way of life. He linked his arm through Maxine's and said, "Then I guess we'll have to settle up soon's he gets home, and be off with the dawn."

"Off," she echoed, suddenly feeling hollow, numb. "Off to Pike's Peak."

Recalling the term being tossed around to describe the newest argonauts, the '59ers, Dicey added, "To Pikes's Peak or bust!"

When Dane came in that evening, he rode straight up to the carriage entrance, directed one of the *vaqueros* to unhitch the team of horses and take them to the barn, and strode through the front door of his home.

Caroline, who'd observed his approach, greeted him as he entered the living room. "Hello, Dane—have you eaten?"

"All I need to for a while," he muttered, distracted. "Where is everyone?"

"Everyone?" she said. "Or just Maxine?"

Ignoring the insinuation, he repeated, *"Everyone."*

Caroline offered a warm smile as she slipped her hand between Dane's ribs and his elbow. *"Everyone* is busy. The boys are upstairs in their room, Maxine and her father are out in the barn doing something to their wagon, and I suppose her brother and that woman are still polishing your leather and silver goods. You should see what they've done to your harness trim and saddles since this morning!"

Disengaging himself from her, Dane turned as if to leave. "Perhaps I'd better take a look now."

Before he could move, Caroline crossed in front of him, blocking his path. "I'm sure that can wait until tomorrow. It's time we had that talk, Dane—your mother *has* left the rancho."

Dane exhaled heavily. "I'm exhausted. I don't think now is—"

"You're not trying to avoid me too, are you?" she asked, cutting him off with a rare display of spunk.

"I wasn't aware anyone had been avoiding you. I'm sure you're mistaken."

"Oh, no, someone definitely has been," she said, slanting her soft gray eyes upward as she slipped her hand into the crook of his elbow again, this time using a firmer grip. "And that someone has been doing so since last night. Don't think I didn't notice the way you rushed into the house and disappeared, or the way Maxine dashed up to her room with Catalina when she came in. She didn't say two words to me or your mother. It was as if she was trying to avoid us on purpose."

Again, he shrugged. "I told you what happened to her—she was probably embarrassed because she thinks she caused us all so much trouble."

"Perhaps," she said, though her expression clearly revealed her doubt. "Why don't we continue our discussion in your mother's sitting room. I think what we have to say to one another should be said in complete privacy."

Dane dreaded the conversation, but he knew he owed her that much. He nodded and allowed himself to be steered into the most English part of the house, the room with the settee in the alcove overlooking Otay Lake.

"If last night wasn't enough," Caroline said, picking up where she left off, "Maxine has been avoiding me all day, too. It's like she's been hiding from me for some reason. Why, even at supper time, she stayed in the barn and ate with her brother and that . . . squaw." Caroline interrupted herself. "That's another thing—I don't like the way that looks one bit. Can't you get at least one of them to come on up to the house?"

Since it was a situation he couldn't condone, Dane nodded. "I'll try, but you must know by now that the McKain family is a little different, not to mention, stubborn. They insist on playing by their own rules."

Caroline lifted her chin. "Since they're staying on del Cordobes property, I should think they could play by our rules, or simply be on their way."

Since he wouldn't even entertain the idea of asking the McKains—any of them—to leave, Dane simply said, "I'll see what I can do."

Gliding up behind him, Caroline kept a quiet, non-threatening tone as she asked, "It's her, isn't it?"

Hoping to steer her off course and avoid the issue entirely, Dane gave her a puzzled look.

But Caroline wasn't giving up, not tonight. "On the off-chance that you don't know who I'm talking about, it's Maxine. Isn't she, not some lost love in San Francisco, the woman you haven't been able to get out of your system since your return to the rancho?"

Dane stared out the window, holding onto his silence as if it were the deed to the family property.

"Do you love her?" Caroline persisted.

At this, Dane drew in a sharp breath, and Caroline circled him, squeezing her slender body between him and the window.

"Well?"

Unable to look her in the eye, he kept his rigid gaze on the distant sheen reflecting off the lake and said, "I don't know how to answer that, or if I should even try. I don't know how I feel about Maxine, myself. This has been a very confusing time for me, very unsettling. I think it would be best if you did not speak to me of such things."

"Oh, *please,* Dane," she said. "I think it's fair to assume that you do love her—at least a little bit. I might add that I got almost the same reaction from Maxine when I asked her how she felt about you."

This got his complete attention. Spearing her with an indignant gaze, he said, "You asked Maxine if she *loved* me?" At her tentative nod, he stormed, "By what right do you think you can ask such a personal question of the guests in my home?"

Although she felt as if she were shrinking inside her black silk dress, Caroline held her ground. "It seemed a natural enough progression in the conversation after she told me she'd spent the night with you."

Dane's disconcerted gaze flickered to the stone fireplace as he quietly said, "That was . . . innocent enough."

"Oh, yes," Caroline agreed. "Maxine explained all that to me, too. Let's see—how did she put it?" She pressed her fingertips against her temple. "I believe she swore on some lucky rocks that you didn't do *loving,* or something like that on her. Not to her or with her, Dane, but *on* her."

"Lovemaking," he muttered under his breath, wondering what else Maxine told her. "She probably said that I didn't do any lovemaking on her."

"Yes, that sounds right." Taking a chance with his hot temper, Caroline added, "I wonder if she can make that same claim today?"

Dane made no denials, but affirmed nothing either.

He just stared at her, the bright blue of his eyes dulled, anguished, and then turned back to the window. "That is something a lady in this house should not be wondering about, much less questioning."

His voice was only a whisper, but the pain in it was loud and sharp, cutting her with a slash of jealousy, and in that moment, Caroline knew for certain, even if Dane didn't. He loved Maxine and loved her well. Loved her, she suspected, in a way he'd never loved anyone or anything before. Certainly with much more depth than he'd ever loved her.

She felt envy's sharp edge as she sidled away, out of his reach. "Perhaps I have been a little too forward with you, but it does seem to me that the term *lady* has been redefined since you brought that family into this house. Is that the way things are going to be around here from now on, Dane? One set of rules for the McKains and another for me and the boys?"

Although he meant to keep it to himself, Dane's groan was audible. "What are you asking of me, Caroline? What is it you expect me to say?"

"Perhaps you've already said it."

Closing the distance between them, Dane slid his hands along her shoulders and gently lifted her chin. "I realize you expected we would be married by now. I—I don't know what to say to you. I am sorry I haven't lived up to your expectations, but I frankly don't know what I can do about it just now. You surely don't want a husband as distracted as I am these days."

Keeping her chin high, even though his hands had moved back to her shoulders, Caroline murmured, "I appreciate your honesty. I'd like a little more of it, please." Trying to hide her disappointment, she pursed her lips and said, "I'm spoiled, Dane. I had the complete, unquestioning love of one man in my life, and now I find I simply cannot settle for less. If you can stand there and tell me that your feelings for Maxine are something of a more . . . *physical* nature than of the heart, that you're free to learn to love me again and only me, then we have a chance. I'll forget everything that's happened between you and her up to this moment and think only of our future together. Can you do that?"

Dane studied her, following each curve of her finely etched features, and tried to concentrate on what he was doing. It was inconceivable to him that a man of his appetites, a man who was so *sure* that Caroline was what he wanted, could be standing here thinking of turning her away. He need only reach out to her and she would finally be his, now and forever. The fact that he could have done just that, and probably should have, many times over during the past few days, didn't make it any easier to understand or believe, but he came to realize one thing; Dane hadn't loved Caroline all these years so much as he'd loved the idea of loving her.

It was a simple enough thing to fathom, now that he really took a good look at himself. Keeping the spirit of that love alive in his heart had kept him from sharing himself too deeply and provided him with an ethereal shield, a fantasy woman no other could dislodge. Until Maxine . . . until Maxine, who'd never made one move, innocent or otherwise, to nudge that ghost aside and claim him as her own.

Now, as he gazed into Caroline's eyes, he wished for his brother's children, and for her, that he could tell the lie, and even live it, but he simply could not. He thought to turn away, but Caroline held him fast—with her arms, then with her words.

"You can't do it, can you?"

Dane slowly shook his head, defeated and relieved at once. "No," he whispered, his voice barely audible. "I cannot. Maxine has turned me—my life—upside down, and right now I have no idea which side is up."

"What are you going to do about it—her?"

This time Dane's groan was meant to be heard, and he drew in a long breath before he could answer her. "I have no idea. I owe her much—I have taken much from her, but this is not a simple thing, not simple at all. Our lives, our worlds, are so different, I have a difficult time imagining a future together."

"A future?" Caroline asked, the word clinging to her throat. "Do you intend to *marry* this girl, Dane?"

Honor demanded that he at least make the offer. After his word to her father, and what had happened at the lake, how could he not? Hedging slightly, Dane quietly said, "It is something I have to . . . consider."

There. He'd finally said it, finally slammed the door to any future with Caroline. A sob rose in her throat and eked its way out.

Dane drew her to him, crushing her to his chest. "I never wanted to hurt you. Please know that."

"You didn't," she managed to say through her tears. "Not really. To be hurt, I would have to be in love with you. I'm glad you told me how you feel *before* that happened—it could have, you know."

"Caroline," he whispered, searching for words of comfort, for some way to reply in kind.

Sensing his dilemma, she pulled out of his arms and turned her back to him. "Please don't offer me any consolatory 'what might have beens,' Dane—not while I'm seeing what is so clear. It's really best this way. I'll make some arrangements for me and the boys to move to San Diego as soon as possible."

"You don't have to do that," he said, again thinking of his brother. "I can have a nice little cottage built for you right here at Rancho Cordoba."

Caroline shook her head. "I'm too isolated here. I want to move to town, to be a part of a community. I've developed a stubborn streak over the years, *Don* Francisco. I'm moving to town, and that's that."

Laughing, Dane strode up behind her, spun her around and pulled her into his arms. Squeezing her, offering a kind of farewell tangled up with an enormous sense of relief, he kissed her softly, briefly.

He was still holding her when he happened to glance up and see Maxine standing in the archway.

18

She'd been wandering around the huge house for several minutes looking for Dane, when Maxine spotted a small room off the main hallway she hadn't noticed before. As she approached it, she saw that it was different from the rest of the house, more exquisite and luxurious, with fine hand-carved furnishings and thick Persian rugs covering the tiled floor.

And then she saw Dane and Caroline—Dane laughing, holding her in his arms, looking happy, blissful even. When he kissed Caroline, Maxine could have been run through with a hot poker and not felt any more pain than she did at that moment. Her mind screamed at her to run, to flee before he saw her, before he could witness the complete and utter destruction of her heart, but Maxine forced herself to stay. She had to watch this, she decided, burn this sight in her mind forever. If this display couldn't teach her to remember who and what she was, to keep what she could and could not have foremost in her mind, then nothing ever would.

Oh, but God how it hurt to see Caroline in his arms, to see that fancy, handsome face smiling down at her classically beautiful features. Why had Maxine been so reckless as to badger her father into this, another fool's errand? And fool's errand it was, she understood that now. Dicey had only been trying to spare her this pain when he'd insisted on paying Dane himself and telling him goodbye for the entire family. But no, Maxine would have none of that. She could handle the Spaniard, she'd told her father, and she could handle her feelings, too. Now that she'd faced up to herself and understood the reality of the situation, none of that would be a problem. No problem at all. Of course not.

"*Maxine?*" Dane's voice, the sound of her own name spoken in that rich, lush tone, jolted her, stunned her to attention.

"Oh," she blurted out, her brain numb. "Ah, I know I ain't—I'm *not* supposed to come in on you like this. I know I've done wrong again and that I've got to get permission to come in here, but I forgot, and I—"

"It's all right, Maxine," Dane said, smiling. "Come on in."

"Oh, no." She took a backward step. "It's not right to disturb you two. I do know that. When you get a minute, Dane—ah, Don Francisco—I need to see you, but only for a second. I won't be keeping you long, but—" She held up her arm, displaying the large leather pouch she had tied to her wrist. "I have something for you. I promise I won't take much of your time."

Caroline glanced quickly at Dane and sighed. She stepped out of his arms and started for the archway. "Come on in, Maxine," she said. "I was just on my way upstairs to check on the boys. I'm sure Dane can spare as much time as you want." She smiled as she passed by her, pausing long enough to brush Maxine's cheek with her fingertips, and then disappeared down the hallway.

Maxine scratched her head, careful not to disturb the long yellow ribbon Catalina had used to catch her hair. What was that all about?

"Rojita? Please—come in."

Maxine whipped her head around at the sound of his crooning voice and took a deep, steadying breath. "Well . . . if this is a good time for you after all, I'd just as soon get this over with."

"You won't do it standing out in the hallway."

Maxine walked tentatively into the room. God but she was beautiful, he thought, allowing his senses free rein to indulge themselves in her as never before. He gave her an expectant smile and watched her every movement as she made her way across the room.

Maxine noticed Dane's odd expression, the curious hint of amusement mingled with something she couldn't identify. She glanced down to her skirt and then back up at him. "I made Catalina put me in this kind of dress, so don't go blaming her again if you don't like it. I told her I couldn't wear one of those fancy ladies' dresses because my ribs were sore and a corset would hurt too much to wear."

Dane straightened his spine, and his smile evolved to a frown. "Are your ribs still sore today, Rojita? And what about the bruise on your jaw? Would you like to see a doctor?"

"No! Oh, no. There's nothing wrong with my ribs or anything else for that matter. I feel fine, really I do. I just didn't want to get strapped into another one of those . . . you know, a corset, *ever* again."

Noting how well the bright yellow daisies and orange sunburst pattern set off her flaming red hair, he grinned wickedly and said, "I have no problem with your attire. You look absolutely beautiful, like an elegant Doña, actually."

Despite the fact that she'd promised herself and her pa not to take anything he had to say too seriously, Maxine shivered at the compliment. "Thanks for saying so, but I'd just as soon not be a Señorita *or* a Doña. I'm just plain Maxine. That's all I am, and all I want to be. Just Maxine."

Dane's brows drew together at her recalcitrant tone, at the defiant set of her chin. What had happened to her today? he wondered. Who or what had taken her spunk, her fire, and turned it into this awkwardly proper stranger?

Dane took a step in her direction to soothe her, but he resisted the urge to put his arms around her. "I stand corrected. You, Maxine, are absolutely beautiful, no matter what you wear."

Faltering in her objective as his words melted her resolve, she swallowed hard, marched over to the window, and abruptly changed the subject. "I never saw this room before. That's a great view of the lake."

Dane followed her and slipped his arms around her waist. "Look at the water," he whispered against her hair. "See how it shines? It reminds me of the way your eyes looked yesterday afternoon, dark and wet, shimmering as if kissed by moonlight. Everything I've seen or touched today reminds me of you in some way. Have your thoughts been of me?"

Dear God, please don't let him talk about yesterday! Maxine couldn't think of it, couldn't allow him to remind her of the passion they'd shared, or she'd dissolve completely. Oh, but the urge to lie back against his broad chest was almost overwhelming, the need to arch her neck and twist her head to receive him was so intense, it was excruciating. If she allowed that to happen, Dane would have to witness yet another commotion—the unladylike display she would make of herself as her pa dragged her, kicking and screaming, off the grounds of Rancho Cordoba.

No, she couldn't think of yesterday. Somehow, she would simply have to pretend it never happened at all. Maxine hardened herself by remembering Dicey's words, that Dane was only feeling sorry for her.

With his strong arms holding her tightly, Maxine's voice quavered once again as she changed the subject. "Looks like fog coming up from the river valley."

Humoring her mood and her evasive attitude, Dane's gaze followed hers out the window. Thick ribbons of night air, heavy with moisture, were creeping over the countryside like a pack of wolves, devouring the hilltops and slopes along the way until the landscape was nothing more than a series of huge, amorphous lumps.

Dane returned his gaze and his thoughts to Maxine. "Fog is not so unusual around here, especially at this time of year. What is unusual," he said, deftly spinning her in his arms until she faced him, "is the way you seem to be avoiding me. What is wrong, Rojita?"

Forced to look at him, Maxine realized Dane was wearing all black again, the shirt open from the collar to where the two wings of coarse black hair met in an intriguing V. In spite of her resolve, her senses supplied the memory of what that hair felt like against her fingertips and then cruelly reminded her of how she'd ached and writhed beneath his powerful body. Maxine gasped, licked her lips, and forced herself to look at something, anything but his dazzling blue eyes or wide, inviting mouth.

Still trying to shake off a tingling sensation as his long, tanned fingers continued to hold her ever so gently, she evaded him again. "There's nothing wrong with me. I—I'm just curious about a few things. How'd your meeting in town go today? Did the governor say he was gonna get those bandits for you?"

"I did not see the governor," he said, his patience ebbing. "I spoke to the Board of Trustees—and no, I do not think they will be of much help. Now that you have my list of conversations for the day, would you mind telling me who *you* have been speaking to?"

"Me? About what?"

"I don't know, but I do know that something is wrong. Something or someone has upset you. You can tell me about it, Maxine." Caressing her shoulders, he assured her, "I promise I will not become angry with you—even if I should discover you joined my *vaqueros* for another round of poker."

Maxine laughed, but the sound quickly became more like a sob. "Nothing's really wrong, Dane. I have something for you." Taking a deep steadying breath, Maxine stepped away from him and pulled open the large pouch. After withdrawing a smaller leather bag, she handed it to him and said, "There's money in there. It's yours. The thousand you gave to get Max sprung and the five hundred Pa lost to you in San Francisco. Count it if you want, but it's all there."

Something about her tone and the offering itself gave Dane a bad feeling. "Thanks," he said, shoving the pouch into his back pocket. "I really didn't expect to be repaid at all, and certainly not this soon. Where did you get the money?"

She shrugged, but the movement was so slight that it looked more like another shiver. "Pa got real lucky in San Diego. We have enough left over to pay you for the wagon wheels, the supplies you bought for our trip, and even maybe buy a couple of things off you before we go."

Go. There it was, the word he'd been dreading. "Go, Maxine?" he said, choking on the sentence. "No one has asked you to leave. You and your family are my guests. You may stay as long as you like."

"Oh, thanks so much for the offer," she answered quickly, her voice too high. "And don't think we don't appreciate that or the hospitality you already gave us. It's just that Colorado and that Pike's Peak strike is calling us, and we have to get moving before there's nothing left!" She laughed, and her voice reached another octave.

His eyes turned cold and dark. "Are you really so set on going off to Colorado?"

Maxine shivered again, this time hard enough to

coax her shawl down low on her shoulders. She tried to feign composure. "Yes I am. We're leaving tomorrow. I've never been to Colorado. It doesn't sound like so bad a place to live, and after we hit our first strike . . ." She paused, wondering if the other information would make her departure more or less painful for them both. Deciding on less, she laughed and added, "Pa says he's gonna find me a man of my own."

Dane heard Maxine laughing, and the sound was anything but music to his ears. He thought of Caroline's assumptions about Maxine's love for him. Could this be Caroline's idea of a woman in love—a woman who could stand before him, laughing as she made plans to leave him, plans which actually included a new man, even though memories of being with him had to be so fresh in her mind and her body?

Dane's fists clenched, and the muscles knotted at his throat. When he was finally able to speak, his voice was hoarse. "A *man*, Rojita? I had thought you planned to find one of those here on my rancho."

"Well . . . ah, as you already know, that didn't work out too good," she said, realizing that telling him her plans had been a mistake. Perilously close to collapsing against Dane's chest and sobbing her heart out, Maxine drew in a deep breath. "People like you—your friends—are a little too fancy for a gal like me. Pa says it's better to find some miner whose ways are more like ours. Says it's time I got hitched up proper, but with someone of my own kind."

His usually velvet voice was rough and scratchy as he said, "And so you agreed?"

Maxine nodded, wondering why he looked so angry,

so blanched beneath his tan. "There's just one more thing. Pa and Max want to keep the clothes you got for them, and me—" She glanced down at her costume. "I really do like this dress. A gal doesn't need to wear all those petticoats or corsets with it. I like it a lot. How much for all the clothes?"

Although she hadn't thought it possible, Dane's expression darkened even more. "Be my guest," he snapped.

He was angry, and Maxine wasn't exactly sure why. "Thank you then, and thank your intended, too. Caroline's been real nice to me, but I'd be willing to bet our lucky nuggets that she's gonna be a lot happier once us McKains are out from underfoot."

Seeing the first glimmer of light, Dane softened his tone and his expression as he said, "You are not in Caroline's way. She and I won't be getting married after all."

"Not . . . *married?*"

Dane slowly shook his head, watching her reaction as he quietly whispered, "No." He was expecting to see relief, perhaps excitement, but what he saw stunned him. Maxine looked horrified, panicked.

"I was afraid of this," she cried, her hands to her cheeks. "I just knew she'd figure out what we done at the pond! Caroline just knows everything. She guesses and she knows—she *knows!*"

Dane reached for her, but Maxine spun away from him. Trying to keep up with her as she paced in erratic circles, he insisted, "It doesn't matter, Rojita—even if she has guessed the extent of our relationship, it simply doesn't matter anymore."

"But of course it does," she cried, tears blurring her vision, threatening the last of her composure. "And it's all my fault! Now I have to fix it. I have to go to her, have to apologize and make her see that I'm the one made you do it." She dropped her voice as she added, "Oh, and I did you know. I ran you to the ground just like a hound on a squirrel, wouldn't let up on you till I got what I wanted, till I got you to do lovemaking on me."

Concerned about their privacy, Dane glanced beyond her to the open archway and then back to her stricken face. "I won't let you talk like that or take the blame—if there's even any blame to be taken. I wanted you as much as you wanted me. We made a mutual decision that has nothing to do with Caroline or her happiness. She and I do not love each other, and that is the reason we are not getting married—the only reason, Rojita, *comprende?*"

Maxine came to a halt. She didn't believe him for a minute, but she did understand. Dane could see her tears, her hysteria, and if she didn't quiet down soon, the whole house would be aware of their indiscretion—if they weren't already. She was causing another scene, humiliating him and herself, again. She had to end this visit—her final moments with him—now.

Maxine straightened her shoulders and said, "Sorry if I got too loud. If you're still offering, I thank you for the dress. I don't need this shawl, so why don't you give it back to Catalina." With that, she slipped it off and tossed it onto the settee, where it settled over the soft velvet cushion like a shroud.

"A properly dressed Doña keeps her *rebozo* around

her shoulders at all times," he said, preparing himself for what he must do next.

"As I already told you, I am *not* a Doña. And I think we both know there isn't much proper about me either."

"There is at least one thing I can think of," he countered, unable to keep his hands off her any longer. "You most definitely know how to give a man a proper kiss."

Then, to her surprise, Dane dragged her into his arms. Maxine tried—not too hard—to resist him, to deny the deep yearning to show him exactly how properly she could kiss him, but she lost the battle the moment his lips came down on hers. She took what he offered greedily, eagerly drinking the sensations, knowing how terribly long this feast would have to last her. When Dane finally pulled away from her, panting, she still hadn't had her fill and knew she would be starving for him again before she could even catch her breath.

"*Dios mio, querida,*" he whispered, his voice husky with desire. "How long have you been saving that kiss for me?"

Trying to ignore her body and its lightning responses to his touch, she twisted away from him. "I was just saying goodbye, that's all."

But Dane caught up with her and pulled her back toward the settee. "No, Rojita. We've much to say to one another, but goodbye isn't part of it. You don't have to pretend with me—tell me what you feel."

Shaking her head, Maxine tried to tug away from his grip, but he held fast. "I don't feel anything," she insisted. "I just have to go."

"No, you do not," he whispered softly. "What if I ask you to stay?"

"It won't matter. I can't stay—you know I can't."

"You can," he heard himself say. "And if you are Doña Maxine of Rancho Cordoba, you must." At her puzzled expression, the words he'd never said before to anyone fairly tumbled out. "On my honor as a gentleman, I am asking you to be my wife."

Maxine's entire system seemed to shut down, frosting over. Had she heard him right? Had Dane del Cordobes, master of all as far as the eye could see, asked her, Maxine McKain, to marry him? Impossible! Why would he?

"Did you just ask me to *marry* you?"

He nodded solemnly. "I can offer no less."

She circled him warily, still stunned, and then reacted the only way she knew how, the only way she could. She laughed, but the sound was bitter, angry.

"If that isn't the biggest load of flapdoodle I've ever heard, I don't know what is." Then, with a toss of her head, she spun on her heel as if to stomp out of the room.

Dane caught her in his arms, bending her backwards as he leaned in close and said, "This is no joke, Rojita. I never joke where honor is concerned."

"Honor?" she said weakly. "I don't know what you mean."

Dane eased the pressure of his grip now that he had her attention. Surely she knew how deadly serious he was. "Back on the trail as we traveled from the eldorado, I made a promise to your father. Do you recall what it was?"

"Pa?"

"Yes, your father. I promised him I would not lay so much as a finger on you. That I would not *touch* you."

Maxine shivered. Her tongue darted out, licking her bottom lip.

"But I did," he went on, his voice soft and low, "didn't I?"

Maxine couldn't speak. She could barely raise her eyes to gaze up at him as she nodded.

"I touched you and then I made love to you—not once, but twice. Remember?" His lips brushed her cheek and settled on her mouth for just an instant, like a hummingbird dipping for a taste of nectar. "I stole your honor, and even more, I suspect. Have I your heart as well?"

Funny that he'd said the word *heart.* Maxine was very aware of that particular organ at the moment, as it was pounding, as if too big to be contained in her chest, close to exploding with an enormous rush of love. And through it all, she could not manage to form words.

Dane smiled down at her, his warm breath heating her lips as he went on. "I would only hope that I served you well as a lover, Maxine, because I have failed miserably as a gentleman. I can do no less for you or your father than to offer my name in marriage. Have I your word that you will become my wife?"

That frozen sensation which had kept her rooted to the spot before now permeated her, sank into her vital organs, and wrapped its icy tendrils around the heart Dane had warmed so thoroughly only moments ago. She'd heard him right. Dane *had* asked her to marry him, but not for the reasons she'd supposed—not for the reasons she'd hoped. He offered himself out of duty, out of *pity*.

"Rojita?" His velvety voice stroked her ears. "What is your answer?"

Maxine gazed up at him, indulging her eyes with one last look at his smooth bronzed features, her hands as she slid them around his neck and down inside the open front of his shirt, and yes, even her lips as she pressed them against his for one final kiss. Then, thinking how cruel this "gentlemanly" thing called honor was, she stepped out of the circle of Dane's arms.

Keeping the word *pity* foremost in her mind, she smiled bravely, if deceitfully, and said, "Thank you kindly for asking, Don Francisco, but no thanks. I've enjoyed the visit here, but there's just too many rules and manners to follow, too many forks and spoons and such for a gal like me. You're better off with someone like Caroline, and I'm better off—without you." She couldn't look at him after the words were out, or she would have reached up and snatched them back. Instead, she twisted away, facing the archway, and worked at forming the final word, "goodbye."

Now it was Dane who was shocked, Dane who felt as if he were standing in a barrel of ice water. "Rojita?" he said. "Do I hear you correctly? Are you saying that you do not love me?"

She bit down on her lip, wondering how she would ever manage the lie. Then she noticed a shadow in the hallway, a short, crooked shadow which seemed to be inching closer to the room. Pa!

Facing Dane again, she swallowed hard and did what had to be done. "Love you?" She laughed. "Why that's just crazy. I have to go now, and all the talking in the world isn't going to change that fact. I gotta go."

"But Maxine, there are so many things yet for us to—"

"Maxie girl?" Dicey's voice drifted into the room, cutting off Dane's objections. "You in there?"

Keeping her gaze on Dane and her back to the archway, she quietly said, "Yes, Pa."

"Time we're a gettin' some rest. Got a long day of travel tomorrow."

She kept her eyes trained on Dane. "Coming, Pa."

Dane took a step toward her. "You can't leave."

Dicey called out. "I'll just be walkin' you to yur room now, Maxie."

"Okay, Pa," she said, resuming her retreat.

"Don't go, Rojita," Dane whispered, his expression riddled with longing and regret. "I don't want you to go."

A single teardrop, as solitary and alone as she felt, rolled down Maxine's cheek. Taking another backward step, hiding herself in the shadows, she slowly shook her head. "It's better that we say goodbye now. Marry Caroline. Have a happy life."

Swallowing a lump the size of his fist, Dane made a final plea. "I'm begging you—please stay."

She wanted to. Oh, how she wanted to.

"Maxie? Dona' make me come in there and get you."

"Coming, Pa."

But just before she turned to run out of the room, out of Dane's life, Maxine took an extra moment. She blew a kiss across the room and whispered so softly that only he could hear, "I'll never forget you." Then she was gone.

Dane couldn't have followed after her if he wanted to. He was frozen to the spot, stunned beyond belief. He'd strolled into his home this evening, his thoughts consumed by both Caroline and Maxine, his mind troubled to think that soon he would break the heart of one of them. Why had it never occurred to him that the heart broken would be his own?

19

The following morning, the fog was still so thick it obliterated the rising sun. Despite the weather, the McKain family was almost ready to begin their journey. Out in the yard, Maxine tossed her freshly packed valise into the back of the wagon and reached inside for her Palo Alto. Dressed for the trail again in her Levi's and oversized man's shirt, she shivered against the damp air and considered climbing inside to look for a jacket.

Then a door slammed. Maxine glanced back toward the house. Was it Dane at last? Much to her disappointment—and relief, she supposed—he hadn't come downstairs to bid them good morning, to see them off, or even more unlikely, to try to convince them to stay. Yet surely he must have heard them moving and known they were up and about. She and Dicey had made enough noise to wake even the inhabitants of the neighboring ranchos as they'd gathered their belongings and made several trips up and down the wooden staircase. Hadn't their clamor disturbed Dane? Was he waiting until the last moment, saving them all from any more scenes like the one they had last night?

When the figure she saw coming toward her through the fog turned out to be her father, Maxine shook off a sharp sense of disappointment and tugged the hat down over her head.

"All set, Maxie girl?" Dicey asked, joining her at the rear of the wagon.

"Just about. How'd you make out in the kitchen?"

He hefted a large flour sack, the contents bulging against the seams. "Manuela packed us enough tortillas and vittles to last us through the next month or so."

Showing her father a smile that was barely this side of a frown, she sighed and said, "Then I guess we'd best be on our way. I'll go tell Max to hitch up the mules."

Before she could back away from the wagon, her brother appeared and shuffled up beside them.

"Morning, Pa. Morning, Maxie." Max yawned, not bothering to cover his mouth, and smacked his lips. "Rosa wants some a that good coffee from the house. Can I go get some good coffee, Pa?"

"Sorry, son. It's time we got on our way. Get the mules harnessed and tell Rosa we'll be a leavin' now."

Max shook his head, the movements quick and jerky, violent enough for Maxine to realize he was in what she liked to call his "stone wall" frame of mind.

Maxine was in no mood for nonsense. She sighed and said, "What is it, Max? Did you forget to collect one of your critters yesterday, or something?"

Again he shook his head, this time harder. "Dane said we can't go. *Don't go* is what he said."

At the words, a nearly identical repeat of what he'd said to her last evening, Maxine rolled anguished eyes in Dicey's direction and bit her lip.

Taking the cue, he turned to his son and asked, "When did you talk to that Spaniard, boy? This mornin'?"

Max nodded. "He come got Alazan."

Dicey's brow puckered. "He took a ride, you say?"

"Yes, Pa. Him and a whole lot of his men. Rode off, they did."

Dicey patted his son's back and said, "Go on, boy— get them mules. We can't be a waitin' around to say goodbye to that Spaniard all mornin'." He took a sideways glance at Maxine. "We said all that needs sayin' to him last evenin' anyways. Got to be movin' on down the road."

But Max rooted himself to the ground like the thick tree trunk his body resembled. "Don't go. Dane *said*."

"Now look here, boy. Dane ain't yur pa, *I* am. I say we're a headin' out. *Now*."

Max's chin quivered, and he slammed his eyes shut and squeezed them hard.

"Dane made him promise," said a female voice which came from nowhere.

Dicey and Maxine spun around in unison to see Rosa peeking around the barn door.

"When Dane talked to Max," she said, "he made him promise on the lucky nuggets that the wagon would not move from this spot until he got back."

Sighing heavily, afraid she would begin to cry, Maxine

folded her arms across her breasts and began dragging the toe of her boot through the dirt.

Dicey scratched his beard, his face puckered into a scowl. "And just how long we s'posed to wait? Did that fancy Spaniard mention how long he might take for this mornin' ride?"

"I think it is more than a ride." With steps, hesitant and tiny, Rosa joined the family and related what she'd heard. "There was some trouble near the west range where most of the cattle are. All of the *vaqueros* went there. Dane went east to check on the man guarding his horses. He said he would ride the boundaries."

Dicey tore off his hat and slapped it against his thigh. "I dona' like this! I dona' like it one bit. What does the man think he'll be a-changin' by delayin' us this way?"

Surely not the marriage proposal! Maxine thought. She had wisely kept Dane's offer to herself. To discuss it with her father would have led to questions and explanations. But what if, for some crazy reason, Dane still insisted that he must make a "decent woman" of her and marry her? Dicey, though not normally a violent man, would probably go after Dane's head when he found out why!

Keeping her voice calm, she said, "I'll go get him, Pa. I'll bring him back or at least get him to take back the promise. Max will settle for that."

"Max might, but that ain't gonna move one inch toward settlin' with me!" He limped up toward Maxine until he was only inches from and level with her gaze. "I had the bedroom next to yurs, remember, girl? Kept me up all night caterwaulin' and carryin' on over that Spaniard, you did."

He'd heard her? Her father had listened to her incessant, broken-hearted sobs during the night? Her cheeks flaming, Maxine averted her gaze and stammered, "I— I'm okay now, Pa. Really I am. Got him out of my system last night. I swear I did. Honest and truly."

Dicey shook his head as vehemently and violently as Max ever had. "I may not be the best pa on the face of the earth, but I do know a losin' poker hand when I see one. We're a-tossin' in the cards where that fancy Spaniard is concerned. You'll not be ridin' off after him and that's that!"

Rosa spoke up again, surprising them all with her new boldness. "Maxine is the best choice to go for Dane. Max is needed here," she said, sparing his feelings, "and you, sir, cannot sit a horse with that knee. It must be Maxine or me. I do not think Dane trusts me, but he will listen to Maxine."

"That so?" Dicey bellowed. "Well just who's *she* gonna listen to if'n I let her tear off after him? Huh? Answer me that—who?"

Rosa glanced at Maxine, a wealth of understanding and sympathy reflected in her expression. Softening her tone, she addressed Dicey again. "I think that today, she will listen to herself. She will do that because she loves this family. Is this not so, Maxine?"

Feeling numb, Maxine nodded. "I want to get away from Dane and California as bad as you do, Pa. You got to let me go after him."

"How about we all go?" Dicey suggested. "We'll just be makin' a little detour on our way out."

Maxine frowned at her father, and turned to her brother. "Go get Rocio ready and bring her to me, Max. Hurry." As soon as he'd disappeared, she finished the conversation with her father. "How we all gonna go if Max won't let us take the wagon off this spot? You gonna move him?"

Dicey picked at his beard in hesitation. "I dona' like the idea of you out there alone with that Spaniard! Damned if I do!"

"I know you don't," she said softly, "but the only other choice we got is to wait Dane out. Knowing him and that stubborn streak he's got, he might just stay out there all day and all night, too. Don't worry about me. I'm gonna be just fine."

He knew he really had no other choice, so he gave her his grudging consent. "You'd best be, girl. You'd best keep yur wits about you, too."

Maxine gave her father a hug as Max returned with the mare.

Helping his daughter aboard Rocio's smooth back, Dicey called out a warning. "I'll give you ten minutes—hear me? If'n yur not back in ten minutes, I'll just be comin' after you, on foot if'n I have to!"

Warming to this rare, protective side of her father, Maxine glanced out at the valley, with its heavy blanket of fog, and then looked back to Dicey. "Best give me closer to thirty, Pa. It will probably take me longer than ten minutes to find him out in that mess."

Grumbling to himself, Dicey offered a short nod. "Just be takin' care of yurself—hear me, girl? Hear me?"

"I hear you."

And for the next ten minutes, she did hear his warning, repeated it to herself several times over, in fact, to drive its message home. Her meeting with Dane this morning would be short and simple: *Take the spell off my brother. We're leaving. Goodbye.*

Maxine was rehearsing these words when she spotted a horse and rider drifting in and out of the fog. He was wearing black, bobbing along atop an animal that blended in with the heavy mist. Even from a distance, she knew it had to be Dane. Urging Rocio into an easy lope, she closed the distance between them.

When he heard a horse approaching and glanced behind him to identify the rider, Dane was not only displeased, he was enraged. His cattle were stampeding in the west range, and out here in the east range, where his huge herd of purebred Andalusian horses should be, he couldn't find one stray filly or even a *vaquero*. Something—something dangerous, he suspected—was wrong. And for all he knew, Chubasco had a hand in the trouble. How could Maxine even think of riding out here alone?

By the time she'd reached his side, his growing anxieties prompted him to forget himself, and he swore as he asked, "What in the . . . *hell* are you doing out here?"

She rolled her eyes, amazed to hear such language coming from his very proper mouth. "I think you know the answer to that. What I didn't know was that a fancy gentleman like yourself could pull such a dirty trick as using the McKains' very own lucky nuggets to get to Max."

Showing her a smug grin, Dane said, "It worked, didn't it?"

"I guess you can see that it did. Now come back to the barn with me and take it off of him. Tell Max we're free to go. Pa's getting all in a twist to get on down the road."

"Sorry," he said with a shake of his head. "Your father is just going to have to find some way to get himself untwisted."

Dane nudged the stallion's withers, guiding him to Rocio's side, and reached out and caught Maxine by the shoulders. "I'm *not* letting you go. We spoke of many things last night," he whispered, sliding his fingers up to her throat and dragging the tip of his thumb across her lower lip. "But there are many more things we did not say, things that must be said. I stayed up half the night thinking about it, and I have made a decision. You, Miss McKain, are not going *anywhere*."

Maxine's eyes closed at his touch. Her tongue met the tip of his thumb, and then she instinctively drew it into her mouth. A shudder coursed from her head to her feet, curling her toes inside her boots. God help her! Would she ever stop wanting this man? She began to shiver, but she couldn't seem to stop herself. It must be the cold, she convinced herself. But she thought of her father and his warnings.

Dropping Rocio's reins, Maxine rubbed her arms and stuttered as she said, "I-it's not your choice or your decision, Dane. The McKains are leaving one way or the other. Together. Please come back to the house so we can get on our way."

"You're the only one who's going back to the house—and you're going right now. It's not safe out here for you. There's been some trouble, and I don't want . . ." The words died in his throat as he picked out a spot of color through the fog. It appeared that a red shirt or bandanna was lying on the ground. Issuing the order from under his breath, Dane said, "Wait here a minute. Don't move. I'll be right back."

"B-but—"

"Don't move! *Comprende?*"

Maxine gulped, and nodded, and Dane galloped off, disappearing into the mist. When he reappeared a few minutes later, he was noticeably shaken, pale despite his tan.

His tone was grim as he said, "It's one of my *vaqueros.* He's been shot. Go on, Maxine. Get out of here—*now.*"

This time she spoke with her heart, not her head. "Not without you."

Dane felt his heart, and every vital organ, swelling with concern, heating with anger. Using that rage to ensure her safety, he jerked the bullwhip off his shoulder, fit the grip to his palm, then pointed it in her direction. "If I have to, I will use this," he warned. "Get back to the house!"

As he drew back his arm to further convince her, Alazan began prancing, nervous and agitated, and then he shied, nearly unseating Dane. "Easy!" he shouted at the stallion, but the animal began to circle, snorting and tossing his silvery mane.

Alazan's warning became clear when the ground beneath them thundered with thousands of hooves— Rancho Cordoba Andalusians, he surmised with a sinking heart, and probably all five hundred, judging from the tremendous reverberations. More ominous than the sound was the fact those hoofbeats were fading, heading away from the ranch, south toward Mexico.

"*Sangre de Christo!*" he muttered under his breath. Sliding the bullwhip back up to his shoulder, Dane clenched and unclenched his fists as he spoke, not really to Maxine, but more to himself. "The cattle stampede in the west ranges was only a diversion! A trick which left our valuable horses practically unguarded."

Turning to Maxine, who hadn't uttered a word, he issued a rapid-fire order. "Go back to the ranch. Get Ernesto and tell him the *bandidos* have taken the entire herd of horses. Have him go after my men. Tell them to start looking for me on the way to Mexico, near the pond where they found us. The trail should not be too difficult to find from there—*comprende?*"

She opened her mouth, thinking for one insane minute of objecting, but the white-hot anger she saw in his eyes changed her mind. Without so much as a goodbye, Maxine kicked Rocio and took off for the rancho. When she arrived at the stables, she slid off the mare's back and hit the ground running.

"Rosa? Pa? Max?" she called out as she burst into the barn.

"What's yur fever, Maxie girl?" Dicey said, nearly crashing into her as she raced down the aisle.

Maxine relayed the story and then turned to Rosa, who'd been listening along with Dicey. "Please, go to the house, find Ernesto, and give him Dane's orders."

Rosa turned on her heel and sprinted out of the barn.

"Maxie?" Dicey said, alarm creeping up his spine. "What are you thinkin' of doin', girl?"

Ignoring her father's question, she approached her brother. "Got a favor to ask you, Max. I want to borrow your *serape*, okay?"

Max hugged himself, keeping the garment squeezed against his chest, and turned his head away from his sister.

"Please, Max? I wouldn't ask if I didn't need it so bad. Dane needs it, too."

As she'd hoped, those final words were magic to his ears. Slowly, still a little bit reluctant, Max lifted it over his head and handed it to her.

"Thanks," she said, sliding the *serape* over her head. Although it was much too large for her, it served its purpose—the generous surplus of fabric covered as much of her as possible, making her look less feminine and, she hoped, more like a *vaquero*.

She hurried from the barn to the wagon. When she began digging through her valise, Dicey grabbed hold of her arm and said, "That's enough, Maxie. If yur even a-thinkin' of going back out—"

"I'm not just thinking about it, Pa," she said, wriggling free of his grip. After finding her knife and looping it and the matching leather holder through her belt, she turned back to him. "I'm doing it. You can't stop me, so's you'd best get out of my way."

"Now see here," he barked, shaking a parental finger in her face. "I'm yur pa and I'm a-tellin' you—"

"Sorry, but this is something you really can't stop me from doing. No use in you even trying." Taking one precious moment, she put her arms around him and said, "I love Dane. You know how much I love him. You can make me leave and you can make sure I never

see him again, but ya can't make me let him die. I'd
rather die myself."

"But, Maxie—yur bein' unreasonable."

"No, I'm not. I seen them bandits. I know the kind
of men they are, how they think. How's a fancy gentleman like Dane gonna face them alone? He needs me.
I'm going after him."

With that, she grabbed Rocio's mane and jerked
herself up on the mare's back.

"Wait then!" Dicey called out. "If'n yur so set on
helping him, at least go a little better prepared." He
reached inside the wagon, lifted the secret boards at
the back, and drew out the rusty old Colt the family
kept for emergencies. Checking the cylinder to make
certain that all six bullets were in place, he limped up
to Rocio.

"Here," he said, handing Maxine the weapon. "Stick
this in the waistband of yur Levi's—just make sure you
don't blow your foot off or somethin'. If anyone comes
at you, anyone a'tall who looks like he might be
plannin' you harm, dona' even think twice about
shootin' a hole in 'em."

"Got it, Pa," she said, stowing the pistol. Then she
blew her father a kiss and galloped off.

Maxine tracked Dane until she came to the south-
ernmost corner of Rancho Cordoba. There, Alazan's
hoofprints became lost in the thoroughly trampled
ground. Following this larger, more obvious trail, she
forged two rivers, the second of which took her out of
the fog and into bright sunshine, and moved into terrain

which steadily grew more arid and harsh, a landscape which resembled something between the shrub-dusted hills of San Diego and the stark Borrego Badlands. When the tracks veered sharply into a narrow canyon, Maxine pulled Rocio to a halt and decided to investigate on foot. She tied the mare to the branches and left her tucked beneath the shade of a mesquite tree.

Hugging her body against the canyon walls and keeping an eye out for the slightest sign that she was being watched, Maxine walked for nearly an hour. She'd just about decided to go back and get Rocio when she spotted what she'd been looking for. Ahead, at the crest of one of the small mountain peaks, she picked out the colorful *serape* and oversized *sombrero* of one of the bandits. Taking off her hat and squashing it between her hands, she flattened her body against the side of the hill and inched her way toward the lookout.

As she moved, Maxine looked for a fist-sized rock. She found a rain-smoothed stone big enough to fill her palm yet small enough to afford her a firm grip. After taking only a few more steps, she figured she was in a position almost directly below the bandit. Then she took a deep breath and put her daring, if not outright insane, plan into action.

Dropping the hat at her feet, Maxine quickly undid her braid and dragged her fingers through her hair until it draped her shoulders and hung down her back. Gripping the stone so hard that her fingers turned white, she prayed that there was only one guard and then staggered out into the center of the wash.

"H-help," she cried, her voice feeble. "Please h-help me." She fell to her knees, listening, still praying, and her reward was the sound of pebbles and sand rolling down the hillside like a tiny waterfall. Someone was coming to her rescue.

Jumping back to her feet to get into position, Maxine kept the hand with the rock buried in the folds of the oversized *serape*. Then she turned and faced the bandit. His pistol was drawn, pointed at her, as he descended the mountain.

Recognizing suspicion along with a healthy dose of surprise in his expression, Maxine fluttered her lashes and made her voice even weaker as she cried out one more time. "H-help me . . . please, h-help me."

When he hit the flat not six feet from her, the bandit's surprised expression became amused and lascivious. Grinning now, he sheathed his weapon with reckless abandon and made his final approach.

When he was within reach, Maxine struck faster than a rattlesnake. She swung her hand, the rock exposed, as hard as she could against his temple. After the collision of skull and stone, the bandit crumpled into a heap at her feet without so much as a groan of surprise.

Maxine made a quick scan of the hilltop to satisfy herself that he was truly alone, and then she dragged him over to the base of the mountain and out of sight. Working quickly, she tore off Max's *serape* and replaced it with the bandit's, ripped the Mexican's shirt into strips, and bound his feet and hands. After she relieved him of his *sombrero* and bright red bandanna, she tied the scarf around her head, and donned the bandit's hat, stuffing her hair up into it. Taking only one more moment to gag the man with the sleeve of his shirt, she slid his pistol next to her father's, making the waist of her Levi's unbearably snug, and then worked her way up the side of the mountain.

When she reached the lookout's spot, a comfortable little niche carved out and smoothed to resemble the seat of a chair, she settled into it and took a cautious look around. Apparently the man she'd knocked out was the only guard—but of what? The camp? And if the bandits were hiding themselves and their ill-gotten stock in the immediate vicinity, were they up the canyon around the bend, or behind her on the other side of the mountain?

Taking the easier route first, Maxine crawled up to the crest of the hill and cautiously peeked over the side. Below, she saw a box canyon, the closed end filled with hundreds of horses restrained by a succession of rope gates. Lining the walls in front of the herd were several small lean-tos and a couple of tents. This was the bandits' camp.

She did a rough count of the shelters and the few men she could see below and concluded that not even half of the bandits were in camp. Where was Dane? Was he sneaking up on them from some other angle, or . . .

The question was answered when she looked directly below her. Dane was tied to what appeared to be some kind of stump or dead tree stripped of its branches.

The thick black hair she loved so much was exposed to the sun, and Dane's head slumped down on his chest, as if he were unconscious. Then she saw some movement. He shifted his weight from one foot to the other, then back again. He looked extremely uncomfortable, if not in a lot of pain.

At the sight, Maxine had to stuff her fist in her mouth and bite down on her knuckles to keep from crying out. She squinted to get a better look at his face. Had he been knocked silly, beaten too severely for rational thought, or would he understand that she was here to help him?

Dane leaned back then, flexing the muscles of his neck, exposing a wide, crooked path of blood which coursed down from his hairline to his collar. Enraged, Maxine slid back down to the lookout's nest and made a vow.

No matter what it cost her—her own life if necessary—she would find a way to set him free. There just had to be a way for her to rescue one bloodied man. There *had* to be.

20

Holding a cup of water in his hand, Chubasco swaggered up to his captive and drove the toe of his boot into his shinbone.

Dane's knees buckled, and then he groaned. Slowly, he opened his eyes and glared at his old friend.

"That is a nasty cut you have, *amigo.*" Chubasco laughed, pointing to the gash just above his left temple, and added, "It is too bad the stallion you ride is so clumsy, is it not?" Dane's chin dropped down to his chest again, but the bandit went on. "You may be pleased to know that your fearless mount did not break his leg in the fall—he has joined the rest of your herd." Chubasco grinned as he corrected himself, "Joined the rest of *my* herd, where I am sure he will be quite happy. Does this news please you, *amigo?*"

"All you need do to please me," Dane managed, even though darts of pain shot through his head, "is to cut me loose and allow me to return my property to Rancho Cordoba."

Chubasco roared with laugher, the sound ugly and cruel. "Why should I return *your* property, *cabrone*? Has anyone returned mine? Do you think they ever will?"

Disoriented, too dazed to make sense of Chubasco's words, Dane said, "Why are you doing this to me? We were friends, *amigos,* remember?"

"Ah, yes, *amigos.* I do seem to recall practicing the *corrida de toros* with the son of a Spanish Army Captain." Chubasco stroked his chin, as if lost in the past. "Ah yes, that boy rode the finest horses I'd ever seen—Andalusians like your great stallion—while I, a poor boy from Mexico . . . was that you, *cabrone*?"

Even though the pressure in his head made it feel as if it might explode at any minute, Dane raised his chin and leveled an exacting gaze toward his old friend. "You know it was me. I can't believe this is *you!* Your bitterness cannot have been caused over some breeding stock my father brought with him from Spain. Why are you really doing this? How could you have sunk so low?"

Chubasco laughed, then took a long drink of water. "Thirsty, *amigo?*" he asked, uninterested in Dane's answer as he formed his own. "According to you and the few noble Spanish Dons remaining in San Diego, I behave exactly as they expect a lowly Californio to behave, *es verdad?*"

Dane studied the man, pleased to note the scabs on his face, remnants of Maxine's battle with him. Suppressing a satisfied grin, Dane tried to reason with him. "I have never considered you as less than my equal, or treated you in that manner either."

After taking another sip of water, Chubasco gave him a grudging nod. "No, *amigo*, you have not—but then you have been gone for how long? Eight, ten years? A lot has happened in that time, has it not?" Leaning in close, his nose inches from Dane's, he snarled, "During that time, Rancho del Sol was stolen—hear me? *Stolen* from the Sanchez family."

Dane shook his head. Whip-like jolts of pain followed the movement. Closing his eyes against the sensations, he quietly said, "I know nothing of this. Why do you punish *me* if your home was stolen?"

Closing in on Dane again, Chubasco spat. "You may not have known of the theft, but you helped drive us off the land—you and your rich committee members up in San Francisco, that is."

Fighting his way through the haze and the sour stench of Chubasco's breath, Dane struggled to remember, to place Rancho del Sol as one of the land grants he ruled for or against during his brief tenure as a member of the United States Land Committee. He could not.

"I—I do not remember your rancho specifically. Did you present a deed of some kind?"

"No," he grumbled, "but you are aware that many rancho owners like ourselves did not have *disenos*. We marked a few boundaries, and the land was granted to us. My family informed the committee of those boundaries, so why was our grant not honored?"

Dane tried to remember, but since 1855, when he'd been appointed to the Land Commission, so many claims had been presented from one end of California to the other, he simply could not recall the circumstances or the judgment made against Rancho del Sol.

Shaking his head more carefully this time, Dane said, "I honestly do not know what happened. I did not have anything to do with the disposition of your land. I can only guess that you did not provide enough proof or find neighbors who were able to testify to the accuracy of your boundaries. How can you hold me accountable for your loss?"

"You were a committee member, were you not?"

"Yes, one of many committees, and then only one of three, but I—"

"But nothing! Our rancho was stolen, claimed by squatters, and you did nothing to help us. None of our fine neighbors did."

"How could they?" Dane flinched, hoping to ward off a sudden dizziness, and then stared into Chubasco's eyes. "Where were you during the fighting and the American takeover? If I recall, the Sanchez family fled to Mexico to await the outcome of the war. To choose sides after victory was assured by one of them, *es verdad?* Your land was left in ruins, abandoned. Did you really expect to win it back so easily?"

Chubasco took a large swallow of water and then spat it in Dane's face. "None of that matters anymore. I am taking back only a small part of what I have lost. Your brother learned that lesson the hard way, and now the little brother will, too."

His pain forgotten, Dane lunged against his bindings. "What are you saying?"

The bandit laughed. "Only that Francisco should have stayed at his home and done what all Spanish

Dons do best—polish his silver. He never should have tried to stop Chubasco. It was a mistake, the same one you are making today."

Dane fought the ropes so hard this time, he could feel the rough twine cutting into his chest as he shouted, "*You* were involved in Frank's death? You killed him?"

Again Chubasco laughed, this time louder, with more pleasure in his voice. "Not I, *amigo*. Your brother was killed by his own cattle. I simply made certain he was lying in their path as they stampeded—as you will be when we drive your horses to New Mexico. They will bring me a fortune."

Although he strained his bonds to their limits, Dane could not burst through the ropes which held him or reach the throat he longed to squeeze between his hands. Thoughts of his brother's unnecessary death and Maxine's indignities at this beast's hands turned his mind murderous, but Dane's only recourse was to hurtle idle threats.

"You miserable *hijo de perra!* You will pay for your crimes. I will make certain that someday you pay, and pay dearly!"

"Such names coming from your aristocratic mouth," Chubasco taunted. "But if there is a son of a bitch here, *amigo,* it is you. You and your *gringa* mother—you and your *gringa puta.*" He touched the scabs on his cheek. "I will find that *peliroja puta* again, and when I do, I will make her very sorry for leaving her mark on me. Then," he added, leering, "after I give her some more of my good loving, I will *kill* her."

Although it took every ounce of strength he possessed, Dane kept the hatred, and the fear, out of his expression, choking back the angry words that crowded his throat. He looked down at the ground and forced himself to say the words, "Do whatever you wish to her. She means nothing to me."

Chubasco laughed and held up the cup. "Of course not, *amigo*. She means no more than this water I offer." Then he inverted the cup. When nothing but a couple of droplets fell from the rim, he shrugged and said, "*Perdona me.* I see that I have been too greedy. I guess you will have to go to your death thirsty after all."

Making a great show of studying the sun's position, Chubasco shrugged and added, "I do not think you will have too long a wait. The rest of my men, along with some of your cattle, should be joining us soon." Then, with another laugh, he dropped the cup at Dane's feet and strode off toward the corral where his men were selecting fresh horses—Rancho Cordoba stock—for their long journey to New Mexico.

Through narrowed eyes, Dane followed the bandit's retreat to the closed end of the canyon, and let his breath out in a long sigh. He had but one chance. His only hope was that Maxine had relayed the urgency of his dilemma to Ernesto and that his *mayordomo* had been successful in tracking his *vaqueros*. Successful and swift, he amended, realizing just how slim his chances of survival were, given the desperation of Chubasco and those like him.

His brother Frank had written to him of the *bandido* problem, about the wild, resentful group of Spanish-Californians left homeless by the "manifest destiny" which had been assured by the American victory. Right or wrong, what had happened to the Sanchez family and others like them, was no different from their own conquest and subsequent domination of the Indians. But of course, men like Chubasco didn't see it that way.

The difference, however, with the exception of those properties which were outright stolen, was that the inhabitants of most ranchos were given the chance to prove ownership, to present petitions or maps to the Land Commission. Those families who could not produce a *diseno* or even find another landholder to testify as to the rancho boundaries had to forfeit their rights. To Dane's knowledge, Rancho del Sol had presented its claim, and that claim had been declared invalid by the joint ruling of the Land Commission. How could Chubasco hold the loss of his land against the del Cordobes family? Did they, in some ways, deserve part of the blame?

Wrapped in his thoughts, his head pounding, Dane was unaware that another bandido had approached him until a finger reached out and poked him in the gut. He jerked his head up and found the most beautiful brown eyes he'd ever seen staring up at him from beneath an oversized sombrero.

"Are you all right?" she whispered.

"*Maxine? Christo!* What are you doing here?"

"Hush!" She glanced around, relieved to see that Chubasco and his men were still too occupied with exchanging horses and saddles to have noticed her arrival. Then she turned back to Dane and asked, "How badly are you hurt? Anywhere besides your head?"

"Get out!" he snapped, his glance darting to the closed end of the canyon. "Run *now*. If Chubasco sees you, he'll—"

"I can't. Your *vaqueros* are spread all over the west valley. No telling when Ernesto can round them up. I'm your only chance. Can you move or think straight?"

Perhaps not as straight as he'd thought, for Dane found himself actually trying to work up a plan using Maxine. "Did you bring weapons?" he whispered, keeping one eye on the bandits.

"Yes." She began to circle him then, muttering under her breath as she walked, "I just knew you were too fancy for this kind a work. That's the only reason my pa let me go—I told him a fancy fellah like you wouldn't know what to do if he caught up to those bandits." Directly behind him now, she slipped her knife between his bound hands and said, "Hang onto this—don't let it fall. I can't spend more than a second back here or I might get noticed. Work the ropes over and see if you can't get them sawed apart."

"I know what to do, Maxine, in spite of what you might think." Working the knife rapidly, and still watching the bandits, he added, "They tripped Alazan with a rope buried in the sand. I was ambushed."

By then, she'd circled back in front of him. "I wasn't."

As Dane tried to come up with a fast retort, he noticed Chubasco glancing over at them. "Quick, Maxine! Do something to me."

"Do something?" She too became aware that they were being observed.

"Anything, whatever a bandit would do."

Maxine doubled up her fist and drove it into his chin.

She'd used less force than she would have if she'd meant business, but the blow still snapped Dane's head back. Horrified, she squeaked out, "Are you all right?"

"No thanks to you. Watch him and let me concentrate on cutting myself loose." Dane closed his eyes and renewed the vicious swipes at his bindings.

As he worked, Maxine kept one eye on the other end of the canyon. When she noticed Chubasco had moved away from his men and was walking in their direction, she said, "Time's up! Here he comes. Are you free yet?"

"No. Run, get away. I can defend myself now that I have a knife."

She ignored his order, knowing what she had to do. Whispering, she warned, "Get yourself ready—I'm gonna bust you in the gut again so Chubasco don't get suspicious." Then she buried her fist in his stomach.

Dane tightened his muscles just before the blow landed, but even though he was prepared, he was surprised at her strength. He gasped and doubled over but continued to saw away at his bindings. Then he heard Chubasco's voice calling from a distance.

"Miguel? Why are you not guarding the canyon?"

"Hurry," Maxine whispered, pretending that she could not hear Chubasco's question. "There isn't much time."

"Miguel? What are you doing?"

The voice was louder now.

Panic gripping him, Dane said, "Do something else to me—do it quick! Kick me!"

Maxine spit on Dane's shirt, then smashed her boot against his shin as requested.

Her foot landed squarely on the spot Chubasco had injured earlier. Dane groaned, and then he felt the sudden release of the ropes. "I'm free," he said, his gaze pinned on the approaching bandit.

"*Miguel!*" Chubasco shouted.

Maxine whipped her head around. Close. Too close. Turning, waving a quick greeting at the bandit, she whispered out of the side of her mouth, "Now what?"

Hanging his head as if defeated, Dane whispered back, "Start walking toward him. As soon as your back is to me, I'll break free, grab you, and put the knife to your throat. Don't move when I do that. I'll threaten to kill you if he doesn't back down. Maybe he'll let us go."

Maxine didn't dare reply. She gave him a barely perceptible nod and then slowly began to move forward. She hadn't gotten two feet before a strong arm circled her waist, another clamped her across the shoulders, and the cold blade of a knife touched the skin at her throat.

"Slide your other arm around my waist under the *serape*," she hissed out the corner of her mouth. "There's a couple a guns in my Levi's."

Relieved to feel the cold steel grip of a pistol, Dane looked up at Chubasco and demanded, "Stop where you are. Don't take another step."

The bandit did as he was told but pushed his hat

back on his head and squinted as he said, "What is this, *amigo?* A knife and my lookout, too? Is that you, Miguel?"

Maxine whispered between her teeth, "What should I say?"

"Nothing," Dane muttered just before he shouted at the bandit, "I'll do the talking, *comprende?*"

Chubasco grinned and held his arms out at his sides, but he took a forward step. "As you wish, *amigo.*"

Remembering the bandit she'd disabled, Maxine suggested, "Why don't you start backing up slow and easy like. Head to the left. There's a horse at the bend in the canyon, the lookout's, I think. If we can get to him, we might just get out of this mess."

"Good idea." Dane began backing up, and Chubasco responded in kind, increasing the length of his steps.

Trying to keep any hint of panic out of his voice, Dane shouted, "Hold it right there, or I'll kill him for sure!"

Chubasco came to a halt, canting his head as he studied the captive in Dane's arms. Resuming his forward progress after only a few moments, he shrugged and said, "If that really is Miguel, perhaps I should let you cut his throat. He is not much of a lookout, is he?"

"That rotten son of a bitch!" Maxine muttered under her breath, unable to restrain herself. "Tell him—tell him that—"

Dane cut her off, ready with an answer. "Are you really so cold-hearted . . ." Dane paused at a word he could hardly spit out in reference to this man, *"amigo?* Isn't it bad enough you have spilled the blood of your old friends and neighbors? Must you cause the death of your own men as well?"

Closer now, Chubasco's grin widened. "I think maybe you are playing a little trick on me and that you do not threaten one of my men. I think, perhaps, your knife seeks to end the life of one of your own *vaqueros.* This *hombre* does not look much like Miguel. If it is him, let him speak to me."

The other bandits, alerted that something was amiss, began to trickle out of the corral and toward their leader.

Sensing they were at an impasse, one that could cost both his and Maxine's lives, Dane adjusted his grip on her shoulders and then dug a pistol out of the waistband of her Levi's. Pointing the barrel outward, although it remained hidden beneath the large *serape,* he increased the speed and length of his backward steps.

With Maxine clutching the forearm he kept pressed against her shoulders, Dane issued a final threat. "Stop right there, Chubasco. Don't take another step, or you will find out exactly whose throat my knife cuts into."

The bandit hesitated. Until Dane's boot came down on a large jagged rock, he thought they might actually have a clear shot at getting away unscathed. But he stumbled, jerking Maxine against his chest. They didn't fall, but the movement flipped the huge sombrero off her head, leaving her long red hair—her identity—exposed.

When she saw the hat hit the ground, Maxine tightened her grip on Dane's forearm even though he'd dropped the knife. She was wide-eyed, unsure of what their next move ought to be.

Dane, equally perplexed, muttered, "*Sangre de Dios*," and glanced to the left, gauging the distance they would have to run under fire before they would be sheltered, however temporarily. He turned back to Chubasco.

The bandit's initial shock had passed. He began laughing, guffawing as he reached for the pistol he wore strapped to his chest. "This is too easy, *amigo*. I can settle all my debts with one bullet. *Adios amigo—vete al infierno gringa puta!*"

Listening for the sound of Dane cocking the gun's hammer but hearing nothing, Maxine cried out, "Aren't you going to shoot the dirty bastard?"

As Chubasco swung his weapon around, arching it toward Maxine, Dane suddenly saw the image of his brother lying trampled into the ground, along with a picture of Maxine's bruised body as Chubasco tried to force himself on her. Rage swelled inside of him, blotting out everything but his anger, and Dane, a man who'd never killed another human being, allowed his reflexes to move on their own.

Although he wasn't consciously aware of pulling the trigger, of his finger pressing against the cold metal, Dane heard the angry retort of gunfire and saw the explosion lift Maxine's *serape* as the bullet tore through the material. Then he watched, stunned as his childhood friend pitched forward, his body jerking as if hit by lightning just before it collapsed to the ground.

Tearing out of Dane's grip, Maxine pulled the second pistol from her waistband and turned to him. "Come on," she shouted, seeing his shock. "We gotta go."

Unable to believe he'd actually killed a man, and an old friend at that, Dane didn't move until other gunshots rang out, echoing off the canyon walls.

This jolted him to action. He grabbed Maxine's hand, and they began to run, side by side. Bullets screamed past them, and they both fired wild shots back toward the canyon as they fled.

Just before they rounded the bend to safety, a barb of fire sliced through Maxine's shoulder, scalding her, searing her flesh, but she didn't stop or even cry out in pain. She just kept on running until Dane pulled her up behind him on the lookout's horse.

She rode with her injured arm wrapped around Dane's waist, the other holding the pistol, firing random shots at the men who pursued them, until they reached the mouth of the canyon.

"Pull up here," she shouted, although by then, Dane had seen Rocio and was in the process of halting the bandit's mount.

Maxine quickly slid down off the animal, collected the mare, and threw herself, awkwardly, onto her back.

Dane, too busy watching for the bandits in the wash they'd just ridden out of to notice her injury, wheeled the bay mustang around, and they were off again, this time heading due north, toward the outer pastures of Rancho Cordoba.

They rode hard, aware that they were still being pursued, but managing to stay out of range of the bandits' pistols. They hadn't quite reached the Army Mail Route when Dane spotted a group of at least fifty rapidly approaching riders.

Pulling the mustang to a halt, he called out to Maxine, "Look what is coming!"

Rocio slid to a stop behind him, and Maxine spun the mare around and trotted up to Dane's side. Glancing first at the riders then back to the approaching bandits, she said, "Hell's fire! Is that more bandits?"

Gunfire cracked over her head from behind. Maxine ducked. Dane grabbed Rocio's reins, and they were off again, still heading north.

Although he knew he was taking a chance, Dane considered the sheer numbers of this new group and just had to believe they were not bandits. Chubasco's camp could not have accommodated this many *vaqueros*.

When they were within a hundred yards of the men, the riders split in half, part of them thundering on by Dane and Maxine to chase down the now retreating bandits, the rest pulling to a halt to await them.

"Ernesto!" Dane cried, relieved and exhausted as he recognized the man. Riding up beside him, Dane spoke in Spanish, quickly informing the *mayordomo* and the other riders who'd stayed behind where the bandits' camp was and what their plans were.

At Ernesto's insistence, Dane chose four *vaqueros* to ride as escorts for himself and Maxine, and the rest took off to the south.

Although her shoulder ached, sticky with her own

blood, Maxine didn't mention it. The wound, painful and irritating, didn't feel as if it were serious. Concealed beneath the heavy *serape,* nobody had even noticed it. Telling Dane about the injury would bring him to her side, a place she could not bear to have him and keep her sanity too. Using this rationale, she kept her silence during the long ride back to Rancho Cordoba.

As the group crested the small butte where the buildings were situated, Dane could see that the grounds were occupied and quite busy. Dicey and Rosa were hitching the mules to the McKain wagon, and Max, much to Dane's surprise, was at work giving Alazan a rubdown.

Chuckling as he rode up and climbed down off the mustang, Dane approached his stallion and began rubbing the animal's muzzle. "So you know a shortcut from Mexico? Perhaps one day you will be so kind as to show it to me."

Max grinned, even though he had no idea what Dane was talking about. "He come back all by hisself just a couple a minutes ago."

"By himself," Dicey shouted in the background. "We thought you was all dead! *Dead!*" Limping up to Maxine after she slid down off Rocio, he gathered her in his arms and muttered, "You been gone better than half the day, girl—I thought . . . you had me twisted up in knots with worryin' about you, Maxie."

Leaning back to kiss her father's cheek, she said, "I told you not to worry about me, Pa. We had a speck a trouble, but as you can see, we come out of it just fine."

Dane and Max joined them, and Rosa stood just behind the foursome.

"Maxine saved my life out there," said Dane. "I owe her a debt that I will never be able to pay. I want you folks to stay on so that I can at least try."

Hearing her father's snort of disapproval, Maxine gave Dane a wan smile and said softly, "Seems like I was just returning the favor. It's time for us to move on."

Dane was determined to make certain the entire family knew the debt was *not* settled, as far as he was concerned, and that he would never let Maxine walk out of his life now. He cleared his throat to speak, but just then, Caroline rushed to his side, calling out his name.

"Oh, Dane—thank God." She linked her arm through his and pressed her head against his shoulder. "We've all been so worried about you—and Maxine, too." She looked over at her and released her hold on Dane.

Max, who'd been studying the *serape* his sister wore, cried out, drawing everyone's attention. "My cape!" he bellowed. "That ain't my *cape*!"

Maxine looked down at the garment, the *bandido's serape,* and shrugged. "I'm sorry, Max," she began, gingerly sliding it over her head. "I had to borrow this one and, ah—"

Dane impatiently took it from her and made a great show of presenting it to Max. "I needed to use the other one, Max. I got this one special for you. I like it better. Don't you?"

Max haltingly reached for the *serape*. He studied it for a moment, a grin slowly replacing his scowl. Then, all at once, he stopped and gasped, "There's a hole in it! This cape got a hole in it! I don't want it." He flung it to the ground.

"A hole, you say?" Dicey limped over, picked up the *serape*, and made a fast examination of it himself. After letting it fall back to the ground, he turned on Dane, fire in his eyes, and said, "That there's a bullet hole, pure and simple. I'm a gonna ask you straight out—was my girl a wearin' this thing when the bullet passed through it?"

Dane glanced at Maxine and then looked back to her father. "Yes, sir, but—"

"No buts! That's twice now—*twice* you almost got my girl kilt! Ain't takin' no chances on givin' you a third." He turned to his daughter. "That's enough for me, and I know you had enough. Now get on up—God in heaven!" he cried, seeing the patch of blood on the shoulder of her shirt, the dried trail spotting the length of the sleeve. Dicey reached out for her, turning her for a better look. "You been hurt! What happened?"

Dane circled Maxine and stood alongside her father. "Rojita? When did you get this? How?"

Backing away from them both, she stammered, "O-oh, hell's fire, you two, it's not that big a deal. It's just a scratch I got when we were running away from the bandits. I guess I didn't duck fast enough for one of their bullets."

Dane raised his eyebrows in horror. "You mean you were shot back there? Why didn't you tell me?"

"*Shot?*" Dicey exploded into the conversation. "That's it, and that does it—damned if it don't!"

Dane nudged Dicey aside, gently lifted the fabric off Maxine's shoulder, and tore it open. A neat crimson groove, looking like a freshly plowed corn row, dented the fleshy part of her upper arm. "*Cristo,*" Dane muttered. "Come into the house. Ernesto will—"

"Hell if she will!" Dicey pushed his way between Dane and Maxine. "We got plenty of doctorin' supplies right in the back of the wagon. Now get on in there with 'em, girl. Yur brother will fix you up."

Dane took her by the hand. "She's coming with me."

"Hell if she is!" Dicey hooked her elbow and began to pull.

Maxine, her head spinning and her heart breaking, felt a great pressure building up inside of her, burning its way to the surface. When she finally opened her mouth, her anger and pain spewed out in a tremendous rush.

"Stop it!" she screamed. "Both of you—leave me alone!" She twirled away from the men, tears rolling down her cheeks, and turned and faced Dane. "I just want to go! Do you understand? *Comprende?* I'm going! I don't ever want to see you or this rancho again!"

Then, sobbing, she climbed up and fell into the back of the wagon.

His features pinched, Dicey turned to Max and said in a quiet voice, "Help yur sister, son. She's got a wound needs tendin'. You get on in there too if yur a wantin' to go with us, Rosa."

For once, everyone did as they were told, and Dicey turned his attention back to Dane. "I'll just be biddin' you adieu now. I thank you fur the good you done us and curse you for the rest. A few folks has walked all over Dicey McKain now and again, but I ain't never been a spot in the road when it come to these here twins. We're done with you. Pure and simple. We'll just be a leavin' now."

Dane was dazed. "Is there nothing I can do or say to—"

"Nuthin'." Dicey backed down the length of the wagon, climbed aboard, and slapped the reins against the mules' backs.

As the rig bumped out of the yard, Caroline walked up beside Dane. He was impassive, unreadable. Her gaze flickered between the wagon and Dane, and she said, "Are you just going to let her go so easily?"

Easily? There was nothing easy about it. His heart felt as if it were being torn from his chest, and with each roll of the wagon wheel, another piece was ripped from his body. If he hadn't really known before, Dane knew now that he loved Maxine more than life itself. But did he love her enough to let her go? Was that what she really wanted? He'd been trying since the evening before to imagine a future with Maxine, but now, for the first time, he had to envision the future *without* her.

Dane thought of never seeing her again, of never feeling the satin of Maxine's skin or those long muscular legs wrapped around his hips. But it was more than physical sensations. He thought of what she'd come to mean to him. How could he live without being able to gaze at those bold features and see that fiery spirit and quick intelligence in her soft brown eyes?

It was asking too much. He'd never known anyone quite like Maxine McKain, never been so privileged to stand beside anyone so real and unpretentious. That he was a better man for having known her was not in question. What kind of man would he be if he let her go?

A gentleman or a fool?

21

The McKain wagon had traveled down the valley for better than a mile from the bluff that supported Dane's home when Maxine finally crawled through the privacy flap at the front of the wagon and joined her father on the bench seat.

"How's yur arm, Maxie?" he asked, trying to keep his tone light and carefree. "Does it need to be stitched up?"

"No," she said, her voice flat. "It's just a scratch. Max put some a that Professor Harrington's Animal Compound on it, then wrapped it up with a pair of his cleanest dirty socks."

Dicey regarded his daughter out of the corner of his eye. Although she'd changed into a fresh white shirt, he could see her dark expression and her quivering chin. If he tried to talk to her, to ease some of the ache in her heart, she would probably begin to cry, so he turned his attention back to the mules and began whistling, "Bonnie Eloise—The Belle of Mohawk Vale."

Dicey hadn't gotten but two bars into the tune when Max pushed the privacy flap aside and said, "Dane's following us, Pa."

Dicey glanced at his daughter, noting that her chin was no longer simply quivering, but trembling. Then he said to Max, "Probably just escorting us off'n his property. Nuthin' to worry about, boy."

Forcing her gaze straight ahead and not looking back for one last glimpse of Dane, was the most difficult thing Maxine had ever had to do. The urge to climb down from the wagon and run straight to him was stronger than any hunger she'd ever experienced, more painful than the bullet that had torn through her flesh. Tears pooled in her eyes, but she willed them to remain inside.

Hearing a sniffle, Dicey looked over at her. "Oh, Maxie, my poor, poor girl. If there's somethin' I can do to ease yur heart, tell me."

"I'm okay, Pa. Really, I am." She knew she'd be reduced to a blubbering fool if he continued to talk that way. "Got some dust in my eyes. That's all. Nothing wrong with me that getting out of this dried up valley won't cure."

Again Max stuck his head out through the flap. "Dane's getting closer, Pa. He's coming right at us."

"Never you mind, son. He ain't gonna do nuthin' but make sure we're good an off'n his land."

Dicey heard the thunder of hooves then, and before he could turn to see how close the Spaniard was getting, Dane was upon them. Alazan pranced up alongside the rig, his *fiesta* harness jingling in time with his gait, providing a musical accompaniment for his master's grand entrance—there was no other way to describe it.

Dane was regal, spotless, dressed as a fine Spanish Don, his hair tousled and topped by a new black hat sporting silver conchos. His blue eyes sparkled with vigor and confidence as he touched the brim of that hat and said, "Good afternoon, Dicey. Something came to my attention after you kind folks left, and I thought I had better get it settled before you got any further. Mind pulling up for a minute? This shouldn't take long."

After sneaking a peek at Maxine, who still sat rigid, Dicey sighed and said, "I s'pose it will not hold us up too much." He reined in the mules, set the brake, and turned back to Dane. "What'd be yur problem?"

"Theft," he answered simply. "I'm afraid your daughter has stolen something from me, and I cannot allow you to leave my property until you settle her debt."

Tossing her aching heart aside, Maxine spun around on the bench, suddenly incensed. "That's a dirty rotten lie, Pa. I give him back everything I ever took!" Then, remembering, she quietly added, "Everything that is except for that ivory brush set. He said I could keep them, but if—"

"That is not the item I'm referring to, Miss McKain," Dane said, his gaze flickering to her features for only a moment before he addressed her father again. "I realize you want to spare Maxine and her brother as much grief as possible, so perhaps we should discuss this in private. Will you take a short walk with me, *por favor*?"

Dicey exhaled noisily. "Are you so sure we got to—"

"I wouldn't ask if I didn't think it was necessary. A moment of your time. That's all I'm asking for. Of course, if you'd rather, I suppose I could turn her over to the authorities in San Diego."

Dicey turned to Maxine and said under his breath, "Musta forgot about *something* you borrowed, Maxie. I'll get it settled up, then we'll be on our way again."

With a sideways glance and short nod by way of answer, Maxine balanced herself on the bench when the wagon lurched at the loss of her father's weight. Moments later, she finally allowed herself to peek at the retreating figures. Dane, dressed in the same black trousers and bolero jacket he'd worn the day of the *fiesta,* strode through the high grass in the meadow, and her father, dwarfed by the Spaniard's height, had to do double time to keep up with him.

When the men stopped some two hundred feet away, out of earshot, Maxine kept a wary gaze on them, watching to make certain the discussion didn't explode to violence. What could she have taken from Dane that would warrant this interrogation? The conversation, though far from heated, was growing more animated, and her father kept glancing back at the wagon—at *her.*

After several long minutes, the discussion came to an end. Maxine saw her father stuff his hands in his pockets and turn to stare out at the valley, away from the wagon. Much to her surprise, Dane was heading back alone, toward Alazan—toward *her.* When he reached his horse, instead of mounting the stallion, he circled the mules and strode up beside her.

"Miss McKain," Dane said in a tone and manner so

polite and correct that he could have been addressing royalty. "Will you please step down here?"

Suddenly petrified, with no idea of what to do, Maxine looked to her father for guidance, but his back was still to her. Finding herself in a rare quandary—speechless—she kept her gaze straight ahead, her lips pressed together, and pretended she hadn't heard the question.

"All right," he said, his voice rife with amusement. "Have it your way, but I want you to know that this is the second hat I'll be ruining in your name."

Curiosity got the better of her, and Maxine turned in time to see Dane remove his hat and send it spinning in a perfect spiral down to the ground. Then she watched him sink down onto it, squashing the crown flat, and place his right knee squarely in the center.

"My dear Miss McKain," he began again, that velvet voice deep and sensual. "After informing your father that you have stolen my heart, he has given his permission for me to ask for your hand. Will you be mine, Maxine McKain? Will you do me the honor of becoming my wife?"

Her heart, her pulse, her entire body seemed to shut down, coming to an abrupt halt like an ore cart crashing into deadfall. Perspiration broke out along her forehead, and her mouth went dry, making it impossible to swallow. He was proposing—*again.* What had he said to her father? Surely he hadn't told him what happened at the pond!

Below her, Dane sighed and climbed to his feet. Kicking his ruined hat aside, he murmured, "I still haven't done it quite right, have I."

Done what right? Maxine looked back toward the

meadow and breathed a sigh of relief. Dicey was coming back to the wagon—slowly, taking his sweet time, but he *was* coming back. Keeping her head turned in Dicey's direction and her back to Dane, she heard him walk away. When he appeared at the driver's side of the wagon, he grabbed Alazan's reins, winked at her, and then walked off with the horse, disappearing from view.

Maxine blinked and rubbed her eyes. When she opened them, she almost could have believed it had all been a dream, a mirage. But then she heard a racket at the back of the wagon. Lifting the privacy flap and peeking through it to the back of the wagon, she saw Dane uncinching Alazan. When he finished, he handed the heavily silvered saddle to Max, and then continued back around the rig, the stallion still with him, until he was standing beside her again.

Chewing on her lip, Maxine's gaze met Dane's for a long, tense moment. Then he softly said, "Well? How many times do I have to ask—will you marry me?"

Maxine glared at him. "I told you already. I don't want your pity."

"Pity? What you have, my darling, is my heart. Now come on down here."

His heart? His . . . love?

An impatient Dane finally clamped his long fingers around her waist and lifted her down off the wagon. Before she could react, much less figure out exactly what was going on, he adjusted his grip and swept her up and onto Alazan's bare back sideways.

Maxine found her voice. "What do you think you're doing? Pa? What's going on?"

Dicey, who'd just climbed aboard the wagon, glanced at Maxine. "Some things you got to decide for yurself, girl. I'm steppin' out a this one."

Vaulting over the stallion's rump, Dane slid up behind her. Addressing her father as he grabbed the reins, he said, "See you folks back at the rancho."

Then he wheeled Alazan around, cautioning Maxine to hang on to him, and loped until they were several yards behind the McKain rig. When Dane felt they'd gotten far enough away from her family for complete privacy, he slowed the stallion to a comfortable walk.

Cradling Maxine in his arms, Dane took a long look into her startled brown eyes and whispered, "What is your answer, Rojita?"

In shock, Maxine peered up at him from beneath the brim of her hat. Incredulous still, she sputtered, "W-well, I don't, I mean I already told you—"

"Yes, yes. You told me you didn't love me and that you never wanted to see me again, but you know what?" She shook her head, looking thunderstruck and adorable at the same time. "I figured out that you love me, Maxine, so don't try to tell me you don't." When she thought to object, he pressed his fingertip against her lips and finished what he had to say. "A woman does not risk her life to save a man unless she loves him very much."

Maxine swallowed hard and blinked to ward off the incoming tide of tears, but it was no use. She knew he could see it in her eyes and feel it in her trembling body. God yes, she loved him, with all her heart. But to say it? To make herself so very vulnerable?

As if reading her mind, Dane nuzzled her ear as he

pulled the ragged hat off her head and sent it flying across the meadow. Working the plaits of her braid loose, he crooned to her, his voice dark and erotic. "I love you, Maxine McKain. Forgive me for not telling you sooner, but the omission does not make my feelings any less true. I love you. I always will. I not only love you, but I need you. Who will ever care enough to save me, should I be taken by *bandidos* again, if not you? You must say yes, Rojita. Because I love you. Say it now."

I love you. Lord, were there any more beautiful words in the English language? *I love you.* She could hear those words over and over and never grow tired of them. Her heart suddenly lurched to life, and the blood thundered in her veins. "And Pa?" she whispered, daring to believe the dream could be real. "He said it was all right?"

Dane laughed. "Only after I offered him an enormous dowry, one so big that a true Scotsman could never refuse it—my holdings in the Central Eureka Mine along with a promise to build Max and Rosa a private cottage of their own at the rancho."

Through a gasp, Maxine said, "You gave *all* that just to get permission to marry me?"

"I would give much, much more for the privilege of calling you wife. Have I your promise?"

Tears exploded, bubbling out of her, and Maxine could no more have held them back than she could have kept the sun from rising. She tried to say "yes," but the word barely came out.

Dane hugged her close, his voice whispering black magic in her ear. "I'll take that as a yes, my love.

You've made me—and our future children very happy."

Maxine raised herself up, catching Dane under the chin. "Children? You mean babies?" Her lip trembled, and she bit the corner as she cried out, "We can have babies?"

Laughing at her exuberance, he said, "As many as you like."

She was so filled with joy now that she feared her heart might explode. "I never thought—I always figured that I'd never—" She swallowed the ache in her throat, but then something else occurred to her. "Lord, what if we have twins! Wouldn't that be something? Twins—just like me and Max!"

Cupping her chin, Dane slowly shook his head. "A lovely, if somewhat frightening thought. Perhaps we should think of other things this day. Things like this." Then he pressed his mouth to hers and kept it there all the way back to the rancho.

AVAILABLE NOW

TAPESTRY by Maura Seger
A spellbinding tale of love and intrigue in the Middle Ages. Renard is her enemy, but beautiful Aveline knows that beneath the exterior of this foe beats the heart of a caring man. As panic and fear engulf London, the passion between Renard and Aveline explodes. "Sweeping in concept, fascinating in scope, triumphant in its final achievement."—Kathryn Lynn Davis, author of *Too Deep For Tears.*

UNFORGETTABLE by Leigh Riker
Recently divorced, Jessica Pearce Simon returns to her childhood home. Nick Granby, the love of her youth, has come home too. Now a successful architect and still single, Nick is just as intriguing as she remembers him to be. But can she trust him this time?

THE HIGHWAYMAN by Doreen Owens Malek
Love and adventure in 17th century England. When Lady Alexandra Cummings stows away on a ship bound for Ireland, she doesn't consider the consequences of her actions. Once in Ireland, Alexandra is kidnapped by Kevin Burke, the Irish rebel her uncle considers his archenemy.

WILD ROSE by Sharon Ihle
A lively historical romance set in San Diego's rancho period. Maxine McKain thinks she's been through it all—until her father loses her in a bet. As a result, she becomes indentured to Dane del Cordobes, a handsome aristocrat betrothed to his brother's widow.

SOMETHING'S COOKING by Joanne Pence
When a bomb is delivered to her door, Angelina Amalfi can't imagine why anyone would want to hurt her, an innocent food columnist. But to tall, dark, and handsome police inspector Paavo Smith, Angelina is not so innocent.

BILLY BOB WALKER GOT MARRIED by Lisa G. Brown
A spicy contemporary romance. Shiloh Pennington knows that Billy Bob Walker is no good. But how can she ignore the fire that courses in her veins at the thought of Billy's kisses?

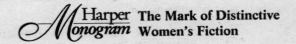 **Harper Monogram** **The Mark of Distinctive Women's Fiction**

COMING NEXT MONTH

MORNING COMES SOFTLY by Debbie Macomber

A sweet, heartwarming, contemporary mail-order bride story. Travis Thompson, a rough-and-tough rancher, and Mary Warner, a shy librarian, have nothing in common. But when Travis finds himself the guardian of his orphaned nephew and niece, only one solution comes to his mind—to place an ad for a wife. "I relished every word, lived every scene, and shared in the laughter and tears of the characters."—Linda Lael Miller, bestselling author of *Daniel's Bride*.

ECHOES AND ILLUSIONS by Kathy Lynn Emerson

A time-travel romance to treasure. A young woman finds echoes of the past in her present life in this spellbinding story, of which *Romantic Times* says, "a heady blend of romance, suspense and drama . . . a real page turner."

PHANTOM LOVER by Millie Criswell

In the turbulent period of the Revolutionary War, beautiful Danielle Sheridan must choose between the love of two different yet brave men—her gentle husband or her elusive Phantom Lover. "A hilarious, sensual, fast-paced romp."—Elaine Barbieri, author of *More Precious Than Gold*.

ANGEL OF PASSAGE by Joan Avery

A riveting and passionate romance set during the Civil War. Rebecca Cunningham, the belle of Detroit society, works for the Underground Railroad, ferrying escaped slaves across the river to Canada. Captain Bradford Taylor had been sent by the government to capture the "Angel of Passage," unaware that she is the very woman with whom he has fallen in love.

JACARANDA BEND by Charlotte Douglas

A spine-tingling historical set on a Florida plantation. A beautiful Scotswoman finds herself falling in love with a man who may be capable of murder.

HEART SOUNDS by Michele Johns

A poignant love story set in 19th century America. Louisa Halloran, nearly deaf from a gunpowder explosion, marries the man of her dreams. But while he lavishes her with gifts, he withholds the one thing she treasure the most—his love.

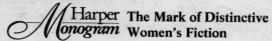 **The Mark of Distinctive Women's Fiction**

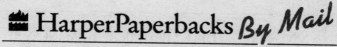

ANALISE

Analise Caldwell was the reigning belle of New Orleans. Disguised as a Confederate soldier, Union major Mark Schaeffer captured the Rebel beauty's heart as part of his mission. Stunned by his deception, Analise swore never to yield to the caresses of this Yankee spy...until he delivered an ultimatum.

ROSEWOOD

Millicent Hayes had lived all her life amid the lush woodland of Emmetsville, Texas. Bound by her duty to her crippled brother, the dark-haired innocent had never known desire...until a handsome stranger moved in next door.

BONDS OF LOVE

Katherine Devereaux was a willful, defiant beauty who had yet to meet her match in any man—until the winds of war swept the Union innocent into the arms of Confederate Captain Matthew Hampton.

LIGHT AND SHADOW

The day nobleman Jason Somerville broke into her rooms and swept her away to his ancestral estate, Carolyn Mabry began living a dangerous charade. Posing as her twin sister, Jason's wife, Carolyn thought she was helping her gentle twin. Instead she found herself drawn to the man she had so seductively deceived.

CRYSTAL HEART

A seductive beauty, Lady Lettice Kenton swore never to give her heart to any man—until she met the rugged American rebel Charles Murdock. Together on a ship bound for America, they shared a perfect passion, but danger awaited them on the shores of Boston Harbor.